DRAGON'S BACK

A. C. EDWARDS

ISBN: 9780-6458-6730-5
A PDS record for this book is available at the National Library of Australia

Dragon's Back: 'Dragon' Series Book 1

Cover Design by Pat Naoum, Red Tally Studios

For Liz, Shannon and Duncan.

There are two kinds of perfect people: those who are dead, and those who have not yet been born.

Chinese Proverb

SIX MONTHS AGO

I shifted the weight on my feet and leaned further back into the darkened doorway.

A typhoon was coming and the rain was falling in fat, heavy drops. My narrow shelter gave me little cover and my legs were wet. Across the street, I could see down Lockhart Road. The neon lights blurred and shimmered in the dark like a wet oil painting and cars crept by in their late-night traffic crawl, windscreen wipers beating futilely against the driving rain. I turned the collar of my shirt up and checked my G-Shock. Half-eleven. I swore in annoyance.

Earlier that night I had picked the target up from outside his apartment and followed him down through Central, onto the MTR and to the bar across the road. I'd been standing in the same spot, watching the same door, for nearly two hours and I was damp, hungry and annoyed.

I couldn't shake the dark mood that had been with me for weeks and now crowded in on me in my rain-wet, urine-stinking doorway. Things were not looking good for me; that was the one certainty of my life. My luck at Mahjong had bottomed out – why I still played was anyone's guess – and my struggling investigations business was on life support. I had no money to speak of and I owed a great deal of money to one of the city's most violent men. I wiped a hand across my face and sighed. No, things were not good.

Despite the rain, the streets heaved with people. Wan Chai on a Friday night is never quiet and it's all up for grabs as the seamier side of Hong Kong ebbs and flows along the hot, neon-lit block bordered by Lockhart and Jaffe Roads.

Expats overflowed in groups onto the footpath outside the popular sports pubs and locals side-stepped them as they sought to get home or to a restaurant, umbrellas up against the heavy rain.

Working girls cruised the streets and those who'd bought a place in a bar sat disconsolately looking for a client. The luckier ones – was it really 'luck'? – were attached to men who studiously ignored them while they watched the football, hooting and shouting at every play. A cacophony of car horns, truck engines and police sirens competed with the duelling racket of music coming from the pubs.

Over the sharp traffic fumes and the sour smell of the drains, the aroma of Cantonese street food – char siu and sui mei, fish balls, fried chestnuts and braised beef offal – wafted down the street and my stomach rumbled, reminding me that I hadn't eaten since breakfast. I may not have even eaten the night before I realised. I really should take better care of myself.

An African pimp sauntered past my doorway and, seeing me, backtracked and looked in. He was big. Bigger than me and I'm no midget. He moved like a panther – all muscle and aggression – and his dark eyes were hooded and glinted in the dark.

There was an air of menace about him despite the friendly smile on his face.

'You lookin' for company, man?' he asked, running his eyes over me, summing me up.

He moved in closer and I glanced down at the front pocket of his jeans from which the handle of a switchblade stood to, ready for action.

I took a breath and pushed myself slightly off the wall and forward onto the balls of my feet. 'Not from you I'm not, so jog on friend,' I said.

He shrugged and flashed me a smile, studying me for a moment longer, before walking away.

I exhaled slowly. I could feel my heart beating in my chest and realised I was wound way too tight – nothing surprising there. Pulling the leather tobacco pouch out of the back pocket of my jeans, I rolled and lit a cigarette, not taking my eyes off the entrance to the bar across the street.

The two men on the door of the bar – Nepalese – weren't tall but they were solid, and their roving eyes and ready stances showed they knew their job. I checked my watch again. Surely he will be out soon, I thought, as I dragged the aromatic smoke deep into my lungs. From nowhere, a rat of doubt started to claw at the back of my neck as I watched the door. I had a dreadful premonition he wouldn't be coming out.

In front of me, the lights changed and traffic slowed to a stop. Taxi drivers instantly hit their horns in annoyance. The blaring, tinny din grated at the inside of my head as I stepped out of the doorway to get a better look at the bar door across the roofs of the halted cars. I was instantly soaked by the rain and the cigarette fell from my fingers in a brown, sodden mess.

'Diu,' *Fuck*, I murmured. Feeling exposed, and conscious of the eyes of the doormen on me, I crossed the road and walked into the bar.

'Insanity' was like most other bars in that part of Wan Chai. It was boisterous, full of drunken expats and a small army of young women all seeking to outdo each other in the chase for drunken expat dollars. A Filipino band was wailing out a pretty good version of 'My Sharona' as I struck out through the tide of girls, each trying to lock eyes with me as I passed.

I spotted a couple of lads I knew from the rugby club – obviously hosting a handful of visitors – and raised my hand in an ironic salute. One of them indicated the guests with an inclination of his head and made the universal rubbing thumb and fingers hand signal for 'money'. The other just rolled his eyes and turned back to his beer.

To my right, a red-faced American was loudly holding court with two friends, swaying slightly on his heels as he struggled to stay upright. Something about North Korea and kicking ass. Half a dozen girls hung on his every word and held him steady, each plotting their own special way of relieving him of his cash at some point later in the evening.

The scene repeated itself a dozen times or more around the noisy, beer-soaked room – each a little morality play but I had no idea what the moral of the story was. It was colourful, loud, lively and all pretty typical for a certain type of Wan Chai bar at nearly midnight.

Reaching the bar, I shouted an order for a lime and soda water and turned around to lean back against the greasy woodwork and scan the room.

The place was packed but I was confident I'd spot my target in a matter of seconds. After a minute or two the rat clawed again, and I swear I could physically feel it. He wasn't there. Slapping a hundred down on the bar I pushed into the crowd to start a lap of the room.

Elbowing my way through, I ignored the curses from the punters and the shocked expressions from the girls. I could see diagonally across the bar and past the entrance to the bathrooms. Another door. Don't let it be an exit, I pleaded with myself as I pushed my way toward it, already knowing it was.

Reaching the door, I pushed hard and it swung open to reveal a dimly lit corridor off to the right. I stepped in and walked quickly along the hall.

By now I knew the bad news. I kicked on a door in front of me and it slammed back. Stepping out, I wiped the heavy rain from my eyes, and stared along a dark rubbish-strewn alley. A large rat scurried past, pausing briefly to look at me before darting into the shelter of a pile of sodden cupboard boxes. Twenty-five metres away a ball of light blazed where the alley emerged onto Jaffe Road.

He was gone and I was standing in the rain looking like an idiot.

1

A WEEK BEFORE, nursing a hangover, I had walked up the three flights of stairs to my small office in a grimy block off Ko Shing Street in Sheung Wan and, juggling my take-out coffee, keyed in the door code.

I stepped in and immediately regretted it. Adele Chung looked up from the newspaper and scowled at me.

'What time is this?' she demanded, imperiously checking her watch. 'It's nearly lunchtime. Also…' she raked me with her eyes 'you look like a hobo. When will you shave and maybe iron your shirts?'

I ignored her as I walked into what passed for my office – more a cubicle separated from my secretary's desk by a waist-high glass panel.

The room was small, with three small desks and cheap office chairs. A worn and over-stuffed brown Chesterfield chair was shoved against the wall by the door and Adele had sarcastically placed a sign above it on which was written 'Waiting Room'. Assorted storage boxes lay scattered around the floor and stacked in the corners of the room, each labelled with thick black pen in my own special filing system that often bore little resemblance to the actual contents.

A year or so ago I had bought a cheap oil painting from Stanley

Markets and the colourful Hong Kong street scene stared down at me from its place on the grimy and streaked wallpaper. A battered three-drawer filing cabinet, on top of which sat an equally battered electric kettle, completed the picture.

It really was quite depressing. I put my coffee down and turned to Adele.

'And jou san to you too, a-yi. *Good morning, auntie.* I'm just fine today, thanks for asking,' I said, taking off my Wayfarers. She clicked her tongue and turned back to her newspaper.

Into her early sixties, Adele Chung was a formidable woman. She stood at a little over 160 centimetres, dressed like the headmistress of a private girls' school, and took no shit from anyone – least of all me. She was the widow of a sergeant who had been killed on duty while working for me years before in the Hong Kong Police Force and had 'adopted' me not long after I gave her a job in my struggling investigations business.

She was a constant thorn in my side and I loved her like my own long-dead mother.

'You call me a-yi,' she said from inside her newspaper 'but you show me no respect. If you did, you'd clean up your act. I'm the nearest thing you have to a mother and you would do well to listen to me once in a while.'

She'd always been able to read my mind.

'Adele, please. Leave off,' I mumbled as I swigged at the near-cold coffee and scratched my head looking distractedly around the office. 'Where's Joey?' I asked, looking for my offsider, and only other employee than Adele who clicked her tongue in reply.

'Bai chi! *idiot*, that alcohol has addled your brain. Joey is in Bali surfing or whatnot...whatever young people do there. I don't even want to think about it,' she shuddered.

I shook my head. 'Oh. Right.' I muttered, chastened. 'I did forget. Back next week, right?'

Adele just pretended she didn't hear me.

I dropped the coffee cup in the bin and sifted through the mail on my desk. Bills, demands for payment, junk mail from my bank offering me an increase in my credit card limit, and a flier from my regular liquor store advertising their new stock of my favourite local craft beer.

'I'll get a case of that,' I muttered, and Adele's head whipped around, her eyes hooded. I held up my hand in surrender then picked up a handwritten note from the bottom of the pile. 'What's this?' I asked, holding it up.

'I don't know,' she shrugged. 'It was under the door when I arrived.'

I studied the note. '*You should pay more attention to Aberdeen*,' was scrawled across it in Cantonese. I scratched my head and turned to Adele.

'What does this mean?'

She shrugged again. Nothing ever seemed to bother her – except, that is, my office hours, my drinking and the state of my shirts.

'Your Cantonese is as good as mine. It says what it says.' She put her paper down and studied me, a faint smile creasing her eyes. 'Perhaps it's a hint to pay your club account – it wouldn't be the first time you were late with that one.'

I shook my head and slipped the note into the drawer of my desk.

'Before you ask,' Adele said, 'my note is about a call an hour ago.'

'Can you tell me anything about it,' I asked picking up another slip of paper. 'Or do I have to guess?'

Adele clicked her tongue again – she did that a lot – stood and walked to the cubicle door.

'A Mrs Sarah Thomas called,' she said. 'Inquiring after your *expert* services. She said something about a 'personal matter'.' Adele shrugged. 'Probably another wayward husband.'

I sighed. Wayward husband. How about a major insurance scam, a missing person or a kidnap? Anything but wayward husbands! Still, I desperately needed the job and the money so, checking the time, I picked up the phone and dialled the number on the note.

2

THE FOLLOWING morning shaved and wearing a freshly-ironed shirt, I rang the doorbell to an apartment on the thirty-eighth floor of one of the many apartment towers in Mid-Levels.

The building was plush and smelled of beeswax and floor polish and the suited concierge eyed me warily as we stood together waiting for the door to open. I was about to break the uncomfortable silence with a comment on the weather when the door opened, revealing a Filipina helper, wearing an outlandish maid outfit that looked to have come from the wardrobe department of 'Downtown Abbey'. She was backlit by a huge window across the room.

I squinted and held out a business card.

'To see Mrs Thomas?' I said. The maid just stared at me. 'I have an appointment,' I added hopefully.

Without a word, she stood aside and ushered me into the main sitting room with a gesture of her hand then disappeared further into the apartment. I walked across the timber floor, the heels of my boots clicking faintly on the wood.

The entrance and the living room of the apartment were well-decorated. Modern and minimalist, with what I took to be Italian-made furniture. My sister is an art dealer – among other things – and

I noted the original, and obviously expensive, artworks on the wall, each discreetly lit by their own small pin spotlight. I decided I would add an extra zero to the invoice if I was given this job – I knew I was going to take it, whatever it was. When you're broke and desperate you find you're less picky than you used to be.

I paused at a small sideboard and glanced down at a framed photograph of a man and woman.

Both were smiling into the camera, arms around each other, holding drinks. Handsome couple, I thought, noting the man was clearly older than the woman, hair greying around the edges, but still in his prime. His eyes looked weak, but who was I to judge? Reaching the large, floor-to-ceiling window I stopped and stared out at the view from thirty-eight floors up on the misty mid-slopes of Victoria Peak.

Hong Kong's skyline was laid out before me. One International Finance Centre and its big brother, Two IFC, reached into the grey sky across which scudded heavy, expectant clouds. I could see the Bank of China Building with its zig-zag design and notoriously bad Feng Shui, then the six Star Ferry piers. Ferries dotted the harbour, making their way to Kowloon and back, leaving foamy, white trails across the grey-blue water.

On Kowloon side, the bustle of Tsim Sha Tsui spread across the foreshore, home to high-end designer stores, watch shops and cheap Indian suits. The sun briefly burst from behind a cloud bank, and the mirrored surface of the International Commerce Centre, soaring high above West Kowloon, fired an eye-searing glare of light back across the harbour.

I scanned across the bustle of TST, all clearly identifiable from here high up on 'The Peak', despite the mist of the overcast day. Behind it all, beyond Kowloon, rose the forested ridgeline of Lion Rock Country Park, running west to east toward Sai Kung and Port Shelter. To the west, from Tsing Yi, the high spans of the Tsing Ma bridge crossed to Lantau Island and the toll road to Hong Kong International Airport.

I took it all in, feeling the usual exhilaration that swept over me when I viewed my city from on high.

Letting my eyes wander back across the harbour and Central to the road below me, I drew in a deep breath as heavy rain started to pelt the window. The view across the city never failed to send a spark through me. I loved the place. It was orderly and chaotic, light and dark, rich and poor. It was my Hong Kong and it was worth everything to me to have been born and raised there.

I sighed. Lost in thought I didn't notice I'd been joined in the room until I heard a discreet cough behind me.

'Mr Jones?' A woman's voice, her voice low but clear. English accent. West End London. Posh but not stupidly so. I turned.

She was in her early forties and stood on a plush rug that looked like I imagined a polar bear would look if it were laid out flat on a floor without its head.

She was dressed in denims, artfully torn at the knees, and a long-sleeved white shirt with its collar turned up and hidden under thick, brown, shoulder-length hair. The shirt's top three buttons were undone. Unbidden, my eyes darted to the string of pearls around her neck and the cleavage of her breasts. I focussed on her eyes as I moved across the room toward her, my hand held out in greeting.

Her mouth was twisted slightly in an ironic grin and her brown eyes crinkled at the corners in amusement. Her nose was small with a slight upwards tilt and her jawline was strong.

I don't know what I had been expecting – if I had even given it any thought – but there was no doubt about it, Sarah Thomas was an attractive woman. We shook hands.

'Good morning Mrs Thomas,' I said. 'Thank you for taking the time.'

'Call me Sarah', she said.

I could tell she didn't mean it. She was holding my business card and glanced down at it then back up at me, taking in my face. Her brow wrinkled slightly in a frown as she examined me in silence for a second or two. I was used to this reaction from people I first met, but it still irked me.

I waited for her to speak.

'Forgive me but you're not...'

'What you had expected?' I said, a little too abruptly. Her face clouded for a second before she quickly regathered herself.

'Well, to be honest, no. With your name, I had expected a middle-aged, retired policeman with a large stomach, receding hairline and red face.' She smiled.

'And instead, you've got a middle-aged, mixed-race Hong Konger with freckles,' I said, smiling back, feeling my temper cool.

'Not at all an unpleasant combination.'

I blinked at her, feeling the smile freeze stupidly on my face. 'Well, we get what we are born with, don't we?'

She gestured to a large sofa on the other side of the polar bear. 'Shall we?'

Once seated, she turned again to me. 'And the *name* you were born with?' she asked. "Galahad Jones'. You have to admit, it is... unusual,' she said, her right eyebrow arching.

'For a Eurasian or just generally?' I inquired, my temper rising again. This was why I never played poker and did so poorly at Mahjong. She flushed, showing a little annoyance herself.

'Generally, Mr Jones,' she said. 'Generally. I think it is fetching and romantic but, as I say, you have to admit the 'Galahad' bit is ... unusual.'

I nodded, conceding the point.

'My father chose it. He was Hong Kong-born English and mum was a mixed-race Hong Konger. Dad obviously liked the sound of the name and my mother also thought it "fetching and romantic". It was a pain as a kid at school with all the Harrys and Toms and Peters and it gets tiring having to explain it every time I meet someone...' I held up my hand and smiled. 'Present company excepted of course.'

'Of course.'

'I admit it has grown on me as I've aged.' I paused and gave a small shrug. 'And I'm not blind to the deeper significance of the name given some of my more 'troublesome' personality traits.'

I shut my mouth with an effort. Why was I spilling all this to a complete stranger and potential client?

Her eyes narrowed and she tilted her head as she regarded me with interest for a moment.

'Mmm, well, let's not go there shall we?' She held up her hand. 'Teresa!' she called, and the maid appeared, smiling, into the room. As soon as she clapped eyes on me the smile disappeared to be replaced with a disapproving scowl.

'Yes, ma'am?' she asked.

'A glass of white and...' she glanced at me. 'A drink, Mr Jones?'

'Just lime and soda if you have it.'

'... and that, thank you Teresa.'

The maid bobbed in a brief curtsey and retreated to the kitchen. We sat on the sofa in silence and I waited for her to speak first. I'm never uncomfortable with silence in company and, over the years, I've found it to be a very useful interview tool.

The drinks arrived and Smiley Maid slapped mine down on the coffee table, just out of reach. She handed her boss the wine, with a smile, bobbed again and disappeared back to her den.

Sarah Thomas sipped her wine and sighed, leaning back into the sofa. I glanced at a clock on the wall behind her. 11.00 a.m., not bad, I thought.

'You disapprove, Mr Jones?' she asked, lifting up her wine glass. I shook my head.

'I'm the last person who should judge when it comes to alcohol,' I said, holding her gaze.

'But never on duty, heh?'

'Something like that.' I cleared my throat quietly and took out my small notebook and pencil. 'Why am I here, Mrs Thomas?'

She sat forward and squared her shoulders, her hands clasped loosely in her lap, and took a deep breath as if considering her opening words.

'I think my husband is having an affair and I want to know if that's true,' she said slowly. Quietly.

'What makes you think that?'

'Lately, he's been coming home late from work, staying only for a short while then heading out again. He gets home hours later – often in the early morning.'

I shrugged slightly. 'Could it just be work?' I signalled around the room with a sweep of my hand. 'I'm guessing he is quite senior, in a well-paid job for a large company. Maybe there's a big project on that's taking up his time.'

She shook her head. 'No, he would have told me if that were the case.' She took up her glass and sipped again at the wine. 'You're right 'though, she said. 'He is senior, and he is extremely busy.' She paused and looked up at the ceiling. 'I don't know... this is different somehow. Something has changed.'

'What has he told you, when he has these *absences*?'

She sighed, her shoulders slumping a little. 'He really doesn't tell me anything. He seems so secretive.'

'What is it he does?' I asked, changing tack, and she reached across to a small table, opened the drawer, rummaged about briefly and pulled out a business card.

She handed me the card and I studied it. James Thomas, Vice President, Operations, AsiaWide Shipping. I slipped the card into my notebook.

'May I ask, how long you and Mr Thomas have been in Hong Kong?'

'Nearly nine months. We moved from London when James was appointed to the role.'

'And you say his 'disappearing' late at night has only started recently? How long ago?' I asked.

She shrugged. 'I don't know. Maybe three months.'

'How often does this happen?'

She screwed up her face as she thought about this for a moment. 'No particular days,' she said. 'It's quite random.'

I jotted a note and looked up. 'Does anything seem to trigger the absences... a phone call maybe?'

She shook her head. 'Not that I can recall.'

'And apart from the late-night absences, any other changes in behaviour?'

'What do you mean?' she asked, an eyebrow arched. 'Are we still sleeping together, having sex? Is that it?'

'Mrs Thomas,' I said soothingly 'that's not what I was driving at ...'

This time she took a long pull on the wine and I watched as the level dropped in the glass. She gazed across the room and out the window. 'No. We are not,' she said quietly. '...and before you ask, we were always close like that.'

I jotted another note and looked up. 'Any other changes? How is his mood generally? Would you say he was stressed, angry, preoccupied...?'

She thought about that for a moment then sat forward.

'Pre-occupied. That's a good description. Something's on his mind and it's crowding everything else out,' she said.

'And you think it's another woman.'

'Jesus!' she exclaimed, throwing up her hands. 'I don't know what to think, but another woman would seem to make sense.'

She paused. 'But it doesn't. That's just not like him. We've been married nearly ten years and I've never known him to look at another woman.'

I let this hang in the air for a minute or two while I made some notes. When I looked up, her wine glass was empty and she was glancing around distractedly for Smiley Maid and a refill. I coughed discreetly to get her attention.

'Forgive me, but are there any financial difficulties? I asked, trying not to look around the opulent apartment. She considered that for a moment, her head tilted slightly.

'We recently lost a great deal in a few fairly risky investments,' she said. 'As risky investments often are, we did very well from them, for a time, but that fell apart about six months ago – not long after we arrived.'

She considered this for a moment. 'But we're doing fine, I'm sure of that,' she said, perhaps a little too confidently, as if trying to convince herself.

I sat perfectly still, willing her to go on. She gently massaged her temples and sighed. 'James has a handle on it, he's assured me.'

I nodded and considered her for a moment. The money angle was interesting but I decided to change direction.

'Have there been any unusual occurrences, at work or here at home? Anything out of the ordinary?'

'You mean besides my husband disappearing for hours at a time during the night?' she asked. I shrugged slightly and she cupped her chin in her hand in thought. I watched her eyes. They had widened slightly. Sarah Thomas knew something and was deciding whether she would tell me or not.

'No... not really,' she said slowly, then affected to suddenly remember as she made her decision. 'Oh...there was one strange thing a few nights ago.' I raised my eyebrows in encouragement.

'The doorbell rang, and James answered it. I thought it strange as we weren't expecting anyone and the concierge hadn't called up first.'

'What happened?'

'I walked out and saw James at the door with an Asian man...'

'Asian? Do you mean Chinese?' I interrupted.

'Yes,' she snapped. 'Are there any other sorts?' I tried to hold a bland expression in response to her casual racism, but I knew I didn't do a good job.

'Perhaps you meant Indian, Pakistani..?' I ventured, to cover my rising annoyance at this pampered, mildly drunk woman.

'No. Chinese...' she said waving a hand in dismissal. 'Anyway, they were both whispering but it sounded urgent, angry somehow.'

'Did you hear anything they were saying?'

'No, I was too far away, and it all happened so quickly. James saw me and closed the door. I asked him what it was, and he told me it was a food delivery guy with the wrong address. I didn't think much about it at the time.'

A food delivery guy? Surely the concierge would head them off at the door and bring it up himself.

Also, food delivery...? I nearly laughed out loud at the suggestion. The

Thomas's didn't get meal delivery unless it was for a fully catered dinner party for ten. She was either hiding something or she really had no idea what was going on around her. I wondered what that was and why.

I was about to speak again when her mobile rang and she answered it. Glancing briefly at me, she stood and crossed the room. With her back to me, she muttered a few words then pressed the phone against her hip and looked back over her shoulder.

'I have to take this, Mr Jones, I'm so sorry. I'll call your office. You can see yourself out.'

I nodded and, feeling like a schoolboy who had just been sent from class, did just that.

The apartment door closed behind me and I paused for a moment trying unsuccessfully to hear snatches of the conversation within. I chewed the inside of my cheek as I pushed the elevator button – what was going on here?

3

A WEEK HAD PASSED since my meeting with Sarah Thomas and, now, I was standing in the pouring rain in a dirty Wan Chai alley chasing her wayward husband.

I kicked out at an empty box as a loud clap of thunder sounded almost directly overhead. 'Fuck it!' I shouted into the storm and swept the hair from my eyes as I walked out of the alley, onto Jaffe Road and hailed a taxi.

I gave the driver my address and took a deep breath to settle myself. As we set off through the busy, wet streets of Wan Chai, I gazed out the window deep in thought.

The Thomas's had recently lost a lot of money... how bad their finances were I had no idea, but could it have something to do with Mr T's unexplained night-time excursions? And who was the 'food delivery guy?'

I didn't for a moment believe Sarah Thomas' version of events – her husband and the unknown Chinese man were probably known to each other and were probably arguing about something at the door. But what? And how in God's name did the Chinese guy get past the concierge and upstairs? The visitor knew the apartment, he knew Thomas, and he must have had pull with the concierge.

Sarah Thomas herself was a mystery. She seemed to lean on the booze – I knew the signs from personal experience – but was that usual or just current stress? Stress about what, exactly?

I had a nagging feeling she was lying to me but I thought that about most people. In all probability, she had no idea what her husband was up to and was more worried about losing him, their bank accounts and expat lifestyle.

Thomas himself had done nothing in the last week but work long hours, visit his club once and go for a jog. He had done nothing at all to indicate he was getting a piece on the side until tonight.

Tonight, he had walked straight from home, onto the MTR and to the bar where he had stayed for God knows how long before unknowingly giving me the slip – he couldn't have known I was tagging him; I was too good for that.

I shook my head and swore softly. He probably walked straight out the back door while I stood, like an idiot, for 90 minutes in the rain waiting for him to emerge with a girl.

That was another thing. There wasn't a girl tonight – at least as far as I'd seen – and I had a feeling there wasn't a girl at all in this picture. Why would he have entered the bar only to leave it by the back door? No-one does that. This looked and smelt wrong.

'Ni dou ting?' the driver asked. *Stop here?*

I nodded, reaching for my wallet. 'Hai, m'goi sai.' *Yes, thanks*. I paid him the fare and stepped out onto the deserted street.

At nearly 1:00 a.m. my part of Wan Chai, bordering Causeway Bay, was deathly quiet. I glanced up and down the street for signs of life. Nothing.

In the doorway of my apartment building, I keyed in the door code. As usual, the elevator took an age to arrive. While it ground its way down to me, and on the ride up to the floor where I lived, I worried away at the tangle of thoughts in my mind before dismissing the effort. It was too late; I was too tired and hugely annoyed at myself for the mess I'd made of things that night.

The elevator slowly shuddered its way up and came to a stop with a bounce. I stepped out onto the landing, turned left to my apartment door, ran my hand over the electronic lock to activate it, and then swiped my door card. The door opened with a satisfying mechanical click and I walked in, letting it swing closed behind me.

I moved through the apartment, leaving a trail of wet clothes in my wake, and took a hot shower. Minutes later, wrapped in a towel, I walked into the kitchen, poured a shot of whisky and stepped out onto the terrace.

The rain had stopped but heavy clouds still rolled their way overhead, and the darker outlines of Mount Cameron and The Peak cut a stencil across the slowly lightening pre-dawn sky, dotted here and there with the twinkling of stars.

I rolled and lit a cigarette and tilted my head to contemplate the stars as the smoke trickled slowly from my nostrils. I threw back the drink, feeling it burn on the way down, and scratched my head.

'What a night,' I muttered to the heavens. As usual, there was no answer.

4

I WOKE with a headache late the next morning and considered staying in bed for the rest of the day. I knew I couldn't – I was never one for lying in – so, cursing, I rolled out of bed and threw on my running gear to hit the roads leading from my apartment up into the hills.

The steep climb of Blue Pool Road, as usual, hurt. My chest was heaving as I sucked in deep breaths, driving oxygen to the tired muscles of my legs. At the top of the hill, I turned right down Wong Nai Chung Gap Road, ignoring the view of Hong Kong laid out below me, as I focussed on hitting my stride. Shaking my head, I promised myself for the thousandth time that week I'd give up smoking and cut back on the booze.

I turned onto the Bowen Road Fitness Trail and headed west with the other joggers and walkers out for their Saturday morning exercise. I could feel my face reddening and the sweat running from under my cap into my eyes.

There had been a time when I could have done this all day, but age had snuck up on me like a pickpocket and experience told me this run was going to hurt long after it was finished.

There was so much on my mind that my thoughts crowded in on each other and swirled around manically competing for attention.

It all started with 'money' and spiralled off from there. My bank account was near empty, I had very little work coming in and I hadn't paid Adele or Joey for nearly two months – not that either would ever complain. Also, I owed money to some very nasty people. A lot of money.

I spat into the bushes on the side of the footpath and tried to focus on the rhythm of my breathing which had now moved from ragged near-death gasps to something resembling a runner's cadence.

I owed money. What the hell was I going to do about *that*? If I didn't come up with near enough to 40,000 USD, and very soon, I was going to end up floating belly-up somewhere off Lamma Island without my head. The thought didn't appeal.

Of course, it was all my own stupid fault. I had a gambling problem – had done since leaving the force. In truth, I probably had it long before that – and my special fondness for Mahjong that I played clumsily and with none of the required presence of mind, didn't help.

I justified my losses in that I wasn't doing it at Happy Valley on a bunch of horses running around a track but in a game that required strategic skill and a quick mind. I winced at the stupidity of that. If I was so damn skilful I wouldn't be so deep in the hole to a particularly violent and unforgiving club operator with triad ties.

I wasn't a bad person, I thought. Just a stupid one – at times. Was it any wonder I lived alone, had few friends, no money and few prospects? A stab of sadness hit me. I ignored it and ran on.

Turning off the trail onto the steep path down the Green Trail, my right knee started to scream. I hit Kennedy Road and turned right to wind my way down to, and across, Queen's Road East, through the markets and down Wan Chai Road.

I checked my Garmin as I ran to the doorway of my apartment building and pulled up, bent over with my hands on my knees, heaving in deep breaths. I loved to run, but I was badly out of shape.

Maybe it was time for something more sedate I thought, but I knew I hadn't the patience for tai chi.

As I keyed in the door code, my mind returned to the pressing problem of the 300,000 HKD and what I was going to do about it. I had to admit; things didn't look good.

Fifteen minutes later, after icing my knee and swallowing down some ibuprofen, I grabbed a beer from the fridge and sat outside on my terrace, in the shade of a large market umbrella. I switched on the Bluetooth speaker, thumbed through a playlist on my phone and hit 'play'. The muted sounds of Carey Morin's blues guitar and gravelly voice drifted across the terrace as I sat back with a sigh and regarded the bright blue sky.

It was clear after the previous days of rain but the humidity was soaring and the cicadas chirruped loudly in a large fig tree that spread its branches over the playground of the abandoned public school across the way. My thoughts turned to Sarah Thomas and her allegedly misbehaving husband.

The night before had been a disaster; no doubt about it. But I'd make up for it tonight, I thought.

I decided I'd call Joey, now back from Bali, and have the Thomas' apartment building staked out on the off-chance he appeared. If he did, we'd be on him from the start. Joey would take it where it led – my off-sider would have no problems with any of the punters in 'Insanity', of that I was sure – get the evidence we needed of Thomas' infidelity, if there was any which I was beginning to doubt, and we could neatly wrap the case. Job done, I thought. I still felt uncomfortable at the nagging feeling that rose deep in the back of my mind. Was it really? Was that all there was to this?

I shrugged. It was easy money and I had already decided that I would pad the invoice. As unethical as that was, I felt no shame at it. I needed the money more than Sarah Thomas did. The fee would allow me to pay a hefty chunk of the money I owed and that should buy me some time while I brought in more work. It all seemed straightforward.

I felt the filtered sun on my face as I closed my eyes and drifted off to sleep. Straight forward, I thought. I had no idea, then, just how wrong I was.

I woke nearly two hours later with a mild headache – drinking beer in the sun after a run is never a good idea. I splashed some water on my face and microwaved some leftover fried rice. Wolfing down my snack, I dropped the bowl into the kitchen sink and headed to the shower. Thirty minutes later, dressed in jeans, desert boots and a T-shirt, I left the apartment.

5

It was still early, and the sun had not yet begun to set. I knew it would be hours before the bars would be jumping, so I decided I would put a couple of kilometres under my belt in a walk to Central for an early meal before I called Joey.

I was rounding the corner onto Hennessy Road when my phone rang. I glanced down at the contact information, grunted softly in surprise and answered.

'It's been a while, Pete,' I said. 'You must want something.'

The voice at the other end of the line sounded mildly offended. 'Why would I want something? Can't I just call an old friend and check in?' it said.

Chief Inspector Peter Toh Luo-yang and I had known each other for years; since I had been a Senior Inspector in the Hong Kong Police Narcotics Bureau and he a young Inspector working organised crime. He and I had hit it off quickly after meeting during an operation in the New Territories and had become solid friends. We had remained so over the years since. Peter was now a senior officer in OCTB – Organised Crime and Triad Bureau – and I hadn't heard from him for a couple of months, but now he just wanted to 'check in'. I was deeply suspicious.

'Go on,' I said.

There was the slightest pause before he answered.

'I'm in your neck of the woods. I know it's short notice, but how about a beer?'

'As a matter of fact, I'm walking to Central now. Want to join?'

'Sure thing,' he said. 'Where?'

I gave him the name of a bar we had often haunted together, hung up and looked back down the road for some transport. A tram was pulling to the stop across from me, headed west, so I ducked across the road and jumped in through the rear doors just as its old bell clanged and it moved off down Hennessy Road. The walk would have to wait.

I didn't own a car and never had. I walked or used public transport everywhere. The tram was my favourite way to get around. It had only a limited route map and was slow, so there was no point using it when you were in a hurry, but I loved the old-world charm of the ancient carriages as they clanked their way through town, windows down, bell ringing, people jammed in against each other in a polite social embrace. A thought of sitting on my mother's knee, as she carried the shopping home on a tram, came unbidden to mind.

In a little over twenty minutes the tram pulled up on Des Voeux Rd and I jumped off. Crossing the street into Theatre Lane, I walked past the ladies polishing shoes and the small alley with stalls of key cutters and shoe repairers, to cross Queen's Road and head up D'Aguilar Street.

Peter had arrived before me and taken an outside high table, in a corner, facing down the street. Good view down the street, with nobody at his back. I would have chosen the same spot.

The place was small, with just a few tables and a bar. A large mirror behind the bar reflected light back into the room, and I caught a glimpse of my father's blue eyes staring wearily out at me. I looked tired. Wine and beer glasses hung in a rack above the bar, and the walls were dotted with old military plaques and pinned with a dog-eared collection of currency from around the world. A Peroni beer poster in a battered frame hung, slightly askew, just inside the open shutter doors. The barman's shirt sleeves were rolled up to reveal muscular forearms and an old-school tattoo of a dancing hula girl. He raised his head from a newspaper and glanced briefly at me as I entered.

Peter stood as I approached. He smiled and raised a hand in greeting. I noticed he'd put on weight since I last saw him.

'Nei hou maa, Gan-Li? *Hello, how are you*? he asked affably, using the Cantonese abbreviation of my name.

'Nei hou Luo-yang. Ngo gei hou. Nei ne? *Hi, I'm not bad, and you*? I replied.

He shrugged, a smile creasing his round face 'Pretty good for an old guy. You know how it goes...'

I nodded and pulled up a stool. 'Beer?' I asked.

Peter nodded and I signalled for two beers. The barman nodded, grudgingly put aside his paper and bent to the fridge.

'Well, this is an unexpected surprise, Pete,' I said. 'To what do I owe the pleasure?' I kept my voice mild but closely watched his reaction.

His eyes clouded briefly before he smiled again and held out his hands, palms up, in a shrug.

'Just touching base, Gal. See how you're doing.' He frowned a little. 'We haven't seen each other for a couple of months...'

I smiled. 'Well, that's nice. It's certainly good to see you.' I was interrupted as the beers arrived. We both took a drink and I rolled and lit a cigarette.

'So, now,' I said blowing out the smoke, 'you can cut the bullshit and tell me what this is about.'

Peter stared at me for a moment, and I could sense he was a little annoyed but, typically, was holding it back well. 'I see you're still on those things,' he said, indicating the cigarette.

'It's my only vice,' I replied.

He arched an eyebrow. 'I very much doubt that' he said, his face serious. 'Look,' he said after a brief pause, 'let me ask you a question.' Another pause. 'Are you in any trouble?'

'Why do you ask that?'

'I notice you don't say "no".'

I shrugged. 'Everything is fine. Work is busy, paying the bills, I've got my health,' I said smiling.

'Paying the bills huh?' Peter said as he sipped his beer. I noticed he didn't look directly at me. At least he had the good grace to be embarrassed. Now I was worried. What was this, a suspect interview?

'Not really a lot to do with you Pete,' I said, my voice still mild. 'Now tell me what this is about.'

My old friend regarded me silently for a long moment, seeming to search my face for clues. Something was bothering him, and Peter Toh was not someone to flap over nothing. He seemed to come to a decision and drew a deep breath.

'Gal, your name has come up in wire-tap transcripts. Triad wire-tap transcripts.'

I didn't answer and he continued. 'Also...' he drew a breath, 'your dad's name has come up.'

Now he had my attention. 'Transcripts?' I asked.

Peter nodded. 'We're running an operation in the New Territories... well Criminal Intelligence Bureau is... nothing specific, but we're looking for corroboration of a tip we've had of a big drug import due sometime soon.' He sipped at his beer. 'To be honest, we don't have much, as good as the wires are, but we live in hope.'

He paused to gather his thoughts. 'Anyway, I don't see the raw material, but I get a weekly summary from CIB. This week, the head of CIB himself brought it to me. He wanted me to know that, among the usual chatter about their day-to-day stuff, your name came up along with a reference to your dad.'

The usual mixture of anger, shame, embarrassment and loss washed over me at the mention of my father. I sat unblinking but could feel my heart racing as I toyed with my beer bottle.

My father was a classic Hong Kong story. He had been born during the war in Stanley Internment Camp and had never known his own father who had been killed just before Christmas 1941 at Wong Nai Chung Gap as the Japanese swept across the Island. He spent his first three years of life as a prisoner in the crowded and unsanitary conditions of the camp before Hong Kong was liberated by the Royal Navy in August 1945.

After the war, my grandmother, still ill from four years of deprivation in the camp, moved into a small apartment in Sai Ying Pun, just off Second Street, to raise her son as she and Hong Kong recovered.

I later learned he was a tearaway kid. Running with a local street gang from the age of seven, he spoke fluent Cantonese, often ditched school and stole whatever he could, whenever he could, from the stalls and small shops along Centre Street.

His first contact with Hong Kong's finest came in 1951 when, aged nine, he was collared by a Sergeant of Police, a large, red-faced Welshman, and escorted home with the evidence of his latest crime – two oranges, a packet of Capstan and a slightly stinking fish – in a bag under his arm.

The Welsh copper soon became close, platonic friends with my grandmother and a father figure to the young Simon Jones. Under his strong and calming influence, Simon started paying more attention to his studies, ran far less with his gang, stole much less than previously and, generally, turned his young life around.

He joined RHKP in 1962 and graduated as a Probationary Inspector in 1963. His first posting was to the old Wan Chai Police station, then located on Gloucester Road, where he soon built a reputation as a tough, but fair, street copper who had the respect of the local people in the district. He was also, from all I had been told in the years since, ruthless and unforgiving with the local triads who preyed on the ordinary citizens of the districts in which he worked.

My thoughts were interrupted as I realised Peter was speaking. '... how this could happen.' I heard him say. I blinked and shook my head.

'Sorry, what?' I said. 'What was that?'

'I was saying: your name just doesn't pop up in a triad conversation for no reason, Gal. I need to understand how this could happen.' He paused. 'A very specific sum of money was mentioned...'

My mind was working fast, trying to figure out what was going on here. I had no idea but the 'sum of money' could have been only one thing. I took a deep breath and stubbed out my cigarette.

'What 'sum of money'?' I asked quietly.

'A lot. Three hundred and twenty-five thousand,' Peter said. He paused. 'But that's not all.'

'Oh, there's more?'

He winced. 'The call was between two known members of Sun Yee On: a Vanguard, and a Red Pole. The Guard asked after you by name. The Pole said that you had been given the payment of three hundred. Vanguard says that's good, to be expected, like father-like son. The Pole says 14K had the father now we have the brat. Chuckles all around, then they move on to other business. Call ends three minutes later.'

I was stunned by the revelation. Why were an Operations Officer and an Enforcer of SYO triad talking about me and the money I owed a Mahjong parlour? Was it just a vague reference to the debt? People owed them money all over Hong Kong, but why call it a 'payment'? And why draw the connection between me and my father?

I noticed we were done with our beers, so I signalled for two more, and we sat in silence until they arrived.

'You said this came from CIB?' I asked. Peter nodded. 'So, am I in the frame for investigation? Arrest? I mean, this is ridiculous...'

'Gal, it is no small thing for your name to be dropped in relation to a payment by two senior triad boys,' Peter, said, pointing out the blindingly obvious. 'CIB wants us to pursue it – and you. You can be sure that it has been noted and they'll be watching you. Closely.'

'Who's leading CI these days?'

Peter drew a breath and shuffled on his chair. I knew this was about to be another piece of news I wouldn't want to hear.

'David Zhou. He heads the unit.'

My skin prickled and I felt a chill as that grenade landed in the space between us.

David Zhou had been a sergeant working in the former Organised and Serious Crime Group with my father and had been the only other person with him the night he was killed. I had always blamed

Zhou for abandoning my father that night – and had told anyone who would listen I believed he had – but the investigation had cleared him based on his statement that he had been acting on orders from my father to scout out another part of the old Kowloon Walled City at the time.

Based largely on physical evidence found at the scene, and Zhou's statement, the investigation concluded Superintendent Simon Jones, 2IC of OSCG, husband to Celia and father of Galahad and Prudence, was killed by 'persons unknown acting for the 14K Triad and likely as a consequence of corrupt dealings with the aforementioned criminal organisation.' Zhou's statement had been the clincher.

I was deeply ashamed of my father for what he had done but I hated David Zhou more.

Zhou had been passed over twice for promotion, largely because of the doubts that lingered over his actions the night my father had been killed, but now he was a Senior Superintendent, and heading up the unit responsible for covert technical and human intelligence on triads in Hong Kong. I had no idea what was happening but, one thing was sure, it did not look good for me.

I decided the best course of action at this point was to deny everything. I wasn't going to spill on the gambling trouble I was in until I could work out what was going on. I rubbed my chin and spoke.

I must have looked surprised – I certainly was – because Peter added: 'Yes, I was surprised at his appointment. Many of us were. Goes to show it's not what you know...'

I nodded absently, not really hearing him.

'I really don't know what this all about, Pete,' I said as I took a sip of the beer. 'Two things are for sure: I have not taken a payment from SYO, or any other gang, and I am not like my father.'

My voice took on a bitter edge. 'Dad was a corrupt copper and he died because of it...I've never taken a back-hander in my life and I don't intend to start now.'

My old friend pursed his lips and scratched the back of his neck. I noticed an ugly yellow pimple on his chin and was staring at it when he spoke again.

'Look,' he said quietly, leaning slightly across the table. 'I know you're not on the take... and I'll do my best to kill any investigation Zhou wants pursued.' He paused and rolled the beer glass in his hands. 'Gal,' he said earnestly. 'If you owe them money, you need to pay it back and get out. Get out from under them. Once they have their hooks into you, they have you for life.'

He stared hard at me for a long moment, then nodded as he said: 'Trust me, I know what I'm talking about.'

As a Chief Inspector in OCTB, he certainly knew what he was talking about, and my friend looked sick with worry for me. He was a little pale and he was rolling his wedding ring with the thumb of his left hand. I wanted to ease his mind but couldn't bring myself to tell him the whole truth so I gave him half a lie.

'Pete, honestly. I have not been paid by SYO and I'm not in any trouble.' I paused. '...that I know of,' I said jokingly, trying to lighten things a little.

'Okay, Gal. I'm sure it's nothing,' he said. 'But Zhou's out for you. You need to watch yourself.'

That bothered me. I could understand why David Zhou would be chasing me, but using a faked wire transcript to do it? Why would two triad gangsters even have that conversation? It just didn't add up.

I mumbled an agreement but wasn't really listening. I was too distracted by what I had learned and trying to figure out what it meant. I was stumped so I filed it away for later examination.

Peter and I hurriedly drank our beers and said our goodbyes, after agreeing to meet again soon for a 'catch-up'. Throwing three hundred down on the table, I walked off down the street toward Central MTR and Peter across the road to his parked car. When I turned back, he was standing in the open door of the car, hand on the roof, watching me.

Before I had walked much further I remembered to call Joey, so I pulled out my phone and tapped the contact. The call had barely connected before she answered – her eagerness sometimes grated on me. Luckily she was at her gym, just around the corner and up Mid-Level Escalators a short way. We agreed to meet in thirty minutes at a small juice bar near the gym so I took my time sauntering along Queen's Road, viewing the high-end goods for sale that I would never be able to buy.

After a short walk, followed by a brief ride up the escalator, I stepped off at Hollywood Road and arrived at the meeting location.

6

I HATE JUICE BARS – especially juice bars attached to gyms.

Juice bars at gyms are always so pompous and judgemental. Feeling like a wet, stray dog that has just turned up at a wedding, I shambled in and examined the board. I wasn't a complete wreck and did, after a fashion, look after myself but I hadn't a clue what half of the hipster ingredients on the board were nor what they would taste like. Apparently, a straight orange juice just wasn't done.

The eager young thing behind the counter was starting to tap her nails on the counter so I hurriedly ordered an apple, carrot and ginger juice and slunk away to take a stool on the counter facing the walkway down Shelley Street. The juice arrived and I sipped at it while I rolled and lit a cigarette.

The disapproving stares, harrumphs and clicks of the tongue were immediate but I shrugged them off. The chances were I was going to meet a sticky end very soon unless I could quickly come up with three hundred grand, so I didn't much care what the gym crowd thought of me.

'What are you doing, boss?' said a stern female voice, Chinese-American accented, at my shoulder. 'Smoking in the gym and winning new friends, I see.'

I swung around on the stool.

Josephine Loh Hu-yung stood next to me, her arms crossed and all 160 centimetres of her giving off a mildly intoxicating blend of disapproval and amusement.

Her yoga mat was slung over a shoulder, her brown skin glistened with a sheen of sweat and the flash tattoos on her arms shone. Her short black hair was dampened to her forehead and her lean, muscular body leaned in toward me as it always did when she was in interrogation mode.

An eyebrow arched inquisitorially and the corner of her mouth curled up in a slight smile, although her dark brown eyes were hooded in a frown. It was very hard not to be attracted to this aggressive, smart young woman – but I did my best.

Joey was Adele's niece and I had given her a job shortly after she had, unexpectedly, left a hitherto stellar career in HKPF where she had been a Sergeant in the VIP Protection Branch of 'B' Department.

There had been rumours at the time of a scandal of some sort but I didn't want to know and had never bothered to ask – being the last person who should ever question anyone about personal scandal. Peter Toh had later told me that she was much missed on her team and had been asked back at least twice to his knowledge.

There was a lot about Joey Loh that I didn't know and about as much that annoyed me. Her age, for one.

She always made me feel old and grumpy and her shiny-eyed optimism made me feel jaded and negative by comparison. She was chatty where I hated to talk and she was an ardent non-smoker. But she was a meticulous investigator, a ruthless interviewer, and a very dangerous person in a tight spot. She was also, for reasons completely beyond me, utterly loyal to me and the shitty little investigations business I ran. I was lucky to have her; she knew it and I knew I should tell her that more.

I butted out the cigarette. 'Ah, the delightful Miss Loh,' I said, switching on my best boyish smile. 'How are you this fine evening?'

She was unimpressed.

'You really don't care if you're unpopular do you...' she said shaking her head in wonder.

'Not particularly,' I agreed.

'You're a sad old man. You know that?'

I inclined my head in agreement. 'It's just as well I enjoy my own company,' I observed. 'I've never much cared for the company of others.'

'Well I do, this is my gym and I'd rather I came here free from the stigma of the attachment to a cranky old gweilo.' She hefted her yoga mat. 'So let's go. Walk with me.'

With that, she spun on her heel and led the way out onto the street and uphill toward Mid-Levels.

'Where are we going?' I asked as she powered her way up the hill, leaving me in her wake wishing I hadn't had that last cigarette. She looked back over her shoulder at me.

'My place,' she said as if it was the most natural thing in the world. It wasn't.

I had never been to Joey's apartment, and I pulled up. I don't know what my face was telegraphing but Joey just looked at me and laughed.

'Boss, don't panic,' she chirped. 'I'm not going to race you off.' Perhaps my face, again, betrayed me and she went on hurriedly. 'I mean, you're a good-looking man, and all, but...let's just say, you're not my type.'

I felt like an idiot – I knew Joey wouldn't see me like that and, to be honest, I didn't see her like that. I don't know what I had been thinking, but I was embarrassed and Joey had covered for me nicely. She turned and strode off up the hill. I tried to keep up and tried not to stare at her ass in her yoga pants.

We turned off Shelley Street and wandered the length of a narrow alley to emerge onto a small public garden and the front door of a small apartment block. Joey keyed in her code, the steel door clanked open and we stepped in.

The smells of close living wrapped around us and I could hear a man swearing loudly in Cantonese, while somewhere above two young children screamed for dinner. Joey hit the stairs – there was no elevator – and I trailed along behind her. The stairwell was dimly lit, and I could smell damp concrete over the noodles, rice and steamed fish. We had climbed four flights and I was starting to suck in big breaths – quietly so Joey wouldn't hear me – when we stopped suddenly.

'Here we are,' Joey said as she pushed an old-school skeleton key into the equally old lock, turned it and pushed the door in with her shoulder.

I stepped across the entrance and froze. After the introduction to the building, I had not expected this.

Joey's apartment was what I imagined an apartment would have looked like if someone had asked a stylist to 'do me 1950s Hong Kong.'

The walls in the small loungeroom were covered in red and black wallpaper and the furniture was classic, traditional Chinese – dark hardwood and ornate. A silk dressing screen divided part of the room and an etched mirror reflected back into the small room, giving it a feeling of size and depth. Light streamed in through two small windows, framed by black, lacquered shutters and a beautiful woman, in a slim-fitting one-piece swimsuit, looked coquettishly out from an old, framed travel poster advertising 'Big Wave Bay – the place to be.' Dust motes danced in the light and I moved across the room to glance into Joey's bedroom while she busied herself in the fridge.

Her bed was large, covered in a gold and red silk bedcover, and dragons chased each other across the cushions thrown artfully against the dark timber bedhead. The only other piece of furniture in the room – if you could call it that – was a lacquered, obviously well-used, wooden Kung Fu training dummy. It resembled more a multi-branched tree than a person, and I could see the rope bindings at its head were stained with years of sweat and rusty, dried blood. I started when I felt a nudge in the back.

Joey held out an open bottle of local pale ale and I nodded my thanks as I took it from her.

'Sit down, relax,' she said, sipping on what appeared to be soda water.

I moved across the room and picked a photo up off a low sideboard. Joey and another young woman laughed into the camera, arms around each other, matching Ray Ban Aviators mirroring the other girl's arm as she snapped the selfie.

'Your sister?' I asked. Joey looked at me with her head cocked slightly and an eyebrow raised.

'No... just a friend.'

I placed the photo down, mumbling something about 'nice' and 'you look happy.' Joey laughed.

'You're almost cute when you're embarrassed, boss,' she said, curling her feet under her on the sofa across from me as I perched on a small wooden chair.

I smiled ruefully. 'Yes, sorry. I'm being a bit of an idiot.'

I paused, suddenly aware of something I had wanted to ask her for months. 'Tell me, Joey: You've worked for me for 18 months now. How are you doing? Are you okay?'

She looked surprised at the question. 'Okay? Sure. Why?'

'Well, for a start, I haven't paid you in nearly two months.'

She shrugged. 'I'm doing all right. I own this place and I have savings stashed away... and there was a pretty decent payout when I left the Job.' She trailed off and her eyes took on a pained expression. I sipped at my beer and waited, quietly, for her to go on. Eventually, she sighed.

'Look,' she said, 'everything's cool. I enjoy the work with you, it's not too demanding and it's good to be close to Adele again...I mean, since mom died.'

'But it's not exactly setting your world on fire, now is it,' I said, stating the obvious. There was nothing about working with me and my struggling investigations company that would have excited anyone. It barely excited me.

Joey nodded. 'No, it's not, that's true. But it's what I need right now. While I get my head around... you know.'

I didn't know so thought I'd venture through that door now Joey had, for the first time, opened it a crack. 'You want to tell me about it?' I asked quietly.

Joey looked at me hard for a moment then shrugged noncommittally. 'Nothing to tell, really,' she offered. It was a lie, of course, but I let it go. 'I fucked up on a job and I paid the price.'

'"Fucking up" in any way doesn't seem like you Joey,' I said. 'I mean, it's just not something you do. Peter Toh tells me the squad wants you back so that's telling me you weren't sacked, but chose to leave...'

She stood up and walked into the small kitchen but shot back at me over her shoulder.

'Boss, not now. Okay? I just don't want to go there. I'm fine, really, and working for you is...' she paused and I could tell she was smiling. '... amusing. Let's leave it at that, huh?'

'Sure,' I mumbled, looking around for an ashtray while I patted my pockets absently to dig out my tobacco pouch. Joey walked back into the room and glared at me with her hands on her hips.

'No smoking!' she shouted and flopped back onto the sofa. I jumped like I'd been hit with a Taser. 'So,' she went on 'what's the scoop?'

'As in the Thomas case?' I asked stupidly, taking the eye roll from Joey in my stride. I sipped at my beer and, seeing nowhere to put it, lowered it gently onto the dark timber floor. I shrugged.

'It's a pile of nothing. She thinks he's fooling around, there has been zero sign of that since I started on it – while you were doing whatever it is you do in Bali that frankly neither Adele nor I want to know.' I sipped at my beer while Joey sighed and rolled her eyes again.

'Anyway,' I continued 'there's nothing in it, waste of everyone's time and I'm about to close it and issue a rather hefty bill.'

I paused briefly, feeling mildly guilty at not telling Joey of my concerns about the case and the many things that just didn't stack up. 'Just one more night on it I think, and I'd like you to cover it. Can you?'

'Tonight?' Joey asked, frowning slightly.

'Yes, if you can.'

She nodded. 'Sure, give me the details. I just need to make a call first.'

'Joey,' I began 'If there's something you have booked, don't worry. I'll cover it...'

She waved her hand in the air to cut me off. 'No, it's totally fine. Give me the details,' she said as she reached for a small notebook and pencil.

I told her everything that had happened on the case, including my disaster at 'Insanity' the night before and she sat silently making notes. When I had finished I sat back.

'That's it,' I said.

Joey nodded and tossed the notebook onto a small table beside her. 'Fine. I'll get on it,' she said. 'I'll call you later with a heads up on any developments.'

There wasn't much more to say so I stood and thanked my young off-sider and let myself out, leaving my half-drunk beer on the side-board next to the photo of Joey and her friend.

I looked at my watch and, as it was still only early evening and I had hours until I expected Joey to pick Thomas up, I decided to grab a noodle soup while I tried to figure out the latest turn of events. I turned left on Queen's Road and soon arrived in Sheung Wan.

The late afternoon had turned dark as the clouds rolled in and rain had started to fall lightly, driving up the already extreme humidity a notch or two. I was sweating freely and watching my feet, not looking where I was going, trying to figure my way out of the mess I was in.

I was completely oblivious to my surroundings and, as I passed the entrance to a small laneway, an arm snaked out and wrapped itself around my throat.

I was jerked off my feet and into the shadows of the alley, my hands scrambling at the vice that held me and was slowly choking the life out of me.

I kicked out and, more by luck than anything, landed a blow down the shin of my assailant and the chokehold relaxed enough for me to duck under it. I tried to spin to face my attacker but wasn't fast enough and a sharp blow to my kidneys dropped me to my knees, followed by another fist to the side of my head that rattled my teeth and exploded a ball of light behind my eyes.

Being on the ground in a street fight is never a good thing, so I tried to get to my feet and face my attackers but blow after blow from bamboo poles rained down on my shoulders, back and legs.

I half stood and covered up to protect my head from the killing blow I expected to be dealt at any moment. Under the storm of kicks and blows I managed to understand that there were at least two, probably three, men now involved in beating the life out of me.

My legs gave out and I slumped onto my hands and knees as blow after blow pounded into me. A pole hammered into the side of my head and I felt my left ear tear. A kick to my kidneys drove straight through me and I collapsed screaming loudly because it hurt. A lot. Then I roared in pain and anger because I was going to die, alone, in an alley, in the rain... like my father.

The beating seemed to go on for hours but was, in fact, probably less than a minute. Then, just as I thought I could take no more, it stopped and one of the attackers knelt down beside me. My vision blurred and his voice was gentle and comforting in my ear.

'Mr Jones, can you hear me?' he whispered. I nodded weakly. 'This is just a reminder of the sum you owe us. We expect full payment in 72 hours. Do you understand?'

I nodded again. The world spun, my eyes rolled back into my head and I slipped into unconsciousness.

More voices. Two men speaking in Cantonese. They were anxious. What had upset them? I seemed to float and could feel my hands trailing along below me as someone touched my head and opened my eyes, one at a time. 'i *told you to stay closer to him. now look!*' – '*i* was *close.*' – '*not close enough you idiot!*' – '*what do we do now? Is he dead?*' – '*no. look he's breathing*'– '*the wounds look bad.*' – '*i've seen worse. he'll be fine.*' – '*so we leave him?*' – '*we leave him. and this time we stay much closer. i'll have to tell the boss and he will not be happy.*' – '*diu...*' Footsteps growing fainter as they moved away, still arguing.

The gritty hardness of the cobbles against my face scratched its way into my mind and I lay there wondering where I was and why I was lying on the ground. The copper taste of blood in my mouth jolted my memory, as did the scorching agony when I tried to roll over.

Flapping onto my back I lay there like a hooked carp, eyes closed, as the heavy rain flooded down on me, washing my face. I opened my mouth and let the rain rinse it before I hawked and spat a glob of blood and mucus onto my shirtfront. Groaning, and wrapping my right arm tightly across my ribs, I sat up.

I immediately regretted the move as my head swam and I emptied the contents of my stomach into my lap. Breathing heavily, and with snot streaming from my nose, I slowly stood and leaned against the alley wall as I waited for the nausea to wash away and the rubbery, lamb-weak feeling to leave my legs.

I mentally checked my injuries and, as bad as they were, I didn't think I needed hospitalisation but I did need somewhere close by to clean up and swallow a box of painkillers. My office, and the med kit, were only a block or two away so, that decision made, I staggered out of the alley. Hunched over like an old man, I shuffled my way in the rain along Queen's Road West toward sanctuary.

An hour later I was sitting in my office, under the yellow glow of the desk lamp, nursing a glass of whisky.

I had arrived at the office and dragged the med kit down from the shelf above my desk, thankful I always kept a fully stocked, paramedic-level kit close at hand. I had stumbled into the shared bathroom down the hall, cradling the red rip-stop bag, and stripped to the waist to bathe, clean and disinfect the wounds I could see and reach. The tear on my ear was pinned together with a butterfly clip, the antiseptic running dark down my jawline, and I turned slowly to look over my shoulder. I could see the bamboo poles had lacerated my back and a number of wounds, ugly gashes across my shoulders and lower back, were bleeding freely.

I tried to reach them with a gauze pad and saline solution but the pain in my ribs when I reached around was like a hot dagger in my chest, so I sluiced my back and shoulders with saline then poured and sipped another whisky, swilling it around my mouth to feel the sting where I had bitten my tongue during the beating.

That done, I settled gingerly in my chair and threw two more paracetamol into my mouth, washing them down with another gulp of whisky, and closed my eyes.

The memory of two men speaking over me as I lay in the alley suddenly popped up like a toy submarine in a kid's bath. Had that actually happened? Who were they? What was it they had said? It was all fuzzy like someone had thrown a gauze curtain over my memory and I was trying to reach back and grab at something that kept shifting, wraith-like, before me.

One thing was clear: the beating was about the debt – I remembered that much.

I had to find that three hundred thousand and I had to find it quick. I had run out of time and there was no way to dodge it: it was pay up or die. The only question was where I'd get that sort of money in that short a time. I had barely asked myself the question when the answer came to me and it was one I didn't want to hear. In fact, I had considered it weeks before and immediately dismissed it.

But there was no dodging the obvious conclusion: I had to get the money from the only source I knew that had it easily to hand. I didn't relish the prospect.

7

PRUDENCE'S EYES widened at the sight of me standing at her apartment entrance. She raised slim fingers to her chin and cocked her head slightly.

'I have questions, Gal. Many questions,' my sister said as she stood back to let me in.

I walked slowly past her, each step an agony as the wounds across my back seemed to tear open with each movement. I gingerly shrugged out of the jacket I had picked up in the office and heard Prudence gasp as she took in the back of my white T-shirt.

'My *God* Galahad! What on earth happened?'

She ushered me across the apartment and sat me on a stool at the kitchen bar – I noticed she didn't offer me a seat on her soft, and very expensive, sofa.

She busied herself in the fridge and poured me a soda water then took a stool across from me. I had hoped for something stronger, but I thanked her anyway.

'I have to say, Gal,' she began 'I haven't seen you for weeks and you turn up here looking like that. I'm not super-impressed.'

She slapped the counter of the kitchen bar. 'Give! What have you got yourself into?'

Prudence was my younger sister but had treated me like a kid brother since the death of both of our parents. To be honest, I liked it – it made me feel that someone, at least, loved me. It was a puzzle to me why I avoided her so much. Shame, probably, and not a little jealousy. Prudence was everything I was not.

She had inherited our mother's beauty and, in fact, looked more Chinese than I did. Much more. She was nearly as tall as me, as slim as a willow and twice as graceful. Her long raven black hair framed a delicate, heart-shaped face from which a pair of dark, perfectly shaped almond eyes viewed the world with keen interest and a hint of healthy cynicism.

She had burst onto the Hong Kong, then international, modelling scene at a young age and had invested her phenomenal appearance payments wisely before marrying the son of one of Hong Kong's wealthiest Tai-pans. I had gone to the wedding, of course, but don't remember much of it through the drunken haze that was much of my life at the time. The marriage lasted just two years before her husband, and scion of that Hong Kong family, was found dead of a drug overdose with a rubber hood over his head in a mistress's apartment.

Prudence had inherited a large portion of his wealth – his family not standing in the way out of shame at the circumstances of his death. Now independently wealthy, one of Hong Kong's leading art dealers and Socialites-of-Note, my sister was at the top of her game and strode through life with both confidence and grace. As I said, she was everything I am not.

I took a deep breath. 'First thing, Pru, have you got a first aid kit here?'

She shook her head. 'No, but the concierge does. I've seen him carrying it.' She stood and reached for the house phone. 'I'll call him.'

I held up a hand. 'Hang on, I don't want it getting about...'

She shook her head. 'Don't be an idiot, brother. Mr Cheng is completely trustworthy, utterly discreet and a darling man. Leave it with me.' She turned away and picked up the apartment phone.

I knew better than to argue, so I shuffled over to her bar and poured a generous shot of very expensive whisky into an equally expensive cut crystal glass.

The concierge arrived swiftly with the first aid kit and I was impressed – it was well-equipped and more than just the pack of Band-Aids and box of Panadol I had expected.

I snatched a series of gauze dressings from it, a bottle of Betadine, cotton swabs and surgical tape and headed to the bathroom with Prudence in tow.

I eased the bloody T-shirt off and, bending over the bathroom sink, let Pru go to work. I could see her face in the mirror. She was concentrating on the job at hand as I directed her, but her eyes were clouded, and I could tell she was a roiling ball of emotions. Finally, she spoke as she dabbed antiseptic into the wounds on my back.

'I'm not going to ask what happened,' she said quietly, standing back to survey her handiwork while she tore open a gauze pad. 'I can see what happened. What I want to know is *why*?'

For a moment I considered lying – it's always easier – but I drew a breath and looked up. Her deep brown eyes caught mine in the mirror.

'I owe money, Pru,' I said. 'A lot of money.' I winced as she gently placed the gauze pad on one of the wounds. 'Three hundred and twenty-five grand, to be precise.' Her only reaction was a slight intake of breath and a narrowing of her eyes, so I went on.

'I got in deep at an underground Mahjong parlour in Yau Ma Tei and couldn't win my way out. I borrowed to try and clear the losses and it just got worse.'

'Okay, that's not good,' she said. 'But I'm sensing there's something else?'

'Yes...that'd be the involvement of a triad in both the parlour and my debt...' I grunted as she slapped the back of my head.

'*Diu*, Gal!' she shouted. 'You *bloody* fool. You're a cop for God's sake... well an ex-cop. What the hell are you doing gambling in a triad parlour? What would Dad think..?'

I spun around to face her, anger rising in me.

'Don't fucking throw Dad in my face, Pru! He's hardly an example of moral rectitude, now is he!' I shook my head and lowered my voice. 'He was bent Pru...when are you ever going to accept that?' I sighed. 'Our father was a corrupt copper and he betrayed us all...'

Prudence closed her eyes. 'He did *not*! It's wrong, it can't be...'

'I've been telling you for years. It's true. The evidence was clear. I never wanted to believe it but there's no other explanation. I went through the file in detail when I was in the Job and it was watertight. What he did was never forgiven and it drove me out of the force. I couldn't go on as the son of a corrupt copper... I wanted to, but the Job just couldn't live with it, or me.'

Prudence just watched me in silence, and I took a deep breath.

'And it killed Mum,' I said quietly. 'It wasn't the bottle of temazepam that did it, it was the shame and the heartbreak.'

She closed her eyes again and I saw a fat tear slide slowly down one cheek.

I stood still, my throat constricted, tears pricking at my own eyes. The sense of loss was almost overwhelming, and my sister and I stood in silence, looking at each other, both feeling the same thing – we were all we had in the whole world. Prudence recovered first.

'Turn around,' she said, sniffing. 'I haven't finished and your back looks like burger mince.'

Fifteen minutes later, I lowered myself into the sofa with gritted teeth and an intake of breath. Pru sat opposite and regarded me expressionlessly, her head tilted slightly. We faced each other across a low coffee table, my back dressed and ribs strapped. Prudence rolled her eyes and shook her head as I sipped at the whisky and swallowed two paracetamol.

'Well, it goes without saying I'll give you the money,' she said.

'Loan...'

'Who are you kidding Gal? "Give". You'll never be able to afford to repay me. And that's okay daaih lou, *big brother*. I'll transfer it to your account this afternoon.'

'Thanks, sai mui, *sister*,' I said softly, my face hot with shame. 'I really appreciate it. I promise..'

'Gal, don't,' she said quietly. 'Don't make a promise I know you won't or can't keep.'

She sighed. 'You drink too much, you're opinionated, you gamble what little money you have...but you're you, and I love you.'

I hated myself then, sitting there across from my younger, wealthy, successful sister. I was supposed to be the guardian of what was left of our family and, instead, she was wiping my nose and bailing me out of trouble. Again.

She was right, of course – what would my father think if he could see me? I swallowed the last of the whisky, put the glass down and stood up. Turning to Prudence I bent and gave her a kiss on the forehead.

'I'm so sorry Pru. Really. I swear to you: I'll get this sorted out and make changes.'

She looked at me sadly and I knew she didn't believe me. 'I know you will Gal,' she said softly as I crossed the room and let myself out.

8

THREE HUNDRED AND twenty-five thousand Hong Kong Dollars is a lot of money – at least it is in my books.

The black sports bag I gripped as I left the bank branch bulged at the seams and weighed much more than I would have imagined. Hong Kong is a safe city – mostly – but I felt vulnerable as I stood at the traffic lights waiting to cross Hennessy Road.

I was carrying more money than I had ever seen and I felt a growing paranoia standing in the open, holding it, waiting for someone to come along and knock me on the head. The lights changed and I crossed the road and hurried toward my apartment to stash the bag, arriving, sweat-soaked, ten minutes later.

I pushed open the apartment door and stepped in. Something on the floor caught my eye and I bent down to pick up a small piece of folded paper. Dropping the bag on the sofa I unfolded the paper and stared at the words written on it in Cantonese. '*we told you, look to Aberdeen. 21/7.*'

For a moment I was lost, then I recalled the note that had been left at my office a week before. Something about paying more attention to Aberdeen. I had dismissed it at the time – probably as a result of the hangover I had been suffering – and had forgotten about it. Now this.

What was going on? Where in Aberdeen and why did the mysterious note-leaver want me to look into it? Were the numbers a reference to the twenty-first of July, the following day? More importantly, how did the note-leaver know where I lived?

Aberdeen? I shook my head in frustration. I couldn't just wander around a district of Hong Kong waiting for something to crop up that I should pay attention to. I shoved the note into my jeans pocket and grabbed a water from the fridge. Something – more than the mysterious dropping of anonymous notes into my life – was ringing bells in my head but I couldn't figure out what.

I walked out onto my terrace, sipping the cold water and closed my eyes, willing my mind to focus. In seconds it came to me and my eyes snapped open. I ran back inside and pulled out a box from under the desk and tipped out its contents onto the loungeroom floor.

Old copies of the South China Morning Post, Oriental Daily, Sing Tao, South China Herald and Metro Daily spilled out around me along with a pile of individual clippings. I crouched down to sort through them, turning first to the clippings.

For years I had kept clippings of different news stories that had caught my attention at the time – a habit I had developed while in the Job – and there were, literally, hundreds of them. I knew what I was looking for, and from approximately what time, so it wasn't long before I gave a small grunt of satisfaction and pulled out a Herald clipping from two months prior.

The story was only brief, a few lines lost in amongst other local news, but I remembered it – I recalled wondering, at the time, why it hadn't been picked up by other outlets. It was almost as if it wasn't newsworthy. '*Undocumented girl dead in Aberdeen*' read the headline. I read on.

'*The body of a young woman, thought to be of Cambodian origin, was found late last night by passers-by on the side of Tin Wan Praya Road, close to the sea wall guarding the entrance to the Aberdeen Typhoon Shel-*

ter. Hospital sources state the young woman died from strangulation. Police sources state the young woman was carrying no identification and fingerprint records show there was no record of her entry into Hong Kong SAR. Police investigations are continuing.'

I dropped the clipping to one side and flicked through the larger pile to find any follow-up on the incident. Nothing. The story had very quickly been dropped, probably for both lack of information and lack of interest. Who cares about a dead, undocumented Cambodian girl anyway?

I scratched the back of my head. Was this what the mysterious notes were referring to? I was drawing a long bow, and I had absolutely no reason to connect the two, but I couldn't shake the feeling they were related somehow. I scooped up the papers and threw them back into the box.

I would get back to the notes, Aberdeen and the dead girl later but I had more pressing matters to attend to – namely a visit to a triad Mahjong parlour to pay a particularly nasty person a very large sum of money.

9

YAU MA TEI lies on Kowloon-side between the more well-known districts of Tsim Sha Tsui and Mong Kok and is mostly overlooked by tourists as they pass through on their way to the Ladies Market or the Jade Market in Jordan.

Like much of the rest of Hong Kong, Yau Ma Tei is a bustling, vibrant district. Unlike much of the rest of Hong Kong, it was also home to a particular underground Mahjong school, run by a loan shark and triad soldier known as 'Jade Tooth', to whom I was deeply in debt.

I stepped off the MTR and slung the backpack containing HKD325,000 as I walked through the late-afternoon commute buzzing through the station.

I was sweating freely by the time I exited onto the street and headed west toward the small doorway I knew was nestled between a convenience store and a Chinese herbalist. It had been threatening rain for days and the Observatory had a T3 Typhoon Signal up, so storms were expected and the humidity was oppressive. My shirt stuck damply to me, I weaved my way through the crowds, past the doorways of stores selling everything from jade ornaments, incense and home goods, to knock-off sunglasses, pet supplies and cheap T-shirts.

Bicycle couriers rode sedately through the traffic, ringing the bells on their ancient two-wheelers, Cantonese fast food in white plastic bags dangling from the handlebars. Delivery drivers competed for what little space there was on the street in their never-ending quest to feed the machine that is Hong Kong small business.

Tempers frayed and singleted, sweating men shouted and swore at each other as they trundled their low metal trolleys, stacked high with goods, through the pedestrian current that, like water meeting a mid-stream rock, flowed around them and on its way.

Two nights before, Joey had tailed Thomas around much of Hong Kong Island, to a variety of bars and a long Italian meal with a group of what appeared to be work colleagues and their wives – Sarah Thomas has been conspicuously absent. Joey had reported the entire night as a bust – nothing out of the ordinary – as the following day had been. I was now convinced we were wasting our time. I decided, as I stepped past a pile of boxes, that we'd close the case and send the nicely padded account for payment (14 days terms please) and Sarah Thomas could work things out with her husband.

I was lost in thought when I was shouldered by a passer-by and the backpack slipped from my shoulder. I caught the strap with my right hand and was slightly turned to re-sling the pack when I noticed two men come to a sudden stop five metres behind me.

Their eyes were on me and they fumbled clumsily as one suddenly turned right to cross the road while his partner took a sudden interest in the ginseng and walnuts outside a herbalist store.

I had not seen either before but they were obviously following me and I was acutely aware of the money I was carrying – and who it belonged to. I spun on my heel and moved quickly down the street, barely stopping to acknowledge the bouncer leaning in the entrance to the 'Lucky Dragon Social Club' as I plunged down the stairs and into Jade Tooth's lair.

It was dim and cool at the bottom of the stairs as I stepped into the empty main room of 'The Lucky Dragon'. The Mahjong tables were covered and staff silently swept and dusted, while an elderly lady put out ashtrays and filled the tea urns with hot water, readying for the people who would soon arrive with wads of cash and an addiction for the deafening clatter of thousands of ivory Mahjong tiles in a noisy, smoke-filled room.

A match struck in a dark corner to my right, briefly illuminating a face as a cigarette was lit. I could see the red glow from the cigarette as its owner dragged deeply, and then a cloud of blue smoke emerged into the room with a faint hissing sound.

'Mr Jones, welcome back,' Jade Tooth said. 'I am assuming that rather over-stuffed bag contains my money?'

Jade Tooth may have acted like a Bond villain but he was far from laughable. In fact, he was probably the most violent person I knew in Hong Kong – and that was saying something. I didn't find his theatrics in the slightest bit amusing, nor was I intimidated by them.

'It's all here, Jade Tooth,' I said, dropping the backpack onto a nearby table. '325,000 crisp dollars. I'll just wait while you count it, shall I?'

Jade Tooth emerged into the room like a snake slithering from a hole. He slid across the room toward me with his slim hips swinging slightly in tight jeans and a black mesh T-shirt stretched across his muscled torso.

An intricate, black-shaded tattoo of a dragon wrapped itself around his right arm from shoulder to wrist and the fingers of his right hand were studded with gold rings. A large gold watch was strapped around his left wrist and the butt of a QSZ-92 protruded from the waistline of his jeans. Jade Tooth was a very dangerous, and slightly unhinged, person.

He smiled, shaking his head, a look of regret on his face.

'Oh, I'm sorry Mr Jones. You didn't get the message?' he said softly. 'A few days ago, you remember. I thought it was quite clear.'

'It was clear, Jade Tooth,' I said, feeling the sting of the tight wounds across my back and shoulders and the throb of my torn left ear. '72 hours to deliver, and here it is.'

Jade Tooth dragged on his cigarette and sighed out the smoke.

'*Interest*, Mr Jones,' he said. 'Did my messengers not advise you of the interest charge?' I stood stock still and he went on. 'I'm afraid that, due to your tardiness in repaying the amount owed, you now owe me a further $50,000.'

He moved to a chair and sat. I stayed silent – there wasn't really much to say.

'You are very quiet, Mr Jones,' he observed. 'Have I surprised you?'

'I haven't got it,' I said quietly, not taking my eyes from his.

Jade Tooth tilted his head and seemed to consider that. 'Hmm... whatever shall we do now?'

The bastard was toying with me.

'Give me three days. I'll get it,' I said, feeling a bead of sweat leave my hairline and trickle down the back of my neck.

He studied the tip of the cigarette before stubbing it out gently in an ashtray. Tapping the end of his nose with his right index finger he pretended to consider my suggestion, then pointed at me.

'You have 72 hours,' he said.

I sighed gently, hoping he didn't notice. The sweat was now streaming down my back, sticking my shirt to my spine.

'If I don't have it in 72 hours,' he went on, 'you and I will take a ride in my boat. Have you seen my boat? It's quite the thing.'

'I don't like boats. You'll have the money.'

'Excellent,' Jade Tooth said, all smiles as he stood. 'Well, I think we're done here.'

I nodded at the bag on the table. 'You don't want to count that?'

Jade Tooth flapped a hand at me in dismissal. 'Don't be silly,' he said. 'We all trust each other here. Right?'

I nodded, turned around and left the room, feeling Jade Tooth's eyes clawing my neck every step of the way.

I pushed past the bouncer who was still lounging in the doorway and out into the humidity of the early evening. I checked my watch. I had until 5:15 p.m. in three days' time to deliver Jade Tooth $50,000 – money I didn't have and had no way of getting. I was a dead man.

I stood on the footpath and rolled and lit a cigarette as the crowd ebbed and flowed around me – I had seriously been thinking of giving up the habit but now was definitely not the time.

As I drew the smoke deep into my lungs, I glanced across the road and straight into the eyes of the two men who had been following me earlier. They had to be Jade Tooth's boys. Something inside me snapped and I surged out onto the road, blind to the traffic that honked in protest, and across to the men who stood stock still, eyes wide in shock, watching my approach.

I had almost crossed the road when a van blared its horn and swung in front of me to come to a halt at the kerb. By the time I got across the road and around the rear of the van, the men were 50 metres down the street and rounding a corner.

I set off at a run, shouldering people aside, ignoring the black looks and shouts of offence and the agonising sting of my wounds tearing open.

My cracked ribs seemed to drive white-hot daggers into my chest but I was at the corner in a matter of seconds, rounded it into the next street and skidded to a halt.

There was no sign of the men in the swirling mass of cars, vans and pedestrians. The crowds washed around me in the dim early evening, lit now by multi-coloured neon signs that flickered and danced, painting faces in the street with their colour. I stood on my toes and looked around. Nothing, the men were gone. I swore softly, turned and headed back to the MTR station and the short trip back to the Island and home.

It was dark by the time I was near home. I was in such a funk worrying about what I'd do with Jade Tooth and his fifty grand that my stomach roiled and my bowels felt loose and hot.

There was no way I could raise that sort of money in that short a time, and I was definitely not going to approach Prudence for it – what little pride I had left wouldn't let me do that. The inescapable conclusion was, that unless a miracle flew its way across the Eight Dragons and dropped itself into my lap, my corpse would soon be feeding the fish wherever the current took it.

I squared my shoulders as I turned into my home street; I needed a drink and tonight I would have more than one.

I stepped into the alleyway that led to the back door of my apartment building and stopped at a faint sound. It seemed to come from inside a pile of cardboard boxes stacked against the wall and blocking the footpath.

I listened, squinting my eyes as one does when listening intently, and heard it again – a soft whine and snuffle came from the pile of boxes. I tossed aside the top boxes and looked down. In an old banana box, filled with litter, sat a brown and black puppy. I leaned in for a closer look and the little creature looked up at me and whimpered softly, its tail wagging. I picked it up and examined it a little closer.

He wasn't tiny but skinny and had a bloated little belly that was a sure sign of worms, and he had sores on his back and hindquarters. I sighed. What was I going to do with this?

'You poor little bastard,' I said softly, tucking him into the crook of my arm, scratching him behind the ear, while I reached into my back pocket for my phone.

I opened my contacts; found the number I was looking for and tapped the number. I had a short conversation with the person on the other end of the line and turned back to the pup.

'I can't keep you,' I said. 'I'll probably be in a worse state than you in a couple of days, but I can get you help. Meantime, let's go inside for some water and a snack.'

An hour later I was sitting on a chair in the kitchen watching the pup slurp down fresh water and chew furiously on a piece of beef jerky I had found in the back of the cupboard, when the doorbell rang.

I opened the door and did a double take. A large Chinese woman stood in my doorway in a multi-coloured kaftan and bright red horn-rimmed glasses that matched her lipstick and dangerously long fingernails. She lifted her right hand, to the tinkling sound of a dozen thin bangles, and thrust it out. I took her hand and shook it gingerly – I needn't have bothered; she had a grip like a tyre mechanic.

'I'm Jenny Lam,' she sang loudly. 'You must be Galahad and this...' she said looking past me at the pup that had wandered out of the kitchen '...must be the little one in question. May I come in?'

I stepped back hurriedly. 'Of course, I'm sorry,' I said as she barged past me and scooped up the pup in one large, manicured hand.

'Oh my *dear*,' she said gently, 'you are a *darling* but you're in need of some TLC, are you not my love?' The pup licked her hand and wagged his tail furiously as she cradled him.

'So you can take him then?' I asked, grateful the pup would be looked after and also off my hands.

She turned to look at me, a faintly disapproving look on her face. 'No, Galahad,' she said. 'I cannot take him. We have no room. It's an epidemic of abandoned animals out there and I'm seeing half a dozen dears like this little fellow every single day. No room at the inn, I'm afraid. No, none at all.'

'Well I can't keep him,' I said helplessly.

'Why?'

'*Why*?'

'Yes, why can you not take him? Forgive me but I see a man who obviously has a soft spot for dogs...' she looked pointedly about the apartment 'lives alone...'

She paused as I muttered something and scooped up an empty whiskey bottle and dropped it into the bin. '...and who could, in all likelihood, use the company and stability a dog companion brings.' She stood back and eyed me placidly.

'Ms Lam...' I stammered.

'Not another word, Mr Jones. You called a friend of mine about the puppy and she called me. She, apparently, knows you and thinks this little pup is your key to redemption.'

'Redemption?'

'Yes, we are all redeemed when we open up our hearts and our lives to help one of God's creatures.'

'Well, I'm sure that's right but...'

She looked hard at me for thirty seconds. I felt as if she was looking straight into my soul and was distinctly uncomfortable at the prospect.

'Galahad,' she said softly, 'I want you to seriously consider taking this dog into your life – it will change things for you, from what I've been told.'

Was everyone in Hong Kong talking about me?

'Ms Lam,' I said sighing loudly, 'If only you knew. Nothing is going to change things for me right now…' I scratched my head. 'But, yes, I'll think about it after you've seen to his treatment with the vet.'

I reached for my wallet and drew out two five-hundred-dollar notes. 'This should cover it and you can take what's left as a donation.'

Her head tilted as she regarded me again. 'I see that your wallet is now empty,' she said. 'I was right about you.'

'Don't be so hasty,' I said as I escorted the large, loud and lovely woman, and what now seemed to be my new dog, out of my apartment.

The door closed, I smiled and shook my head. I was staring at the prospect of an especially gruesome death in a little over 40 hours but the pup and a boisterous woman in a kaftan had lifted my spirits immensely. Still, the meeting with Jade Tooth had left me shaken – as had the certain knowledge his men were tailing me and had been the ones who delivered the beating. I still needed that drink.

10

MUCH LATER THAT EVENING, after a number of drinks in a cop bar in Wan Chai, I climbed the stairs to a high-end cocktail bar in Wan Chai and waited patiently to pay the exorbitant entrance fee and get the inside of my right wrist stamped by an attractive Ukrainian hostess. Stepping through the heavy velvet curtains was like stepping back seventy years into a slightly seedy speak-easy.

The décor was traditional Chinese. Dark, hardwood yokeback chairs, and porcelain vases and jars, lacquered screens and wedding cabinets, Imperial Lions and exposed timber ceiling beams abounded – all artfully and dimly lit in a soft green and white hue by suspended glass versions of the traditional oil-paper umbrella.

The place was packed with well-heeled drinkers, both Hong Kongers and expats, sipping their artisan cocktails in the din of conversation over which played a loud techno version of an Edith Piaf track. Waitresses glided through the crowd, trays skilfully balanced on raised hands, dressed in figure-hugging black and red cheongsam, their hair immaculate in wavy and curled 1940s styles.

I moved to the bar and made some elbow room while I waited to order.

Glancing up I took in the two attractive women, dressed in green and black cheongsam, each lounging on a separate shelf fixed to the back wall, sensually moving their hands in time to the beat of the music, while decorously covering their faces with ivory and silk fans.

The bar was a stylish and intoxicating mix of Cirque du Soleil meets 19th century opium den – it wasn't really my thing, and I rarely ventured through the velvet curtain, but I was there that night for a reason. I leaned in and shouted an order for a Whisky Sour and looked up into the eyes of one of the girls on the back wall.

Angel Yeung Mei-ying had her fan raised but her eyes crinkled in a smile of recognition and I smiled back. With a dramatic flick of her wrist, she snapped the fan shut then gently tapped it onto the square face of her vintage watch and held up five fingers. I nodded, picked up my drink and stepped back from the bar.

I smiled at a security guy who unclipped a red velvet rope that cordoned off a small lounge area from the rest of the room and stepped through.

Settling back into a couch, I took a long pull on the drink and closed my eyes as the sherried single malt washed through me and Piaf's techno 'La vie en rose' beat at my senses. My eyes were still closed when I felt the couch sink and the scent of jasmine and bergamot wafted over me as a light kiss was planted on my cheek. I smiled and opened one eye.

'Hi,' I croaked, my throat constricting as it always did when Angel Yeung was near me.

'Hi yourself Gal,' she said, smiling. 'It's been for ages, darling. Where have you been?'

I shrugged. 'You know. Here and there..'

She rolled her eyes and turned to the security guy.

'Tony,' she called. 'Glass of bubbles please my darling. Toot sweet!' The bouncer smiled and lumbered off and Angel turned back to me.

She squinted as she looked at me. 'Who beat you up?'

She was both observant and direct. I scratched the back my head and winced. 'Jade Tooth's boys. Small matter of a wee debt...'

'Three hundred and twenty-five large isn't a *wee debt* Gal, especially where Jade Tooth and those shit-heads in SYO are concerned.'

My eyes widened in surprise – although I really shouldn't have been. 'How did you know that?' I asked as her champagne arrived and the security guy handed it to her with a little bow.

'Thank you my love. Tony you are such a *dear*,' she said then turned back to me, slipping her arm around my neck. My heart started to thud and I sipped the whisky.

'Gal, do you need to even ask that?' she said. 'One: I know everything that goes on around here and, Two: you already know why that is, right?'

I shrugged again. 'Well, we've never *actually* discussed it, Angel. It's just my professional hunch based on...well, a bunch of things.'

'How long have we known each other?' she asked, leaning in to whisper in my ear.

'Not long enough,' I replied. 'Too long.'

Angel nodded. 'And all of the time,' she whispered, 'you've known I was 14K. Sure, you've probably tried to deny it, force it down – being an ex-cop and all – but you've known. Every time we've been to dinner, every time we've been to the movies, every drink, every hike we've done... every time you've bedded me, you've known.'

She smiled and leaned back, her hands in the air. 'There, it's all out in the open. Better, huh?'

She was right. I had known all along.

Peter Toh had confirmed Angel was 'peripherally connected' to 14K not long after she and I had started seeing each other, and he had warned me off. Typically, I hadn't listened to Peter and, equally typically, I had denied it to myself and justified it endlessly until the fact my girlfriend was a triad associate had been laundered Persil white.

I also wasn't blind to the fact that it was 14K who had killed my father. That I was seeing one of their women, regardless of how 'peripheral', was just another of the many reasons I had to despise myself, but it was useless resisting. She had her hooks deep into me and I was too weak to do anything about that.

I took another pull on my drink and smiled at her.

'You're right, of course,' I said. 'Always known, but always denied it. You're too important to me to let a small thing like criminal connections get in the way.'

She tossed her head and laughed, then sipped at the champagne. 'Oh dear Galahad, whatever am I going to do with you?'

'Marry me?'

That got her. She sat back and stared at me, a frown creasing her brow.

'Ahhh,' she smiled after a few seconds, wagging her finger, 'you nearly had me there,' she said, punching me lightly right on top of what I suspected was a broken rib courtesy of Jade Tooth's lads.

I winced and bit down on the inside of my lip. Angel threw back the rest of her champagne and stood up.

'I have to get back to it, Gal,' she said, looking at her watch. 'You hanging around?'

I checked my watch. It was nearly midnight so I shook my head. 'No, I'll head home. I need to be up early and attend to something. Great to see you, Angel.'

She bent down and kissed me lightly on the lips. 'I'll let myself in later, Gal. I'll try not to wake you.'

'Angel, that would be cruel and unusual treatment, and I won't have it,' I said as she smiled and walked away.

11

THE NEXT MORNING I woke feeling surprisingly good considering how much I'd had to drink the night before. My eyes still closed I rolled over and froze as I came into contact with a body. Through the fog of sleep, the memory came back to me.

Angel had let herself in around 4:00 a.m. and I had lain there, in the dark, feigning sleep, as she slipped out of her cheongsam, the whisper of its silk pooling on the floor in an alluring hiss. She had showered and quietly, gently, slipped into bed beside me. I had kept my eyes closed, my heart hammering, as she slid up against me.

'I know you're awake,' she had whispered. 'You're holding your breath.'

I exhaled and reached for her. 'You're like some sort of ninja,' I said hoarsely as I leaned in to kiss her.

Her long, wet hair draped across my chest as she rolled onto me, our mouths locked, and I lay back in the thrall of my triad girl.

Now the sun poured through the blinds and I leaned across and kissed the nape of her neck. She purred like a cat as I moved back the covers and climbed out of bed, rubbing my hair and stretching. I padded across the apartment into the kitchen and flicked on the coffee machine then headed for the shower.

Fifteen minutes later, I was dressed and standing on the terrace in the early morning light as the birds hopped and pecked at the seed I had put out. I sipped at the coffee and dragged on the first cigarette of the day, feeling both the caffeine and nicotine go to work on my system.

I blew out a cloud of cherry-scented smoke and looked up at the sky, still blue before the clouds of another humid day rolled over. I had a little over 36 hours to get the money to Jade Tooth and I was rolling this worrisome fact around in my mind when my phone rang. I checked the screen before answering it.

Sarah Thomas. In two weeks I had come up with zero evidence of any misbehaviour on her husband's part. Whatever he had been up to – if ever there was anything – was now all done. I had thought I'd never hear from Mrs Thomas again and Adele had been preparing her invoice only the day before.

My wounds were still healing and I suspected the cracked rib was probably worse than I had thought – Angel's wild physicality the night before hadn't helped. It stabbed at me when I raised the phone to my ear.

'Mrs Thomas. Good morning. What can I do for you?'

'It's started again,' she said without preamble. 'Last night. He went out at nine and got back this morning just before dawn.'

'Has he said anything to you about it?'

'He said he was out drinking with some of his friends, but I just don't believe it...'

I sighed, probably too loudly and I'm sure she heard me. I really was over the whole thing. Joey had picked up some regular protection work in the last few days that was billing quite well, so I had little patience, or time, for Sarah Thomas and her husband.

'Mrs Thomas,' I said. 'I'm sorry but there is really nothing more I can do for you. I can follow your husband for another month and still not...'

'*Please*,' she shouted down the phone then paused to gather herself. 'Please,' she said quietly. 'Just one more night. Just one more try. I'm sure it has started again. It's almost like it's a monthly thing ...'

That set off a bell in my head and I scratched my chin. A monthly thing. If it was, it wasn't a girl, it was something else – something on a schedule?

'Ok, Mrs Thomas,' I said. 'One last night then I'm off the case and we'll send you the account. Do we agree?'

The phone was silent for seconds and I thought the connection had been lost before she spoke. 'Yes, we agree,' she said in a hiss, through clenched teeth. 'You *really* have not been much use to me, Mr Galahad Jones.' She ended the call and left me staring at my phone and wincing a little in embarrassment.

That night, at a little after 8:00 p.m. James Thomas left his apartment building and walked downhill to the Mid-Levels Escalators. He seemed to be in a hurry and didn't glance back, which was just as well as I was in close, not wanting to lose him. Once he hit Queen's Road he turned right and headed east. Minutes later we were on the MTR heading east on the Island Line and I knew where we would get off.

The train pulled in at Wan Chai Station and Thomas stepped off, moving through the dense evening crowd, with me two metres behind him and slightly to his right. He picked up his pace and was walking quickly, stepping and dodging his way through the crowd, stealing frequent glances at his watch. I was pleased to see that. It told me that, whatever he was doing, he was running late and I wouldn't have long to wait before all would be revealed.

Unsurprisingly, we stepped out of the MTR onto Lockhart Road. Thomas headed west and five minutes later he stepped through the front door of 'Insanity'.

I had a decision to make and I made it quickly. If I followed him in, he was likely to go straight out the back door and would spot me when I followed him into the corridor leading to the alley. He'd certainly spot me in the alley once I emerged behind him.

I ran to the corner and turned right onto Jaffe Road, slowing to a walk when I saw a black Mercedes parked at the alley I was aiming for. The street was heaving with people and I came to a halt. Leaning against the wall, I rolled a cigarette while I watched the car and the alley entrance.

In less than a minute I was rewarded with the sight of Thomas emerging onto the street and heading to the parked car. He was carrying a green backpack – that explained why he had gone through 'Insanity' first; he had to pick something up. But what and why? I drew on my cigarette. 'Curiouser and curiouser, said Alice,' I muttered.

The back door to the Mercedes opened and Thomas ducked in. I looked around frantically for a taxi as the Merc pulled out into the traffic on Jaffe Road. Luckily spotting one, I hailed it and leapt in. Rolling my eyes, I pointed to the Mercedes and snapped at the driver; 'Follow that car!

For fifteen minutes the black Mercedes wove its way through Hong Kong traffic, starting from Wan Chai and then making its way into the Western Harbour Crossing. As we entered the tunnel it dawned on me.

I guessed where Thomas was heading and only ten or fifteen minutes more would tell me if I was right or not. Sure enough, after emerging onto the tunnel toll road and heading northwest for a little over ten minutes, the Mercedes turned off the West Kowloon Highway, with Stonecutters Island on our left, and down Container Port Road.

We were headed to Kwai Chung Container Terminal and, probably, Thomas' office at AsiaWide Shipping.

I knew now, for certain, that this was never about an errant husband and a girl. Something else was going on and I wanted to know what.

The Mercedes stopped briefly at the well-lit security gate before entering, so I directed to taxi driver to pull over in a patch of deep shadow, on the access road among half a dozen parked cars with a view of the gate. The driver shrugged, did as I asked and switched off the engine. I stepped out of the taxi and reached for my phone. It answered, as usual, in two rings.

'Joey, I'm with Thomas at Kwai Chung,' I said with no greeting. 'Can you get on your bike and get down here? I may need you if we have to split a tail when he comes back out.'

'I'm not doing anything important boss, thanks for asking,' she replied. 'Luckily for you, I have no life.'

'Yeah yeah. Can you get out here?'

There was a pause while she probably checked her watch. 'Sure,' she said. 'I can be there in about twenty minutes. What's happening?'

'I'll tell you when you get here,' I said. 'Just get here quick – I've no idea how long Thomas will be inside. Check your phone; I'll share my location with you.'

Without waiting for Joey to reply, I ended the call. I rolled and lit a cigarette and leaned against the warm bonnet of the taxi to watch the gate. Fat drops of rain began to fall, splatting onto the warm bitumen of the road to throw up that familiar, earthy scent and thunder growled in the hills above Kam Shan Country Park.

My train of thought was soon derailed by the sound of a motorbike kicking down through the gears as it rounded the bend behind me. I had been considering what Thomas' covert late-night visit to his office might mean and had drawn a blank but, given his actions to get there, I was certain it wasn't something legitimate or legal. Time would tell, I thought, as I ground out the cigarette under my heel.

Joey pulled up beside me and flipped up the visor of her helmet.

'Hey boss,' she said, her muffled voice breaking the sudden silence as she flipped the kill switch on the bike. 'What's up?'

I was about to answer when the gate alarm sounded and a large truck hove into view inside the terminal, heading for the gate. I squinted into the light enveloping the gatehouse as the truck pulled up, a shipping container sitting on its tray. Joey and I exchanged a glance – was it anything? Joey spoke first.

'So it's a shipping container. This is a container terminal after all. Probably nothing to...' I held up my hand silencing her.

'Behind the truck,' I said pointing. 'Can you see it? The Merc. It's him'

Joey nodded. 'Right,' she said snapping down the visor of her helmet. 'I'll slip in behind you. If they split, I'll take the truck and you take Thomas. Good to go?'

I looked at Joey and smiled. As usual, when the job was on she switched from annoying skater-girl to a focussed and competent operator. For the fiftieth time that week I thought how lucky I was to have her working for me, so I gave her a thumbs up and climbed into the taxi, while she started the bike and swung it around in a tight circle to face back up the road.

The truck passed us and I examined the shipping container as it slipped by.

It looked like any other standard ISO shipping container. It was painted blue, 2.5 metres wide, about 2.5 metres high and 6 metres in length. I noted the louvre vents on the door of the container as the truck passed and was surprised to see a small air conditioning unit at the upper rear of the container.

I wasn't a logistician but I knew that, while it was an available option, it was rare to see air conditioning on a shipping container. If this was Thomas' shipment, what was he moving that needed climate control?

As the truck moved up the road and past Joey, Thomas passed me, sitting in the rear of the black Mercedes. I could see clearly, for the first time, that another man sat in the front passenger seat, his muscled frame clear in the streetlight, and was on the phone. Thomas was mopping his brow with a handkerchief despite the fact the car would have been controlled at a comfortable 23c inside. He was sweating something, I mused, and we would soon find out what.

I gave the taxi driver a tap on the shoulder and he pulled out slowly, 50 metres behind Thomas and his escort, and we set off in their wake with Joey on her motorcycle dropping in smoothly behind us.

Before long we were on Lung Cheung Road that runs across the top of Kowloon's outer districts, skirting the foothills of Lion Rock

Country Park, and heading East. The Mercedes was still tucked in behind the truck and container and we were trailing along behind, three cars back. If I could, I would have told Joey to move out in front of the truck and break up, what seemed to me, the obvious tail on Thomas.

The traffic was heavy enough and my guess was we had gone unnoticed, so I relaxed a little into the back seat of the taxi and watched the tail-lights of the Mercedes while I tried to think of a plan of action for when it reached its destination.

We had been driving for a little over twenty minutes, still heading east, when the truck and Mercedes turned right off the main road. The traffic suddenly thinned out and we were exposed, trailing along directly behind Thomas. If they were awake they could not fail to spot us now. We had travelled perhaps another 200 metres when the Mercedes suddenly slowed and the truck sped away.

Joey reacted quickly and swung out to pass the car and sped off after the truck, swerving to miss a large, grey SUV that was entering from the left.

I had barely registered that she had safely pulled that off, when the SUV accelerated and smashed into the left rear wheel of the taxi, spinning us across the road.

I was flung to my right and whiplashed back to the left. My head swung viciously against the window and lights exploded behind my eyes. I could hear the driver screaming over the sound of tearing metal and shattering glass as the taxi flipped onto its right side and skidded to a halt, the engine racing as the driver's foot pressed leadenly on the accelerator.

Dazed, I unclipped my seatbelt and hugged the passenger seat headrest to stop myself from slipping to the downside of the taxi. I tried the door handle. It was jammed solid. I could smell petrol from the ruptured fuel tank and could hear it splashing out onto the road somewhere behind me. I glanced around frantically for an out.

Bending myself double, I crabbed into the front of the cab. I examined the driver, still in his seatbelt and tilted to the downward side of the taxi. He was obviously dead, with the remains of his head a gruesome paste on the road and broken glass of the driver's window. I moved his leg and the engine revs eased off, so I leaned across the body and switched off the ignition. The engine ticked hotly in the sudden quiet.

Jamming my back into the gap between the driver and passenger seats, I bent my knees and kicked out at the windscreen. It didn't budge so I kicked again and again, swearing with the effort, until, finally, it dislodged and popped cleanly out. I turned and slithered out backwards onto the road.

I was moving to my knees when my feet were grabbed from behind and I was dragged across the glass-covered bitumen, my hands and right cheek tearing painfully. I came to a stop and rolled over on my back, trying to sit up, but I had barely moved when a foot planted into my chest and kicked me back down.

Ignoring the pain of my torn hands and knees, I rolled away and quickly stood to face my attacker – by now I was beginning to connect the 'accident' with the truck and Thomas' getaway. There were three of them. Chinese. Jeans, white T-shirts, tattoos. Triad soldiers.

Two of them moved in, fanning out to flank me, while the third stood back observing. I cuffed at the blood running into my eyes and moved into a solid boxing stance, my eyes flicking around my attackers trying to gauge the first move. It came quickly and it didn't come as it does in the movies; one at a time. On a cue I didn't register, the two gangsters rushed me.

The man on my left was closest so I pivoted on both feet and drove my right fist into his face, feeling the cartilage and bone of his nose fracture as a spray of blood exploded into the heavy night air. I swung away, not seeing him fall back to crack his skull on the road, as his companion rained blows into my midriff and face. I covered up as best I could, trying to defend myself, looking for a chance to strike out.

I stepped in close to him and stamped down with my right boot, hearing a satisfying squeal as the heel of my boot gouged down across his shin and cracked across his instep. He dropped to his right knee and reached around to his back pocket to draw out and snap open a knife. I stepped back and kicked out hard, connecting with his jaw. It shattered with an audible crack, like a piece of cheap roof tile.

I had barely regained my balance when I felt a blow across the back of my head and dropped heavily to all fours, gasping with the pain and sudden nausea that swept over me. My eyes were blurred and I could feel blood running down the back of my neck as I fought the wave of unconsciousness that threatened to swamp me.

Hands patted my pockets and drew out my wallet.

'Who are you?' said a disembodied voice in halting English as I vomited onto the road. 'Let's see.' The gangster was rifling through my wallet and I was trying hard not to faint. 'Mr Jones...you journal-ist?' I nodded dumbly.

'Where are you from,' he said in Cantonese. 'Who do you work for?'

I shook my head and spat vomit and saliva onto the road. 'I don't understand you,' I mumbled thickly, then grunted as he kicked me, hard, under the ribs.

'Well it doesn't matter now,' he said conversationally, still speaking Cantonese. 'I don't know what you're doing and I don't care,' he said as he racked back the slide of an automatic, chambering a round. 'Normally it's not personal, orders are orders, but I'm going to enjoy killing you, you filthy half-breed bastard.'

I gave in then and flopped onto my back looking up at my killer and the handgun he had pointed at my face. It was over and I wouldn't even hear the shot. I closed my eyes, took a breath... and heard a woman's voice.

'Not so fast, pig shit,' Joey said quietly in Cantonese.

The soldier turned slowly to face her, lowering the handgun to his side, and smiled sardonically.

'What's it to you, little sister?' he asked then shrugged when she didn't answer.

'Diu, whatever. You have come along at the wrong time. I'm going to kill this one,' he said waving the handgun in my direction, 'then I'm going to have some...' was as far as he got before Joey launched herself off her back foot and sprang forward, kicking the gun out of his hands. It landed by my side and I fumbled it up, my eyes tearing and another wave of nausea washing over me.

The gangster lowered himself into a fighting stance and attacked Joey, his fists flying. Joey blocked with her forearms and turned away his strikes by gripping and twisting his thumbs and wrists, but the soldier kept coming.

Both fighters were a blur of movement as they traded blows and kicks. The soldier was stronger but Joey was faster, and her strikes were hitting home more as she danced and spun out of range of her opponent.

'Pretty good for a girl,' he sneered. 'I'm still going to kill your boyfriend and have fun with you before I put a bullet in your head.'

Joey remained silent, balanced on the balls of her feet, bouncing slightly at the knees. She cocked her head and lifted her right hand, palm up, to wave the soldier in with her fingers. I had seen Bruce Lee do that in a movie when I was a kid and it was a cheeky move that infuriated the gangster.

He spat in anger and reached into his back pocket to draw out a knife. He snapped it open and sprang again at Joey who again blocked his strikes; the knife a blur as he flicked, stabbed and slashed with it.

I struggled to my knees and raised the handgun. My grip was unsteady and the gun wavered as I placed the front sight hesitantly between the gangster's shoulder blades. As he moved in on Joey, I took up the first pressure on the trigger.

The gangster feinted with his right, stabbing out at Joey's face with the knife in his left hand, but she easily blocked it and delivered a stinging strike to the side of his head. The blow rocked the gangster but he came on. In the blink of an eye, he changed hands and grip on the knife and delivered an undercut thrust, designed to gut Joey, while feinting with his now empty left hand.

Joey looked to have misread the strike and was extended, off balance. The soldier cried out in triumph as the knife slashed up toward Joey's stomach.

I squeezed the trigger and the handgun bucked once, but there was nothing in my sights.

In an instant, Joey had stepped in, spinning past the gangster on the ball of her left foot to back-kick him in the head with her right foot. The knife clattered to the ground as the gangster dropped to his knees. Joey now had him in a choke hold, bent backwards, his throat in the crook of her left arm, as he struggled to stand upright.

Thunder rolled loud from somewhere above Lion Rock and I felt a fat raindrop, followed by another, hit my face. The night was thick and the air crackled, heavy with portents of doom.

The gangster reached back and grabbed Joey's hair, yanking hard as she squeezed his windpipe. It was enough to loosen Joey's grip and he spun away, diving for the knife. He came up with it in his hand and rushed Joey, who was in my line of sight. Before I could react, he raised the knife to bring it down into Joey's chest and she stepped into him.

Lightning flashed overhead and, in a fluid motion, Joey deflected his knife arm, crouched then struck him, hard, under the nose with the heel of her right hand. The gangster's nose exploded and the delicate bones shattered with a loud cracking sound, driving deadly shards upwards into his brain.

He was dead before his body slumped to the road.

It was raining heavily as Joey closed her eyes and took a deep breath. Exhaling slowly, she turned to look at me, her figure momentarily illuminated in another flash of lightning, the rain plastering her hair to her face and her t-shirt stuck wet and bloodied to her body. She crouched by the dead man.

'You okay?' she called to me over the noise of the storm. She rolled the corpse over and drew out a wallet to examine the contents.

'How do I look?' I managed to reply.

She glanced briefly at me. 'Like shit. Can you drive?'

I nodded, picked up my wallet and stuck the handgun in the waistband of my jeans. 'We need to get out of here,' I said as I quickly checked the back seat of the taxi for anything I might have dropped and hurriedly wiped the door handles with the tail of my shirt.

Joey dropped the wallet back on the gangster's body as she stood and spat, once, onto the road.

'I hate triads,' she muttered and threw an arm around my shoulders to guide me to the damaged SUV. Throwing open the driver's door, she eased me into the seat, ran the seatbelt around me and clipped it in.

'Your place,' she said and I gave her my door codes before she gave me a quick wink and ran off into the dark where, I guessed, she had left her bike. I turned the keys, gunned the engine and spun the steering wheel. The SUV swung around, its tyres screeching in protest, and I drove out of the darkened road, leaving the dead and injured behind me in the rain and dark.

12

AFTER WIPING the SUV clean and dumping it in a side street on the other side of Wan Chai, I headed to my apartment and met up with Joey who had been sitting quietly on an upturned milk crate outside the shop next door.

'You could have let yourself in,' I said as I punched in the front door code, but Joey just shrugged silently, staring at the wall.

We rode the elevator to my apartment in silence and I showed Joey out onto the terrace before walking into my bedroom. I pulled the handgun, a Chinese Type-92, from my jeans and unloaded it, dropping the magazine out onto the bed and catching the round that ejected as I racked back on the action. I slid the round back in with the others, then clicked the magazine home before wiping the weapon clean again and stashing it in my bedside drawer. That done I headed into the kitchen.

I poured two large whiskies and moved out to the terrace where Joey sat silently looking up at the starless and cloudy late-night sky. She didn't look at me as she accepted the glass so I rolled and lit a cigarette, sipping on my whisky, and leaned back into the soft terrace furniture with my eyes closed.

We sat like that for a minute or two before Joey sighed and spoke.

'He was the first person I've killed,' she said, sounding bemused, and threw the whisky back, holding out the glass to me. 'More.'

I went inside and brought out the bottle and put it down on the table. Joey picked it up and poured a heavy shot. I dragged on the cigarette, letting the smoke stream idly from my nose as I silently watched her.

'It was easy, in the end,' she said matter-of-factly. 'One strike and *poof*,' she clicked her fingers. 'A life gone.' She sighed and looked at me. 'Ever happen to you?'

I nodded. 'A couple of times. Not lately. It's never nice but you do get used to it,' I promised, hollowly.

'I don't want to get used to it,' Joey objected, throwing back the whisky and reaching out for my cigarette. I pulled it out of her reach and she shrugged. 'I want it to sting like a bitch.'

'It will. For a while. But then it'll fade and you'll think about it less and less until it just becomes one of those 'things I've done' that pop up in memory now and then.' I sighed heavily. 'Look, Joey, I was dead if you hadn't turned up out of nowhere and done what you did... It really was him or you. *Both* of us,' I added in emphasis.

I dragged deeply on my cigarette, realising my hand was shaking a little. I stubbed the butt out in the ashtray and squeezed my hands together.

'You saved my life, Joey,' I said quietly. 'At the risk of your own life, you saved mine.'

I could tell she was troubled but she seemed to gather herself and sat a little taller in the chair. She put down the glass and pushed the bottle away from her.

'Well,' she said brusquely, slapping her thighs with her hands. 'We can dwell on that later, right now there are a few immediate issues we need to consider. Like, for instance, the fact there is one, possibly more, triad gang-bangers and an innocent cabbie lying dead on the road in Chuk Un and we're in the frame for it all. Thoughts?'

I shrugged. 'They obviously made the tail at some point and called in the cavalry. It was aimed at me I'm sure...the guy with the gun was surprised to see you. The others didn't see you so, if they survive their injuries, this will all be down to me.' I tried to make light of it and grinned. 'Excellent for my reputation!'

Joey shook her head. 'Boss, don't be an idiot! Those guys were triad. This will be laid at your feet and you know damn well what that means.'

I knew all right, but given my situation with Jade Tooth it hardly made things any worse. I felt a stab of guilt, again, about not levelling with Joey on that.

'Let's look at this clearly,' I said. 'Before you arrived Gun Boy was asking who I was. He had no idea, even after he saw my ID. They don't know who I am,' I said shaking my head.

I thought back over the past fortnight and the fact that Thomas had been so elusive despite our best efforts.

'They *may* know I've been on his case since the very start,' I said. 'If he's doing something for them – and it's pretty obvious he is – it would be normal practice for them to have baby-sitters on him 24/7. They could have made me but...'

'Why haven't they moved against you before this?' Joey asked.

I considered that for a moment. I had been asking myself the same question.

'I don't know,' I admitted. 'I just don't think they knew who was following them tonight. The hood with the gun certainly didn't – he thought I was a journo. Even if they've made me following Thomas around before this, I guess they didn't see me as a threat. It's not as if I was anywhere near to what he was doing, so maybe they just thought I was a pest and nothing more.'

'Until tonight,' Joey said.

'Until tonight.'

Joey's eyes widened. 'They must know where you live,' she breathed.

Apart from being beaten near to death by a couple of Jade Tooth's hoods, I had noticed nothing out of the ordinary, certainly not any tails and I was usually pretty alert to that. I thought about that for a moment... Someone *had* been following me, I was sure, but so discreetly and very light touch that I'd been unable to spot them.

A vague memory came back to me of concerned voices as I lay semi-conscious after the beating by Jade Tooth's lads. Something told me it wasn't the people Thomas was mixed up with. Had it been, they would surely have removed me from the picture long ago.

'They *might* know where I live. If they've been following me they'll know for sure but I just don't think they have been. As I say: they probably haven't connected me with Thomas and are unlikely to connect me with them tonight. I think we've still got some space to dig into this.'

Joey nodded. 'Yeah probably,' she said. 'But now they know, whoever you are, that you dodged the ambush tonight, so you've got a target on your back. It won't take them long to find you.'

'If I'm much more alert and keep my head down, I think I've still got time to find out what Thomas is up to and let Peter Toh know.'

I wiped my face; I was tired and my mind was fogging. The whisky didn't help. 'The hell with them Joey,' I said. 'I'm not running,' I said. 'Besides,' I added lamely, 'I've got nowhere to go.' I rolled and lit another cigarette.

'I wish you'd stop that,' Joey said.

'It's my only vice... besides what's it to you?'

Joey smiled for the first time. 'You're my employer and I saved your ass tonight... I have a vested interest.'

I shifted in the chair and scratched my head. 'Yes, well...' I mumbled. 'Look, we have to work out what's going on here – what Thomas is up to. How do we do that? What are our next steps?'

Joey shrugged. 'Dunno. The container would seem to be key – I mean you just don't drive around Hong Kong with one of those for no reason. Find the container and we find the reason.'

I pursed my lips and nodded. 'Hai-yah, *Yeah*, maybe. My gut feel is, whatever it was for, it's now back inside Kwai Chung; but you're right... the container is key. So let's look at that. Pass me the bottle...'

Joey poured herself a small shot and pushed the bottle to me. I poured myself a much larger one – by now I was feeling a lot less pain than I had been an hour before.

'So...' I began. 'What do we know, what don't we know?'

I ticked the items off on my fingers. 'One: Thomas is involved in something shady. What that is we don't know. Two: it's fair to assume Thomas is in deep with a triad. Which one we don't know. Three: Thomas and a triad babysitter took an air-conditioned, 6-metre, ISO container for a drive this evening. We don't know where they ended up; Four: Thomas works for a shipping company and shipping containers are used, funnily enough, to ship stuff. So...'

'So,' Joey jumped in, 'whatever was in that container had just been shipped or something was in it about to be shipped.'

'Hai-yah,' I agreed. 'The questions now are: what commodity are we talking about and had it just arrived or was it being prepared for export?' I took a sip of the whisky and closed my eyes. 'Dammed if I know.'

'Maybe the triad angle,' Joey offered. 'I mean, if we know who it is Thomas is working with maybe we can figure out what their interest would be.'

'Good point, but I mean triads are triads: it's all about gambling, drugs, extortion, smuggling and prostitution. Doesn't matter which one we're looking at – that's their core business.'

'Exactly!' Joey exclaimed. 'Look at that and match it with the container. Gambling? No. Extortion? Unlikely. Drugs? A definite starter and smuggling, yes. Prostitution? No...'

I held up a hand. 'Wait. Why "no" on prostitution?'

Joey shrugged. 'Because it's all street-based, it's in the bars...'

'Yeah, but what about the raw material... the girls? They're mostly not local so where do they come from?'

'They fly in through HKIA,' Joey offered.

'They used to, but visas and border protection efforts here – and in the usual countries of departure – are a lot tighter than they used to be. Definitely not as many girls coming in that way anymore. Sooo..?'

'They're being smuggled in,' Joey said.

I nodded. 'They're being smuggled in. That container had an AC unit on it. I thought that was strange... and drugs don't need climate control – nor do they need an entire 6-metre container.'

I sat forward excitedly. 'Sure, something else may have needed that AC but my bet is there were girls in that container. Thomas is smuggling in girls for triad prostitution...'

Joey's face creased in a frown of disgust but she held up a hand. 'Good theory, but we gotta long way to go before that's a 'known', as you like to call them. We need to find evidence.'

'True,' I acknowledged. 'Maybe I'm reaching.' I paused for a moment. 'Ok, let's look at the 'where',' I said standing up. 'Hang on a moment,' I shot back over my shoulder as I walked inside. 'I need something.'

I heard Joey mutter something unintelligible as I rummaged around in one of the boxes under my desk. Before long, I drew out what I was looking for, with an 'ah ha!' of triumph, and walked back to the terrace waving it in the air. Joey looked up and frowned.

'What on *earth* is that?'

'*This* is a map,' I said. 'We used them in the olden days.'

Joey pointed to her phone. 'It's all on there, boss. Everything you ever need is on there!'

I moved the whisky bottle and glasses and spread the old motoring map of Hong Kong on the table, orienting it to the north. I examined it for a moment then stabbed my finger down.

'We were here,' I said, indicating a spot on the map, 'when the truck and Thomas pulled away and I was side-swiped. We were heading south when that happened.' I paused and peered at the map, willing it to speak to me. 'Where did they go?'

Joey leaned over and studied the map. She traced a finger along a main arterial.

'Heading south they would have driven down here,' she said moving her finger. 'Toward the harbour or...' she flicked her hand 'they hooked east and headed over the hill, toward Sai Kung.' She shrugged and reached across the table for her glass.

'Could have gone pretty much anywhere,' she concluded, throwing back the remains of her whisky.

A sudden thought erupted over me like the thunder that was now rolling in across Victoria Peak. I felt a jolt as a number of pieces of the jigsaw slipped into place.

I looked up slowly from the map and stared at Joey for a moment before darting back inside. I had what I wanted in seconds and strode back out to the terrace. I passed the small piece of folded paper to Joey with an instruction to read it.

'*We told you, look to Aberdeen. 21/7.*' She recited. 'What's this?'

'That,' I said pointing at the paper in her hand 'arrived under my door yesterday.'

I sat and sipped at the whisky while I told Joey of the first note left with my office mail, the second note that she held and the dead undocumented Cambodian girl.

'That girl was found dead two months ago and that's around the same time Thomas started acting strangely...' I could see Joey was about to object so I held up my hand. 'The twenty-first of July is today.' I stood and leaned over the map and traced my finger along a route.

'What if Thomas and the truck carrying the container carried on south to the harbour, entered the Cross Harbour Tunnel, took the Wong Nai Chung Gap flyover, and entered the Aberdeen Tunnel?' I stabbed the map. 'They went to Aberdeen, and my bet is they weren't delivering – they were picking up a shipment and we missed it.'

'Shit,' Joey breathed. 'What if you're right? What *if* it was a shipment of girls? Where are they now?'

I just shrugged and shook my head as Joey stood. A loud clap of thunder broke over us and the first sluggish, warm drops spattered onto the dust of the terrace and my parched plants. The heavy wet velvet night closed in around us and we both looked up.

'It's been threatening for weeks,' Joey said. 'It smells like a typhoon,' she added softly, still looking skyward.

I glanced at my offsider. She was tough and resilient in many ways but the events of the night had changed something in her. I could see it and I was sad about it. I had to say goodbye to the skater girl, at least for a while, I thought.

I gathered up the map, folding it along its worn creases.

'It's always threatening this time of year,' I replied, trying to lighten the moment. 'I'm only surprised we haven't had one yet.'

Joey nodded. 'It'll come all right,' she said, her voice laden with portent. 'When it does it will be big.' She shook her head and turned to face me. 'Time I was gone, boss,' she said. 'Gonna get a few hours sleep if that's okay with you... Call me if you need me.'

I nodded. 'Sure. I have some thinking to do and I want to catch up with Peter Toh in the morning and see what, if anything, OCTB are making of the incident tonight.' I paused before adding: 'I also think we need to rattle Thomas' cage a bit.'

I patted her lightly on the arm.

'Thanks again Joey. Really. You're amazing and I don't know what I'd do without you.'

'I know,' she said as she turned and let herself out.

Minutes later I heard her motorbike gun into action in the small laneway below my terrace and roar off into the night, leaving me alone with my thoughts of Jade Tooth, the money, shipping containers and a dead Cambodian girl.

13

At a little after 1:00 am, the T8 typhoon we had been expecting for nearly a week finally swept in from the south and slammed into Hong Kong with all the force of a flight of angry dragons swooping across the Pearl River Delta to batter and dominate.

Within the hour the storm had grown to a T10 – the strongest we had seen in years – and the gale-force winds clawed furiously at the city, tearing down signs, shredding the foliage off trees, and carrying away anything not bolted or tied down, along with much that was.

Heavy rain drove in horizontally in drenching sheets that soaked the city and flooded the streets as the winds swept over the hills and howled down the mighty canyons of high-rises that shook with the impact. The seas to the south of the Island, and Victoria Harbour itself, were whipped into a frenzy that quickly overcame seawalls to wash furiously at waterside apartment buildings, flooding their underground garages and nearby roads, effectively cutting off thousands of residents. Cars were overturned, ancient fig trees were uprooted and towering building-site cranes collapsed onto streets like broken Meccano sets.

The city's inhabitants hunkered down in swaying apartment towers and squat low-rises to ride out the storm as it shrieked and screamed around them like a frenzied mo gwai; the demon from Chinese mythology that is said to breed during times of rain. I slept through the whole thing.

I awoke to a grey, misty morning, with rain still falling lightly. Everything was eerily quiet across my neighbourhood, like the still on a battlefield the morning after. I made a coffee and walked out onto the terrace to view the damage, thanking whatever sense I had had the night before, after the best part of a bottle of whisky, to tie down my furniture and plants. Everything looked mostly intact so I threw up the umbrella and sheltered out of the drizzle to roll and smoke a cigarette while I sipped my coffee.

To my right, clouds hung low and full over Victoria Peak and, to my front, the dark ridgeline of Mount Cameron and Mount Nicolson brooded wet and green over me. I glanced east and saw a mist-shrouded Jardine's Lookout standing silent sentinel over Wong Nai Chung Gap and the road down into Aberdeen.

Nothing moved. Not a bird or a rat or a person. Then, as I watched and listened, the city seemed to heave a great sigh of relief and, like a stunned animal, began to emerge from its shelter to face a new day.

14

By my reckoning, I had about 30 hours to find $50,000 for Jade Tooth and I still had no idea how I was going to do that. So my mood was as grey and wet as the city around me when my phone rang. I ignored it, dragged deeply at the cigarette and swigged back the last of the espresso as I wrestled with the problem.

Even if I had an answer to Jade Tooth, I didn't know what my next moves would be regarding the dead and injured triad soldiers and the dead taxi driver. To cap it off, I was no wiser on the problem of Thomas and what he was up to, almost certainly, with one of Hong Kong's criminal societies. I was picking away at all of this, with a germ of an idea coming to mind, when my phone rang again. Swearing softly, I walked inside. I was mildly surprised, given the early hour, when I checked the contact information as I answered.

'Hi, what's up?' I said, trying to sound chipper but I had a nasty feeling what was coming.

'Don't "what's up" me, Galahad Jones,' Angel Yeung's voice hissed at me. 'What the *fuck* were you up to last night?'

'I'm not sure what...'

'You listen to me, you idiot... we've cleaned up the mess so the cops won't know anything other than a tragic single-vehicle accident. We'll look after the cabby's family... that *poor* man!'

I closed my eyes. 'They're all dead?' I asked, fearing the worst.

Angel snorted. She wasn't happy. 'No. We dropped one off outside Saint Teresa's emergency. The other two...well, let's just say their bodies won't be found. You really excelled yourself this time. *Diu*!' The phone was silent for a moment.

'Wait..!' she added. 'Have you still got their vehicle?'

I sighed. 'I'm not a *complete* idiot, Angel. I dumped it,' I said. By now I was thoroughly confused. 14K cleaned up the mess? Why? How did they even know?

Angel sighed down the line. 'Okay, message me where and we'll deal with it.'

'Anything else?' I asked sarcastically.

'Yes. Can you *please* just keep your head down for two days? Just stay home...'

'Angel, what's going on?'

'I would have thought it's obvious, Gal, she said, sounding exasperated. 'Even to a blockhead like you.'

Pieces of the picture were starting to slot into place, like a Tetris game, in my overhung and foggy brain. Angel's involvement and references to 'we' were an obvious sign of 14K involvement in what I was mixed up in, but there were so many questions. I didn't know which one to ask first; or even what they all were.

'To be honest, Angel, nothing's very clear this morning...' I said, feeling a headache coming on. 'What happens in two days?'

'I'll call you, give you a time and I'll swing by and pick you up.'

'Where are we going?'

'You have an important meeting to attend.' I heard Angel draw in another long breath. '*Jesus*, Gal. What a mess. Just stay out of trouble, okay?'

She hung up and I put my phone down on the table. The good news was two triad bodies hadn't been found by their bosses – but their men had disappeared and that had happened while they were following someone who had been following Thomas.

They would know, by now, that someone was getting close to what Thomas was doing. I was betting my life they wouldn't know who, yet, but the odds didn't look great. Outside, the rain was falling heavier and the mist had lowered and closed off what little view I had of the hills. I sighed and headed to the shower – I had work to do.

~

The foyer of Hong Kong Police Headquarters is a bright and airy place – if heavily secured and, to the uninitiated, imposing. Arsenal House was the last piece in the development of HKPHQ that began in the '80s and ended up a rambling compound in Wan Chai, with its various wings and the old Caine House where my office had once been.

It always struck me that, despite being a modern building, Arsenal House still smelt like any other old police station – a mixture of boot polish, wax and Brasso that I found somehow comforting. I was getting old and nostalgic, I thought ruefully as I stepped in through the large double glass doors.

I folded and rolled my wet umbrella and strode across the marble foyer toward the reception desk behind its ballistic glass. I drew out my Hong Kong ID Card and handed it to the young constable on the desk.

'Galahad Jones to see Chief Inspector Toh, OCTB.'

The constable looked me up and down, fighting hard to keep the disapproval off his face. 'You have an appointment?'

'No. C.I Toh is a friend and I ...'

'No appointment, no entry,' he said, handing back my ID. 'Thank you. Good day.'

I was about to snap a reply when a uniform, wrapped around a short, slightly round middle-aged man, emerged from a room behind the constable and its owner greeted me.

'Mr Jones, sir. I thought it sounded like you. It's good to see you again. It's been a while.'

I smiled. 'Station Sergeant Wong, good to see you too. How are you these days? Mandy and the kids all well?'

Billy Wong shrugged expressively, a wide grin on his face. 'Ah, you know Mandy, sir. She's unstoppable – still wants me to retire. The kids are good too. Both graduated. I've got two lawyers in the family now,' he said, rolling his eyes.

'I'm sorry to hear that Bill,' I laughed. 'I'd keep that quiet if I were you.'

He chuckled briefly then added: 'My nephew, you might remember him: Michael? He graduated a while back and now works for Mr Toh in OCTB. He's heading up the New Territories South desk.'

'That's great Billy,' I said. 'The Wong family will be running the place soon!'

Billy Wong chuckled again then turned a serious face to the young constable, by now thoroughly perplexed by our exchange. 'Issue Senior Inspector Jones a pass and buzz him through.' He turned back to me. 'It was C.I Toh, right sir?'

I nodded and Billy gave me directions although I knew the way. I thanked the constable, who handed over the pass like he was holding a soiled nappy, waved briefly to Billy Wong and moved through the access control to the lifts.

Minutes later I stepped from the lift and walked along a bright corridor to an office with Peter's nameplate on the wall by the door. Tapping on the door frame I put my head around the corner.

'Knock, knock. Nei hou,' I said brightly. 'Got a minute?'

Peter Toh looked up from his laptop, a slight frown on his face. 'What happened to your face... and how did you get in? No appointment, no entry.'

'Yes, so I was told. Billy Wong's on duty downstairs. He 'facilitated' my entry.' I ignored Peter's reference to the bruises and scratches on my face in the hope he also would.

'I'll have to have a word,' Peter growled. 'Can't have civilians just wandering about the place.'

I grabbed at my heart. 'You wound me, Pete,' I said as I sat down slowly in the one remaining chair in the office, my body aching. 'Seriously, have you got a minute?'

Peter sighed and rubbed his eyes. 'Hai-yah. *Yeah*. Of course. Sorry. Just a lot on and not getting anywhere with any of it.'

'What's happening?' I asked.

'What's not happening,' Peter said. 'First, there's the...' he pulled himself up, wagging his finger at me. 'That's none of your business.' he sighed. 'Look it's great seeing you, and don't get me wrong, but why are you here?'

I had been wondering how far to go when Peter asked me that. I thought I might be onto something big and I needed his help, so I decided to tell him everything... up to a point.

Taking a breath, I laid it all out. The gambling debt to Jade Tooth, meeting Sarah Thomas and taking her brief, the beating Jade Tooth's boys had given me, borrowing the money from Pru, following Thomas pointlessly around Hong Kong for a fortnight, the mysterious notes at the office and home, the dead Cambodian girl, the $50,000 I had to pay Jade Tooth in a little under 30 hours, and, finally, watching Thomas drive out of Kwai Chung with a babysitter and a blue, six-metre shipping container.

I stopped and sat back, eyeing Peter for a reaction. He didn't move for over a minute while he doodled on a notepad on his desk. I sat perfectly still. Finally, he looked up and gently put down the pencil.

'Is that all?' he asked quietly.

I kept my eyes locked on his and lied. 'That's it,' I said. 'That's enough, wouldn't you say?'

He pouted and scratched the back of his head.

'I would say, the only thing in all that that isn't blind conjecture is the money you paid Jade Tooth. At least it clears you on the triad wire transcript. I knew it had to be rubbish. Turns out you're just a bad gambler, and a worse Mahjong player.'

I shrugged sheepishly, and he went on. 'Jade Tooth is Sun Yee On – always has been – so the guys on the wire would have been having a chuckle about having you over a barrel.'

Peter stopped and looked out the window to the city skyline

around Wan Chai and Admiralty. Lights were already coming on against the gloom of the storm-broken morning. He seemed to be wrestling with something. He turned back to me.

'They can't know we have a wire there,' he said. 'Everything coming out of SYO right now is pretty good stuff. A lot of low-level chit-chat but some solid, actionable stuff that we are working on. No decent arrests yet.'

I looked at him and tried changing tack. 'Do you think I might be on to something with the girl angle?' I asked.

Peter considered that for a moment. 'Possibly. But we've chased this down endlessly and there's just nothing there. You've got nothing solid, have you.' He paused and slowly spun his pen on the glass top of the desk. 'You don't even know where that container went...*Do* you?' He stopped and looked hard at me. 'Why didn't you follow it?'

I waved my hand dismissively. 'Engine problems. I was on my own, and the damn taxi conked out. By the time we got it going again, Thomas and the container were long gone.'

I was conscious of a bead of sweat on my upper lip and I was sure Peter could see it. I sat looking disinterested but was a ball of nerves inside.

I could have told him I did, indeed, follow the truck and lost it in city traffic but I just didn't want any connection between me and what had occurred along the truck's route. I wasn't sure Peter even knew of the dead taxi driver or the one injured and two by-now-disappeared gangsters, and I didn't want to go there. No matter the friendship, you just don't admit to a Chief Inspector of Police to a role in the deaths of two triad soldiers... self-defence or not.

Peter was still looking at me, his face blank but eyes hooded and suspicious. 'Where were you, last night Gal?'

I shrugged lightly. 'Here and there...home mostly,' I said levelly.

Peter sighed and pinched the bridge of his nose. He knew I was lying, but he said nothing as he turned again to look out the office window.

'So the girls...'I pushed on. 'Have you heard of anything like this? Smuggling them in via commercial shipping?'

Peter turned back to me and waggled his hand. 'Yes and no,' he said. 'There are always whispers but we've never had a scrap of intelligence on it from CIB or our own informants. We have a team on it but it's a bit of an urban myth, if you ask me.'

He spun his chair again to turn his face from me and look out the window. He seemed a little jumpy. I put it down to fatigue.

'It's pretty clear,' he went on, still looking out 'that the bars are being stocked with enthusiastic amateurs who fly in through HKIA on a Visitor's Visa... or from visa waiver nations.'

'That's rubbish, Pete,' I objected. 'Ask any gweilo down Wan Chai and they'll tell you girls are thinner on the ground these days. Things are a lot tougher for them to get out of their home countries and into Hong Kong.'

Peter Toh nodded. 'CIB is convinced the triads play almost no role in girls' entry to the SAR.'

'What do *you* think?'

'I back CIB's assessments – I have no reason not to.'

He was still staring out the window, his back to me, and something started scratching at the back of my mind. David Zhou, CIB, SYO wiretaps falsely accusing me of being on the take, no intelligence on a human trafficking operation that I was sure was happening... Peter's voice dragged me back.

'I deal in facts. I have no intelligence, let alone solid evidence, that the triads are importing women into sexual servitude in Hong Kong. We're looking at it but until I have something solid, it's just not happening, Gal.'

Peter turned to face me and rubbed his eyes. My friend looked tired.

'Look, Gal,' he went on. 'I trust your instincts but you're wrong on this one. Believe me. Just let it go.' He held up his hands as he saw me about to object. 'Hold on...Okay? You get something worthwhile then come to me and I'll take a look.'

'Okay,' I said, standing to leave. As I reached the door I turned around. 'Is Fat Johnny Tong still around these days?'

'Yes. Why?'

I was surprised. I would have bet the dragon had got him by now, recalling Tong's long-held habit of smoking heroin.

'I thought I might have a chat. You never know what he might come up with...'

'Waste of time,' Peter Toh growled, waving his hand at me. 'You can't trust a word that junkie says... Now get out, I've work to do.'

I was walking the hallway toward the elevators when a figure rounded the corner and came to a sudden halt in front of me, a look of surprise on his face. I stopped and regarded him for a moment, drawing a deep breath to calm the anger I felt welling up. It was a physical reaction I could not avoid every time I thought of David Zhou, and now he stood before me in the sterile fluorescent light.

Zhou took two steps toward me, clutching the files he held against his chest like a shield.

His eyes, in a sharp, acne-ravaged face were dark and regarded me like a barracuda watching as a minnow swam by. His hair, greying now I noted, was cut short and stood in spikes across the top of his head that crowned a face that scowled at me, his mouth turned up bitterly in the corner. David Zhou did not like me, never had, and I knew why – I had worked hard to blacken his name after my father's death. I spoke first.

'David. It's been a while,' I said, doing my best to keep my face impassive.

He winced slightly at my use of his first name and stepped in closer, his face now just centimetres from mine. I could smell the garlic and chilli on his breath and could see two long, wispy hairs that grew from one of the larger acne scars on his right cheek.

'It's *Senior Superintendent* to you, Jones,' he hissed. 'You forget yourself... but then you Joneses always did.'

That was a strange thing to say, but I didn't rise to the bait.

'I haven't had the opportunity,' I said mildly 'to congratulate you on your command of CIB. You must be very proud.'

Like all small men, Zhou couldn't help but puff up at that. He preened a little and smiled at me.

'Yes, I am honoured to have been chosen,' he said. We studied each other for a moment before he continued. 'If I may say so, CIB has excelled under my command, being responsible for the arrest and conviction of many senior triad members.'

'Really?' I said, thinking of the reference Peter Toh had made to the lack of serious arrests. Was Zhou just a petty bureaucrat, picking the low-hanging fruit – and, from what I knew of the man, that seemed likely – or was there something else? I pressed on.

'I had heard much of what came out of your unit was idle chit-chat and that any arrest and convictions had been of low-level soldiers for minor offences.'

Zhou's face turned red, but I went on. On a hunch, I wanted him angry, and with a man like David Zhou it wouldn't take much.

'It seems to me, and others, *Senior Superintendent*, that there is not much of use coming out of CIB. Why is that?'

Zhou poked me in the chest. He landed on one of my bruised ribs and I bit down on a wince.

'You listen to me you bastard,' he whispered, his voice sibilant. 'People, very high up, are extremely happy with the job I am doing and I don't need your, or anyone else's, approval or acceptance.'

He drew a breath and his face twisted in a satisfied smirk. 'Interestingly, I have information at my disposal of your criminal connection with Sun Yee On. Perhaps it's time I used it.'

Zhou could make things very uncomfortable for me if he pushed an investigation, but I wouldn't give him the satisfaction.

I shrugged. 'Go ahead David,' I said quietly. 'You and I both know what you have on that transcript is bullshit and won't sustain an investigation, let alone a conviction.'

Zhou was shaking now, and his breathing was rapid. 'What I have will certainly be enough mud to stick, you smug bastard.'

I would have bet my last dollar – and I was very nearly down to that – that Zhou would, somehow, use the transcript against me. Was it that he genuinely thought I was tied in with SYO? As the commander of CIB, that would certainly be a reason for him to dislike me more than he already did.

Zhou made to step around me but I put out a hand and pressed against his chest. He stepped back, a look of shock on his face, and, for a moment, I thought he was going to strike me.

'You *really* hate us both,' I said, feeling my face redden. 'My father and me. It's clouding your judgement David.'

Zhou's voice raised in the empty corridor. 'I didn't hate your father you fool, but he was a ...nuisance!'

He suddenly stopped and clamped his jaws shut with an audible click of his teeth. I was certain I saw a flare of panic in his eyes as he pushed past me.

'You, however, I don't like,' Zhou muttered as he walked swiftly away, elbowing past two uniformed officers who had emerged from an office.

I watched, stunned, as he disappeared from view. We Joneses 'forget ourselves' and my father was a 'nuisance'? My instincts were right: I had angered Zhou, deliberately, and he seemed to have slipped with what I was sure was a serious revelation – but what that was and what it meant, I didn't know.

I shook my head and, after a brief ride in a crowded elevator and a wave to Station Sergeant Wong, I left the building.

15

Back on Arsenal Street, it was raining lightly and, looking up, I could see the claws on top of Two IFC were hidden in low cloud.

Victoria Peak was blanketed in a thin gauze of mist, behind which lights of the higher apartment buildings shimmered. On Hennessy Road, neon street signs flashed their bright colours through the rain and office workers threaded their way back and forth under a carapace of umbrellas that rippled like the scales on a dragon.

Delivery men pushed their trollies through the crowd, oblivious to cars, the press of bodies around them and the clinging drizzle that soaked their grimy white singlets. Trams rumbled and dinged their way along Hennessy, moving easily through the molasses-slow traffic of red taxis, delivery vans, and luxury cars.

I checked my watch. My head was spinning after my confrontation with Zhou and I needed to go to the office to ready a few items for later use, so I flagged down a taxi. Easing into the back seat, I sat back in the air conditioning as the driver crept his way through Admiralty and Central to Sheung Wan.

In fifteen minutes we had threaded our way through the worst of the traffic and turned into Ko Shing Street, so I paid off the driver and stepped out into the rain, turning my collar up for the brief dash into the vestibule of my office building.

I shook myself and ran a hand through my wet hair then climbed the three flights of stairs to my office, punched in the door code and stepped in, dropping my umbrella in the stand by the door. Adele Chung looked up from her newspaper.

'Good *afternoon*, Galahad,' she said, folding the paper. 'It's so nice to see you in the office.'

'I don't come into the office, Adele, because I'm busy. It's called "field work",' I replied, only half-jokingly. I really didn't need, nor want, a lecture but I knew my a-yi was going to deliver one. It's what she did best.

'Mmm,' she said, looking at me over the rim of her glasses. 'Clean shirt. You look half respectable today, I must say. Been visiting?'

I nodded and walked across the room to my desk. 'I've been to Wan Chai to see Peter Toh,' I said, rummaging about in the drawers.

Adele pointed at my face. 'What happened there... and there?' she asked, indicating the butterfly dressings I had cinching together the gash above my eye and on my ear. She waved her hand. 'And all the other nonsense on your face. What happened to you?'

'Minor disagreement with someone,' I said without looking up, opening and closing desk drawers and scratching about in their contents. 'Nothing to worry about a-yi.'

Adele's eyes narrowed. 'Please tell me Joey wasn't involved in this *disagreement*. I also note she is not in today.'

'No, she's got a sleep-in because I had her working most of the weekend. She's fine. Really.' I winced inwardly. Adele would murder me when she found out what I had dragged Joey into the night before, and she *would* find out.

I slammed the desk drawer shut and looked up. 'Where's my press pass?'

Adele stood and crossed the room, slowly opened the top drawer of my desk, put her hand in briefly and dropped my fake South China Herald ID onto the desktop.

'Here,' she said, a faint smile crinkling her mouth. 'How do you manage to get out of bed and outside each morning?'

I scooped up the pass and dropped it, and a small black notebook, into a black satchel under my desk. 'I manage just fine, thank you,' I said moving for the door.

'Can you do something for me please?'

Adele nodded and picked up her own notebook and a pen.

'Call Sarah Thomas. Set up a meeting with her in the next few days – here or there, doesn't matter.'

I was halfway out the door when I stopped and looked back. 'Oh, and send her that damn invoice,' I said. 'We need the money,' I muttered as I closed the door behind me, hoping I would still be around in two days.

The rain had stopped by the time I stepped out of Mong Kok MTR, and the sun was steaming the wet pavement as I walked east along Prince Edward Road, past the Police Station. I had worked briefly in that station and Prince Edward-Mong Kok-Yau Ma Tei had been an exciting policing challenge.

The area had it all: Triads, youth gangs, student activists, street prostitution, markets, bustling tourism and thousands of small businesses competing with each other to eke out a living in Hong Kong's cut-throat economy.

I liked the area, and always had; it was real Hong Kong to me. With a slight spring in my step, I turned down Flower Market Road, past the rows of flower shops and horticulture suppliers, before coming to a halt at my destination. I checked my watch and walked in.

The Yuen Po Street Bird Garden was alive with the trills, squawks, warbles and screeches of thousands of caged birds. Mostly middle-aged and elderly men wandered about, alone or in pairs, observing the birds and discussing their plumage, song and habits. The shade of the gardens and the bird song made it a tranquil place to take tea and just sit and think, so I sat on a concrete bench under a large tree, and ordered a tea from a nearby stall.

My drink quickly arrived and I sipped at it, feeling the tension of the past few days wash away as I gazed idly around the gardens.

It wasn't long before I spotted a familiar figure moving in the shadows, hunched over to peer into a cage at a collection of madly hopping finches. Despite the light, I knew straight away who it was. I had found Fat Johnny Tong.

The wiry figure stood and moved slowly away, pausing briefly to eye the birds in the other cages as he passed. Fat Johnny Tong was every bit as emaciated as the last time I had seen him nearly a year ago. If anything he was worse.

His collarbones and shoulders pushed against his sagging short-sleeved shirt and his arms were straw thin, ending in unusually large hands with long and slender fingers. His hair was long and lank, pushed back off his forehead and tucked behind his ears that poked out like the open doors of a small car, and his high cheekbones stood out like razors, tightly stretching the skin of his face into an awful grimace.

He had always affected a long moustache, and wispy chin beard, that he stroked as he shuffled in my direction through the aisles of bird cages. His shirt and trousers were loose-fitting and he seemed to disappear within their folds. I could see the deeply ingrained grime in them from where I sat.

As he rounded a cage and stepped out into the light, I saw he had a cloth satchel slung over his right shoulder and he clutched a small brown paper bag in his left hand. He spotted me and froze in his tracks, glancing nervously to his left and right.

I patted the concrete bench next to me and he shuffled forward and sat down. The stink coming off him was eye-watering.

We greeted each other in Cantonese as Fat Johnny opened the paper bag and took a handful of bird seed out that he scattered on the ground for the marauding sparrows. We sat in companionable silence for a minute watching the birds feed before Johnny spoke, still staring at the avian feeding frenzy at his feet.

'Did you know sparrows mate for life?' he asked, his voice clear and melodic, strangely at odds with his destroyed physical appearance. 'They are very loyal.'

I sat silently watching the fat little birds grasping and squabbling over the seed. I thought they were angry little bastards, probably *because* they mated for life.

I finished my tea and signalled to the stall owner who came and collected the empty cup. Reaching back into my hip pocket, I drew out my tobacco pouch and offered it to Johnny.

He took it gently and rolled and lit a cigarette. He exhaled the cherry-scented smoke slowly, his eyes closed, just as I imagined he did when he was chasing the dragon in some filthy back-street squat.

'It's been a while, Mr Jones,' he said quietly, still watching the birds. 'Are you well?'

I was almost touched by Johnny's concern for my welfare – he certainly had his own problems. 'I'm okay Johnny,' I said. 'The usual. You know.'

'Ah, yes the *usual*,' he muttered, scattering some more seed. 'How is your usual going these days, Mr Jones?'

I shrugged. 'Up and down. A little of this and that.' I ground out my cigarette. 'Anyway, my skinny friend, I have some questions,' I said, feeling that Johnny was taking control of the conversation. I didn't like that.

'Answers cost,' he said.

'I haven't got any money.'

He nodded. 'Yes, I had heard that... but, apparently, you *do* have a rather large debt to a rather nasty person.'

I shouldn't have been surprised at Johnny knowing that. He was the guy in Hong Kong if you wanted to know anything. Fat Johnny Tong knew everything and everyone. As they say: he had friends in low places. I sucked at my teeth.

'Yes, I do and I have about 26 hours to find a solution to that,' I said.

'Jade Tooth is an evil man, Mr Jones,' Johnny said quietly. 'He is responsible for what I am today.' He dragged deeply on the cigarette.

'He's a nasty piece of work, no doubt, 'I replied. 'But, Johnny, no-one but you is responsible for the way you are. Own it.'

'You're not going about things the right way if you want me to answer your questions,' Johnny objected, flicking away the stub of the smoke and helping himself to my tobacco pouch that sat on the bench between us.

I watched as his spidery fingers wove their way around the tobacco and cigarette paper, that he delicately licked and then lit with a match. Once he was done, he leaned back and looked at me.

'Okay, Mr Jones. As it appears I have no option, ask away.'

'Tell me about girls being smuggled in to work the bars,' I said, getting to the point before Johnny's mind wandered off.

'What makes you think they are?'

'I'm asking the questions, Johnny,' I said. 'Focus!'

He paused and ran a hand through his greasy hair. 'I hear things now and then,' he admitted. 'Nothing concrete, but there are whispers of a big operation bringing in girls on a regular basis.'

'Who's doing it?' I demanded.

Johnny chuckled. It sounded like the wind rattling through a clump of dead bamboo. 'Now, that information will cost you a great deal, Mr Jones,' he said and flapped a hand, making a face. 'Besides, I don't really know.'

'Take a guess...'

'I don't think so.'

'Okay,' I said, changing tack. 'Where are the girls coming from and how are they getting here?'

He scratched his ear and dragged on the cigarette. By now the birds at our feet had had their fill and hopped away to do whatever it was sated birds did.

'Mostly Vietnam, I think,' he said.

'Anywhere else? Cambodia?'

'Yes, probably,' he shrugged. 'Laos. Thailand... who knows.'

'How?' I asked again.

'The whispers would have it they are coming in by sea, containerised like shipments of pork.'

I winced at Johnny's simile. 'Where are they coming in to? Where are they ending up?' I asked, by now sure this was what I was facing. I was getting excited about running it down. Johnny held up his hand.

'I don't know, Mr Jones and don't care to know,' he said, taking the wind out of my sails. 'Whoever is behind this is very powerful and very dangerous. They make Jade Tooth look like a weekend amateur, quivering in his designer sneakers.'

He paused and shook his head. 'No, I'm not about to go poking about in their business. I value my life...as miserable as it is.'

I relented a little. I still didn't get how this would work in practice. I was working on the assumption the girls were brought in by sea, which Johnny had just confirmed, so that probably meant a freighter or container vessel – and that was where Thomas came in – but I couldn't figure out how they got ashore from an ocean-going vessel.

'So, how do they do this?' I asked. 'Surely they don't just land a container full of women at Kwai Chung, open the doors and march them out...'

I scratched the back of my neck as a bug nipped it. I hoped it wasn't bird lice. Johnny had a bemused look on his face as he turned to me.

'Mr Jones, come on!' he said in a faintly scolding tone. 'Think about it. How have most shipping imports happened for years in this city?' He chuckled, shaking his head.

I stared at him as realisation dawned. I could have slapped myself.

Mid-stream operations were a Hong Kong peculiarity, having been devised as the city's explosion in shipping traffic outgrew the Kwai Chung terminal. It was a simple, yet ingenious, solution to a difficult logistics problem whereby specially built cargo lighters, flat-bottomed barges equipped with cranes, tied up alongside container vessels to load and unload cargo. The lighters were mostly, but not all, unpowered and relied on Hong Kong's tug fleet to manoeuvre them from ship to shore where they cross-decked to trucks.

I recalled that most of these lighters were unloaded at Tsing Yi but that didn't fit the direction of travel of Thomas and the container.

There was a wharf at Hung Hom on the Kowloon foreshore, I

remembered. That could be it...But, what about the notes? What did the references to 'Aberdeen' mean? What about my theory that Thomas had taken the container across to the Island?

I slowly let out a breath I hadn't been aware I was holding. 'Where,' I asked quietly. 'Where are they coming in?'

Johnny licked the tip of his index finger and made a show of judging the wind. 'Southside,' he said.

'Aberdeen?' I pressed.

He shrugged and raised his eyebrows but said nothing. That was good enough for me. It all made sense: the notes – although I still had no idea where they had come from – the direction of travel when I had last seen Thomas and the container and their likely route from there. Aberdeen. There was only one thing left.

'Any ideas when the next shipment is due?'

I realised I was leaning forward eagerly on the bench, my hands on my knees, willing an answer from my heroin-torn informant. I sat back to calm myself and not spook Johnny.

He looked up into the grey-blue sky for a moment. 'You have always been good to me, Mr Jones.' He said, turning back to face me. 'I don't know why, but you have.' I sat silently.

'Do you remember a few years back?' he asked. 'When you and Mr Toh saved me from that beating in Om Yau?' I nodded silently. 'That was Snake-eye Chung, may God rest his disturbed soul, and he would have killed me if you had not stepped in...'

'I can't have just any old shit-head beating up my informants, Johnny,' I said lightly.

He waved his hand as if swatting away a fly. 'Whatever... Anyway, I have never forgotten it.'

He paused again and ground out the cigarette under the heel of a worn and filthy shoe.

'I really don't know *if* or when the next shipment will happen,' he said. 'It could be any time. Tomorrow...next month. I can't ask around about it, Mr Jones... It's just too dangerous. I'm sorry.'

I sagged a little on the bench, disappointed. This was the nearest I had been in weeks to what was really happening with Thomas. I was so close to him, and his backers, I could smell it, but without at least a reasonably accurate time frame I was stumped. I couldn't just hang around Aberdeen district hoping I'd stumble on the operation whenever and wherever it happened.

I looked at Johnny and I knew that was as far as I was getting today, so I grabbed up my tobacco pouch and stood. Reaching for my wallet, I drew out $500 and offered it. I winced to see my wallet, yet again, empty.

'Get yourself some noodles and some water, Johnny. You look bloody terrible.'

The scrawny addict on the bench gently took the cash and slipped it into his shirt pocket. His eyes were yellow and watering as he looked up at me.

'That's $500 less you have for Jade Tooth,' he said quietly.

I shrugged. 'What's $500 between friends, hey?'

Fat Johnny Tong nodded and smiled faintly. 'Indeed,' he said. 'Thank you, Mr Jones.'

I looked down at him. 'I may send my offsider to speak with you at some point...'

'The biker girl? Ex-cop?'

Again, I wasn't surprised he knew about Joey. Johnny Tong knew everything.

'Yes,' I said. 'If I do she'll introduce herself with the password...' I looked around. '"Dove". Talk to her as if you're speaking with me. Got it?'

Johnny nodded.

'Call me,' I said, and turned to walk out of the gardens leaving Johnny staring at the small grey feathers and husks of bird seed being blown about in the soft breeze.

16

IT WAS RAINING AGAIN the next morning when I awoke and I could hear it pattering on the tiles outside and the rhythmic tick of water dripping inside the downpipes.

There was no wind to speak of, although Hong Kong Observatory had again raised the T3 Typhoon Signal the night before. It was typhoon season and the big storm of two nights before seemed forgotten as the city bustled its way into a new day in the rain and rising heat. I lay in bed for a while, my hands behind my head, luxuriating in the feel of the warm duvet wrapping me against the chill of the air conditioning in my small apartment.

My head ached dully, my mouth was tacky and dry, and my stomach churned as I closed my eyes against a hangover I knew was going to take hours to subside. The problem was, I didn't have hours to spare.

Today was the day I had to pay Jade Tooth the fifty grand I didn't have. I felt the bile rise in my throat at the prospect and I fought the panic that welled in me as I realised it could well be my last day on earth.

Groaning, I swung my legs to the floor and slowly sat, holding my head in both hands to still the vertigo. The skin on my back pulled and I could feel scabs tearing as I leaned forward. My ribs ached as I moved. All in all, I felt terrible and I knew I looked it.

After a minute or two the room stopped spinning and I stood and walked gingerly into the bathroom, leaning with my hands against the sink as I stared at my reflection in the mirror.

My face, unshaven and haggard, stared back at me. I looked a mess, but then I almost always did. Dark bags hung from my bloodshot eyes and the crow's feet at their edges seemed to be deepening. My broad shoulders were slumped and I slapped at the belly I had developed in the past months, scowling at the middle-age that was creeping up on me.

Not for the first time, I wondered at the very English freckles that still dotted across the nose and cheeks of my faintly Chinese features. My hair was still dark but I could see grey flecking it and I sighed.

The bruises on my face were yellowing and the cut over my eye had remained closed so I gently peeled away the butterfly dressing and dropped it into the bin. My ear looked better if a little dog-eaten.

I turned to examine my back in the mirror and could see the purple bruises were fading and that most of the scabbing had fallen off, leaving me with some fresh pink scars where the bamboo poles had shredded my skin.

I stared into the mirror again, trying to work up anger for Jade Tooth and his thugs, searching for the warm feeling a vow of revenge brings. I couldn't find it.

When all was said and done, it was all my own stupid fault: I knew what I had been getting into the moment I started racking up a debt and I had paid the price. I could hear my mother's voice scolding me, as she used to when I was a boy, with a favourite proverb: '*One who stands straight doesn't fear a crooked shadow*.' She was right, of course, but it seemed I had never learnt that particular lesson.

I stepped into the shower, turned the taps to full and put my hands against the wall, head down, as the hot water beat down on my back and neck. I softly swore 'never again' and castigated myself for, again, getting drunk, alone, at home. I knew it wasn't a good sign, that solitary drinking, but I had always preferred my own company when needing to get away and find some space in a bottle.

Through the blinds, I could see an empty whisky bottle slowly filling with rainwater on the terrace table, and an ashtray sitting on the edge of one of the large pot plants, brimming with butts and dirty water. The whole scene was depressing and not a little pathetic.

I stepped from the shower and towelled myself down then, feeling near human, padded into the kitchen to make a coffee. With the espresso in my hand, I opened the kitchen window and leaned against the sill, staring out into the rain while I sipped the rich, black brew.

Where to start, I wondered. By 5:00 pm that day I had to either have $50,000 in Jade Tooth's scaly hands or have come up with a convincing reason otherwise – and I did not, for a moment, believe Jade Tooth would accept anything but the money. I couldn't see any way out of it: I would just have to confront him, call his bluff on the debt and see where it led. Nowhere good, I was sure.

Today was also the day that Angel would pick me up and take me to an 'important meeting'. I had no idea where, or with whom, that meeting was to be but I had a feeling it would be with someone who would push me deeper into the puzzle that had emerged since I first took Sarah Thomas' job. I realised, not for the first time, that the Thomas case was not only a thorn in my skin that I picked at constantly but would also somehow be the saving of me.

Not 'redemption' in Jenny Lam's sense, but my way out of the bind I was in with Jade Tooth, his triad backers, my failing business and a life that was generally coming apart at the seams. I didn't know why I thought that, but my senses told me Thomas was key and I was determined to chase him down.

Having arrived at that place, I felt a little better so I peeled a banana and shoved it into my mouth while I pulled on my clothes to face the day. I was bending to lace up my desert boots when the security buzzer sounded. I checked my watch and frowned – it was early and I wasn't expecting visitors.

I checked the small CCTV screen and groaned aloud, pushing the button to buzz the person, and her package, into the building. Two minutes later the doorbell to my apartment rang and I swung open the door, despite not feeling in a very welcoming mood, to greet the woman who stood there.

'Galahad, good *morning*!' Jenny Lam beamed, her voice loud in the silence of my apartment. 'How are you this fine day?'

She was dressed in another multi-coloured kaftan and she elbowed me aside as she surged into the apartment like an over-loaded schooner under full sail, waving me away with a podgy hand and dangerously sharp, bright red nails. As she breezed past I looked into the large box she held, and there sat the black and tan pup I had given into her care the previous week.

I sighed and rolled my eyes. I really did not need nor want the dog – I had too many things going on and, besides, there was a very real chance I wouldn't be around to feed it come sunset.

'Jenny,' I began. 'Look, I've been meaning to call you but I've been very busy. I just can't...'

She held up a hand, with a bitten-off 'ah!' silencing me and put the dog gently onto the floor.

I watched it toddle into the kitchen and squat on the tiles in front of the fridge, then wander off leaving a small puddle in its wake.

'Did we not agree, the last time I was here, that you needed this little darling in your life and would take him?' she asked gently.

I lifted my hands, palms up like a supplicant. 'Jenny, I can't take this dog,' I said, sounding more determined than I felt. 'I have too much going on and, to be quite honest, I simply don't know if...' I trailed off and looked away.

She gazed around the apartment that, frankly, looked a disaster then examined me closely for a moment before she spoke.

'I don't know what troubles you have Galahad, they are none of my business, but I *do* know you need this dog in your life. He will give you a reason to win in your struggles and come home today and each day after that. He will give you a reason to care for yourself as you care for him.'

I looked over at the pup as it snuffled its way around the kitten, searching out the smells and crumbs on the floor before it gambolled into the loungeroom to roll around at my feet.

I bent and picked it up, holding it at arm's length as we stared into each other's eyes. He had put on weight and looked bigger and rounder than he had only a week before. The pup's front paws paddled as he reached out to me and he tossed his head with a little bark.

I hadn't owned a dog since I was a kid and, suddenly, my eyes misted over and my throat constricted. That all seemed so long ago, in a happier time that I only ever recalled in dreams. There was no doubt, I could use a little of that.

I sighed and put the pup down. Jenny Lam stood watching me quietly

'Okay Jenny,' I said, smiling slightly. 'You win. I'll take him.' The large woman danced a short jig, clapping her hands, and I went on. '*But* I have a full day today and won't be home for hours...'

'That's not a problem Galahad,' she said. 'I have his crate, bedding and favourite toy in the car. I also have the first week of food for him and all your veterinary paperwork on his shots.' I must have looked confused which, given the hangover, was how I was feeling, so she went on.

'I've watched him closely the last week and you need not worry, he's really quite independent and doesn't need constant company. He's happy to sit in his crate and sleep or play, so you can go to work.' She paused and sat on the sofa, her hands trailing the floor to let the pup nip and lick at her fingers.

'Yes, it's true,' she continued. 'Things will change and you will need to work out a routine that includes him. He needs to be a part of your life from this moment on. It won't be easy at first but you'll quickly adapt and, I *guarantee* you, it will be worth it!'

I didn't know what to say so I just nodded as she stood and moved to the door, telling me she would be right back with everything I needed.

I stood over the pup and watched as he chewed the corner of the sofa with his tiny teeth, making faint growling noises as he did so. I chuckled as I watched him and knew that, if I lived beyond the end of the day, my life would never be the same.

Two hours later I left home and headed to the MTR to travel across to Yau Ma Tei to confront Jade Tooth.

When Jenny Lam had left, after taking me through the pup's feeding routine, and his next schedule of shots, I had set up his crate with his blankets and a soft toy crocodile, placed his food and water bowls in the kitchen and laid sheets of newspaper on the floor by the terrace door. The last had been an immediate success as I watched him sniffing around and, as he squatted, grabbed him up and placed him on the paper, rewarding him with a scratch behind the ear and a small dog biscuit when he peed.

I had remembered a training tip I heard years ago from one of the handlers in the Dog Squad and, as the pup peed I murmured a word to him over and over. It's called "cueing".

Despite what Jenny had said, I didn't want to leave the pup alone so I called a friend and asked if I could 'borrow' his helper to dog-sit for a few hours. He agreed and a smiling middle-aged Filipina woman arrived shortly after. I left minutes later as she rolled on the floor with the pup clambering all over her.

'What's his name?' she called after me as I was leaving.

I looked back and shrugged. 'I don't know,' I said and I closed the door.

17

IT WAS DRIZZLING LIGHTLY as I threaded my way through the wet market on Bowrington Road, dodging the umbrellas, toward Causeway Bay MTR. The humidity was soaring and by the time I hit the air conditioning of Times Square, my shirt was sticking to me and my hair was plastered to my scalp.

As I walked, I could feel the scabbard of the small, double-edged dagger I had clipped inside the back of my jeans. I rarely ever carried a weapon of any sort but, on the spur of the moment, I had tucked the fighting knife away thinking that if Jade Tooth was to attempt to do what I thought he would, I was prepared to do what I could to take him with me. If that happened, I hoped Jenny Lam would look after the dog.

I wondered, smiling grimly to myself, how much of my free-flowing sweat was down to the humidity and how much was fear at the prospect of facing down Jade Tooth, on his own ground, in the next hour.

It occurred to me that no-one knew where I was going so I took out my phone and called Joey. I gave her my destination but didn't tell her why I was paying a visit to Jade Tooth and asked her to check in on me in three hours. Unsurprisingly, she insisted she back me up but I told her it was something that needed doing on my own and I could hear the suspicion in her voice as she reluctantly agreed. I gave her instructions to call Peter Toh if she couldn't reach me and hung up feeling a little more reassured.

I ducked into a convenience store and bought a can of energy drink that I guzzled greedily, replenishing the fluids in my dehydrated body, then rode the escalators underground to the Island Line and onto the platform where, seconds later, I stepped onto a westbound train.

The train was crowded and the carriage swayed as it sped its way down the line. I looked out over the heads of my fellow travellers as they bowed to the small screens of their phones, no-one making eye contact with anyone else.

Much had happened in the past few days so I tried to focus my mind to pick at the threads of it all. I had made major progress in discovering from Fat Johnny that girls were, indeed, being smuggled into the city and that this was most likely occurring on the south of the Island.

But I still did not know who was behind it nor when the next shipment was due, and the latter was key if I was to convince Peter Toh to investigate – it would be a big case for OCTB and I knew Peter would latch on to it aggressively once he had something to work with. I had to find that something.

There was a lot bothering me about all this and I scratched away at it like a scab as I hung onto the swaying red handle in the middle of the aisle, bumping now and then into passengers beside me and apologising with a small nod. What was the extent of Thomas' involvement and on whose orders was he working?

I was assuming he had been suborned into working with whichever triad was heading the operation – and it had to be a triad, this all seemed far too big for an 'independent' – but I had no clue as to how. That was an angle I would try and develop when I got in front of Thomas in the coming days.

Did Sarah Thomas know what was going on? I doubted it but had no real reason for thinking that – maybe she was in it up to her neck.

Would the next shipment go ahead? Given whoever was behind it was facing the inexplicable disappearance of two of their men during what was supposed to have been a fairly straightforward 'stop and mug', there was every chance it would be postponed. If it did go ahead, and that was also likely given the pipeline was probably already full of orders, where would it be and when?

I rubbed at my temple, trying to soothe away the mounting headache and shook my head... it was all academic really because, in under thirty minutes, I would be standing in front of Jade Tooth and things were likely to get ugly.

There was something else nagging at me, clawing away in the dark recesses of my hangover – something Peter Toh had said. Was it CIB and their intel? I couldn't latch on to it and my head pounded.

Additionally, the confrontation with David Zhou had disturbed me deeply – I just hadn't had time to focus on it yet. What did he mean by my father was a 'nuisance'? In his anger, he had accidentally revealed something to me, but what was it?

I wiped my clammy face, and decided to focus on the more immediate issue to hand as the train pulled into Admiralty and I interchanged onto the Tsuen Wan Line.

A little over ten minutes later, I stepped out of Yau Ma Tei station and onto the street, surprised that the rain had stopped and the sun had burst through the clouds, heating up the steaming footpath and throwing a hot, wet blanket over everything.

I moved off through the crowds, not really taking anything in as I focussed on the street in front of me, each step taking me closer to 'Lucky Dragon Social Club' and Jade Tooth. I could feel my pulse racing and a tightening of my chest. I relished the familiar feeling that prepared me for the violence to come.

Taking deep breaths and exhaling slowly, I willed my mind to calm and my heart rate to slow, feeling each step I took, each contraction of my muscles and beat of my heart.

The streetscape faded from my awareness and all I could see was the entrance to the Lucky Dragon. One of Jade Tooth's thugs leaned casually in the doorway. He pushed himself off the wall and faced me as I walked up. We looked at each other briefly before he placed a hand on my chest pushing me away.

'We're not open, man' he growled in Cantonese. 'Take a hike.'

Without a word, I grabbed his hand with both of mine and twisted down and away. I heard and felt his thumb snap and he yelped in pain as he dropped to his right knee, his arm up and injured hand still twisting in my grip. I kicked at his left knee and he cried out again as his kneecap dislocated and his leg fell away to lay him flat on the footpath, writhing in pain.

I stepped over him and down the darkened staircase.

As I rounded the corner at the bottom of the first flight I ran into another of Jade Tooth's boys, surging up the stairs. As his face drew level with my feet I kicked him, hard, under the chin and watched as his eyes rolled back in his head and he fell away. Stepping across the prone body, I reached down and drew out the handgun from the waistband of his jeans and tucked it into mine, leaving the grip exposed.

I was about to turn away when he groaned and started to move so I grabbed a fistful of his shirt, drew him up and punched him hard between the eyes. I released the shirt and he collapsed with a thump onto the stairs.

Moving down, I emerged from the staircase and into the main room with its covered tables, tea urns and the stale smell of old cigarette smoke. This was the second time I had been in the club while shut and, unlike the raucous, sociable atmosphere when it was open and filled with people laughing and shouting over the clattering of Mahjong tiles, the empty room gave off an air of menace.

It looked and felt every bit the lair of some dark creature from Chinese mythology.

I glanced around and spotted Jade Tooth sitting at a table across the room, in a pool of light, a pile of cash in front of him. One of his men stood at his shoulder and, on seeing me, hurried across the room to block my way. Jade Tooth held up his hand and clicked his fingers. The thug stopped in his tracks and moved aside.

I stepped further into the room, my shoes susurrating faintly on the sisal matting, and stopped a safe distance from Jade Tooth's boy who glowered at me, ready to spring forward on command.

Jade Tooth looked genuinely surprised to see me and I bit down on a feeling of confusion. Focus, I told myself.

'Mr Jones,' he said, eyeing me closely. 'I would say it's a pleasure to see you but I admit to being a little perplexed.'

He flicked a match and lit a cigarette. I watched the dragon on his right arm as it writhed, alive to its master's own movements. Jade Tooth dragged deeply on the cigarette and exhaled slowly, letting the smoke wreath his head, his unblinking, reptilian eyes never leaving mine.

'Why are you here?' he asked finally.

Now I *was* confused. 'The fifty grand. The interest payment,' I said.

'You have come to pay me?'

I took a deep breath, feeling the handgun and knife pressing against my skin. I judged the distance between me, Jade Tooth and his soldier.

'No,' I said quietly. 'I've come to tell you I don't have it. You're not getting your money.'

Jade Tooth blinked at that. I could almost hear his eyelids rasping against his glassy, dark eyes. I tensed, and my right hand started to creep back.

For a long moment, he didn't move then, suddenly, he leaned back in his chair and tilted his head back to let out a howl of laughter. He coughed slightly and wiped at his eyes as he sat forward on the chair, his arms on the table and hands clasped. Jade Tooth shook his head and chuckled.

'*Diu*, man! You really don't know, do you,' he said, disbelievingly.

I stood silently, still on my guard and glanced at Jade Tooth's soldier who stared back menacingly. His boss went on.

'Mr Jones, your debt has been paid. Just this morning. In full.' He waved his hands like a magician at the cash on the table. 'In fact,' he added, 'this is it.'

When I didn't answer he stood and walked slowly toward me.

'I knew you didn't have this money,' Jade Tooth said lightly. 'To be honest, I was looking forward to what that would then give me licence to do – you really are quite a nuisance.' There was that word again.

He grimaced. 'But when this arrived this morning I was forced to re-assess.' He dragged again on his cigarette. 'You have a clean slate, Mr Jones,' he said through the smoke. 'We're even.'

I shook my head in disbelief. 'Who paid it?' I asked.

Jade Tooth shrugged. 'I really don't know,' he said. 'The bag was dropped off by a boy early this morning. By the time my men had checked it out, he was gone. One thing is for sure: you have rich and generous friends.'

'I don't have any friends, Jade Tooth.'

He shrugged again, disinterested in my personal life, and turned back to the table of cash.

'Well, the fact remains: I have the money and you're off the hook. For now...' he paused as a low groan sounded from the stairwell behind me. Jade Tooth looked back over his shoulder.

'From the sounds of things, you have also, inadvertently exacted your revenge for the chastising those two gave you in Sheung Wan.'

He gestured with his chin to the stairs. His goon glared once more at me and moved off to give what help he could to his mates, leaving Jade Tooth and me alone. He glanced at my waist, indicating the handgun in my jeans.

'There'll be no need for that, Mr Jones. We're all friends here... although I would like you to return it before you leave.'

He sat down and resumed counting the money, making a notation on a small notepad at his elbow. I stood staring dumbly at him. After a long pause, he glanced up at me and waved his hand languidly.

'You can go now, Galahad,' he said still counting the cash. '

I nodded slowly and turned away, my heart racing.

'I look forward to seeing you at our next Mahjong tournament,' Jade Tooth called after me, laughing, as I walked from the room and made my way cautiously past the two casualties on the stairs.

Emerging out onto the street, I blinked against the glare of the sun then turned and tossed the handgun back down the stairs. I was stunned and stood rooted to the spot while I rolled and lit a cigarette, my hangover forgotten.

That morning I had woken to the very real prospect of a bullet in the head – if I was lucky – but now I had got my own back for the beating at the hands of Jade Tooth's goons, my debt had been paid and I had been allowed to leave, untouched.

I shook my head and dragged deeply on the cigarette, feeling dizzy with relief and the usual post-action crash. I badly needed a drink so I headed off toward Shanghai Street and a bar that I knew would be open at that hour on a weekday.

I had not gone 20 metres when a black Mercedes S-Class pulled up alongside me. I had barely registered it when I felt a hand on my shoulder and the barrel of a gun jab painfully into my left kidney.

The back door of the vehicle swung open and a hand clamped on my head, pushing down as I was bundled into the car with my assailant clambering in beside me. The door slammed shut, the central locking clicked down and the car sped off south down Shanghai Street.

It had all taken about 10 seconds.

18

I LOOKED at the man sitting next to me, then at the driver and another man seated in the front passenger seat. None of them appeared tense – in fact, they seemed quite relaxed, which struck me as odd seeing as they had just kidnapped me off a crowded street.

All three were Chinese and they were obviously confident none of this would be an issue for them, and that worried me. The man in the back seat next to me slid on his seatbelt and gestured wordlessly, that I should do the same.

Yes, I thought, can't have me being injured in a car crash.

I was about to ask my captors to introduce themselves when the front passenger picked up his phone and hit a speed dial number. He spoke lowly, but clearly, in Cantonese. A faint memory came back to me...that voice!

'We have him,' he said then paused, listening to the person on the other end of the call. 'No... he's fine. Amazingly. You should have seen what he did to ... yes. Sorry, ma'am. We will be fifteen minutes with this traffic.'

He hung up and turned in his seat to face me, a faint grin on his face.

'You really have been a handful, Mr Jones,' he said in heavily accented English, shaking his head. 'Jade Tooth's men won't soon forget you! *Wow*.. what a demon!' His voice tugged again at my memory.

The one next to me grunted.

'A pain in the ass, if you ask me,' he added in Cantonese.

As soon as he spoke, it came back to me and I heard them both again in my head. '*i told you to stay closer to him. now look!*' – '*i was close.*' – '*not close enough you idiot!*' – '*what do we do now? is he dead?*'

These were the men who had found me after Jade Tooth's boys had beaten me half to death and had been worried that the 'boss' wouldn't be happy. Who were they and who was their boss?

I smiled politely at the man in the front seat. 'Where are we going?' I asked lightly.

He stroked the thick, dark beard on his chin. 'For a short drive, Mr Jones. Don't worry. Sit back and relax.'

I decided to accept his advice, so I relaxed into the luxurious upholstery of the Mercedes, feeling the air conditioning cooling my face and watched as Kowloon slid by me as we headed south along Nathan Road.

I was surprised, given my situation, to find my eyes growing heavy. Ordinarily, I should have been on edge to have been snatched off a street – not that it had happened to me before – but I sensed I wasn't in any immediate danger so I saw no point in fighting it. I let myself go and drifted off to sleep.

Almost immediately, it seemed, I was prodded awake and the car doors were opening. I rubbed my eyes and looked about. We were parked in the taxi rank at the Star Ferry Pier in Tsim Sha Tsui and the driver stayed behind the wheel as my two escorts climbed out of the car.

The smiley one with the beard opened my door and bowed slightly as I stepped out. I could see he was squat but powerfully built. His partner moved ahead and took up position by a small gate in the sea wall rail slightly down the promenade from the eastern-most Wan Chai ferry.

This was a private vessel pier where tourist junks and private boats briefly tied up to take on passengers. Sure enough, as I followed along behind Smiley, the bridge of a super yacht came into view, the very top of it poking above the upper deck of the public walkway. I hated boats and my stomach churned slightly at the thought of being whisked away on this one, as big as it was, to parts unknown.

The gate was opened for me and my two escorts held back as they gestured for me to cross the gangway and board. Before I did, the bearded gangster quickly ran expert hands over me and drew out the knife. With a click of his tongue, he tossed it into the harbour. A young man in a slim-fitting grey suit, white shirt and dark tie, waited patiently for me.

I noticed another two alert, smartly-dressed young men: one above me on the upper deck and one at the bow.

When I stepped aboard, Slim Grey Suit gestured wordlessly for me to follow as he led the way to the stern and a large, covered lounge area.

As soon as I was aboard, the ropes securing the vessel to the pier were slipped and the engines roared as the skipper steered us out onto Victoria Harbour. The deck swayed slightly under my feet, my hangover returned in a flash and I felt as if was going to vomit. I closed my eyes and swallowed down a wave of nausea. Taking a deep breath, I stepped onto the rear-deck lounge area indicated to me by the smart young man in the grey suit with a sweep of his arm.

I had taken one step in when I froze.

On the left of the covered area, under a large black ceiling fan, sitting on a long lounge, one arm draped languorously across its back and dressed in a white shirt, designer jeans and black Louboutin heels, sat Angel.

She arched an eyebrow and smiled ruefully at me as I stepped in. I just frowned at her and turned my attention to the other person in the room.

The man who rose from a large cane chair and crossed the deck toward me, hand extended in greeting, wasn't young. He was, perhaps, in his mid-sixties but he carried it well. He was Chinese, slim and tanned and his tailored white shirt sat flat against his stomach, stretching slightly across his chest. He wore a pair of dark, slim-fit linen pants and black deck loafers. The magnificent Patek Philippe I glimpsed on his left wrist completed the picture.

This man wasn't just rich, he was probably the richest of Hong Kong's super rich and I knew him by sight. I put out my hand and shook his.

'Good afternoon Mr Lee,' I said in Cantonese. 'You will forgive me if I don't say it's a pleasure to meet you.'

Lee Pak-chun was the Chairman and CEO of one of Hong Kong's mightiest corporations. YunCorp dominated shipping, finance and industry in the Special Administrative Region and a very large slice of the Mainland – mostly centred on Guangdong and Hunan provinces – and Lee's personal worth was reported to be in excess of US37 billion.

He was also, although it wasn't widely known – or perhaps it was, but was ignored because that's the way Hong Kong rolls – the Mountain Master, the leader, of 14K Triad.

My eyes slid to Angel and I swallowed. Sitting alone on a super yacht with Hong Kong's leading Tai-pan, and most powerful triad lord, was not something usually done by a person only 'peripherally involved' with organised crime. She was in as deep – or as high – as it got and it was something, I knew with a rising sense of dismay, I would have to confront at some point.

'Mr Jones,' Lee said brightly, his accent educated and English. 'Welcome aboard. Please come this way,' he said as he offered me a chair facing his. 'I do hope the circumstances of your arrival were not too distressing...'

I glanced at Angel. 'Well, it *was* a surprise,' I said. 'I presume,' I went on, talking to Angel, 'this is the "important meeting" you mentioned?'

She nodded. 'Yes,' she said sternly. 'And, if I recall, I also asked you to stay out of trouble. Instead, you chose to wander, alone, into Jade Tooth's den and challenge him for the money you owed him.'

I bit down on the terse reply that sprang to my lips and took a deep breath. 'What's happening here Angel?' She just looked at the man across from me, so I turned my attention back to him.

He poured three glasses of an extremely rare Bollinger Vieille Vignes from a chilled bottle and carried one to Angel, who accepted it with a smile. A pang of jealousy stabbed at me as I watched her toast him silently.

I was becoming more annoyed by the minute but I was at least smart enough to realise that would not help me, given my current position – I hadn't been blind to the grip of the automatic that had protruded from the young man's grey suit jacket. I wasn't really holding any winning cards in this game so it was best to play along.

A glass of champagne was passed across to me and I sipped gratefully at the complex and powerful flavours, closing my eyes briefly in appreciation. I opened my eyes and, although I was mad at her, winked at Angel, who grinned and winked back.

Things could be a lot worse, I thought. I sat back and looked passively at Lee.

'Of course,' he said, 'you know Ms Yeung.'

I nodded. 'Yes, you could say that. We're acquainted.'

Lee tutted. 'Now Mr Jones no need to be coy. I am well aware you and the beautiful Ms Yeung are "an item". It's quite all right, really...'

'Well, thank you for your permission,' I said levelly.'

He grinned and sipped at his champagne. He sighed contentedly and smacked his lips. 'Delightful,' he said. 'What you may not be aware of, Mr Jones, is the fact that Mei-ying is my Straw Sandal. Did you know that?'

I swallowed and flashed a look at Angel. That explained a lot. She was Lee's Liaison Officer, one of the upper echelon of the triad. I felt sick again and looked at her. 'Nei saa ngo,' *You've been playing me*, I said bitterly.

She shook her head and smiled sadly. 'No, Gal. I'm protecting you,' she replied. I wanted to laugh but decided against it.

I turned back to Lee, the exquisite champagne ashes in my mouth. 'Do you mind if I smoke?' I asked, pulling out my tobacco pouch and rolling a cigarette without waiting for his reply. I flicked my lighter and lit the cigarette, using the first, long drag as a moment to gather my thoughts.

An ashtray was placed silently on the table in front of me and Pistol Boy stepped back to his place by the rail. I ashed the tip of the cigarette and looked up.

'Tell me, Mr Lee. Why am I here? It's been a very long day, I'm tired and eager to be home.'

Lee smiled slightly and opened a humidor behind him, selecting, cropping and lighting a fat Cohiba. He puffed out the smoke and rolled the cigar gently in his fingers, inspecting the tip. Finally, he spoke.

'I have a business proposition for you, Mr Jones,' he said, still studying the ash at the tip of his cigar.

'I don't do business with criminals, Mr Lee. I'm sure you know that.'

He nodded. 'Yes, I know that. Everyone knows that of you, Mr Jones. However, I think you'll find you are *already* doing business with me.'

I sat back in the chair. 'The fifty grand to Jade Tooth. It was you.' Lee shrugged slightly and raised an eyebrow. 'Why?' I asked.

'A number of reasons, but, first, because Mei-ying asked me to.' I resisted the urge to look at Angel and Lee went on. 'But I confess I have my own, less-than-philanthropic reasons. In short, Mr Jones, I believe you can do me a great service – and I am prepared to pay very handsomely for it.'

I didn't like the way this was going. My father had been a crooked copper and 14K had killed him, presumably when he crossed them at some stage. Now their Mountain Master, no less, was assuming the apple didn't fall far from the tree.

Maybe he was right. I sipped the champagne and dragged on my cigarette; a transparent delaying tactic but I needed the space to think. Lee sat patiently.

'You're not listening to me, Mr Lee,' I said eventually. 'You may have had my father in your pocket – well perhaps not *you*, but your predecessor – but that's not me. I'll repay you the fifty thousand...'

'Do I look like I need your money, Mr Jones?' he said mildly. 'I could not care less about a paltry fifty. I couldn't care about one hundred times that.'

He drew again on the cigar. 'The debt is paid, no strings attached, as my favour to Ms Yeung. You are under no obligation. You have but to say and we will turn the boat around and drop you wherever you wish.' He paused before adding 'And...I think you do your father a great disservice. He deserves your honour, not your condemnation.'

That got me and I blinked in surprise.

'May I go on?' Lee asked politely.

I looked about me and saw that we were rounding the eastern tip of the Island and passing Chai Wan, heading south toward Cape D'Aguilar and the open ocean. The sun had broken through again, shining warmly on my face, and the champagne was washing its magic through my body. I looked at Lee and nodded.

'First, what did you mean about my father?' I asked.

Lee held up a finger like a school teacher making a point to a recalcitrant class. 'That will come, Mr Jones, I assure you. But allow me to lay out my needs and how you might assist me to meet them.'

I nodded again and Lee took a deep breath before beginning.

'As you have probably worked out by now, someone with whom James Thomas is working is engaged in large-scale trafficking of young women into Hong Kong for the purposes of sexual servitude.'

He saw the surprise on my face and chuckled. 'As soon as we saw you first speaking with Sarah Thomas I knew I had been granted an opportunity that rarely comes along. I commend you; you have pieced most of it together quite quickly – probably with a little help from our anonymous notes and, I dare say, Johnny Tong.'

He paused. 'The incident the other night in Chuk Un, however, was ... unfortunate.'

I shrugged, beyond caring at that point. 'The two men who picked me up this afternoon,' I said. 'How long have they been following me?'

I realised they were also the two men outside of Jade Tooth's club who had disappeared into the crowded street when I had chased them.

'They were watching Thomas when you arrived so it was a simple matter to move them to you, by way of your protection and to keep me apprised of your progress.'

'They didn't do such a great job of protecting me, did they,' I said, remembering the agony of the split bamboo poles beating me senseless in a Sheung Wan alley.' Lee shrugged, looking a little embarrassed.

'So what does all this have to do with me?' I went on. 'Why do you need me to have figured this all out and why bring me here now?' I asked, sensing I already knew the answers to the first two questions.

'Let me take your last question first,' Lee said. 'You have been quite tenacious and seem to have assembled most of the facts but, unfortunately, you have been a little slow and events seem about to overtake us, hence my decision to have you here today as my guest.' He smiled again, warmly.

'I'm sorry to have let you down,' I said sarcastically. 'I would have moved much faster had I known it was important to you.' Lee ignored the comment and continued.

'To your first two questions, it's quite simple: We want the trade stopped,' he said.

I nodded, although I could not fathom why he would want that. 'Fair enough. But why not just stop it yourselves? Or, now here's an idea, why not tip off OCTB or CIB?'

Lee smiled again and again held up his finger.

'We could, *possibly*, stop it ourselves but the last thing I want is an open war,' he said, shaking his head. 'No, that would not do. Secondly, we do not really know all the facts. Yet. Besides, if we did, do you think your friend, Mr Toh, would have acted on an anonymous, uncorroborated tip, regardless of how specific? Or worse yet, a tip from a triad?'

I shook my head, agreeing it was unlikely.

'And...' he went on 'Criminal Intelligence Bureau is another matter altogether.'

I felt the familiar clawing again at the back of my mind when I thought about the CIB wires. They had revealed, falsely, I had taken a bribe, but I remembered Peter's insistence they provided him and OCTB good, actionable intelligence. Finally, there was my troubling chat with David Zhou.

'What does that mean?' I asked.

'Patience, Mr Jones.' Lee paused and blew gently on the tip of the cigar, gently fanning its burning core. 'Now, where was I?

'You want the trade stopped,' I said.

'Ah, yes... So you can perhaps see why we couldn't go to OCTB. It has to come from somewhere else. Somewhere like you and your dogged, if unconventional, methods and close association with Mr Toh. If you were to provide Peter Toh with evidence, I am quite sure he would act.'

I remembered Peter telling me, only the day before, to go to him if I found anything solid. I nodded.

'So why not get to Thomas and lean on him to take it to the cops?' I asked. 'Why not just tell me; why the puppet show with you pulling the strings?'

Lee raised an eyebrow. 'Would you have believed us if we had just told you?' he asked mildly.

I conceded the point. 'No, probably not.'

'As to Thomas giving up the operation: perhaps he may but then it would, in all likelihood, just shift and we would be back at the start. Besides, I need this to ... play out.'

He paused for a moment and sipped at his champagne.

'So, there you are. We needed you to figure it out – with a little help – then tell Chief Inspector Toh who would then take action and, bingo, a competitor's wicked trade in innocent young women is stopped.'

Lee puffed on his cigar.

'Competitor. Which triad? I asked. 'Who is doing this?'

'Sun Yee On.'

I thought back to the wires and the rat scratched again, this time wildly as if its very life depended on it getting out. I wasn't sure how much to reveal so decided to play it safe.

'Surely CIB has sources inside SYO,' I said. 'If the triad were running this operation then word would get back to CI and to OCTB. They would be shut down overnight.'

Lee smiled and he looked at me a little pityingly. I heard Angel chuckle softly over in her corner.

'They *do* have wires inside, Mr Jones. I know that for a certainty.' Here it comes I thought... 'But, ask yourself, if that is the case why do those devices reveal nothing? Why is there no word of this coming out of SYO?'

The pieces were clicking into place in my mind so fast I could almost hear them. But it still did not make sense.

'SYO knows about the wires,' I said. 'So it's also possible that someone in CIB is playing a double game?'

Lee made a gesture as if to say "See, now you have it" and nodded.

I asked the obvious question. 'Who?'

There was that finger again. 'All in good time Mr Jones, I promise. Although I admit I cannot be sure. Let us first examine the more immediate issues.'

'Which are?'

'Firstly, as I have said, events seem to have overtaken us so I decided to bring you here and speed things up as best I can and, secondly, as I have already told you: I want the trade ended. That is all.'

'The trade ended? So you can take it up?' I challenged. 'So 14K can take over; a seamless transition into a profit stream to which you haven't had access?'

Lee took the Bollinger bottle out of the ice bucket and walked over to Angel, topping up her glass. Again, she toasted him silently and I bit hard on my tongue. Moving back to the table he filled my glass and, the bottle empty, he signalled to the man at the rail for another. The soldier glanced at me and then back to Lee.

'It's fine,' Lee said to his man then looked at me. 'We're all friends here,' he added.

It was the second time I had heard that from a villain that day, the only difference was Jade Tooth was small fry and they didn't get much bigger than Lee Pak-chun.

I was distinctly uncomfortable at the notion of "friendship" with this man and knew my earlier misgivings had been on the money: I was sliding deeper and deeper into a morass from which there looked to be no escape. Lee sat down and puffed his cigar to life.

He was about to speak when my phone rang. I checked the contact details and answered.

'Hi,' I said. Joey's voice sounded concerned on the other end.

'You okay boss? You hadn't checked in so I thought...'

I looked at Lee who was examining his fingernails in boredom and, probably, annoyance. 'All good here,' I said. 'I'm just talking to a couple of friends. I'll tell you all about it on Monday. Go enjoy your Friday evening, and have a good weekend.'

Joey acknowledged, muttered something about another weekend with nothing happening and hung up. I dropped my phone, face down, on the table and looked up at Lee. 'You were saying..?' I said rolling a cigarette. I really was smoking too much, I thought.

Lee huffed, a little annoyed at the interruption.

'I am sure it will surprise you,' he said 'to know that we want no part of an organised slavery racket. True, it is very lucrative but the risks are high. We invest in corruption, Mr Jones, and, with our focus in recent years on white-collar activities which pay far greater dividends, we have decided the risk of dabbling in the slave trade far outweighs the benefits.'

He paused while taking a sip of his champagne.

'My *God* that is good,' he sighed. 'Anyway, in simple terms, I want the trade stopped for two reasons,' he ticked them off on his fingers.

'One: the dent in SYO's coffers at the loss of this significant slice of their operation will nearly cripple them. They will, in all likelihood, never rise to challenge my society again. And two: the operation draws heat – a great deal of it – and by shutting it down we ease that heat, thus allowing us – *all* the societies in fact – to get on with business.'

I studied Lee closely. The operation drew heat? As far as OCTB and Peter Toh were concerned it didn't exist except in my fevered imagination. Also, Lee wanted the smuggling operation to 'play out'. Why? What was Lee's angle here? He was telling the truth I thought, but only up to a point; he was definitely holding something back. There was something that didn't quite fit.

I had the nagging feeling this went much further than an operational inconvenience for 14K, but I put the thought aside as I recalled something he said earlier.

'You said events have overtaken you, the reason you decided to speed up my clumsy investigations. What events?'

Lee nodded as if he were waiting for me to ask that question.

'You are familiar with the shipment a few nights ago,' he said. I nodded. 'Although you did not get close to it,' he added pointedly. 'Well, it was a small one – a trial run, if you will. We believe another shipment, a much larger one, is due sometime very soon. We do not know the date or time, nor the location – but we suspect it to be Aberdeen.'

He smiled, spreading his hands. 'You see?' he said. 'There is no time to waste. You must work your magic, Mr Jones.'

I stood to stretch my legs and moved to the rail to gaze out at the sea and passing headland of Cape D'Aguilar. The sun was setting. The headland and coast were in shadow, the sea darkening as it slipped past the boat to leave a glistening, phosphorescent trail in its wake. I dragged on my cigarette and flicked it into the water, watching its bright tip instantly extinguish.

I could feel the grip of the moral quicksand I was in as it tightened around me. I was standing on a criminal lord's super yacht, possibly on the point of agreeing to help him bring down a competitor triad. I turned back to Lee, briefly catching Angel's eye as I did so. She looked worried – probably for the safety of her own position, I thought uncharitably.

'Okay,' I said. 'Let's assume I agree with all that – God help me. You still haven't told me why I would help you.'

'I know the offer of a great deal of money won't work with you, Mr

Jones. Is it not enough for you to see the trade in young women ended? Lee challenged me.

'Of course it is. But that's not the point.' My voice started to rise so I took a breath to control myself. '

You're the 489 of 14K Triad, for God's sake,' I said, using his triad numeric title from the traditional *I Ching*. 'I've always hung my own personal respect – what little there is of it – on the fact I was honest. Stupid, but honest. I swore years ago I would never be like my father.'

My face flushed as the anger finally got the better of me. 'A man who, incidentally, you and your gang of thieves murdered. So, no, I won't help you and never want to see you...' I glanced at Angel '... either of you, ever again.'

I stood my ground, leaning against the boat's railing, breathing deeply and watching one of Lee's men who had moved into view as soon as I raised my voice.

Lee sat back in his chair and studied me hard, unblinking, for over a minute. The silence stretched out uncomfortably before us.

Finally, he spoke, his face composed and voice level but clear so I could hear it above the sound of the engines and the sea rushing past the yacht's hull.

'You asked me earlier about your father,' he said. 'Well, I see now is the time for me to tell you.'

He signalled, with a flick of his hand, to Angel who stood and moved into the main cabin of the yacht, disappearing from view. Lee sat silently until Angel returned.

With her stood a well-dressed man, a little younger than me, fit & healthy with broad shoulders, a slim waist and lively eyes. His otherwise handsome features were marked by an old scar that ran, in a jagged line, the length of his face from the corner of his right eye to the point of his jaw. It gave him a slightly rakish look but there was no doubting it had been a serious injury at some time. He looked at Lee who nodded and smiled.

'This, Mr Jones,' he said indicating the man, 'is my son, Lee Zhang-yong. Jason. He is my only son and he is everything to me.'

The other man nodded and bowed to Lee, making a fist and palm salute, then moved to sit on the lounge next to Angel. Lee smiled approvingly at the man and turned back to me. He puffed on the nub of his cigar and began to speak.

The young boy was nearing his seventh birthday and had been playing with friends in the old Kowloon Walled City, doing all the things young boys do when left without supervision. They kicked their football through the crowded alleyways and streets of the Walled City, bouncing it off people and shop stalls and, generally, leaving a trail of indignation and minor damage in their wake. One of the boys, at 13 the oldest of the gang, kicked the ball hard, ricocheting it off the wheels of a stall cart and the boys watched as it disappeared into the doorway of one of the many derelict buildings in the ever-changing streetscape of the City. The older boy turned to the youngster and pointed into the doorway. 'Go get it, kid,' he said and leaned back against the window of a shop to watch as the boy darted under the bamboo scaffolding and into the darkened doorway.

The sound of a car grinding through its gears and revving its engine came to the boys as they stood waiting for the return of their friend and their ball, and they looked up the street to watch as a dented VW Beetle lurched its way down the narrow street. The driver was having problems with the gearbox and the engine revved in low gear as the car bunny-hopped forward. As the boys watched on in amusement, the car suddenly lurched forward, its engine racing and accelerated along the street.

It knocked over a street stall and flung aside two people who tried desperately to dive out of its way, before careening into the bamboo scaffolding at the precise moment the boy was exiting with the ball under his arm and a smile on his face. The scaffolding collapsed and the car, now jammed against the brick wall of the doorway, started to smoke and flames licked the underside of the rear of the vehicle. As the scaffolding collapsed it brought down a load of bricks and cement bags, sand and gravel that partially buried the front of the car and the doorway as fire spread quickly to the back of the car, threatening to engulf the unconscious driver.

The boys leapt forward, calling their friend's name but there was no answer and they were driven back by the flames as the grown-ups around them struggled with the battered door of the car and dragged the driver clear. The boys stood rooted to the spot, overwhelmed and unable to act, calling their friend's name again and again with no reply. From nowhere a large gweilo policeman ran forward, throwing aside his dark uniform cap as he leapt the wall of flames, his face sheltered in the crook of his arm.

His partner, a Chinese Sergeant, gathered the boys into his arms and shepherded them back across the street and to the safety of a store doorway before running back to the burning vehicle. The Sergeant tried to move forward but was forced back by the flames, that by now had taken hold of the car, the scaffolding and the doorway of the building. He pulled the radio from his belt and shouted a demand for assistance. It was mayhem in the street as people ran for cover, choking on the smoke, and the flames threatened to spread to the ramshackle, mostly wooden, structures that made up the majority of the Walled City. In the distance the wailing of sirens could be heard as fire engines crept their way into the City, negotiating the maze of narrow streets and alleys.

Suddenly, from the flames and smoke, a giant in khaki uniform emerged. His face and arms blackened, his uniform torn, and his fingers bleeding from where he had desperately clawed at the rubble that had covered the little body he now held in his arms. He staggered forward and shuffled slowly up the street, his partner in tow, to a clear area where he placed the young boy gently on the ground.

The Sergeant swore under his breath as he took in the state of the boy's face. Through the blood, it looked as if the entire right side of his face had been peeled away, and the lad's skin and cheek flapped against his jawline. Both the policemen could see the boy's teeth through the horrific wound. The big officer unbuckled his Sam Browne belt, dropping it on the pavement, stripped away his uniform tunic and pulled off the singlet he wore underneath. Gesturing to this partner to gently take the head of the unconscious boy, the gweilo policeman tenderly lifted the flap of skin and muscle back into place then gently wrapped the right side of the boy's head in the sweated and charred singlet. It wasn't as sterile as the policeman would have liked, but stopping the bleeding was critical.

That done, he gently rolled the boy into the Recovery Position then snatched up an umbrella from a nearby stall, opened it and stood above the boy to shelter him from the blazing sun in the smoke-filled street. The shouting, panicked crowd surged around the policemen and the unconscious boy, but the men stood firm like two boulders in a raging torrent, covering the broken and bleeding boy and protecting him from harm.

Lee stopped and watched as I glanced across at his son. The scar stood out all the more now that I was focussing on it. Although I already knew the answer I asked the one question on my mind.

'The gweilo officer was my father?' My throat felt tight and the words caught as I spoke.

Lee nodded. 'Yes, he was your father. He was a Superintendent in the Organised and Serious Crime Group at the time but, as was his habit, he had put on his uniform and patrolled the community of the Walled City that day. Had he not, my son would have died.'

I did a mental calculation and frowned. 'This must have all been shortly before...'

'Shortly before your father was killed,' Lee finished my sentence. 'Yes. In fact, it was only two weeks. Jason was still in hospital when your father was murdered.'

He sat back silently, waiting while I worked out the staggering implications of what I had been told.

I took a deep breath and exhaled slowly. 'So 14K didn't kill my father. He didn't work for you.' I said flatly, my mind whirling.

'He did not work for us, nor did we kill him. In fact, from the day he saved Jason we had a team on his every movement, for his protection. As you know he was very unpopular with the gangs, and completely dogged in his pursuit of them...Us. He never knew it but our men shadowed his every movement at work and at home to ensure his safety... and that of his family.' He shifted slightly in his chair. 'Sadly, we failed,' he added.

'So he wasn't on the take?' I asked quietly.

'Far from it, Mr Jones. He was the most scrupulous of men, a devoted servant of the community and sworn enemy of the societies – including my own.'

I felt dizzy. Everything I had come to believe about my father since I was thirteen years of age was a lie.

The disgrace I had carried into the Police College and the job, and the pain and anger I had held in my heart for a man who had betrayed his oath and his community, for a father who had betrayed his family. It was all built on a lie. I drew in a sharp intake of breath as I realised, with a jolt, that also meant the vast report into this death and his corruption were false.

The evidence of his corruption, evidence found on his body and supposedly discovered in later raids on SYO operations, was as bent as it accused him of being. I shook my head.

There was just too much to take in, too many pieces to connect, but I swore to myself that would come. Right now I needed to focus on Lee, what he was telling me and what he was offering. I sensed there was one last piece of bait he wanted to dangle before me.

'If 14K didn't kill my father, who did? Do you know?'

Lee nodded and looked out at the now darkened ocean as the yacht, now heading west, ploughed its way toward the lights of Stanley.

'We know who pulled the trigger, and we know who lured him there,' he said. 'I have always known.'

'And you sat on that knowledge for all these years? You let a good man's name, a man who saved your son, be blackened and trampled?'

Lee grimaced and had the good grace to look shamefaced. 'Yes, we did. *I* did. I can't answer why I did, nor why I didn't find the time and occasion to let you and your family know. It shames me.'

'My mother killed herself over *her* shame, Lee...' I said bitterly. 'You knew all along, you let our family suffer and now you ask me for my help? Well, *fuck* you!'

That seemed to slap Lee like a blow across the face. I doubted anyone ever spoke to the 14K Mountain Master like that and it gave me some satisfaction to needle him. He pointed his finger at me, prodding the air as he replied.

'Yes, you are entitled to be angry, to even hate me. None of that matters to me. I admit to making a mistake when it comes to your father and your family, and I regret it. Deeply. If I can, I will make amends but I will not beg for forgiveness. Mistakes happen, Mr Jones. *Life* happens. Do you want to know who killed him? *Do* you?'

I nodded silently and Lee went on.

'Well, for that piece of information, you will have to deliver me the service I have requested of you.'

He saw I was about to object and held up his hand. 'No... I will not reveal the final piece to you and risk your anger and thirst for revenge derailing my plans for SYO.'

He sighed and then lowered his voice, his tone conciliatory.

'Mr Jones, help me do this and I swear I will help you take revenge for the death of your father and restore his good name.'

Like a master angler, Lee had thrown the lure out into the boat's wake and I had swallowed it deep, hooking myself inextricably in the process. It was now easy for him to reel me in, gaff me and land me onto the deck of the boat. For that information, the name of the person who murdered my father, he knew I would agree to anything, do anything. Like it or not – and I did not like it, not at all – I was Lee's man for the immediate future.

'Okay, Mr Lee,' I said finally. 'I'll help you but know this: if you don't give me what I want, you will be next on my list and no amount of this...' I said waving my hand around the opulent boat and the bodyguards 'will stop me.'

Lee extended his right hand to seal the bargain.

'Agreed,' he said. 'I would expect nothing less from you, Mr Jones.'

I just looked at him and turned away to lean on the railing, leaving him standing there with his hand out.

19

IT WAS late evening by the time I got home. It had been a long day and I felt the physical and emotional fatigue of it tug at me as I keyed in the code to my apartment and opened the door.

My friend's helper lay on the sofa, watching TV with the pup asleep beside her. She smiled and lowered the snoring little creature gently onto the blankets in his crate. I asked her if there had been any problems and she shook her head. The pup was very well-behaved and a real joy, she assured me.

Somehow I doubted that but I would find out for myself in the coming days. I thanked her and handed her the cash I had remembered to take from the ATM across the street, and she left.

The sound of the door locking into place woke the pup and he whimpered softly then toddled out onto the loungeroom floor, stretching and arching his back, before trotting into the kitchen to grab a mouthful of kibble and a drink of water. I stepped out onto the terrace, holding the door open and whistling quietly.

'Come on… boy,' I said.

I really had to name this thing if I was keeping him, I thought. The pup waddled past me, onto the terrace and sniffed at a nearby pot plant before dropping into a squat to pee. I had grabbed a beer out of the fridge before walking out, so I flicked the lid off with the bottle opener hanging from a string beside the barbecue and sat down on the terrace lounge to drink and smoke and gather my thoughts.

Lee's boat had arrived at Stanley an hour earlier. Angel had stepped ashore and taken me by the arm, her face serious.

'I didn't know, Gal. I really don't know anything about your dad,' she had said. 'I had no idea. You have never spoken to me of him, and Mr Lee has never discussed it with me. I knew only he was a policeman, like you, and nothing else. I swear...'

I shrugged out of her hold and glared at her.

'Here I was thinking you were a poorly paid dancer in a club when, all this time, you've been a senior member of a triad.'

I nearly laughed at the craziness of it all. 'You've played me so your boss could get what he wants. You put your hooks in me, knowing all along what Lee was planning, the game he was playing, and you led me into it. You disgust me.'

Angel's eyes lowered and I knew she was hurt but I could not have cared less. 'Gal, it started like that when we first met...'

'When you first targeted me, you mean.'

She sighed. 'Yes. That's the way of it. I admit. But I quickly moved beyond that and developed a real ... affection for you.'

I paused at that. It was the first time she had made what even came close to a declaration of her feelings for me.

I had looked about and hailed a taxi that swung across the road and pulled up alongside me. I opened the door and climbed in.

'Don't call me, Angel,' I said looking up at her standing straight and beautiful in the orange glow of a streetlight. My heart lurched at the sight of her.

'I'm too pissed off. Strictly business from here on and I'll call *you* when I have anything you need to know... although I'm sure your stooges will have passed that on anyway.'

I stopped to take a breath and lowered my voice. '

'That's another thing, you can call your boys off. I want no shadows. Not anymore. If I see them I'll deal with them and your boss won't like that.'

I shook my head. 'A triad Straw Sandal,' I said in disbelief. 'Who would have thought..?' and, with that, I had slammed the taxi door and ordered the driver on.

Now on my terrace, sipping on the beer, I thought it had been quite a day. I had escaped Jade Tooth's near-fatal financial penalty and been cleared of the significant debt, shared a bottle of champagne with Hong Kong's most powerful crime lord, had my suspicions regarding Thomas confirmed, and had discovered my father was not a corrupt copper but, in fact, a much-respected policeman – at least by his enemies. His former colleagues still thought he was a disgrace. I was also much closer to discovering who really killed him. I swigged the beer.

That all seemed on the upside but, on the downside, it looked like I had sold my soul to the devil and had lost the woman I had come to realise I loved.

I knew if I was to accept the pact I had made with Lee, and wanted to keep Angel, I had some serious wrestling with my conscience ahead of me. I had no idea how I would rationalise my working for a triad but I instinctively knew I wanted the situation with Angel to be resolved. The whole mess was a dilemma to which I could see no immediate solution.

I shook my head and looked up at the night sky as if pleading for answers. The sky was silent and the only sound I could hear was the clank of a tram as it snaked its way past the front of my apartment.

I felt the pup clawing at my jeans and I looked down at him. He sat and looked up at me, his head tilted and ears pricked.

I sighed deeply. 'If you're going to stay, you'll need a name,' I said.

I swigged again at the beer and ran through a list of possible names, saying them out loud as the pup sat and listened. None of them did anything for me, or him for that matter, and I was about to give up when a memory sprang unbidden to my mind.

I am sitting on my father's knee, he in a high-backed cane chair on the veranda of our home in Kowloon Tong. It is a hot and humid evening; the crickets are making a din in the yard and a light breeze whispers through the large Bauhinia that stands guard over the front gate. Inside, my mother's voice is cooing to a distraught baby Prudence as she feeds her. She is also instructing our helpers in readiness for the dinner party that night, in her polite but born-to-rule voice high-ranking Hong Kong Chinese women all have. My father's ancient Labrador lies at his feet. He is reading to me, from Le Morte d'Arthur, *his voice low and mellifluous. My eyes are heavy. Galahad, Bors and Percival are on the Grail Quest performing miracles, fighting evil and saving damsels. My head swims with the images, for I am Galahad, a knight fair and true. I sleep and my father carries me in his arms to my bedroom and tucks me into bed, kissing me on the forehead. I wake a little later and smell cigar smoke wafting the house like a light blanket over the bright chatter of the dinner party on the back lawn. I smile and drift back to sleep.*

The pup clawed me once again and I blinked back to the present, feeling tears welling hot in my eyes.

My brief daydream had been the first time I had thought of my father in that light since his death and it felt like a release, a rare moment of joy to think of him as a loving parent rather than a corrupt policeman who had brought shame on his family.

As fraught as the deal with Lee was, it gave me the chance to discover what had really happened to my father and to avenge his death. I knew I would do nearly anything to have that.

I bent to the pup again and he backed up and yapped a little bark.

'He was the son of a king and a great knight,' I said as he stared up at me. 'One of Arthur's finest. Galahad's right-hand man in the Grail Quest, together to the death. So it really can't be anything else.'

I scratched him behind the ear. 'That crazy woman was right... without each other, we really would be on our own, so welcome to your new pack, boy. It's not big, but it will do us both for now.'

The pup's ears twitched and flicked at my voice and I put down the empty beer bottle and stood.

'Come, Bors,' I said as I walked off the terrace and inside, my new companion in tow. That night I slept fitfully, lost in dark and fragmented dreams, with the word 'nuisance' ringing in my brain.

20

ON SATURDAY MORNING I woke early and headed into the hills to run and clear my mind.

The meeting with Lee had revealed much but had given rise to even more questions – many of which I could not even frame. The news of my father's innocence had brought both immense relief and a renewed surge of white-hot anger. Anger for my father, my mother, Pru and me. Anger at my career destroyed, a father stolen and a family broken. I felt it rising from deep within me and, at that moment, in my thirst for revenge, I could have done anything, killed anyone.

I shook my head, and re-focussed on the immediate issue of 'what now?'

I was getting deeper and deeper into an immensely complicated criminal enterprise, a web of deceit, murder and revenge. All I could see as I ran, my breathing laboured and sweat flowing freely into my eyes, were mirrors within mirrors reflecting away into infinity. A major human trafficking shipment was due to arrive sometime in the next five days and I did not know where or when – although I still put my chips on Aberdeen as the 'where'.

I needed help but I felt I had exhausted my resources. Who else could I turn to? Who else might have heard, or be interested in ...?

The answer came to me like a punch in the gut and I pulled up suddenly on the running track, another runner who had been trailing me taking evasive action with a shout to avoid a collision.

I checked my G-Shock. It was still early, so I had time to catch him over morning coffee, if he still took it where he had for years. I spun on my heels and ran as fast as I could down the steep hill, my knees screaming, back on to the road and headed for home. Arriving there in a matter of minutes, I impatiently rode the elevator to my floor and surged into my apartment.

Bors lurched off his mat by the door but I just ruffled his head quickly and ran to the shower. Ten minutes later I had locked the door, stepped out onto the main road and hailed a passing taxi, giving the driver the address of a small coffee shop in Wan Chai.

I impatiently tapped my knee as the taxi crawled through the morning traffic, busy as usual despite it being a Saturday, and checked my watch. I had ten minutes before, according to his long-set morning schedule, the man I needed to see would leave and I did not have his phone number – as far as I knew he still refused to carry a mobile phone.

The taxi finally pulled into the curb just off Johnston Road and I swung open the door as I handed over a hundred and told the driver to keep it. With a sigh of relief, I saw him sitting at his usual table, hidden behind an open newspaper, an espresso by his right hand and an ashtray at his left.

I stepped forward and tapped on the table. The newspaper slowly collapsed as he brought his hands together and a pair of piercing blue eyes, hidden under eyebrows that looked like shaggy caterpillars, regarded me coldly until he recognised me and a wide smile cracked his jowly and tanned face.

'Well, bugger me,' he said in a light voice, the accent distinctly Oxbridge and posh. 'If it isn't Galahad Jones. To what do I owe... etcetera?'

He waved a hand languidly and I took a seat. 'It's been a while dear chap,' he said, picking up his espresso and flicking a lighter to a cigarette.

Alastair Xavier Chard had arrived in Hong Kong in the late-seventies as a young, good-looking, long-haired junior reporter with The Times, initially covering the social rounds and odd jobs for that revered broadsheet, but soon graduated to the police beat where he cut his teeth on the city's seamier underbelly before moving across to the South China Herald – one of Hong Kong's newspapers of record since 1910 – where he remained.

Rumour had it that he had been one of Hong Kong's more notorious lotharios – on both sides of the fence – and had left a trail of broken hearts behind him as he cut a swathe through the expat community. He also quickly became The Herald's leading investigative journalist in Southern China with an extensive personal network of the high and the low right across Hong Kong; greater than anyone I had known, including Johnny Tong.

He was known as a scrupulously honest man who was fiercely protective of his sources and he had eyes everywhere and in everything. Alastair Chard was, in every sense, the archetypal old-school foreign correspondent: hard drinking, slightly overweight and florid, a chain smoker, brash and loud, with a doctorate-level swearing vocabulary and sartorially inclined toward rumpled linen suits and stained ties. I liked him very much and trusted him completely.

I rolled and lit a cigarette and signalled the waiter for two espressos. 'Hi Alastair,' I said. 'How are you?'

He looked at me like a bird eyeing a worm. 'How am I?' he asked. 'Fucking *marvellous* old man, but I confess to being a little baffled. What are you doing at my fucking breakfast table – it's been, what, four months?'

'Closer to five.'

'Right, five months. Now here you are. All prick and toenails, invading my space and, doubtless, about to ruin my morning. You have a way of doing that, you know...'

'That's a bit harsh.'

'But fucking fair, old boy.'

The coffees arrived and we both sipped appreciatively at them, eyeing each other. I was going to sit quietly and wait for him to speak first but I realised I was trying it on against a master of the pregnant pause. He would sit like this all morning just to prove a point, so I gave in.

'Well, Alastair,' I began. 'It's by way of asking for a bit of a favour. Information really.'

He dragged deeply on his cigarette and stabbed it out brutally in the ashtray. 'Information? Assuming I have this *information*, and am prepared to part with it, I will receive what, exactly, by way of quid pro quo?'

'My undying gratitude and fealty.'

'Fuck your sworn oath, Galahad old cock. I was thinking more along the lines of something I can use. You know, to squirrel away in my bag of "I fucking know stuff."'

'Oh, I think you can use this Alastair,' I said equably. 'In fact, if things pan out the way I'm thinking you'll be known far and wide as the greatest journalist in Asia Pacific.'

He lit another cigarette and drained the espresso. 'I *am* the greatest journalist in fucking Asia Pacific, you ill-educated twat,' he said serenely. 'Now, enough foreplay, what have you got for Uncle Alastair and what do you wish in return?'

So I told him.

Leaving out my close encounters with Jade Tooth, the fact I had been involved in the deaths of two triad soldiers and my cosy chat with Lee Pak-chun, I quickly brought him up to speed on the Thomas job up to that point, what I knew, what I suspected, and ended with my meeting with Fat Johnny Tong and the brick wall I had hit on time and place of the next import.

Alastair didn't blink the whole time I spoke but studied me inscrutably. I was sure he could see I was holding back.

'So,' I said. 'I'm pretty sure this is happening and a big one is coming in soon. I want to be there, get what's needed to have Peter Toh involved and get this bloody thing stopped.' I sat back and waited, gesturing to the waiter for two more coffees.

Alastair picked at his teeth and made a pained expression with his face, as if badly constipated.

'You're holding something back, you little scrote,' he finally said. '*Aren't* you?'

I nodded. I had also, for reasons unknown to me, held back Peter Toh's insistence the CIB intell was good and that I was barking up the wrong tree.

'Yes, Alastair, I am. But I do that for two reasons: one; some of this stuff you just don't need to know. It's personal. Two; I'm still not clear on a few things so I don't want to share any half-arsed theories. Yet.'

'Oh, Galahad, you silly fucker. I'm a journalist. I *deal* in 'half-arsed'. But I take your point. For now. I know what you are about to ask so I shall just dive in and you can divulge the rest of your sordid little escapades at a later date. Shall we?'

'Fair enough. Shoot.'

'You are about to ask me what I know about any of this. Is this really happening? *Are* girls being trafficked into Hong Kong for sucky-fucky in Wan Chai and other points north? If so, *who* is behind it, *when* are they doing it again and *how* can you, brave Galahad, the purest of Arthur's knights – what a bunch of cunts *they* were – stop it?' He sat back and swallowed the fresh espresso that had just arrived, somehow also lighting a cigarette at the same time.

'That's about it, Alastair. Seriously though ...'

He leaned across the table and stabbed a podgy finger at me. '

'I *am* serious you fucking halfwit. I could not be more serious. If you hadn't guessed already, you are mixed up in some very, very nasty shit. *Very* fucking nasty indeed.'

He dragged hard on the mangled cigarette in his nicotine-stained fingers.

'Are you really sure you want to do this, Galahad?' he asked quietly. 'This is a door through which, once you step, there is no return.'

I leaned forward. 'I am, Alastair. The thought of that Cambodian girl, being throttled on the side of a road, dying alone, keeps coming back to me...' I sighed. 'I can't let this go.'

Alastair rubbed his nose with the back of his hand. 'Okay. Your fucking funeral Mr Jones.'

He gathered his thoughts for a moment then continued.

'There have been serious whispers about this for nearly two years now – probably about twenty months. The word is the girls are being brought in – as you say – mostly from Cambodia, Vietnam, and Laos, by ship. But no-one has had any idea exactly how – ships, of course, were always guessed at – or who. That is, until you seem to have stumbled, flat-footed cunt that you are, on the secret.'

He lit yet another cigarette and dragged ferociously on it, spitting the smoke out impatiently as if he needed to get immediately to the second drag, which he did.

'I agree with your 'best guess'. It's SYO. I've always hated those bastards since one of their junior shitheads in a white T-shirt fire-bombed my car in Ma Tau Wai in '92.'

He shook his head and smiled, reminiscing about his good old days on the crime beat. 'Fuck me,' he said quietly, still grinning.

'Anyway, word is it's SYO – no real surprises there – but the other word my dear Galahad, is they have some *serious* cover on this. Someone, *very* high up, is flying a very effective Combat Air Patrol over the SYO forward line of troops.'

'Very high up? Where?'

Alastair shrugged. 'Police, government, both? No-one fucking knows. It is one of the closest-held secrets I've heard of since arriving in this beautiful and ever-so-exciting city.'

I frowned as I thought back to Lee hinting at an SYO source in the Police; probably in CIB, at Zhou's insistence his intel was solid and Peter's urging that there really was nothing to see here. Was that it? Was the top cover for SYO coming from inside the police force? Was Peter being deceived and was that deceiver Zhou?

'What would be your guess?' I asked.

'My guess would be the coppers aren't interested because they don't really know, and there's a reason for that. Someone must know and they're killing it. *But*,' he held up a finger. 'My *other* guess is there's someone else. Someone much bigger. But I've got nothing to go on for that. Not even a morsel of bullshit rumour.'

'Do you have any idea when this might happen again?' I asked hopefully, already knowing the answer. He didn't.

'If I knew that, you fucking dullard, do you not think I'd be doing something with it?'

He shook his head. 'Fuck me, Galahad, you can be dense sometimes. I've been sniffing around this like a horny tom cat for a few months because what I want is the big exposé that will get some action down at Arsenal House, make me even more fucking famous than I am now and, like you, I am desirous to see the end of this *dreadful* fucking trade. Don't you think if I knew anything specific I'd be doing something about it?'

'Of course, Alastair. Sorry,' I muttered, wondering where to next. I had run face-first into another brick wall.

Alastair lit another cigarette – he really was going for some sort of world record, I thought as I rubbed my eyes. I was tired and feeling completely lost. This thing was going to happen and I wouldn't be there to do anything about it.

'Sometime this week,' Alastair said, casually flicking a page of his newspaper and affecting to study the print.

I laughed out loud. 'You crooked old bastard,' I said. 'I knew you knew!'

'Not so fast my ripe little boy scout. I don't *know*, but I've heard from a few different sources it's sometime this week.' He paused. 'To be honest, Galahad, I'm surprised we haven't crossed paths on our respective hunts on this one.'

'Well we're on it together now, Alastair,' I said standing up, suddenly feeling like there was a chance, just a slim one, we could discover the where and when of this thing. 'I'll be sure and let you know whatever I hear.' I waved and walked off to the taxi rank. As I was about to open the door of a taxi, I turned around.

'I just remembered,' I shouted. 'I haven't got your number.'

'I've got yours old boy, he replied. 'I'll call you, never fear.'

I turned back to the taxi and climbed in, the door closing behind me.

'And *I'll* pay for the coffees shall I, you stingy fucker!' Alastair shouted as the taxi pulled away. I didn't need to turn around, I knew he was smiling.

~

I spent the rest of the weekend with Bors, walking him on the leash through Happy Valley and Wan Chai, furthering his toilet training, instructing him on the finer arts of 'sit', 'stay' and 'come', and sitting with him propped at my feet in a bar as I enjoyed a reward or two for my diligence.

Despite the mess I was in, the troubling thoughts spinning like razor-edged tops in my mind, missing Angel with a longing I could feel deep in my chest, and the constant gnawing at the problem of where and when the next shipment of unfortunates was to arrive, I was reasonably happy, if a little tightly wound. It was also the first weekend in memory that I had not drunk myself to sleep. It's true what they say about canine companionship.

Late Sunday afternoon the weather began to close in again, with heavy grey clouds rolling in from the south, with a sharp spike in humidity and the threat of yet another typhoon in the air. Sunday evening was brooding and dark, matching my mood.

Grabbing a beer, I sat on the terrace with Bors, contemplating the week ahead and my next steps down a dark road with Lee and my own Grail Quest for the truth about my father.

21

I WAS in the office early on Monday morning, so early that Adele had not yet come in, and I used the solitude to gather my thoughts before Joey arrived for the scheduled meeting. Joey was my immediate issue: how much was I to tell her?

Would it endanger her to reveal all I knew? Would it drive a wedge between us once she knew what I had agreed to do and with whom? I gave myself a mental slap – how could I not be anything but completely truthful with her? She had, after all, nearly been killed – and *had* killed – protecting me.

I decided quickly that I would fully trust Joey, her impeccable instincts and her nose for investigation. I felt relieved by that decision, and I now felt I wasn't in this entirely on my own. I only hoped Joey would understand my decision about working with 14K.

I pulled a piece of paper from the drawer in my desk and started to write on it as I tried to sort the maelstrom of thoughts in my mind.

I wrote 'Thomas' in the middle of the page, then connected him with a straight line to 'Sarah' and a thick, heavily underscored line to 'SYO', which in turn was connected to 'girls', who I connected with 'Aberdeen' 'dead girl' and 'mid-stream?' and back to 'Thomas' and

'Asia Wide'. Off to the margin of the page, I wrote '14K', 'Lee' and 'Angel' – all connected – and drew a dotted line to 'girls'. Fat Johnny Tong got a place and I linked him with a dotted line to 'girls'. Jade Tooth also got a guernsey – connected to 'SYO' – but I circled him and even gave him an asterisk.

I stared at the page but my mind wandered in the silence of the office and I doodled absently, not really taking in what I was doing.

I was still scribbling when the office door opened and Joey walked in.

'Hey, boss!' she called cheerily as she threw her rain jacket across the old Chesterfield. 'Happy Monday.'

She was carrying two take-out coffees and walked the few paces across the office to my desk and sat down opposite me, offering me one of the brown cardboard cups.

'Double-shot latte, not too hot and "none of that skimmed bull-shit". Just the way you like it,' she said.

I thanked her and rolled and lit a cigarette before sipping gratefully at the strong brew.

'Get comfortable,' I said. 'And strap in because I'm going to tell you a whole lot of stuff now that will both surprise and, probably, shock you. Ready?'

'Let me have it,' she replied, leaning back in the chair, stretching out her legs and crossing her ankles. So I did.

I told her everything. I laid it all out for her; from my gambling debts, the beatings, Pru's money, the confrontations with Jade Tooth and his men, and discussions with Peter Toh to 14K watchers at my back, my early-evening cruise with Lee Pak-chun, my relationship with Angel and Angel's real involvement with 14K, confirmation of the trade in young women into Hong Kong, my father's connection to Lee and his family, his murder at the hands of persons yet unknown – but almost certainly now not 14K – the likelihood the shipments were coming in through Aberdeen via mid-stream operation, SYO's involvement, my deal with Lee and, finally, my meeting with Alastair Chard.

I finished and dropped the now-empty coffee cup into the bin. I sat back and waited in silence as she stared at me, her face expressionless. After what seemed an age, Joey nodded a few times and scratched the back of her head.

'That's it?' she finally said.

'I'd have thought that was a bit to start with.'

Joey stood and started pacing around the office. I had expected some sort of comment, most likely an explosion when I revealed my agreement to work with Lee, but she padded and prowled the small space like a caged tiger: silent, sinuous and deadly.

I rolled and lit another cigarette, letting the blue smoke trickle slowly from my lips as I watched her. She paced for five minutes, without a sound, before she finally stopped near Adele's desk and turned to face me. I braced myself.

'Okay, I get that,' she said levelly. 'Where do we start?' she asked, as casually as if she was asking me what noodles I preferred.

I couldn't hold back the grin as I looked at my young off-sider and replied. 'Well, I thought we could start with Thomas, I think he's the key – and probably the weak link. What do you think?'

'Perfect,' she agreed, grabbing up her rain jacket. 'Let's get going before Adele comes in and starts ordering us around.'

As I stood, I glanced down at the piece of paper on my desk and froze. There, among the patterns, swirls and geometric shapes of my doodling, written in capital letters above the mind map, and twice underlined, was a single word: 'NUISANCE!'

My breath caught in my throat and I felt my heart thump as I stared at it.

That one word that Zhou had uttered – and I was convinced he had done so accidentally – screamed out at me. I felt sick, and my eyes swam for a moment, as a conclusion too shocking, too crazy, to even consider sprang to mind and pieces of the jigsaw, some many years old, started to fall into place. Joey paused at the door and looked at me, concern on her face.

'You okay boss? You look like you've seen a ghost...'

I grabbed up the piece of paper, folded it and shoved it into the back pocket of my jeans. I bent and snatched up a small black satchel from under my desk and slung it over my shoulder.

'I think I have, Joey,' I said. 'I really think I have.'

We left the office, locking the door behind us, rode the cranky old elevator to the ground and stepped out onto Ko Shing Street for the brief walk into Central.

22

JOEY and I talked as we walked, war-gaming our next moves and sketching out a plan for the next few days – from there, we agreed, we would see where things took us. I let Joey take the lead and come up with the plan. I knew it would be a good one and I had nothing much to add, other than the occasional suggestion, so I just nodded a lot as I scratched away at the slowly-forming idea in my mind.

I was still wrestling with it when we turned a corner onto Bonham Strand and I heard a woman's voice call out.

'Joey? ...Oh my *God*!'

Joey froze beside me and her eyes glanced left and right. She quickly regathered herself and stepped toward a woman who was approaching us, her arms out in an embrace in which she enveloped Joey.

I stood silently with a polite smile on my face but I noted Joey's uncomfortable reaction to the casual encounter. The woman held Joey close and kissed her, lingeringly, on the lips then pulled back to look at her.

'My God, Joey! It's been so *long*. Where have you been? Why haven't you returned my calls you *bad* girl?'

Joey stiffened a little but smiled and took the woman by the arm.

'Irene, I'd like you to meet my colleague, Galahad Jones.' She turned to me. 'Gal, this is Irene...'

'Irene Sheh, yes I know,' I said, extending my hand. 'It's a pleasure to meet you Ms Sheh.'

Irene Sheh was the embodiment of the classic Hong Kong power woman. She was tall, stunningly beautiful, immaculately dressed, incredibly wealthy, one of Hong Kong's Top-Five socialites. She was also the wife of a senior member of the Hong Kong Government, and she was known to be one of the most powerful background voices in Hong Kong politics. She regarded me inquisitively, holding my hand in a firm, dry grip.

'Mr Jones,' she purred. 'The pleasure is all mine.' She turned to Joey, her short-cut bob swishing her face, a wide smile showing her perfect teeth. As beautiful as she was, I couldn't help thinking of a crocodile – she looked like a man-eater.

'My, but he's a handsome one Joey. Where did you find him? Is *he* the reason for you breaking my heart...?'

Joey rolled her eyes and flushed a little. 'No, Irene,' she said. 'We work together. In fact, Galahad is my boss. Aren't you, Gal?'

'Yes, I'm her boss,' I added lamely.

'Well, I can see working with you would be an *absolute* pleasure Mr Jones,' the older woman breathed.

I was struggling to hold in the laughter that was bubbling up inside me, although I was mildly uncomfortable at the weirdness of the encounter so, desperately wanting to be gone, I looked at Joey, raising my eyebrows in question.

Luckily, Irene took the initiative. She grabbed Joey again, pulled her in close and kissed her deeply. Joey responded in kind, her right hand gripping one of Irene Sheh's perfectly formed buttocks and I tried, unsuccessfully, to look elsewhere.

Their intimate clinch over, Irene and Joey parted with a wave and promises to 'catch up soon', and Joey and I walked off down the Strand in silence.

The silence stretched out, becoming more uncomfortable by the second until finally, Joey spoke.

'I suppose I owe you an explanation,' she said, matter-of-factly.

I shook my head. 'Nope. You don't owe me anything, Joey. None of my business.'

Joey sighed. 'No, I need to tell you because it's relevant to why I'm here, working for you.'

I had guessed it the moment I saw Irene Sheh kiss Joey, but I stayed silent and gave the barest of shrugs as Joey and I walked side-by-side through Central toward the MTR. She seemed to be arranging her argument and, from the corner of my eye, I could see her lips moving silently. I felt terrible for her so I thought I'd kick it off.

'So,' I said quietly. 'My guess is Ms Sheh is the reason for your sudden departure from the VIP Protection Branch...?'

Joey shrugged and grinned a little sheepishly. 'We were doing a protection job on Mr Sheh and Irene... a conference in Beijing. Very high level and very long days. As the lead female on the team, I was allocated as CPO to Irene. Sheh was hardly around, Irene was bored. One thing led to another and...'

I stayed silent and Joey stopped, holding up one finger.

'I slept with her *once* Gal!' she said a little too loudly before lowering her voice. 'Just once, but word got out. Sheh hushed it up but demanded my team leader's head so I gave him mine instead. It was only fair.'

I nodded. 'And you've stayed away from his wife until now?'

'Yep.'

'From the looks of your goodbye just now, it doesn't seem like you plan to keep that distance,' I observed drily.

Joey shrugged and grinned. 'I guess not,' she agreed.

'You're playing with fire there, Jo,' I said. 'Sheh is a powerful man and his wife won't hesitate to drop you under a tram if her position looks threatened.'

I scratched the side of my nose. 'You couldn't find a safer girlfriend?'

Joey laughed and clapped me on the back. I was sure she felt relieved at this finally being out in the open between us. I, frankly, didn't give a damn about Joey's sexuality but was relieved I didn't have to blunder around the subject any longer, like the dinosaur I was.

'That's a laugh, coming from you! she said happily. 'Danger is the spice of life, boss. You taught me that.'

Thirty minutes later, and across the harbour, the two of us emerged out of the MTR onto Nathan Road. My stomach was cramping with hunger as I realised I hadn't eaten since the night before, so I suggested an early lunch. We took a table by the window in a small noodle and roast bar, and each ordered a wanton noodle soup and an iced lemon tea.

While we waited, I dropped my satchel onto the table and, digging about, drew out a plastic ziplock bag that held a phone sim card that I removed and placed on a piece of tissue on the table in front of me. I moved aside the soy sauce bottle, pulled a toothpick from the small dispenser and popped the sim tray from my phone. I swapped the sim cards – being careful to wrap my normal sim in tissue and drop it into the ziplock bag – and powered the phone back up.

Within seconds my phone screen came to life so I dug back into my satchel, pulled out the business card I had taken from Sarah Thomas when we had first met and dialled the number.

After three rings the call was answered by a female voice in both Cantonese and English.

'Good afternoon, AsiaWide Shipping, how may I direct your call?

I chose English and plummed it up. 'Good afternoon, this is Michael Davis,' I said, giving the name on my fake press ID card, and winking across the table at Joey. 'From South China Herald. I wonder if I might speak with Mr James Thomas, Vice President, Operations?'

'May I ask what it is in relation to?' the young woman asked politely, but coolly.

'Yes, we're doing a series on expats in industry and business in

Hong Kong and their influence on the direction of the city. I was wondering if Mr Thomas might care to be interviewed.'

There was silence at the other end of the line so I pushed on. 'Very soft human-interest stuff, nothing too penetrating. I promise.'

'Please hold on. I will speak with his assistant,' said the cool and polite voice so I held the phone to my ear and thanked the waiter as he placed my noodle soup and drink on the table.

I dropped some chilli oil into the soup and began to eat noisily. I really was much hungrier than I had thought. I had just chomped down on a steaming hot wanton when the voice was back.

'Mr Davis, would next Tuesday at 10:00 be suitable?' she asked

I sighed regretfully. 'I'm so sorry, but I was hoping to get to see him today. My editor has just dropped this on me and he is really pushing for a quick turn-around. Would it be possible..? Just 20 minutes. I'd be ever so grateful.'

A little less politely now, the young woman instructed me to wait while, presumably, she went back to Thomas' assistant. She was back in seconds and gave me a time that day and I glanced at my watch. Two hours. I thanked her profusely and hung up.

There was always a risk they would call the paper and double-check but I had used this ruse a number of times in the past and had not been rumbled yet, so I was confident I would be fine on this occasion. I swapped the sim cards back out, and snapped the burner sim in half, dropping the pieces into my pocket.

I looked across at Joey.

'I see Thomas in two hours,' I said as Joey sucked up a mouthful of noodles. 'I'll do it on my own, but can you do something?'

'Name it,' Joey mumbled around the noodles, flicking an errant one into her mouth with a finger.

'Track down Fat Johnny Tong. This time of day he's probably at the Bird Garden or Kowloon Park. Put the screws on him for info on that shipment Lee told me of. Johnny knows, I'm sure of it.'

Trust me, if he knows I'll get it out of him.'

I gave her the password. 'Be nice to him, Joey,' I added, seeing

Johnny in my mind's eye. 'He's a poor, weak bastard with a shitty life... and we need the information he has, somewhere, in his head.'

Joey belched softly and stood up, giving me a dismissive wave.

'Lunch is on you,' she said as she left the restaurant without a backward glance.

Taking up my spoon and chopsticks I tucked ravenously into my meal, while I played out in my mind the possible scenarios for the conversation I was to have, in person, with James Thomas that afternoon. Whichever way it went, I thought, the meeting would not pass without result – something would come of it, I was certain.

23

THE SUN WAS SHINING BRIGHTLY and a light breeze blew in from the east, and wispy, white clouds raced across a kerosene-blue sky – something Hong Kong had not seen for many days. I slipped on my Wayfarers and looked out of the taxi window.

There was a taste of autumn in the air, although it was still July and the temperature was far from mild. At least the humidity had dropped a little, I thought, as I tried to smooth my collar and then pulled my damp shirt out from my armpits.

Hong Kong slid by me as the taxi cruised along Jordan Road then right onto West Kowloon Highway. To my left, beyond the breakwater, the harbour glittered blue and placid, a different place altogether from the vicious typhoon-whipped nightmare of a few days previous. Ferries, small pleasure craft, and reclamation barges towed by fat, little tugboats dotted the harbour, and sampans weaved their way across the shimmering waters like beetles scuttling the surface of a pond.

Watching the barges I soon saw a mid-stream lighter, its crane tilted back and deck laden with shipping containers, being slowly towed by a tug toward its dock at Tsing Yi.

The reason for my visit to Kwai Chung, and the dark purpose

behind Thomas's smuggling operation, flooded in on me and my mood soured. My resolve hardened as I swore, again, to do whatever I needed to take down Thomas and end – or at least significantly dent – the disgusting trade in young women.

Just before noon, I rolled down the window of the taxi and presented my phoney press pass to the bored security guard at the gate to Kwai Chung. He glanced briefly at his list and ticked off 'Mr Davis to see Mr Thomas – business meeting', noting the time of my entry. With barely a glance at me, he handed back the pass, pressed a button to raise the boom gate and waved me through.

Unsurprisingly, every berth in Kwai Chung was occupied and an army of giant gantry cranes serviced the docked container vessels; lifting, moving and lowering shipping containers into massive yards where they were then picked and whisked away to bonded warehouses to be cleared before the trip to their final destination.

As I watched, I saw a small white van disgorge a number of Customs officers, resplendent in their khaki summer uniforms that looked much like the old HKPF uniform, and I wondered further at the smuggling operation's choice of mid-stream unloading when they could just as easily dock at Kwai Chung. It was not as if SYO didn't have the reach to make payments to corrupt Customs officers who would turn a blind eye to the shipment, that sort of thing certainly happened.

I decided that it didn't matter why, although it was probably just a matter of convenience and heightened secrecy. The fact remained it was happening and I was going to stop it.

Before we had gone much further along the service road, dodging the synchronised mechanical dance of the wharves, we came to a low, three-storey building, painted white and looking more than a little shabby around the edges. High up on the wall sat a large sign proclaiming the building was home to AsiaWide Shipping.

I paid off the taxi and stepped briefly into the light and heat of the dock before walking into AsiaWide's cool, modern reception area, on the walls of which hung the obligatory photographs of container vessels and shipping containers all proudly bearing the name of the company.

I showed my fake journalist ID to the receptionist, who scrutinised it much more closely than the security guard had before passing it back to me and indicating a leather couch on which I was to wait. I had barely sat when a door opened and a young woman emerged and moved toward me, her hand extended.

'Mr Davis?' she asked, her voice firm and professional. 'I'm Emily Yang, Mr Thomas' assistant. If you would like to follow me..'

I shook her hand and fell into place behind her as she swished her way back through the door and along a corridor, flanked by open-plan desk spaces at which sat AsiaWide's staff, busily tapping away at their spreadsheets and Gantt charts.

The atmosphere in the office was subdued and I felt as if I had stepped into a medieval monastery's scriptorium as the monks, their fingers blackened with ink, bent over their vellum manuscripts, writing and illustrating.

I blinked to clear my mind as Ms Yang stopped outside a door and knocked, twice, on the frosted glass pane. We stepped in and I stood, face to face, with a man I had followed all over Hong Kong but never seen at close quarters – James Thomas.

He stood behind his desk to shake my hand and gestured me to a chair. He looked harried and worn. In fact, James Thomas looked ill.

His stylishly long, greying hair was lank and oily and his eyes were red, staring out at me from atop heavy and dark bags. The skin of his face was waxy, and coated with a thin sheen of perspiration, despite the chill of the office air conditioning.

As he had reached across the desk to greet me I had noticed ugly yellow stains under the arms of his tailored, but badly rumpled, shirt that was cuffed up at the wrists, revealing an expensive watch and dark red splotches on the skin of his hands.

He ran a hand through his hair and I saw that it trembled slightly and he blinked constantly, his eyes now watering. If I didn't know better I would have said Thomas had the plague and I should beat a hasty retreat from his office, followed by an iodine bath.

James Thomas was on the edge and it would not take much of a push from me to tip him over.

'Well, Mr Davis,' He began, his voice surprisingly firm and well-modulated if a little weary. 'What can I do for you?'

I decided the best approach was to ease into it. I didn't want him collapsing on me.

'Thank you for seeing me, Mr Thomas,' I replied. 'As I explained to your assistant, my paper is doing a series on expats in industry and business in Hong Kong and their influence on the direction of the city. I was hoping to speak with you, get your views, find out a little about you...' He looked up sharply at that. '...and include you in the series. Very light touch, nothing controversial, I assure you.'

'Why would there be anything controversial,' he shot back.

'There wouldn't be. Just a figure of speech.'

Thomas sighed and massaged his temples slowly. 'Forgive me. I'm just a little overworked at present. Lots happening.'

'Nothing too serious I hope...'

Thomas shot me another look, his eyes hooded.

'No, nothing serious. Just some shipments coming in that I...' he tailed off and fidgeted with a pen on his desk, spinning it like a compass dial.

If I kept up like this, I thought, Thomas would crack and give me everything inside the next five minutes. I decided to give him a break and steer things in a less provocative direction – at least to him, as tightly wound as he was.

I took out my notepad and pen. 'So, can we start by you telling me how long you have been with AsiaWide?' resting the notepad on my knee I began to write as Thomas spoke.

After nearly ten minutes I had his full, sanitised, back-story.

His early days in shipping in the UK, his delightfully happy marriage to Sarah (*she's such a wonderful woman, you know*) and the great excitement of the posting out to Hong Kong (*Gosh, the Far East really is as exotic as they say.... But I can see you know that*). The job was a challenge and very rewarding (*we are one of the largest shippers in this part of the Region and it's always go, go, go*) but sometimes kept him away from his beautiful wife for longer than he would have liked. And so on.

I tapped my lip with the pen and stared up at the ceiling pretending to think for a moment.

'What about your biggest challenges? Is there anything you deal with that is especially stressful?'

I waited while Thomas stared back at me, a look of mild shock on his face as if I had slapped him.

'What do you mean?' he asked quietly, a slight tick emerging in the corner of his right eye.

'I don't know... a particularly stressful shipment? A tough one on you personally, perhaps?'

'Personally? Why would it be tough 'personally'?'

I shrugged. 'Perhaps a shipment that you would rather not be involved with...'

Thomas surged out of his seat and leaned forward, his fists on the desk. 'What in God's name are you driving at? I think you best go, Mr Davis...*now*!'

I didn't move from my chair. To hell with it, I thought. I looked steadily at him and kept my voice low.

'You better sit down, Mr Thomas.' He blinked but remained standing so I went on. 'I want to talk to you about AsiaWide shipping, facilitated by you, being involved in the smuggling of undocumented women into Hong Kong for...'

'*Out*!' he roared thumping the desk with both fists. 'Get out! This is outrageous! I'll be complaining to your editor and to the Press Council...' he hissed through clenched teeth, picking up the telephone on the desk.

I leaned across and stabbed a finger on the handset cradle.

'I don't think you'll be complaining to anyone, Thomas,' I said. 'Now sit the hell down and listen to me – it will be in your interest to do so.'

'Who *are* you?' Thomas asked shakily as he slumped into his chair and rubbed his eyes.

A frantic knocking sounded on the door which burst open to reveal Ms Yang, her eyebrows raised in question. 'Mr Thomas...?'

Thomas waved her away. 'It's okay, Emily. Really. I was just telling a story and got carried away.'

His assistant left, softly closing the door and we both listened as the sound of her heels on the timber floor receded down the hall. We sat in silence. I watched Thomas and he breathed heavily, his shoulders slumped as he seemed to shrink into himself. I almost felt sorry for him.

'Now,' I said quietly. 'Let's start at the beginning shall we?'

Thomas groaned and shook his head. 'I can't. They'll kill me. Christ, they'll kill Sarah!'

'Much like they killed a young Cambodian woman in Aberdeen?'

Thomas looked confused. 'What do you mean?'

'So you don't know about a young Cambodian woman, smuggled into Aberdeen then strangled on the side of the road? I asked savagely.

He shook his head. 'I only bring them in... I mean I only provide the licences and route the ships. I ...'

'You just make it happen, huh? You don't get involved in the dirty work, you don't know what happens to the girls once they get here. Is that it?'

Thomas looked up, his eyes wide. 'Please,' he begged. 'Please don't. I can't tell you anything. They'll...'

'They'll kill you?' I spat. '*I'll* fucking kill you right now if you don't start talking.'

I watched closely and saw the moment Thomas cracked. His eyes widened and he bit his lower lip, nearly drawing blood, and he sank a little deeper in his chair. He groaned in despair and then took a deep breath, as if he were about to dive into a bottomless pool – which, in effect, he was.

'Not here,' he said shakily. 'I promise I'll tell you everything, but not here.'

'Where? When? I asked quietly. I had him now and needed to bring him in gently.

He paused, thinking. 'The water fountain, in Victoria Park, the day after tomorrow at 2:00 p.m.'

'Why so long? Why not tomorrow?'

He shook his head. 'I have meetings with *them* most of the day tomorrow. If I miss that they will be on to me.' He paused then: 'I'll know more then, too…' he offered eagerly, like a kid offering his teacher a fresh apple.

I wanted to throw up.

I leaned forward and studied him. I was fairly sure he had made the decision to come clean, most likely in the hope it would go well for him – he probably thought I was police, and I wasn't about to disabuse him of that notion – and he certainly was as close to a breakdown a man can get.

Nevertheless, I was taking a gamble letting him out of my sight when I was so close.

'If you bullshit me, Thomas, if you don't turn up, I will find you and your lovely wife and it won't go well. Never mind the bloody triads.'

He nodded mutely, spent with the effort of his decision and now shivering in fear. I picked up my notepad and dropped it into the satchel. Turning for the door I shot back over my shoulder.

'Just be sure you're there. I'll be waiting.'

I closed the door quietly, the reflection of James Thomas slumped across his desk clear in the glass panel of the door and walked slowly out of the building.

24

SHADOWS WERE LENGTHENING and the sky was thickening with clouds, dark and expectant with rain, as I paid off the taxi, stepped out onto Johnston Road and wound my way through the mid-afternoon pedestrian crush. The usual mixture of the elderly, hunched over on walking canes or holding the arm of a family member, mums with prams, shouting school kids and bare-chested delivery men competed for space on the narrow footpath. Shop spruikers called out their wares in rapid-fire Cantonese, urging the punters to step in and snap up a bargain, and old men sat quietly on upturned milk crates, smoking and chatting.

Vans, high-end cars, motorcycles and the ubiquitous red taxis moved slowly up and down the road, billowing exhaust, and the sound of revving engines and honking horns added to the cacophonous din. Sweat dribbled slowly down the back of my neck and from my armpits, soaking my shirt but slightly cooling in the faint breeze that wafted down the road.

Flicking on my Wayfarers against a sudden burst of sunlight, I was content to plod along with the flow while I contemplated the meeting with Thomas.

Head down, I shuffled along in the tiny steps common with Hong

Kong folk in a crowd, wanting to neither stride ahead nor collide with anyone. I checked my watch. I had ten minutes to make the short trip to Southorn Playground, where I would meet Joey and we would discuss the day's events and plan our next steps.

I pulled out my phone, thumbed the contacts until I found the one I was looking for, and hit 'call'. The phone rang two or three times before it was answered.

'Wai? *Hello?* Gan-Li?' Peter Toh asked.

'Nei hou Luo-yang,' I said. 'Who else would be ringing you from my number?'

Peter grunted. 'True. Sorry. What's up?'

'Are you sitting down?'

'Aren't I always?'

'I've been to see Thomas,' I said. 'Very interesting, Pete.'

There was a long silence on the other end and I thought we had been disconnected when Peter spoke. 'You *did*? When?'

'Today. This afternoon. I just left him...'

Another silence. 'What happened? What did he say?'

'He cracked, Pete. It's him. He as good as admitted his involvement to me. To be honest, it didn't take much. He just crumbled and flipped.'

'His 'involvement' you say? What did he say? Any names, dates... you know, *details*?'

I paused slightly, this wasn't going well and I was beginning to regret calling Peter so prematurely. After all, I really had nothing concrete except a brief half-admission by a sick man, confused and under pressure from someone who had forced their way into his office. At least that's the way his defence silk would put it in court... and that's what mattered to Peter Toh.

'Not exactly,' I conceded. 'Words to the effect that he was involved but nothing more before he clammed up and I left...'

'Well, Gal, you've got nothing...'

'Hang on! I left *after* he agreed to meet and give me everything.'

Another pause. 'When are you meeting? Today?'

I told Peter that Thomas had agreed to a meeting in two days' time and the reasons why. Peter was silent while I spoke and I assumed he was taking notes. When I gave him the time and location of the meeting I could hear him tapping his pen on his desk before he replied.

'Okay. That sounds great Gal. Good work. Meet him, get him to talk then bring it to me. I'll take a look at it then wheel him in for a proper interview under Caution. Keep it to yourself Gal – very important.'

He took a breath, that I could hear over the phone. 'You haven't told anyone, have you?

A voice in my head shouted 'don't!' so I lied. I don't know why I did, I had no rational reason to, but I did. It wasn't as if I was trying to steal his thunder; the arrest and the fame would be his but I did not want him to know I had spoken to Alastair Chard and that Joey was in deep.

'No, Pete. Just you and me.' I felt dirty.

He seemed to relax a little. 'This is good, Gal. Really. Well done. If you're right, we'll soon roll this up, hey?'

'Thanks, Pete,' I said, feeling unduly proud at my friend's praise. It was good to be right and to bring another bad guy in after all this time. I would meet Thomas, get him to divulge enough for reasonable grounds for Peter to act, and that would be that.

The conversation over, we agreed I would visit his office late afternoon after my meet with Thomas, Peter wished me luck, and I hung up.

I had a nagging feeling of discomfort as I headed off down Johnston Road, and I was distracted as I meandered along, lost in thought.

Suddenly, I felt a sharp jab in my side. I instantly spun about into a slight crouch, right arm drawn back, to confront my attacker. A kid with a skateboard under his arm let out a cry of alarm and backed away, his hands raised, to disappear into the crowd that stared disapprovingly at me.

I shuddered out a deep breath and shook my head. I hadn't realised how tense I was but the events of the past few days had wound me as tight as a watch spring. Now I was jumping at shadows and threatening to thump kids in the street. It wasn't a good look. I scratched my ear, embarrassed, as I picked up my pace and hurried through the crowd toward the rendezvous with Joey.

Right on time, she entered the sports ground and, looking about, quickly spotted me sitting alone in the stands and made her way around the grounds and up the steps to sit beside me.

'You're sweating,' she said without preamble, as she flopped down on the hard concrete step. 'You look like a damp old gweilo.'

'It's summer. I'm hot,' I replied, mildly offended.

Joey shrugged. 'Must be the English blood in you,' she dead-panned. 'It still can't handle anything but the cold and drizzle of your ancestral island.'

I frowned. '*Hong Kong* is my ancestral island,' I snapped, a little waspishly, feeling the heat rise to my face.

Joey immediately realised she had touched a nerve so she patted my knee and looked me in the eye. 'Sorry boss, really. Just kidding. You're as much a Hong Konger as I am...'

I let out a sigh. 'No, I apologise Jo. Childish of me.'

I scratched the back of my neck. 'Hong Kong's a melting pot and I've never had any real issues. So many of us have mixed heritage. I just get touchy about it now and then. It's stupid, I know.'

She seemed to think about this for a moment, gazing out across the sports ground to watch a group of teenagers playing four-on-four basketball.

'You know,' she said. 'I think You should be looking at it as a blessing. Rather than being caught between cultures, you're accepted across both. You're able to easily walk in both worlds. That's pretty cool.'

Joey was right and I knew it. My life had certainly not been one of torment because of my mixed race - so many of us were in Hong Kong - and I knew it was foolish of me to be touchy about it – I just couldn't help it sometimes. Still, Joey's insightful comment was food for thought and I mentally committed to sort myself out once and for all as far as this subject went. Perhaps I should have spoken, but I didn't so we sat in companionable silence for a minute or two watching the football.

'So,' I said finally. 'Did you find Fat Johnny?'

Joey shivered. 'Yes, I did. What a wretched specimen. Poor man.' She shook her head. 'He wasn't keen to speak to me until I told him you had sent me and gave him the password you gave me... that was a good move by the way.'

'Why, thank you. I do have them now and then.'

'Mmm, indeed,' she said, sounding doubtful. 'Anyway, the bottom line is he has no idea. He agreed he had heard vague whispers about next week but nothing else.'

I winced in disappointment and swore softly under my breath. 'I had hoped he'd know something... and we're running out of time.'

'No word from Lee, I suppose?' Joey asked. I shook my head and rubbed my eyes with the heels of my palms, trying to focus.

'How did you go with Thomas?' Joey asked, breaking into my thoughts.

'He's a mess, Jo,' I said. 'It was simple enough to get under his skin and rattle him.' I remembered Thomas's drawn features and the smell of fear he gave off. 'It was almost as if I had given him a chance to unburden himself. I nearly felt sorry for him.'

I reached for my tobacco pouch and started to roll a cigarette. As I did so, the thought occurred that I had no idea what I was going to tell Sarah Thomas. I'd certainly have to tell her something once her husband was arrested for his crimes.

This had all turned into much more than a wayward husband, I reflected. As they say, be careful what you wish for. I also silently thanked God Adele had sent Sarah Thomas the invoice earlier in the week – I only hope she paid, and quickly.

Joey sat forward excitedly. 'You mean he spilled it? He fessed up?'

'Not in as many words, no,' I admitted. 'But he revealed, obliquely, his involvement and we've set a meet for the day after tomorrow at Victoria Park. He's supposed to give it all up then.' I paused. 'After that, I'm taking what I have to Peter Toh.'

Another thought bubbled up as I fiddled with the cigarette paper.

'I'll need you there to run counter-surveillance on him,' I said. 'His business partners might be tracking him, in which case we'll need to abort, and bloody sharpish.'

I was about to light my cigarette when Joey punched my arm and pointed to a *No Smoking* sign on the wall behind me, a look of disapproval on her face. I sighed and put the cigarette into the pouch and shoved the pouch into my back pocket. I stood and looked down at her.

'It's been a hell of a day,' I said. 'I need to smoke and drink. How about we move across the road? I said pointing in the direction of one of my favourite bars, only metres away on Amoy Street.

Joey nodded and skipped away down the steps. I followed slowly on my dicky knee, feeling old.

That evening passed in a pleasant blur of good company, conversation and copious quantities of alcohol. I had never socialised with Joey and found her, unsurprisingly, to be engaging company, and I soon relaxed into it as we became more and more informal as the evening wore on.

Given our recent shared experiences, we were now less employer and employee and more partners, and that seemed to please both of us. After a few drinks at the bar, we wandered up Tai Wong Street and took a seat at the high bar of a small Vietnamese restaurant where we attacked Pho and rice-paper rolls, washed down with bottles of chilled Saigon Beer. As we ate and drank, Joey's jokes and tales of her escapades became more and more risqué and I found I was enjoying myself.

After dinner, we walked around the block to Ship Street and spent the rest of the evening moving from bar to bar, in each one proposing a fresh toast to ourselves and our success. We had discovered the smuggling operation, Thomas had cracked and was going to reveal all to me in two days' time and I was going to take that to Peter Toh and the case would close. Girls saved, Galahad Jones and Josephine Loh heroes of the hour. It was brilliant. *We* were brilliant!

On and on we toasted and the night became hazier and hazier, a dizzying whirl of light and sound, sometimes elating, sometimes nausea-inducing.

Both of us were increasingly over-amused at our crappy jokes, and drunker, louder and more demonstrative as the hours wore on. Both forcing gaiety and abandon, aided by the alcohol, in a battle against our personal demons and the darkness that so often threatened to engulf us.

Eventually, Joey stumbled into a taxi after slapping me on the back in farewell, and I decided to walk the 1500 metres home in an attempt to sober up.

I arrived at my apartment building a little after 1:00 a.m. and stumbled into the elevator and up to my apartment where Bors greeted me by tripping me onto my backside and licking my face. I took him for a short walk around the block, then fed him, showered, swallowed down two paracetamol against the headache I knew was to come, and collapsed into bed with Bors curled up next to me.

As I lay there I smiled, recalling the toasts and silently repeated them into the dark with an empty hand. I had no idea just how premature those toasts were and just how much they tempted the gods. We should not have done it.

25

TWO DAYS later I sat on a park bench in the shade of a large Cotton Tree, close by the water fountain in Victoria Park. Hong Kong's large public park in Causeway Bay glittered, emerald green and peaceful, as office workers taking their lunch chose places in the expansive shade to rest and revive.

To my left, under the spreading branches of another large tree, a small group of elderly people went through their choreographed Tai Chi routines, their slow and fluid movements rotating smoothly between the elements of the weapons forms, breathing and awareness.

On my right, a young mother stopped her pram and leaned in to pat and smile at her youngster, adjusting the small shade umbrella as she did.

I slipped on my Wayfarers. The sun shone brightly and, the hour nearing midday, it was hot and humid. The sky was clear and blue above me and, glancing up, I could see no clouds above the hills over Tai Hang.

I checked my watch. 11:55.

A slight breeze blew through the gardens and birdsong rose sweet and clear above the loud hum of traffic from Gloucester Road. From behind me the ever-present sound of concrete cutting and pile-driving at building sites broke across the tranquillity of the park, and police sirens wailed somewhere down near the harbour.

Everywhere was bustling activity as Hong Kong offices broke for lunch and the streets heaved with workers heading for the noodle bars and ramen joints.

I glanced up and saw Joey in the distance as she passed the Statue of Queen Victoria, scanning the park for signs of surveillance. I had seen none, and Joey would call if she did, so no news was good news.

I ran through the approach I would take with Thomas as I glanced again at my watch. 12:00. Any minute now.

I would gentle him along, befriend him, show him I was the only person he could trust, the only one he could tell. I would be his confessor and I would absolve him. I re-checked the old digital recorder in my satchel on the bench beside me. It was charged and ready to go.

Joey appeared on the footpath about 200 metres away, looked at me and imperceptibly shook her head. No sign of surveillance. There was also no sign of Thomas but I was not unduly concerned; it was still early and a slight delay could be expected. I sat back on the bench, my hands on my knees and tried to look like any other person seeking some peace and solitude in the park.

As the minutes ticked by with no sign of Thomas, a prickle of anxiety shivered up my spine. I cast frantically around the gardens and could see no sign of him, nor of Joey. 12:27. I picked up my phone and tapped Joey's contact. She answered immediately.

'Anything?' I asked, trying, but failing, to sound calm.

Joey replied in the negative and I hung up.

By now my right leg was jiggling nervously and my foot was tapping the concrete. I was sweating freely, and it wasn't just because of the heat and humidity. I could feel panic starting to bubble up inside me.

What had I done? Instead of heavying Thomas in his office, when he was at his weakest, vulnerable to my questioning, I had cut him loose. I had not even taken his bloody phone number, for God's sake!

He had failed to make the meet and now, in all likelihood, had gone to ground where I would never find him. I could have punched myself in the face.

Instead, I stood and called Joey again, telling her to make her way to me. She arrived in two minutes and we talked through our options.

Thomas wasn't here, so where was he? He wasn't likely to be at work; he knew I would find him there. He could have run for a bolt-hole, in which case we were cooked, or he may even be at home. For all we knew, Thomas didn't know his wife had engaged me to follow him so he might be thinking he was safe at home until he could work his next moves. If he wasn't there, would Sarah Thomas know where he was? Either way, we had to start there.

I told Joey to head to the office and stand by for me to call and, with a quick 'roger that,' she left the park. I looked, hopefully, around one last time.

There being no sign of Thomas, I snatched up and slung my satchel and walked quickly from the park, a sinking feeling deep in the pit of my stomach.

26

After another anxious crawl through traffic, the taxi swung into the avenue-like driveway of Thomas' apartment building. Turning in, we almost drove straight into a police blockade behind a line of blue and white crime scene tape. The earlier shiver of anxiety up my spine turned to a spasm of pain at the base of my skull. I didn't believe in coincidences, and this did not look good.

I stepped from the taxi and approached the two constables behind the tape, who regarded me suspiciously. I tried to look over their shoulders to make out what might be happening, but one of them shifted his position, blocking my view.

'Can I help you sir?' the constable asked politely, showing no signs of actually wanting to help.

I couldn't lie and tell them I lived there; that would be exposed in ten seconds, so I tried the next best thing.

'Oh yes,' I said mildly, looking every bit the concerned citizen. 'I am supposed to be having lunch with a friend of mine. I was to meet him now and we would go together in his car.'

'And the name of your friend, sir?'

I paused. 'Thomas. James Thomas.'

The constables shared a quick look and the one speaking to me turned and walked away a few paces, talking quietly into the handset of his radio. The look between the two men told me everything I needed to know.

They were there because of Thomas and, right now, he was probably upstairs, in handcuffs, being cautioned. It must be Peter, I thought bitterly.

He had moved early and, in doing so, had deprived me of getting what I needed from Thomas to pass on the Lee in exchange for information about my father's killer. I was furious; selfishly so, I knew, but that didn't lessen the anger that welled up within me. The constable on the radio turned slightly to look back at me then turned away again. I saw him nod as he spoke into his radio.

Clipping his radio handset to his shirt, he walked back to his partner, his eyes fixed firmly on mine.

'If you would just wait here, sir, Chief Inspector Toh will be down presently,' he said.

I swore under my breath. Thomas had been arrested – and that was a good thing – but I was out of the game, and that was bad.

My hands shook as I rolled and lit a cigarette, hoping the nicotine would calm my nerves. I did not have long to wait before Peter appeared in the portico of the apartment building and, whistling to the two constables, waved me on.

I ground out the cigarette and, stepping under the raised police tape, walked toward Peter, hoping my face was expressionless. I stopped at the bottom of three steps and looked up slightly. Peter stood there, hands loosely by his side, a stern look on his face and I could see he was breathing rapidly.

'Well, Pete,' I said levelly. 'This is a coincidence... or is it?'

'Don't get snarky at me, Gal,' he snapped. 'I know what you're thinking, and you're wrong.'

'I am?'

Peter nodded. 'Yes. It *is* to do with Thomas but not what you think. I'm not here to arrest him.'

I swallowed hard. This was getting worse and worse. There was only one other reason I could think of for Peter being there, if not to arrest Thomas; and I shuddered to even consider it.

'You better come in,' Peter said. 'Touch nothing, say nothing, speak to no-one unless I tell you. Got it?'

At the door to the Thomas' apartment we were met by a member of the government's Forensic Science Division, who handed Peter and I a set each of hooded disposable overalls, latex gloves and disposable over-shoes. On Peter's direction, we both robed up and, Peter leading the way, we stepped into the apartment. Into hell.

The sharp iron tang of blood hit me like a physical blow, which wasn't a surprise as the room was painted with it.

Over the blood I could smell something else; the rich stench of human faeces. I swallowed down hard as my throat filled with bile and saliva. The plush white rug I had walked over weeks before was red and dripped with gore that crept thick and sluggish across the timber floor like a rising crimson tide. Blood was sprayed up and across the walls behind the rug like a demented Jackson Pollock and it coated the nearby furniture.

In the centre of the rug, a look of horror on her face, lay Sarah Thomas.

Her eyes, wide open, were glazed and milky like those of a dead fish. Her mouth was gagged with gaffer tape that had been wrapped around her head. She was spread-eagled across the rug, her legs apart, and her skirt was hitched up over her waist, her panties hanging loose from her right ankle. I could see, on her inner thighs, the glisten of semen tinged pink with blood that still seeped from between her legs. I averted my eyes, to examine the rest of her body.

Her shirt was ripped open and her bra had been forcibly torn open to reveal her breasts. With horror, I saw the clear red indentations of vicious bite marks, so deep and brutal they had drawn blood and, on one breast, had torn the flesh. She looked as if she had been savaged by a wild beast.

Between her breasts were the killing wounds, now plugged with congealed blood that had mounded slightly like cooling lava. She had been stabbed in a frenzy and I could count six wounds from her right breast, across her sternum and on both sides of her ribcage. The stab wound in her throat was more like a slash, the knife probably having entered then been pulled across before being ripped free. The white of her trachea could be seen through the destroyed muscle and flesh. I swallowed again and rubbed my eyes, willing myself not to vomit.

'In here,' Peter said quietly and led the way out for the lounge-room into the corridor to the bedrooms.

I steeled myself as Peter indicated a darkened bedroom into which I stepped to find James Thomas.

Again the walls were plastered with blood, only this time more. Much more.

The room was a charnel house of blood and shit and torn flesh. Thomas lay, face up, across the blood-soaked bed. I took in the scene at a glance and turned and threw up on the floor, hearing Peter click his tongue in annoyance by the door.

With the back of my hand, I wiped the vomit and drool from my mouth and chin, then turned back to Thomas' corpse.

Like his wife, his eyes bulged out of his head. The gaffer tape gag had slipped in his desperate death throes and his mouth was wide open in a rictus of fear and horror and agony. At first, I did not know what I was looking at as it appeared his mouth was wider than it should be then it hit me and I gasped audibly.

His throat had been slit, literally from ear to ear, and his tongue had been pulled through and out to rest, pale and flaccid, in the cleft of his neck just above the clavicle.

'Jesus Christ,' I breathed then clamped my mouth shut as I felt bile rise again in my throat.

I wanted to get out of the room and away from this nightmare but my professional curiosity got the better of me and I allowed my eyes to travel down Thomas' body. What I saw chilled my soul.

Thomas' shirt had been torn open and he had been gutted, from below the ribs to below the navel, and his intestines had been pulled clear to glisten blue and wet in the dim light of the room. His bowels had been torn open in the attack and his legs were coated in shit, that mixed with the congealed blood in a demonic brew.

Something caught my eye so, breathing through my mouth I bent for a closer look, hearing Peter move in behind me. I peered into the tortured stomach cavity then pulled out my phone, triggering the flashlight. There, jammed into the shredded intestines and bloodied stomach lining, soaked in blood but clearly recognisable, was a tightly rolled bundle of $500 notes. Thomas' final payment.

'Seen enough?' Peter asked.

I nodded weakly and followed him from the room and out the front door of the apartment where we peeled off the foetid over-garments and dropped them into a Hazardous Waste bag proffered by the Forensics Officer.

I leaned against the wall of the corridor, feeling the marble cool the back of my head, and closed my eyes. I knew Peter was studying me but he could wait. I needed to pull myself together. Finally, I opened my eyes.

'Now do you see, Gal?' Peter said, his voice tight. 'This is why I warned you to stay away.' He waved a hand at the door to the apartment. 'That could be you next, lying there like a slaughtered pig. *Diu*!'

I didn't know what to say so I kept my mouth shut.

'You want to know what has happened here, Gal? *Do* you?' Peter demanded. 'I'll tell you. You blundered into Thomas' office like a rookie constable, spooked him, he ran to his masters and told them. Then this. They murdered Thomas and his wife to shut them up.'

'This wasn't murder, Pete,' I said. 'This was sadistic. Ritualistic. We've both seen some things but *never* anything like this.'

I rubbed my eyes again feeling as if I might be going into shock. 'And Sarah Thomas...? Jesus! She had no idea what was going on,' I said wearily.

But I knew he was right. I had killed them both just as effectively as if I had held the knife.

'That doesn't matter Gal. *Fuck*! We're talking about triads here! They don't give a damn who knows or who doesn't. They just want to clean house!' He lowered his voice and sighed deeply. 'And by the looks of things, they've done that.'

'So you finally admit Thomas was into the smuggling? That it's *real*? I shouted, taking out my own self-loathing on my friend. '*Now*, you'll act?'

I could see the muscles of Peter's jaw working as he fought his anger but his face was impassive. He leaned in and poked me in the chest. Hard.

'Listen to me. I'm only going to say this once. Stay away from this. Drop it and leave it to me and actual professional police investigators. You've done enough damage and, if you value your life, you'll walk away. I can't protect you, on this.'

He sighed again, and put a hand on my shoulder, his voice low and eyes pleading.

'Please, Gal. Walk away.'

So I did just that.

I nodded and mumbled something like an apology and walked, like a whipped dog, to the elevators where a constable met me and escorted me out of the building and into the mid-afternoon sun. I called Joey and tersely told her it was all off and that I would speak to her later.

I badly needed a drink so I walked off downhill into Soho to a bar on Staunton Street. Pulling up a stool, I rolled a cigarette to burn the taste of death from my mouth and the stench of it from my nostrils. I leaned back and signalled to the barman for a beer.

When it hit the bar in front of me I swallowed it in two giant gulps, drowning down the horror of the afternoon and the deep disappointment of my own failings.

Wiping my mouth with the back of my hand, I signalled for another and gave the barman the wind-up 'keep them coming' signal with my finger. It was a long afternoon alone at that bar, and I don't remember leaving.

27

LATE THE FOLLOWING MORNING, nursing a headache and with my stomach churning, I walked into the office, dropping my satchel on my desk without a word to Adele and Joey who just watched me in silence.

I slumped into my chair and leaned back, my hands behind my head, and studied the ceiling. I sat that way for five full minutes and the silence in the office was oppressive, but I could not have cared less. I was deeply disappointed, both in the situation and with myself.

Thomas and his wife had been brutally murdered, I had no idea if or when the next shipment of girls was coming so I had nothing to give Lee. Nothing with which to buy the information I so desperately wanted; the name of the man who killed my father. Now I would probably never know. As hard as that was to consider, the personal embarrassment and shame I felt were all the more difficult.

I had blundered around Hong Kong like a boy scout on a quixotic crusade to take on the city's most powerful triad, foil their human trafficking master plan and save the day. I had honestly believed I would do that.

All I had managed to achieve was to dig myself into a dirty deal with an opposing triad lord and get Thomas and his wife killed in the most horrible of ways. If that was not all bad enough, I had also involved Joey in the, as yet undiscovered, killings of two men.

I felt my face flush as the magnitude of the folly washed over me. I had been blind, and hubris had brought me low. I knew it, and Adele and Joey knew it. I could barely bring myself to face them. Finally, Adele could take it no longer.

'Galahad... Joey has told me everything,' she said quietly and held her hand up as I leaned forward over my desk to glare at Joey. Had she told Adele about my deal with Lee? I desperately hoped not; Adele would never forgive me for that.

'No, do not blame her,' Adele said. 'I made her tell me. I have not seen either of you for days and I'm not stupid. I knew that something serious was happening.' She smiled a little, her eyes warm. 'I was worried about my sai lou, *children*.'

There was another thing to add to my list of recent screw-ups. I had left Adele out of the loop. Not that I did not trust her; of course I did. I told myself I had made a conscious decision to keep her in the dark for her own protection. Or so I thought. Perhaps I was just a thoughtless bastard, unaware of the hurt that might have caused her.

'I'm so sorry a-yi,' I said. 'Please forgive me.' I walked across the room and hugged her close. She pushed me away with a click of her tongue, a mock frown on her face.

'There is nothing to forgive zai zi, *son*. Stupid boy.'

I smiled weakly. I really did not deserve a woman like Adele Chung in my life.

'Something bad has happened, hasn't it?' Joey asked from her desk, her face serious. 'I can tell...'

I nodded, sat down and told Adele and Joey everything that had happened from the time I had left Victoria Park the day before. When it came to the scene at the Thomas' apartment I left out the detail, telling them only that Thomas and his wife had both been killed, presumably because I had spooked Thomas to confess to his masters who, in turn, did not take it well.

I gave them both a summary on where that left us on the case –

effectively with nothing – and that it was over. I finished by looking at Joey.

'I've been warned off, Jo,' I said. 'Peter Toh is furious and will probably arrest me if I stick my nose into this again... not that there is anything left to stick my nose in to.'

I shrugged. 'It's all up to him now,' I added.

I smiled wanly at Joey. 'Would you mind ducking downstairs and grabbing me a coffee? I'm dying here...'

She rolled her eyes and mumbled something about 'self-inflicted' then stood and was almost at the door when there was a knock on the glass and the door opened.

Our local postman stepped in, greeted us all with a smile and dropped a small pile of mail on Adele's desk. I sighed. More bills, I thought, wondering uncharitably whether or not Sarah Thomas had paid hers.

I walked back to my desk and was fidgeting around with some papers when Adele walked over and dropped two letters and a small, flat parcel on my desk. I ignored them until Joey returned with the coffee then, sipping on the strong brew, I sifted through them.

The first, a marketing flyer, went straight into the rubbish bin and the second was, as expected, a bill; this time for my cell phone. That one went into my desk drawer and I picked up the small package, examining the outside and shaking it slightly.

My name and the office address was written in pen, in a neat hand, on the front of the envelope and, turning it over, I saw there were no sender details. It was postmarked Central late afternoon three days previous.

I opened my pocketknife and slit the top of the envelope. A black, hardcover notebook dropped onto the desk. It was dog-eared and slightly soiled, with an elastic closing strap and a place-keeper ribbon that poked out the bottom. I fished around in the envelope and dug out a single piece of paper on which a brief note was written in the same hand.

Mr Jones,

I assume you are the same man who visited my office today. I found your business card a few days ago and my wife told me why she had engaged you. I admit, it did give me a laugh to think of her assuming I was having an affair. I am not a complete fool and soon put a few things together that led me to you. You were the one following me when I left the club and again when I left the terminal with the container. Doubtless you have been following me for weeks. Sadly, you have stumbled into something much bigger than an unfaithful husband. As they say, 'if you are reading this letter I am, in all likelihood, dead.' If I am not I will have met you as planned and we will discuss the contents of this notebook as soon as possible, as I don't know how long I have until my masters discover you came to my office – at which time it will be the end for me. I send you the notebook because I wish to make amends. I know I can never truly make up for what I have done, the pain I have caused, but I hope this notebook will go some way to easing my way in the hereafter.

Yours sincerely,

James Thomas.

I lowered the letter and whistled softly, my heart racing, as I picked up and opened the notebook.

I leafed through the first few pages, then flipped through the entire notebook. Every page was covered in a tight scrawl in pencil – some of it fading and smudged – and my eyes widened to see that not a single page contained a legible word. The entire notebook was written in a meaningless jumble of capital letters, in five-letter groups.

I dropped the notebook and swore. I am no cryptographer but I knew what I was looking at. It was a cipher. The notebook was, probably, the key I needed to finally uncover what was happening and who was involved; and, if so, it was also my trump card in my dealings with Lee. But first I had to unlock its secrets so I resolved to study it later in the day when I was alone.

I held it up by one cover and shook it, making a soft grunt of surprise in the back my throat as two business cards fell out. I peered at the first and saw it was Thomas' own card with 'Wendy' and a

Hong Kong phone number written on the back in a feminine hand. So he was playing around after all, I mused. That might be of some use so I slipped it back into the back of the notebook along with the second business card, which was from an air conditioner installer and repairer. That one would certainly be of use, as it was probably the person who had retro-fitted the shipping container I was now sure had transported the trafficked women.

I called Joey over and handed her the letter and the notebook. She studied them both while I rolled and lit a cigarette and drank the remains of my coffee, my hangover forgotten against the excitement that was coursing through me.

Joey looked up. 'Is this what I think it is?' she said, her eyes shining with excitement.

I shrugged. 'I think so but we won't know until ...*if*... I can break the cipher.'

'Well, you had better get on it, then,' she said, sounding like one of my old teachers.

I agreed and slipped the notebook into my black satchel, grabbed my tobacco pouch and headed to the door, stopping briefly to kiss Adele on the cheek. 'I'll do this from home,' I shot back over my shoulder as I opened the door. 'I'll be in touch.'

Out in the corridor, I decided to take the stairs and was a flight down when my phone rang. I dragged it clear of my pocket and stared at the contact information, letting the phone ring. It rang on insistently, echoing loudly in the stairwell. I took a deep breath and answered.

'Hello Angel,' I said, my voice cool. There was silence at the other end before Angel spoke. She got straight to business.

'So the Thomas' are dead?'

I wasn't surprised she knew; she and Lee would have known minutes after the police arrived, perhaps even before.

'As you have called off our watchers,' she said 'I can only assume you visited Thomas at some point and it led to this...'

'Do you want me to find out what's happening, or not?' I snapped. 'To do that, the fastest and most effective way was to get to Thomas.'

'Did you get anything from him?'

I was going to reply in the negative when I remembered the notebook.

'As a matter of fact, I did. I'm working on it now and…'

'What did he tell you?' she interrupted.

'I'm not sure yet, Angel. Nice to chat,' I said a little patronisingly and hung up.

In my mind I could see her seething, holding her phone in her hand and I chuckled, childishly satisfied to have scored a point. The phone rang again and I sighed and answered it immediately.

'I told you I'm working on it,' I said. 'I'll call you when I have something.'

'You'll call *me*?' asked a male voice, the sound of traffic in the background. 'That's gratifying Mr Jones, but perhaps you may wish to hear what I have to say first.' Fat Johnny Tong. I rolled my eyes.

'Sorry Johnny. What is it? I'm kind of busy,' I said as I stepped out of the building and onto the footpath. The day had clouded over and it was grey and gloomy, with the smell of rain in the air.

'I assume, Mr Jones, you are not too busy to hear the details of the next shipment,' Johnny said, a smile in his voice.

I came to a sudden stop. That was news I wanted to hear.

From the deep and depressing hole I had been in when I woke, to the notebook and now this, the day was looking up. I told Johnny to go ahead and listened as he laid out the date and time a ship was due at anchorage south of Hong Kong island, in the calm waters between Ap Lei Chau, the island across the channel from Aberdeen, and Lamma Island. I was surprised that he also had information about the size of the shipment. I was staggered at the numbers.

The traffickers were bringing in nearly 150 girls in a one huge operation.

Young women torn from their families and homes and shipped across the sea into slavery. One hundred and fifty young souls lost. How many people had to be involved in a conspiracy of this size, both in Hong Kong and across other countries in South East Asia, to make it work? Could I even hope to stop something of this scale?

Johnny finished by giving me the precise landing point at a remote park on the water at Kellett Bay. I was stunned. I finally had it; the information I needed to observe and track the traffickers was in my hands. Johnny Tong had really come through.

'Thanks, Johnny,' I said.

'You owe me, Mr Jones. You really do. I just hope I live long enough for you to pay up' he said before ending the call.

I looked at my watch. We had nearly 14 hours until the landing; I figured 12 hours before we needed to be in place, so there was sufficient time to make solid preparations. I punched Joey's contact on my phone. As usual, she answered inside three rings.

'It's on,' I said without preamble. 'I've had a call from our skinny friend. We have plenty of time but I want us together and standing-by in case he calls and brings the times forward. I'll meet you at my place in two hours and I'll give you the details. Bring both the go-bags; we're going to need them.'

Joey acknowledged and hung up and I made another quick call. Unsurprisingly, this one took longer to answer. When it did, my sister sounded clear and calm at the other end of the line – I could imagine her in her studio, placidly eyeing a new collectors' piece she had acquired.

'Gal, big bro!' she said, delight tinged with suspicion in her voice. 'What's up, what have you done and what do you need?'

She was right to lead with this; after all, in recent months I had only seen her when I needed something from her.

'Pru, listen I can't explain but can I borrow your car? Tonight?'

She did not hesitate. 'Of course you can, Gal. I suppose I should not ask what for?'

'Probably best not,'

'Okay,' she sighed. 'Just look after it for heaven's sake. Want me to drop it over to you?'

'I was hoping you could.'

'I'll see you in 90 minutes, does that suit?'

'Perfect,' I said. 'Thanks, sai mui, *sister*. I owe you.'

'I'll add it to the list,' she said before hanging up.

28

THIRTY MINUTES later I let myself into my apartment and greeted Bors who dragged himself, stretching, from his mat, his tail wagging. By now I had engaged a dog-sitter who visited Bors twice a day during the week to play with him and take him for a long walk. I could ill afford it but I couldn't leave him, pining alone at home for hours at a time. I made up for it, whenever I could, on the weekends when we would take long walks in the hills above Wan Chai and Happy Valley then sit together in a bar, him with his water bowl and me with a pint.

I made a coffee then walked into my room.

Opening my wardrobe, I reached up to the top shelf and pulled down a large black bag. Hefting the bag's weight to my shoulder, I grabbed my coffee and walked out onto the terrace. I rolled and lit a cigarette, sipped at the coffee and unzipped the bag. Taking out my Digital SLR camera I checked that both it and the spare battery were fully charged. I removed the standard lens and clicked home the large, low-light telephoto lens, turning to the hills above me to test range and focus.

Satisfied with that I placed the camera back in the bag and took out a set of night vision goggles, checking they were not visibly damaged and the power pack was correctly seated. There was other equipment in the bag but that was all I needed from it, knowing the go-bag Joey would bring had the rest of my usual operational gear.

I rolled another cigarette and glanced at my watch.

There were hours ahead of me so I convinced myself one or two light beers would be fine and walked inside to the fridge. My thoughts were a mess and they needed ordering so, seated back on the terrace, I flicked the top off a beer and sipped at it while I pondered the night ahead and what it might bring.

I could not believe my luck that Fat Johnny had come through with the information.

I had no idea where and how he came by it but I had to trust in it – and him – for now. It all came down to what happened tonight and I was determined to make up for my many blunders on this job. There was simply too much at stake not to. I ran through in my mind what was in front of me, mentally ticking each off as I worked through the web of inter-woven factors.

A shipment was coming in tonight and I knew where and when, but so many things could still go wrong. A last-minute change of anchorage, timings, or landing place would throw my plans into disarray. I had no idea what sort of reception committee the traffickers would have for the arrival of the container, nor of the security they might put out to prevent anyone from seeing, let alone getting close, to their activity. I did not know where they would go after they had landed the girls and I did not know how many vehicles, or of what type, they would use.

Assuming a number of vehicles – and I did, seeing as I expected them to be landing 150 women – which would I follow and how would I decide that?

There would only be Joey and I, so if a convoy split into more than two packets we would not be able to follow them all; and the one we did not follow could turn out to be the key. I dragged on my cigarette and sipped at the cold beer, feeling it cool my throat against the humid and overcast afternoon.

With all that, if we got lucky and followed the vehicles to their destination, what then? Would there be a vantage point from which we could observe them and, if so, how would we get to it without being seen ourselves? Then there was the question of what I was to do with the information I gathered tonight. Where would I take it and to whom would I give it?

There was no point giving it to Lee; he would probably soon know anyway and, besides, he wanted me to gather enough to prompt the police into action that would roll up the SYO operation. So, that left the police; and that raised the question of Peter Toh and David Zhou. I had a nagging feeling about Zhou – and that 'nuisance' reference still rang in my head – but I was still prepared to consider that he was, in fact, just an incompetent fool.

Peter Toh was a different matter.

He had been characteristically cautious when I first told him of my theory; unlike me, he had never been one for diving in without knowing the depth of the water. Something wasn't right with Peter; I had known him too long not to notice. But, I decided, cautious and methodical had been the way Peter operated for many years and it was obvious he was on the case.

A thought flitted manically like a bat, darting and weaving across my consciousness, so suddenly it gave me a start and I paused with my beer mid-way to my mouth. It came and went so quickly I wasn't even sure what it had been.

I took a deep breath. I needed to focus on what lay immediately in front of me, and that was tonight's little jaunt over to Aberdeen. I was walking back to the kitchen when the front doorbell rang.

'I feel like a food delivery guy with both of these on the bike,' Joey said as she pushed past me in the open door with our two go-bags – black, military specification backpacks.

'Hi to you too,' I said, walking back into the kitchen and opening the fridge. 'Drink?' I called over my shoulder as I reached for a beer.

Joey called out for the same so I carried them onto the terrace and handed her one. We raised the bottles silently to each other and drank.

Joey belched quietly and licked her lips. 'That's good,' she sighed. 'Hot today. Looks like rain too.'

I was about to answer when the front door intercom rang. Checking the screen I saw it was Prudence so I picked up the handset and told her I would buzz her in.

'No don't bother,' she replied. 'I need to get back. Just come down and I'll give you the keys.'

So I hung up, took the elevator to the ground floor and stepped out onto the noisy street. As usual, Prudence looked stunning. She was immaculately groomed in designer jeans and a white T-shirt and I noticed not a drop of perspiration on her face – sweat was always a little too common for my sister. She smiled in greeting and kissed my cheek.

'Big bro,' she said. 'You look like shit.'

'Why change at my age?'

She held out the keys of her Mini Cooper S to me. 'It's parked around the back in the laneway. The tank is full and I've left some sandwiches and a couple of bottles of water in the back.'

She pulled a face that made her look like my mother when she was chastising me. My heart lurched a little as I took the keys.

'Thanks, Pru,' I said. 'What would I do without you?'

'Probably go gallivanting about on some mysterious quest without food or water, I expect.' She sighed. 'Don't thank me, Gal. Just be careful, whatever it is you are up to.'

And with that, she kissed me again on the cheek and turned to walk off down the road, hail a taxi and disappear from view. I stood on the footpath for a moment, watching as her taxi turned the corner, then walked back inside. Minutes later was back on the terrace with Joey.

'So... as I was about to say: why don't you take off the bike jacket? Get comfortable We've got a long wait before we head out.'

Joey's eyes flicked away to study the beer bottle in her hands. 'No, I'm fine, boss. Really.'

I had noticed the slight deformity in her jacket when she walked in so I decided to just tackle it head on.

'You're not taking off your jacket because you are carrying. Right?'

She winced a little then grinned sheepishly.

'You got me,' she said. '*But*, you know I'm licensed so it's not an issue and let's face it: the last time I went out with you we could very well have used it. I'm taking no chances tonight.'

I swigged on the beer and studied her for a moment. She was tough and competent; more than capable of looking after herself, but I had got her into enough trouble lately and I did not want her risking herself, again, for me.

'Look, Joey, if anything happens tonight, in particular if I get myself into trouble, you are not to get involved. I want you to run.' She looked at me blankly. 'I *mean* it,' I said more sternly. 'I'm in too deep, but nothing that happens tonight is worth your life. Got it?'

Joey bit her lower lip then nodded. 'I get it, boss. Promise.'

'Now take your bloody jacket off and get comfortable!'

She smiled and slipped off the heavy biker jacket to reveal the Glock at her hip. She unclipped the holster and placed it on the table between us.

'Happy now?'

I nodded and we turned our attention to checking and testing the contents of our go-bags after which we ran through scenarios for the night in front of us.

The more we worked through the possible directions the evening might take us, and their 'what ifs', the more it was obvious this was going to be very much a 'take it as it comes' operation and we would have to be clear-headed and quick on our feet. I only hoped we were up to the task.

Overhead, the clouds had merged into a dense blanket of dark grey, pierced only here and there by the slowly setting afternoon sun and, off into the distance, we could hear thunder begin to rumble over the hills and out to sea.

29

I ADJUSTED my position slightly to ease deeper into the leaf mulch among the trees. The ground was damp and the smell of decayed vegetation was strong in the air that swarmed with mosquitos. I had lathered myself in repellent before entering the trees but the bugs still whined about my head and savaged me through the cotton of my shirt.

The sun had set hours before, the night was moonless and thunder rumbled and growled in the hills above me. The dark had settled over the park like a black hood but I could clearly make out the still waters leading into Aberdeen Harbour. The lights on Magazine Island glinted and shimmered, silhouetting the high-rises on Ap Lei Chou.

I hit the light on my G-Shock. 0115. We had been in place for two hours and now there were only 45 minutes until the expected arrival of the cargo lighter. I made myself as comfortable as I could, wriggling my belly and moving a knee off the sharp pinch of a small rock.

Behind me, all was quiet in Kellett Bay with no traffic on the road and only the occasional bark of a dog, and the gentle chirruping of crickets, to break the still of the night.

I glanced to my left, not seeing Joey but knowing she was in position a few hundred metres further east in case the lighter failed to land where I anticipated, instead choosing to head deeper into Aberdeen Harbour. I did not think that would happen because they would not want the eyes of the population of the sampan fleet and house boats upon them; as they would be, even at this hour.

Somewhere in the dark a child cried out in a nightmare and I could faintly hear the voice of its mother shush it back to sleep. It was a comforting sound and I felt my eyelids grow heavy. I scratched at my face and closed my eyes momentarily against the fatigue that was setting in, despite the mounting tension I was feeling.

My eyes snapped open at the sound of a voice in my ear. I had been asleep! Cursing myself, I lifted my wrist and keyed the mic that was connected to the wire that ran up my arm under my shirt to the radio on the back of my belt.

'Say again, Two,' I whispered.

Joey's voice, faint but clear sounded in my ear. 'This is Two. I say again: we have four minibuses arriving now. 20 seaters. Moving west down the street toward you.'

'Roger. Thanks out.'

I frowned into the dark. That was only room for 80 so they were either bringing in fewer women than expected or planning on two trips. If the latter we would be in trouble having to either split up – not a good idea – or gamble on taking the first load or wait for the second, that we did not even know was coming. I made a decision and keyed the mic again.

'Two this is One. You'll have done the maths. If they are doing two loads we can't risk waiting for it not to turn up and lose the first load. We'll go with what we have in hand.'

Joey acknowledged and ended the transmission. I was moving the go-bag beside me, readying myself to take out the NVG and the camera when her voice burst again, urgently, in my ear.

'This is Two. Disregard. The vehicles have pulled up short. They're not coming to you. Stand by...'

I waited anxiously for a few seconds.

'They've pulled into a vacant lot beside the old sewage works. Not quite inside Aberdeen Harbour.' She paused, then her voice again calm and clear. 'Lights off now, drivers and a team of...eight, debussing. This is it.'

'Stand by Two... I'll be with you shortly.'

Swearing, I stood up and grabbed the heavy go-bag, shrugging into its shoulder straps and loped off through the trees. Coming to the road I looked up and down then darted across, in a pool of shadow cast between two streetlights, to bash my way into the scrub on the other side of the road.

There was a narrow footpad off to my right through the dense bush so I headed down it, in a half crouch, toward where I knew Joey was lying. After five minutes of feeling my way forward in the dark, I was starting to worry. Had I somehow overshot Joey's hide? Suddenly, a voice hissed at me from the ground.

'Gal...here. *Diu*, you sound like a herd of elephants coming down the road!'

I quietly threw myself flat and laid the go-bag beside me, unzipping it and taking out the NVG and camera. I was relieved to see the vacant lot was not well lit and the minibuses stood faintly in the dark; good, the NVG would do their job well so I powered them up and lifted them to my eyes.

Through the lit green image, I could see the minibuses had their windows obscured by what looked like black plastic and their registration plates had been partially, or totally, obscured with mud. Turning my attention back to the men, I counted 12, in three small groups, lounging around the buses smoking and talking quietly.

I scanned the group and saw that three of them were holding a bunch of what looked like straps of some kind so I zoomed in and saw they each held a number of quick-cuffs, each already double-looped to quickly secure two small hands.

I handed the NVG to Joey, indicating with my hands that she should take a look. She lay perfectly still with the device to her eyes then swore softly, shaking her head, and handed them back.

'Fuck, I hate triads,' she whispered.

Taking in the scene again, I was pleased to see that none of the party looked to be on alert and it was clear they had no spotters out. They were confident. That was all to our benefit; I just hoped they were that casual wherever they were about to take the women.

While I watched, one of the men lifted a phone to his ear, listened momentarily then called out to the rest of the group who broke up and took stations by the water and by each bus.

I shifted my attention beyond the shore and could see, on the limits of the NVG range, a small shape that was backlit by the lights across the water, heading in our direction. I watched as the shape slowly took form and breathed deeply, nudging Joey. It was a small, self-powered cargo lighter, its derrick crane cranked back, carrying two shipping containers. As the lighter moved to within 300 metres I could see the markings clearly on each container. AsiaWide Shipping. I nudged Joey again.

'We're on,' I whispered. 'Remember, no heroics. We watch and follow. No matter what.' I handed her the NVG.

She didn't answer but I could feel her tense up beside me and the anger seemed to radiate off her as we lay together in the hastily constructed hide. I pulled out the camera and switched it on, focussing the telephoto on the slowly approaching lighter.

I took photo after photo as, metre by metre, the lighter crept toward the shore until its engines reversed and it slowed to rock forward on its own wake, its tyre-covered nose gently kissing the low stone wall across the seafront of the vacant lot.

The crew on the lighter threw ropes to the men waiting onshore who lashed them off to two arrays of steel pickets I could now see had already been hammered into the ground. As that happened, the derrick swung up and around while the crew busied themselves securing straps and chains to the first container in readiness for it to be lifted clear of the deck. I had to give it to them; it was all done swiftly, smoothly and in total silence.

Slowly, with the clink of chains and clanking of the derrick, the first container swung out from the lighter and lowered gently onto the ground with a soft thump. My camera clicked and whirred. Now, two of the men holding the quick cuffs stepped up to either side of the container, with the third standing off to the side in reserve. With a loud thunk, the securing arms of the container were thrown up and the doors were opened. I focused the camera on the doorway and gritted my teeth.

From where we lay, we could clearly hear the cries and moans from within the container and I was sure I could smell the stench of the cramped and foetid interior.

Slowly, one at a time with the snapped orders of the men, young women stumbled and fell their way out of the container. Those that fell were dragged to their feet and the quick-cuffs expertly slipped onto their emaciated wrists and cinched tight. Those who walked out were likewise cuffed, and all were pushed toward the waiting minibuses.

As we watched, a young woman burst from the container and tried to shoulder past the two waiting goons, only to be knocked to the ground and kicked repeatedly before being dragged up bloody, cuffed and thrown on a bus.

I felt Joey start to rise next to me and I pushed her down firmly, shaking my head as she looked at me with tears glistening in her eyes.

With the first container emptied of its dishevelled and distraught cargo, the process was repeated with brutal efficiency. Joey and I lay there stunned at what was playing out before our eyes. My camera recorded everything.

Once all the women were loaded, and the men divided up to each minibus, the drivers held a brief conference in readiness for their departure. I patted Joey on the back, took up the go-bag and slipped silently out of the hide to retrace my steps along the footpad through the bush.

I moved as quickly as I could, hearing behind me the reverse alarms of the minibuses as they began to back out onto the road. I sprinted across the road between the streetlights and skidded to a halt beside Prudence's car, fumbling with the key fob in my hand to press the unlock. Swinging the driver's door open, I threw the bag into the back seat and slid in behind the wheel. I sat still and tense, waiting for Joey's call. It didn't take long in coming.

'One this is Two, she said, not bothering to hide the volume of her voice now. 'They are moving. Four-vehicle convoy. I have them in sight and about to follow on.'

I acknowledged and gunned the engine, reversing onto the road in a cloud of dust, from the track where I had hidden the small car.

In seconds I was speeding east down the road looking for the tail light of Joey's bike that hove into view as I rounded a bend and sped past the vacant lot. She was holding a good distance behind the minibuses, their tail lights small red dots about four hundred meters further on.

Now all we had to do was hold our position, not give ourselves away and not lose them as they wove their way through Hong Kong to their destination; wherever that was.

We headed up through Aberdeen and soon entered the tunnel through the hills to the north side of the island. I saw Joey's brake light flicker up ahead, as she eased back further from the minibuses in the near-deserted and well-lit tunnel, so I also backed off on the accelerator. As long as I kept Joey in sight I was confident we would be fine; she would not lose them while remaining a cautious distance back in their wake.

Emerging out into Happy Valley, we skirted the racecourse and headed along Wong Nai Chung Gap Flyover, still heading north. I was sure the buses would turn right when they got to the end of the road, taking them down into the Cross Harbour Tunnel, so I grunted in satisfaction to see Joey's bike lean to the right as she negotiated the downwards bend at the spaghetti junction over Gloucester Road. Another tunnel and we were Kowloon Side.

I was surprised to see we were heading east again, toward Kai Tak and Kowloon City, as I would have bet they would have gone the other direction, toward SYO heartland in central-north Kowloon.

The headlights of the car swam across deserted shop fronts and lit the darkened streets, momentarily blinding the occasional lone pedestrian heading home after a late night or starting their long day at work. There was little traffic and the roads were largely deserted with the exception of the flood-lit market distribution streets that were stacked high with large styrofoam boxes and swarmed with men carrying and sorting produce for early delivery to the wet markets in the area.

The first drops of rain smacked against the windscreen, smearing the dust and I resisted the urge to hit them with the wipers as I focussed on the road ahead, seeking out Joey's bike as she ducked and weaved through the narrow streets, relentless in her pursuit of the buses.

My eyes felt gritty and I desperately needed a cigarette but my blood surged with the excitement of the hunt, all thoughts of fatigue were banished, and I slapped down the gears of the Mini to speed around a tight corner, stuck to the road like a kid's slot car.

In minutes we had turned right again and were headed east on New Clear Water Bay Road toward the hills that led down to Ho Chung Valley. That really did surprise me and I could not immediately think where our final destination might be.

I was mulling this over in my mind, not really concentrating on what I was doing, when I came around a bend in the road just in time to see Joey's bike slide to a halt, its brake light screaming red into the dark.

I slipped down through the gears, braking heavily, and came to a stop behind her as she kicked down the bike stand and walked back toward me. She flipped up the visor of her helmet and leaned in on my open window.

'They just turned off,' she said excitedly, a little out of breath after the hard ride from Aberdeen. 'About 300 metres up and then doubled back into the dark. There's a small service road in there that heads up to the Suicide Cliff walking track, then another road that is full of housing development.'

I nodded, pursing my lips in thought.

'I don't think they will go as far as the housing estate,' I said quietly. 'Too busy, too many nosey neighbours. They have to be stopping somewhere on the service road.' Joey nodded her agreement and I went on. 'Let's head in but take it slow; lights off, rolling stops, no brake lights. I'll wait here.' Joey nodded. 'Go find them Jo,' I said.

Joey slapped the window sill and gave me a quick wink. In moments she had mounted her bike and slowly headed off into the dark so I stepped from the car and waited nervously on the side of the road; taking the opportunity to roll and light a cigarette.

I paced back and forth, scuffing at the gravel under my feet, dragging hard at the cigarette as I waited for Joey's voice to sound in my earpiece.

A few more drops of rain started to patter onto the roof of the car and puff into the dust while the night sky, like a waking dragon, growled and rumbled faintly overhead. I ground out the smoke and pressed the light on my G-Shock. Nearly 0330. Christ, where was she? After what seemed like an hour, but in reality was only 10 minutes, the radio crackled to life and Joey's voice whispered in my ear.

'This is Two. I have them. They have pulled into a compound at the end of the service road. I can just see the roof of two of the buses. You better get up here. Fast.'

I was diving for the car when Joey spoke again. 'I know the perfect spot to overlook this place – I've seen it before when I've been hiking this track. Move up to me – you'll see the bike – and I'll show you where to park.'

I was already moving and I keyed the mic twice in acknowledgment. Almost immediately on turning into the service road, I came upon Joey who waved me to a small dirt track, partly obscured by brush, into which I backed the Mini. I leapt from the car and threw the backpack onto my shoulders.

With a nod, Joey turned and ran off into the dark, heading up a narrow gravel path with thick bush on either side that reached across the path, tugging at my clothes and scratching my face as we passed.

Joey suddenly disappeared and I stopped dead, peering into the dark, wondering where she had gone. She hissed from my right, and I turned to see her standing on a small path that was barely a scratch through the bush; it was beyond me how she had seen it.

As we cautiously felt our way down the footpad, the thick vegetation making it near impossible to see, a deafening thunderclap sounded immediately overhead and the heavens opened, soaking us in seconds. The noise of the storm covered any sound we might make so Joey picked up the pace and, seconds later, I bumped into her back as she stopped.

'This is it,' she said pointing to her right as she dropped into a squat.

There, immediately below us, clear and unobstructed, sat the compound and the four minibuses. I didn't need the NVG; it was all clearly laid out under floodlights not much more than 75 metres from us. I wiped the rain from my eyes and lay down next to Joey, pulling the camera from my bag and started reeling off shots.

Thunder boomed overhead and the rain swept across us in sheets as the wind whipped at the trees, torrents of muddy water rushing downhill to soak us in filth.

The compound was about the size of half a rugby field, bounded on three sides by a 3-metre concrete block wall, topped with razor wire and what looked like cemented-in broken glass. I was not surprised to see that the back boundary was only secured by a 2-metre high chainlink fence – it was common for properties backing into the bush to be much more lightly secured; I could never work out why, but it kept happening. The fence itself was poorly maintained, rusted out in places and showing more than a few gaps in the wire. There were two strands of rusted, loose barbed wire running along the top, in places also broken and sagging down.

The entire perimeter, and inside of the compound, was well lit. A large light tower stood in each corner with an array of floodlights shining out brightly in all directions. Three sides of the perimeter had smaller poles between the corner towers, on which smaller spotlights were attached to ensure that illumination overlapped the length of the wall. I noted with interest that was not the case along the rear boundary, and that a large patch of darkness existed in the middle where the corner tower lights did not quite reach.

Along each length of the left, right and rear boundaries sat long, low concrete-block buildings with tin roofs; looking much like old army barracks. A smaller brick building sat off to the left-front near the gate and, across the compound off to the right, was a slightly larger tin shed, into and out of which I could see a number of men moving, burdened down with an assortment of stores.

The minibuses were parked in the centre of the compound. It was clear the first two buses were empty.

As we watched, the doors of the third bus swung open and two men stepped out, followed by the first of the women who staggered out, shielding their eyes from the glare of the lights, to be hustled by other waiting men toward one of the three barrack blocks.

As the lines of women reached each barrack block they walked past a small group of men who handed them each a blanket, a large and a small bucket, a plate, bowl and cutlery, and a large black bin liner that bulged with some other contents.

The women dumbly accepted these offerings, their heads down and shoulders slumped, and were quickly pushed through the door to the barracks from where we could hear other male voices raised in command for the women to find a place and settle in.

I lowered the camera briefly to rest my eyes and I could hear Joey muttering and cursing next to me.

I was about to speak when two black Mercedes sedans turned slowly into the compound, their tyres crunching over the gravel and three men stepped out of what I was, by now, considering the office building to shelter from the rain under a canvas awning.

The steel gate slid closed behind the vehicles as other men stepped from the barracks to watch and, for a moment, all was still and quiet except for the rain and the occasional cry from the barracks.

Whatever was happening here, I sensed the new arrivals were important. I lifted the camera and steadied the telephoto as I continued to photograph the scene.

The cars came to a halt, the passenger doors opened and two men stepped out of each vehicle, each throwing up an umbrella against the driving rain. I photographed the two facing me as they began to move around the cars toward the office block. The other two passengers had their backs to me but there was something about one of them that made me zoom in for a closer look. He stood with his back to me with others moving around him with umbrellas, obscuring my view. Just as he was turning into profile two others moved across my line of sight, and then he was walking with the rest toward to office.

The hairs stood up on the nape of my neck and I felt a slight shiver down my spine as I watched him.

Even in the half-light of the centre of the compound, there was something about the set of this man's shoulders and the way he walked that was ringing alarms in my head. I kept the telephoto trained on him, willing him to turn and give up his identity.

Slowly the group walked toward the office then, as they sorted out to move one by one through the door, the man turned his face slightly to his left at something one of the group said. My camera whirred and my blood chilled for, in that instant, I saw his face clearly.

The acne-ravaged face, the dark hooded eyes and the bitter twist of the mouth were unmistakable. There, in the bright light of the building, stood Senior Superintendent David Zhou.

I swallowed hard, feeling my throat constrict. What was Zhou doing here? Whatever it was it wasn't police business, certainly not by the way he was being greeted and… with a burst of clarity the word 'nuisance' leapt into my mind.

I hissed to get Joey's attention, still looking through the viewfinder of the camera.

She didn't answer, so I reached out with my left hand to pat her shoulder but my hand hit only mud and leaf mulch. I spun my head, looking urgently to my left and right, then rolled over onto my back to look behind me. Her bag lay just out of my reach but she was gone.

I shook my head, annoyed – if she needed to relieve herself she should have done it where she lay.

Wincing as a rock dug into my hip, I rolled over onto my stomach to keep watch on the compound. As I did so, a movement immediately below me and slightly off to the left, in the dark shadow of the rear boundary fence caught my eye. I peered through the rain then raised the camera and swore savagely. It was Joey.

She was bent over, stepping through a gap in the fence, holding the damaged chainlink away from her head and shoulders as she squirmed through. That done, she crouched and looked about. I held my breath. *Christ*! What was she doing? She was going to expose both of us and, worse, get herself killed. I had to get down there and drag her back.

30

STILL SWEARING, I shoved the camera back into the go-bag and stowed it against Joey's bag, hoping we would be able to find them again in the dark when we returned. Taking one last look at Joey, still crouched by the fence, I slid down the hill on my backside, the mud and slush aiding my descent down the short drop to the fence line.

I hit the bottom of the slope and was about to crawl across to the fence when I looked up and froze; a guard, wrapped in a poncho, was rounding the corner of the barrack block, the beam of his torch playing out before him.

He would be on Joey in seconds and I could do nothing about it.

Holding my breath, I watched as the beam of light crept closer to Joey but she had seen it and darted across the unlit ground and flattened herself against the wall where the shadow was deepest.

The guard walked closer, his head down against the driving rain, until he was in line with Joey and his torch beam began to swing toward her.

In a heartbeat, Joey stepped from cover and launched a kick at the guard's head, collecting him on the temple. As he collapsed, she silently stepped in close, grabbing the falling man's shirt and struck him once behind the ear. She lowered the unconscious guard gently to the ground and turned back to the building.

A pair of small legs were hanging from a small window in what was, from the smell of it, the toilet block of the barracks. The guard's radio was squawking on the ground and I watched, frozen to the spot, as Joey pulled at the legs, desperately trying to dislodge the little torso that was stuck fast in the window frame.

Shaking myself, I doubled forward to the gap in the fence, pushing the mesh away and hissed into the dark

'Joey, for *fuck* sake, Let's go. Come *on*!'

She didn't turn or acknowledge me as she worked away at the little body that was slowly easing out of the jam. With a cry that could have been heard miles away in Sai Kung, the body came out and fell into Joey's arms. A young woman, clad only in a pair of cut-off denims and a cropped T-shirt, stood shivering in shock, eyeing Joey with fear.

Without a word, Joey put her arms around the girl's shoulders and bundled her toward the fence.

'*Come on*!' I urged, dragging the girl through the gap and holding the wire up as Joey dived through. 'Back up the hill. *Quickly*!'

As we disappeared into the dark, slipping and clawing our way back up the slope, grabbing at bushes and tufts of grass for support, another guard turned the corner of the barrack block, waving his torch left and right, calling out the name of his colleague.

We had not gone 30 metres when he came across the unmoving form on the ground, shouted an alarm into his radio and shone his torch uphill. The powerful LED played across the bush and we hugged the ground as the light swung over us without stopping. Moving was a risk, but we could not stay where we were so, praying the guard's night vision was shot, we slithered upwards on our bellies, the young woman panting in fear.

After what seemed an age, we emerged onto the thin track, amazingly beside both of our bags that we threw onto our shoulders. I looked back down the hill to see half a dozen men pouring through the gap in the fence, their bright torches waving into the night like air-raid searchlights.

Joey took in the scene at a glance and grabbed at my shirt, her hair plastered to her skull and the rain beating on her face.

'Take the girl and get out of here! I'll buy you some time...'

'Joey. No! Come on, we'll...'

'Gal' she said through clenched teeth. 'They will be on us any minute. I know these hills so I'll lead them off.'

I shook my head and started to speak, but she pushed me in the chest and turned away to run up the hill angling away from the girl and me.

I stared after her and saw her torch switch on and start waving frantically around the bush as she ran. The pursuing guards saw it too and, with a shout of triumph, they peeled off to the right after the panicked light that drew them on like moths.

Grabbing the girl by the shoulder, I ran off in the other direction, ignoring the tearing of the bush on my face and arms as I pushed our way along the narrow path. The rain was falling heavier and we could barely see as, feeling our way forward, we stumbled through the dark.

With an ear-splitting crack directly overhead, a flash of lightning vividly lit our way for a split second, burning the image of storm-flogged bush onto the back of my retinas. Anxiety rose in me at the thought of missing the intersecting hiking path but then, just as a dark voice in my head was screaming at me that we were lost, we stepped from the grip of the bush and onto the wider, gravelled track.

I grabbed the girl and we ran downhill, sliding in the mud and loose stone underfoot. Heedless of injury, we fled toward where I had hidden the car at the base of the track.

We had not gone far when I saw a light bobbing up the path toward us and heard scrabbling in the gravel as someone panted their way up the path. I dragged the girl into the scrub and forced her down, my hand over her mouth. Moments later a lone figure ran past us and onwards up the hill.

I counted slowly to 30 then heaved the girl to her feet and we continued our stumbling run downhill.

In moments we burst out into the small recreation area at the start of the track, nearly colliding violently with a wooden park bench. We turned right and ran along the darkened road to the track where I had hidden the car.

I stopped the girl briefly and looked back up the hill. All was dark. The rain stung my face and the girl shivered. Then, some distance uphill and still angling away from us, a single light flickered in and out of the dark, followed closely by six more. Joey was being hunted and the dogs were closing in.

As I watched, Joey's light extinguished and the pursuers paused as they tried to gauge what had happened. She was now off and running, on her own, in the dark. I muttered a short prayer to whatever gods were out there that night to watch over her and turned back to the girl.

I offered what I hoped was a reassuring smile but she stared back at me like a frightened rabbit. We were still far from safe, and the noise from the compound sounded in the night like a kicked-over hornets' nest.

I unlocked the car, helped the girl in and slid behind the wheel. I started the car and we rolled, sedately with headlights off, down the service road and out onto New Clear Water Road, where I gunned the engine and the Mini flew off into the night.

31

Water sluiced off the windscreen as the wipers worked overtime and rain beat at the roof of the car with a sound like marbles hitting tin. I flicked on the high beam and the incoming rain seemed to rush at us as it lashed the road ahead. I could see nothing through the glare thrown up by the lights in the rain, but I dared not slow down. I dropped a gear and the car leapt forward.

The girl sat silent and rigid in the passenger's seat, her eyes wide, staring at the road ahead.

Keeping one hand on the wheel I reached behind me and fumbled about until I felt the plastic bag Prudence had left. I pulled it across to the front and dropped it into the girl's lap. She looked at me and I mimed eating and drinking, pointing at the bag. Hesitantly she opened the bag then tore off the wrapping on a sandwich and attacked it ravenously.

I had not yet worked out where we would go. The addition of an undocumented woman had not been part of my plan for the night and I had no idea what to do with her.

I slapped down through the gears, as an idea began to form in my mind, and we sped toward Kowloon with the dawn starting to crack bleakly behind us.

32

AFTER A MAD DASH through the city, I pulled the car over to the side of the road, and switched off the ignition, listening to the ticking of the engine as we sat in the early-morning silence. Nothing moved around us.

I threw open the door and beckoned the girl to join me at the entrance to a renovated low-rise apartment block. The security door was locked tight. I pressed the call button of the apartment insistently, three or four times. I was about to give it another burst when an annoyed voice, blurry with sleep, answered.

'It's me,' I said.

There was a long pause before the security lock clicked open and I ushered the girl inside where she trailed after me. I jogged up the two flights of stairs and knocked on the apartment door that immediately swung open.

'I had nowhere to go,' I said quietly. 'May we come in?'

Angel stepped back, pulling her silk dressing gown closed at the neck as she spied the girl standing at my shoulder. I took the girl to the loungeroom and sat her in a chair then guided Angel, who had still not uttered a word but eyed me with a suspicious look, into the kitchen.

I rubbed my eyes, feeling the adrenalin of the past hours washing off me. I was bone tired. Angel busied herself with the coffee machine, poured two espressos and handed me one.

'Now,' she said, one hand on her hip and the other holding the small coffee cup. 'What is going on?.. Although I am almost scared to ask.'

I threw back the hot, rich coffee and sighed.

'She's a trafficked girl. We got her last night ... well, we didn't *get* her, she's not a pet cat.'

I shook my head briefly to clear it, then started again, telling Angel everything that had happened from the moment I received Johnny Tong's phone call to our arrival at her apartment. When I was finished I stood back and waited as she stared at me, a stunned look on her face.

Slowly, a smile started to curl at the corners of her mouth and she made the sound someone would make when they find a fifty in their sock drawer.

'Holy *shit*, Gal,' she breathed. 'You did it? You witnessed everything and rescued a girl into the bargain...'

'Well, to be fair, Joey rescued the girl...'

'Does she speak English?'

'I have no idea. She hasn't said a word since we found her.'

She dismissed this with a wave.

'I'll work something out.' She paused and rubbed her chin in thought. 'Okay, we need to think this through...'

'I already have. I need you to keep her here. Safe and out of sight. I don't know for how long. Can you do that?'

After a moment's hesitation, she nodded so I went on.

'I have a few things to do. First, I have to find Joey then I have to see Peter Toh and tell him what's gone down. If he moves quick enough he might still be able to catch them at the compound...'

'I doubt that. After your little Rapunzel escapade, they'll shut that place down quickly. Hell, it's probably already deserted.'

'Still, the quicker I tell Peter the better chance he has of rolling them up. Once he has those bastards under lock and key, it's only a matter of time before one of them gives up the rest of the plot to save his own skin.'

Angel didn't look convinced. I had been wrestling with the next subject on the drive over, so I thought for a moment and decided to tell her about Thomas' notebook and letter. As I spoke her eyes grew wide.

'A notebook? Written by Thomas, in a code...? Oh my God, Gal, do you know what this means?

'I think so but I won't know for sure until I can break the cipher and decode the notebook. That's a priority.'

'Give it to me, Gal,' she whispered, her eyes shining. 'Give me the book. I'll give it to Mr Lee and his people will figure it out.'

I looked hard at her, feeling my stomach churn at the reminder of Lee and my dirty deal. If I had been playing Mahjong – and the stakes here were bigger than anything I had played for at Jade Tooth's place – the contents of the notebook were my *uk teng*, my one-shot win. There was no way I was surrendering that to Lee unless I got what I wanted for it. Besides, an idea was forming in my mind about what the notebook could be best used for.

I shook my head.

'No,' I said expecting her to explode but, thankfully, she just pouted, her dark eyes limpid. My heart skipped. We stood looking awkwardly at each other for a moment, each unsure what to say or do next, then Angel stepped closer and kissed me lightly on the cheek.

'Are you okay?' she whispered, her breath hot in my ear.

My skin tingled and I felt a flush rising up my neck. I was kidding myself if I thought I could ever free myself from this woman's spell; if I even wanted to. I nodded dumbly and stepped back.

'I have to go,' I said more abruptly than I had intended. 'I need to speak with Lee, and soon, so I'll be in touch. Look after the girl.'

Angel nodded and I saw sadness briefly cloud her eyes before she turned away and went to sit next to the girl, taking her hand and murmuring gently to her. I let myself out and, in minutes was again weaving through the traffic headed for home.

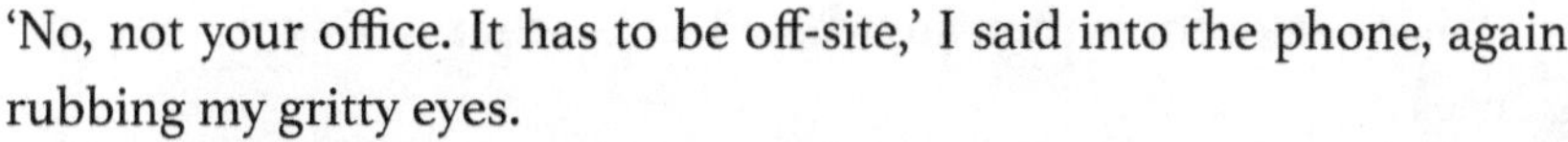

'No, not your office. It has to be off-site,' I said into the phone, again rubbing my gritty eyes.

I had arrived home and parked the car in the back laneway, then called Joey's number again and, again, the call rang out. I was deeply worried and feeling sick at the thought of what might have happened to her had she been caught. What the hell had I done, involving her in this madness?

With an effort, I had pushed those dark thoughts to the side and called Prudence to ask if I could keep her car for another few days. She had not sounded impressed but had relented with a suggestion to "buy your own fucking car" before she hung up.

That done, I had then made a coffee, rolled and lit a cigarette, and walked out onto the terrace to make the next call.

'Why the secrecy, Gal?' Peter Toh asked. 'Just come in...'

'You'll see Pete,' I said. 'It's not safe for me at Arsenal. If you want what I have, you will meet me where I told you and you'll be on time. I'm in no mood this morning to fuck about.'

There was a long silence at the other end of the line before he spoke.

'I'll be there,' he said, and I could tell his teeth were clenched.

I hung up and dragged deeply on the cigarette then wandered inside, stripped off my filthy clothes, watching in mild disgust as Bors immediately rolled on them in delight. I headed to a long, hot shower.

As I was towelling myself down I could hear my phone ringing from the kitchen so I skidded my way through the apartment and snatched it up, staring in relief at the contact.

'Joey? Thank *Christ*! Are you okay? *Where* are you..?'

'I'm fine, boss,' she said, her voice weary. 'I just got home. It took a while but I lost those stupid bastards in the hills.' She paused. 'Where's the girl?'

I hesitated briefly. No point in lying. 'At Angel's place.'

'Nice. From one triad to another,' she said sarcastically. I couldn't blame her.

'She is safer there than anywhere I know, considering the circumstances.'

'I guess you're right,' Joey said. 'Look, just checking in. I need to shower and sleep. Do you need me for a few hours?

'No, I've got a bit to do so take the day. I'll call later. And Joey...'

'Yeah, boss?'

'Keep your head down... and thanks, yet again. You were amazing. Another one I owe you.'

'I'll add it to the list, shall I?' she said and hung up. Why were all the women in my life saying that to me?

33

PETER TOH REGARDED me silently across the table, as I sipped a coffee and rolled a cigarette. A patch of sun broke through the thick, grey clouds and warmed my face. My eyelids felt like lead weights. I was fading fast but there was still so much to do.

'So let me get this right,' he said eventually, as I sat back in my chair on the terrace of the coffee shop in Central. 'Yesterday you got a tip from "someone" and, acting on that tip, you went, alone, to Aberdeen and staked out a vacant lot onto which two shipping containers of trafficked women were landed?'

'Correct so far.'

'You then, still alone, tailed the women to a compound on the way to Sai Kung where you recorded further activities clearly pointing to the place being a holding area, or camp, for the women.'

I nodded. He sucked at his teeth. 'That's some tale, Gal. Anything else?'

I still don't know why I lied to Peter – at best, not completely filling in all the details – but I needed to leave Joey out of all this and, more tellingly, a voice in my head was shouting at me not to mention the rescued girl. That would lead to Angel and then to 14K and my cosy relationship with the triad.

I also knew I was holding the girl like the notebook; using her as a bonus tile in the game, although I didn't yet know if, or how, I would play it.

'It's all on here,' I said, waving a hand at my camera. 'There's something else,' I said, switching the camera on and thumbing through the viewer to the image I wanted. 'This.' I passed over the camera.

Peter studied the playback screen for a long minute, his face completely impassive. Eventually, he swallowed and put the camera down on the table between us.

'That's David Zhou,' he said levelly. I nodded and waved for another espresso.

'Now you can see why I didn't want to come in,' I said as I sat waiting for Peter's reaction.

He leaned forward on the table. His fingers steepled and studied me hard. The silence stretched out and I resisted the urge to shift slightly in my chair, holding Peter's eyes with mine. His face was unreadable. Then, suddenly, he smiled at me and clapped his hands together.

'This is *brilliant* Gal,' He said. 'I've long suspected something was wrong with Zhou, but I had no idea it could have been this bad. With what you've got here we'll be able to roll this lot up and Zhou with them. Great work.'

Peter was still smiling but the smile didn't quite reach his eyes and, just for an instant, I saw anger flicker across them. It was gone as quickly as it came.

'Well that's great,' I said enthusiastically. 'Case closed, hey?'

'Yes. Mind you, I am still annoyed you did not listen to my advice to step away from all this... but, I guess I should be thanking you.'

'No need for that, Pete,' I said. 'Just glad I've been able to help and that you can shut this thing down.'

'Yes, shut this thing down,' he murmured then, as an afterthought: 'I take it you will give me the SD card?' I had already made a copy of the card so I nodded.

'Of course. Take it now,' I said, popping the card free from the camera and handing it to him. He dropped the card into his jacket pocket then stood and made to leave.

I remained seated and, while he was still bent over, pushing his chair back, I spoke, casually watching the tip of my cigarette as I knocked the ash off into the ashtray.

'There's something else.'

He froze, still bent over, then slowly sat back down. He grinned hesitantly. 'Something else?'

I exhaled a cloud of cherry-scented smoke. 'Thomas mailed me a notebook before he was killed.'

Peter sat perfectly still as he waited for me to continue.

'There was a handwritten letter with it,' I went on. 'He could see the writing on the wall. It was an apology of sorts and a "righting of the wrongs".'

'What is in the notebook?' Peter asked quietly, his eyes unblinking.

'I honestly don't know. It's in a cipher. It could be anything... diary, ledger, both?' I shrugged. 'I don't know.'

'Who else knows about this? The compound, the notebook...' Peter's voice was quiet.

'No-one,' I lied. I had been doing that a lot with my friends lately.

Peter rubbed his jaw and scratched under his chin. 'Gal, that's evidence. You need to give it to me.'

I held up my hands. 'I will. But let me have a go at cracking the cipher first... save you some time huh?'

I had no intention of giving him the notebook – that was going to someone else – but I would give Peter a full transcript of its contents. He would have to be happy with that.

He sat in his chair as if carved from marble, although his eyes were granite. I could tell he was angry and was fighting to control it. There was something else there. I moved to ease his mind.

'Pete, look, I'm not out to steal this pinch from you. The investigation, the arrests, the credit, that's all yours. I've come too far on this so let me have this one last go at it. Yeah?'

He still did not move or speak as he wrestled with a decision and choked down the anger I could now see rising on his otherwise inscrutable face.

I knew then our long friendship was probably over and I was sorry for that, but there was too much at stake for me to lose the notebook. Peter leaned in close, across the table, his hands pressed hard against the glass.

'Time and again I have warned you off this,' he hissed. 'Again and again. But you just won't listen.'

He seemed to sag a little in resignation at my pig-headedness; or was it that he had come to a difficult decision?

'Okay, Gal,' he said. 'Have your fun. Play your games. But mark my words: when this blows up in your face – as it most assuredly will – remember who tried to warn you.' He shook his head, his face a mask of bitterness and regret. 'I want that notebook in my hands, complete, by close of business tomorrow.'

With that, he abruptly stood, his chair screeching back against the tiles, and stalked off.

34

I RUBBED my hands across my face, enjoying the brief moment of rest it gave me, and dropped the pencil on the desk in frustration. Thomas' notebook lay open in front of me.

I had been poring over it in the small study nook of my apartment for two hours and had made no progress. I was feeling the pressure. Somehow I had to crack this code and decipher the notebook before I was due to hand it to Peter Toh the following day.

I reached down and absently stroked Bors' ears. I could not believe how big the mutt had grown in the short time since I had taken him in. With me seated, and him standing, his head, came up to my hip. Jenny Lam's voice sounded in my head, warning me that I was going to need a bigger apartment.

I stood and started to pace, my hands on my head as I prowled up and down the narrow length of the loungeroom.

I was playing music and the low-sung, laid-back voice of Kenny Wayne Shepherd flowed through the apartment like molasses. I found myself nodding hypnotically to the beat as I picked away at the problem of the notebook.

I knew what I was looking at. It was a substitution cipher. And probably a relatively easy one given Thomas' background and the likely rushed times in which he made notebook entries.

A friend of mine, one of Her Majesty's retired spies, had explained basic ciphers to me years ago over drinks at The Foreign Correspondents' Club and we had laughingly played games with them in our future email and SMS messages.

Substitution ciphers aren't a complicated beast. They involve the simple substitution of the first few letters of the alphabet, using a keyword of any length but usually of about five unrepeated letters, then writing all the remaining letters in the alphabet in the usual order, skipping any that appeared in the key.

I knew all this, and I was certain that Thomas' notebook was written in a substitution cipher but I did not know the key. I was staring at the lock and had nothing with which to turn it.

I continued to pace, mumbling to myself, repeating the word 'key' over and over. Bors lifted his head and watched me briefly before returning back to his usual recumbent position on the floor.

The key would be a word, a simple one Thomas would remember but one, if written or mentioned, would seem innocuous enough to go unremarked. How could Thomas expect me to decode a cipher when I didn't have the key? How could he expect me to even begin to know what that key *was*? Christ, it could be anything...

As I reached the end of another lap of the room, I glanced outside at a bird picking away at the seed on the terrace wall and froze, a grin spreading slowly on my face, as the answer loomed in my mind.

Thomas *didn't* expect me to figure out the key. He had to have given it to me, and the only thing he had given me was the notebook, the letter, and the business cards.

I nearly ran to the desk and scanned over Thomas' letter, hearing his strained voice in my head as I did. Nothing stood out to me and I was sure that was the point: Thomas meant the key to stand out for me. It wasn't the letter.

I shook the notebook to drop out the two business cards that were tucked in the back. I snatched up the first and studied it. The air conditioner repair man's name was Chinese, too long and included repeated letters. As a cipher key it was no good. I picked up Thomas' business card and turned it over, my heart racing. "Wendy" leapt off the card at me as if it were a Mong Kok neon sign.

"Wendy". Five letters, non-repetitive and innocuous. Was this it? I sat and grabbed up a pencil, pulling a notepad in front of me and wrote the substitution cipher using "Wendy" as the key.

A B C D E F G H I J K L M N O P Q R S T U V W X Y Z
W E N D Y A B C F G H I J K L M O P Q R S T U V X Z

I turned then to the first page of the notebook and, running my finger along the lettered groups, wrote each onto my pad, then, below each, decoded the groups using the cipher.

Slowly, laboriously, words started to appear on the page. Words that were names, streets, days and months, districts and buildings. Something, however, was missing. Some of the decoded groups were gibberish. I looked at the page in front of me, then it dawned on me.

I had words that were names of things and places but I had no numbers. The nonsensical groups had to be numbers and that posed a fresh problem for me. I now needed a number key. I felt my eyes pulled toward the business card that lay face up on the desk. Wendy's phone number! After a couple of attempts, mostly to sort out the position of the zero in the ten-digit stream and then overlaying the first ten letters of the alphabet, I thought I had a workable solution.

1 2 3 4 5 6 7 8 9 0
4 7 2 6 3 5 9 1 8 0
A B C D E F G H I J

I applied it to the as-yet unclear letter groups, switching between the alpha and the numeric codes, and bit by bit, as if scratching a lottery card, what was previously unseen became clear.

I now had dates and dollar amounts. I sat back and scratched my head, a deep sense of satisfaction washing over me. I had cracked it.

Now all I had to do was decode the entire notebook. I looked down at Bors snoring at my feet.

'This is going to take a while, boy,' I said. He didn't move, but grunted softly, his eyes rolled back in his head and his pink and black tongue protruding slightly between his fangs.

35

THE SUN WAS SETTING against an already cloud-darkened sky by the time I finished decoding the last page of the notebook and ran some copies off. I flicked through the pages of my notepad, shaking my head at the story of corruption and criminality they told.

I had in my hands a complete record of the trafficking operation, stretching back almost two years, with enough detail to blow the lid off the whole thing and put a lot of people behind bars for a very long time.

The breadth of the operation across the city and the depths it plumbed into Hong Kong's criminal underworld was staggering. I had been around long enough, and knew my city well enough, not to have been surprised but I was. I was beyond surprised.

The clock was ticking and I needed to figure out my next steps, although I already had the outline of a plan buzzing around in the back my mind.

I clipped his leash to Bors' collar and we headed out into Happy Valley to stretch our legs and clear my mind. Out on the road, street lights and neon signs flickered against the lowering gloom, and the first fat drops of rain started to splat onto the footpath and patter off the shop-front awnings as we wandered around the racecourse, Bors sniffing everywhere and cocking his leg on everything.

By the time we got home, it was dark and raining heavily. I towelled Bors down and fed him, then boiled some water and ate a pot of instant noodles on the sofa.

Swallowing down the noodles, I poured a large whisky and carried it out onto the terrace to drink and smoke under the market umbrella. The rain pelted against the shelter and flooded across the tiles of the terrace and out of the spouters, cascading down to the street. Below me, the rubbish washed along the gutters of the laneway and I could see the dark shapes of a rat or two ducking for cover.

I thumbed a playlist on my phone and the sound of Robert Johnson's voice and steel guitar on a scratchy recording belted out 'Crossroads' into the night.

Thunder rumbled across the hills that ran the spine of Hong Kong Island and the occasional crack of lightning flash-bulbed the jagged skyline. The song's lyrics reached out to me as the singer knelt at the Crossroads, seeking God's mercy only, later, to be "sinking down." I knew how he felt.

Unbidden, thoughts of my father sprang to mind and, along with them, an aching sadness. Sadness that Prudence and I had spent so much of our childhood without him, without his calming influence in the home, and sadness for my mother to have had him ripped from her so young; a searing emotional experience from which she never recovered. Most of all I was saddened beyond belief that I had spent most of my life hating my father, blaming him for a crime he had never committed. I had ground his memory into the dirt and done nearly everything I could to make sure everyone knew it. I hated myself for that.

With a deafening crack that seemed to explode directly above me, lightning tore the sky and I stepped from the shelter and looked up into the rain, letting the deluge wash over me.

My throat was constricted and my chest was tight as I fought for a moment against the welling tears before giving myself over and letting them flow. They were instantly washed away in the warm tropical rain that pummelled me and the city.

Leaning against the low wall, I hung my head, rainwater running from the end of my nose, and sobbed.

Eventually, I seemed to have cried it out so, the night being as heavy as my mood, I shuddered out a deep sigh and wandered inside. I rubbed Bors' snout then collapsed fully clothed, and wet, onto my bed to fall instantly into a disturbed and febrile sleep.

My dreams that night were of death and brutality and betrayal. Young women wrenched, screaming, from their families in faraway villages, to be strangled on the side of a deserted road, their tongues thick and eyes bulging. James and Sarah Thomas lying eviscerated in a tide of blood. As I leaned over to look at each of them their eyes opened and their mouths worked silently like hooked carp. David Zhou pressed the cold muzzle of an automatic into my forehead and muttered "nuisance" over and over while another malign presence stood behind me. I was chasing my father and another figure whose face I could not see. But, no matter how hard I struggled to run, they were always just out of reach. I shouldered my way through the crowds that pressed in on me, every face eyeing me silently as they passed. I called out again and again but the spectral image of my father disappeared from view, and I was left standing in a suddenly empty street with a man's laughter ringing in my ears.

The insistent ringing of my phone woke me and I rolled over, groaning, to drop my feet to the floor. I picked up the phone and checked the contact, groaning once more. I tapped the screen and put the phone to my ear.

'So you're awake,' Angel said without introduction.

'It would appear so,' I croaked, looking about the room for a bottle of water. Not seeing one, I stood and shuffled into the kitchen to pour a glass. I cleared my throat. 'Christ, what's the time?'

'7:30 and time you were up...'

I scratched my chin, looking absently around the kitchen. 'You are never up this early!' I observed. 'So how's the girl?'

'Her name's 'Chaya'. She's Cambodian, from a village in Kampot province. She's very quiet but we are managing to talk a little. She speaks a little English. She's eating but mostly sits and stares out the window... Poor little thing.'

I thought for a moment. 'Do you want to come over and get Bors? He might cheer her up.'

'Bors?'

'My dog, you haven't been introduced.'

Angel chuckled throatily. 'Well, we shall have to fix that. Yes, I think that's a good idea. I'll come over and pick him up.'

'Fine. You'll have to let yourself in because I'll be out.'

'You have a meeting in three hours. You'll be picked up from home so please make sure you are there.'

I guessed who the meeting was with and wondered vaguely what had brought it on. Probably just Lee wanting a progress report. I really didn't have time for that, but it tailed nicely with me needing the name from Lee before I handed over the notebook contents to Peter Toh.

'Okay,' I said. 'I'll still be out so you better make it four hours...'

'Gal, don't be an idiot! *He* sets the times of his meetings, not you.'

'If he wants to see me and hear what I've discovered, and what's happening next, he'll bloody well have to adjust his diary, Angel. Four hours.' I hung up and threw the phone onto the kitchen bench.

Muttering to myself, I made a coffee and lit a cigarette, coughing as the first hit of the day snagged at my lungs and heart.

Out on the terrace it was, again, a grey day with the sky leaden and heavy. The humidity was already climbing and a fat stillness blanketed everything.

Above me a black kite soared and circled in a thermal, occasionally flapping his large wings to take elevation. His shrill, whinnying call echoed off the buildings as he turned his head this way and that, relentless in his hunt for live prey and carrion in the streets and alleyways far beneath him.

As I watched, squinting into a ray of sunlight that had broken the clouds, I felt the first beads of sweat of the day form on my forehead and upper lip. I hadn't checked the Hong Kong Observatory for days but I didn't need to; there was a typhoon coming. It had been building for days and would be big.

Bors padded out to stand beside me, his claws ticking on the tiles of the terrace. Without looking down I knew he was eyeing me patiently, waiting for his morning walk and breakfast. His needs were simple, I thought. Food, exercise, loyalty and love. Lucky him. My needs were far more complex and the coming days would see me pushing them as hard and as far as I could. None of them involved loyalty or love.

Moving back to my desk, I gathered together the photocopies of my notes from Thomas' decoded notebook, along with copies of the photos I had taken at the smugglers' compound and organised them into three packages.

I slipped one package into an A4 envelope and wrote Peter Toh's name and work address on the front. I stopped at the next package and stared at the blank envelope, thinking hard. I wasn't sure whether I should send this to who I had in mind, but the dark thoughts that had been closing in on me lately swam back to the surface. I decided that the package needed sending – if I was wrong I could explain it later but if I was right... I sighed. It really was too hard to contemplate.

I wrote a long note and slid it and a pack of the documents into the envelope and wrote the recipient's name and address on the envelope's front. I looked at it again for a moment, wondering if I was doing the right thing and praying silently it would not be needed.

I slid the last package of photocopies into the final envelope and left it blank – I would soon be delivering it personally.

An hour later, showered and dressed, with Bors walked and fed and rolling happily on his mat, I stuffed Thomas' notebook, and the three envelopes into my satchel and walked into my bedroom.

Pulling open the drawer of the bedside table, I looked down at the triad handgun, gleaming grey and deadly in the half-light of the room.

I snatched it up, feeling the grip cool and reassuring in my hand. Dropping out the magazine I rolled the top round gently with my thumb and pushed down, testing the magazine spring. Snapping home the magazine, I turned the weapon over in my hands once more, my thoughts whirling, then shoved it deep into my satchel. Without a backward glance, I left the apartment.

36

'I NEVER TOOK you for a cat person,' I said, lowering myself into an over-stuffed armchair, upholstered in a faded floral print. Alastair Chard stood in a threadbare dressing gown, belted loosely across his prodigious belly, and scowled at me.

'I hate the fucking things,' he said dismissively as a large grey Persian with an impossibly bushy tail wove its way in and out of his legs.

On the sideboard, sitting on a tarnished silver drinks tray between a decanter of whisky and two cut-crystal glasses, a brown and white cat stared placidly up at Alastair who absently scratched it behind the ear.

'If I could, I'd drown every last one of these fucking creatures in the harbour,' he growled, picking up the Persian to place it gently on a cushion.

'Before I ask,' he said, turning for the kitchen, 'just what the *fuck* your reason is for turning up on my doorstep and disturbing my morning routine so early, I suppose you want a coffee.'

'Very generous of you.'

'Don't be a smart bastard, Galahad or I'll kick you out on your spotty half-Chinese arse,' he replied from the kitchen over the sounds of clinking glasses and the espresso machine warming up.

'I'm quarter Chinese, Alastair you fat English bigot.'

'Whatever..,' his disembodied voice replied. 'And, I'm not fat...'

I looked about the loungeroom as I waited for him to appear with coffee and attitude.

Across the room a worn, dark brown leather Chesterfield ran most of the length of one wall, stopping at a roll-top desk that was cluttered with papers and books and upon which sat the largest black cat I had ever seen. I stood and walked over to it, negotiating the crazily stacked piles of books that lay all around the room. I crouched down to look at the cat – more a small Panther – and it raised its head and flattened its ears, a deep growl echoing up from its throat. I gave it my best alpha-male stare and it didn't flinch but stared balefully back at me.

'Nice kitty,' I murmured and turned back to the room.

The sky seemed to have brightened a little and sunlight streamed in through a large window, illuminating the room around which dust motes danced and swirled. I looked out the window and down over the south side of the island.

Alastair's bungalow was built at the turn of the twentieth century and was perched high above Middle Gap Road, hidden largely from his neighbours by an unruly and overgrown jungle that passed for what he called 'The Garden'. Alastair had never invited me to tour the house but had, in the past, deigned to host me deep in his garden, on its weed-cracked and mildewed terrace.

It was rumoured that the bungalow had been gifted to the mistress of a senior colonial official shortly before the war and had been the scene of frantically hedonistic parties in 1941 as the Japanese closed in on the territory. From what I could see of Alastair's loungeroom, much of the furnishings were left over from that time. I could almost hear the gay laughter, the clinking of glasses and the gramophone playing, all trying vainly to drown out the sound of Japanese bombers passing overhead. Everything about Alastair Chard was a little dog-eared and worn and harkened back to a time long gone; a time of empire and faded glory.

Another cat, a large ginger, lay curled on the window sill, his ears torn and his face scarred from battle, the tip of his tail flicking contentedly as he slept.

The floor of the room was a dark hardwood, nearly black in colour, covered in two places by large Turkish rugs that, like everything else in the room, were frayed and faded. On the sideboard beside the 'whisky cat' stood a number of framed photographs, most of a much younger, and fitter, Alastair rubbing shoulders with the great, the good, and not so good of Hong Kong society going back over forty years.

I picked one up and studied it, not recognising the beautiful Chinese woman, dressed in a long figure-hugging Cheongsam, smiling out from the black and white print.

'Seen enough, have you?'

I put the photo down gently and turned to Alastair. 'Who is this? I don't recognise her.' I waved my hand at the rest of the frames. 'Most of these I recognise, but not her.'

Alastair put my coffee and an ashtray down on a small side table and flopped heavily into the Chesterfield. He shrugged and waved a hand dismissively.

'Just someone I loved once. Long ago...'

I sat in the lounge chair and sipped at my coffee, watching him as he adjusted his dressing gown and lit a cigarette. He gazed back at me for a moment.

'That's it. Just a woman...' he muttered.

Alastair's eyes took on a faraway look and a slight smile creased the corners of his mouth. It was none of my business so I let it go, turning instead to my satchel and drawing out the last of the envelopes, the previous two having been dropped in my office on the way over.

Alastair dragged deeply on his cigarette and ashed it violently.

'So now we turn to the purpose of your visit, do we? But before we do, I have a question for you, Galahad?'

'Sure.'

'What the *fuck* was your role in the recent bout of the 'Hong Kong Knife Skills Championship' at the Thomas' place?' He shuddered and shook his head. 'Fuck me, I've seen some bad stuff in this city of the years, some truly *awful* shit, but never anything like that.'

The sight and smell of the charnel house in the Thomas' apartment, and a flash replay of last night's dream, played through my mind and I swallowed.

'The day after I met you,' I said 'I shook him down in his office. He as much as admitted his involvement to me. We set a meeting for two days later when he was going to give it all up but he never showed.' I shrugged. 'They got to him first.'

'*Fuck*, Galahad! Yes, you could say that... they got to him all right. Fucking hard to focus on other things with your tongue pulled out through your throat and a wad of five hundreds shoved up your arse.'

I rolled and lit a cigarette, using the pause to gather my thoughts and let Alastair calm down a little before I went on.

'That's one of the reasons I'm here. But I'll get to that shortly. For now, you should know the importation happened two nights ago.'

'And you're just telling that *now*? Fuck *me*, I thought we were working together on this!'

I held up a hand. 'Calm down Alastair. Look, yes I should have called but I've been a bit busy as it happens.' I dragged on my cigarette and drained the coffee, waving the empty cup at Alastair.

'Jesus *Christ* you're insufferable,' he said, standing and gently pushing the brown and white cat aside so he could pour a whisky. He raised the glass at me with an eyebrow cocked questioningly.

I checked my watch: 0845, so that was a "no" to whisky, although I felt I could use it. I shook my head. Alastair sat and sipped at the drink. Both he and the giant black cat glared at me in silence.

Resting the envelope on my knees, I took a deep breath and launched into a retelling of the events of two nights previous.

I told Alastair of our stakeout in Aberdeen, the arrival of the mid-stream lighter and the two shipping containers full of women, of our wild chase across Hong Kong and Kowloon to the camp, Joey's rescue of the girl and our escape. When I was done I sat back in the chair and rubbed my eyes.

'So there you are,' I said.

'There I am *where*?' Alastair replied, his voice exasperated. 'I think it's fair to say I have some fucking questions.' He held up a finger. 'The first one: who else knows about this?'

'Peter Toh.' I wasn't going to tell him about Angel.

'Okay so, by now he's cleared that place and got everyone under lock and key. At least in theory.'

'Meaning?'

'Well, you bloody idiot, it's now nearly 36 hours since your escapade and, presumably, about 24 since you told Toh. So why didn't I know? Why didn't I hear about a huge police operation, arresting a fistful of triad shitheads and saving a few hundred weeping and bedraggled women?'

I blinked. 'What are you saying?'

'I'm saying Peter Toh either didn't move fast enough or he didn't move at all. No idea which, but either way no mass arrests and no mass rescue.'

I shook my head. 'No way Peter would not have acted. They must have beaten him to the punch and abandoned the place before he got there...'

'And yet, Galahad, not a peep on the streets or from the usually voluble Police PR machine about the mounting of any operation.' He arched an eyebrow. 'Strange, no?'

I stared dumbly at him, my mind spinning. I simply could not accept Peter's lack of attention to this, nor that it pointed at anything untoward. It was unthinkable. There had to be another explanation and my bet was his operational reconnaissance failed to find any sign so the op wasn't mounted in the first place. Peter would be hunting them across Hong Kong now. I was sure of it.

'My next question,' Alastair went on. 'What did you see in the compound?' he indicated the envelope on my knee. 'I might be old but I'm not completely fucking demented... One assumes *that* is something of note?'

I nodded. 'Correct. I'll get to that. Next question?'

'Peter Toh has the girl?

I shook my head, unsure what to say.

'Where is she, Galahad?' Alastair asked quietly. 'It might not yet have filtered through the lump of shit between your ears that you call a brain, but she is quite important to proceedings at this point.'

'She's safe at a friend's house.'

Alastair sat stone still, regarding me quizzically and I could hear his brain ticking over. He had a mind like a steel trap so it didn't take more than a few seconds before he replied.

'Ah, I see,' he said quietly. 'That "friend" would be your little piece of triad totty...The alluring, and slightly scary, Ms Yeung.'

I squirmed in my chair at his crude reference to Angel.

'And *that*, my old cock, brings me to my next question: What is 14K to you and what is their part in what you're doing?'

'Like I said last time Alastair: some of this stuff is very complicated and very personal. I plan on keeping it that way.'

He exploded at that. 'Well then, you fucking *clown*, you can plan on whatever it is you are doing from here on doing it without *me*!'

I held up my hand and tried to interrupt. 'No, shut your fucking mouth Galahad and listen.' He lit a cigarette and dragged angrily on it, squeezing the life out of it in his clenched fingers.

'You come poncing up to me last week, your sweaty hand down the front of my shorts, full of promises like a Wan Chai whore... your "undying gratitude and fealty" wasn't it? Now you want me to do whatever it is you want me to do, quite possibly drawing myself into some very, very nasty shit... do you recall my reference to that you dim little cunt? ...Without being given the benefit, the fucking *courtesy*, of the full story.'

He laughed out loud, more a frog's croak, and shook his head sadly. 'Fuck me, you've got more front than Harrods...'

I held his gaze, clenching my jaw. He was right, of course, I was asking much and giving little. But how do you admit to a friend – and a journalist – that you're in neck deep with a triad in pursuit of a personal vendetta? No matter which way you cut it, it wasn't a good look. I heard Alastair fiddling around with the whisky decanter so I looked up.

'Yes please,' I said quietly. Without a word, Alastair poured two drinks and handed one to me, his brow knitted in a deep frown.

Once he was seated, Alastair lit another cigarette and swirled the whisky around his mouth. The panther slunk fluidly down from the desk to sit next to him, its pitiless eyes still watching me murderously.

'Let me make this easy for you, shall I?' Alastair said quietly.

I nodded and he went on, watching my face closely for a reaction as he spoke.

'You blundered into this thing with Thomas, obviously through your girlfriend, then you're reached by 14K who have enlisted your help to bring down SYO by breaking their smuggling operation. Correct so far?'

I nodded.

'Now, I ask myself: what's in it for you? You might be a bit of an idiot, Galahad, but you're at least, mostly, honest. I can't see you engaging enthusiastically with a fucking triad unless there was something big in it for you... Now, what could that *be*?'

I opened my mouth to speak but he held up a hand.

'No don't tell me, let me guess...' he drained the whisky and put the glass down on a small table at his elbow. His face was knotted in a frown, but his eyes were sympathetic.

'This is about your dad, right? 14K didn't kill him but know who did and will give you that name if you give them SYO.'

I drew a deep breath. 'It's not just 14K, Alastair. This is coming straight from Lee Pak-chun.' I knew he was surprised by that but he didn't blink.

'Well done, *you*. 14K's fucking Mountain Master himself. No half measures with you Galahad, I'll give you that.'

I winced and shrugged ruefully, my palms up in supplication. 'So where to from here Alastair? Are you still in? I'll understand if not and will let myself out quietly.'

He shook his head, tapping the fingers of his right hand on the arm of the sofa. Another laugh-croak and the panther looked at him.

'Fuck it, Galahad. I told you last week I want to blow this open and be even more famous than I am now – if that's even fucking *possible*. And I see you are sporting what I assume to be a tasty little morsel of evidence that will allow me to do that. So, yes, I'm in.' he waved a liver-spotted hand, ash from his cigarette flying everywhere. 'We'll work out some plausible deniability bullshit later to try and bury the 14K angle ... although your frequent tupping of the delightful Ms Yeung will make that somewhat problematic.'

I wanted to tell him that it was over between me and Angel but I couldn't bring myself to even admit that might be the case. I still had no idea what I was going to do in that department.

I took a small sip of the whisky, feeling its warmth flare out down my throat and into the pit of my stomach, then handed Alastair the envelope. He drew out the photographs and leafed through them.

'Christ, it looks like bloody Stalag Luft III,' he muttered, flicking from page to page. Seconds later his head snapped up and he waved a sheet at me.

'That's fucking David *Zhou*!' he shouted. 'The commander of CIB! Jesus Christ, Galahad! You've done it. After all these years, you've finally surprised me.'

He looked down at the photo and shook his head.

'That explains why nothing about this operation has ever, seemingly, reached police ears. Zhou was on the inside all along.'

Still staring at the picture, he scratched the panther behind the ear, it slit its eyes in pleasure but didn't take them off me for an instant.

'I always hated that bastard,' Alastair muttered.

'You think he was placed there to knobble CIB while this puppet master you spoke of pulled his strings?'

'I don't know. Honestly, no idea but you'd have to think so wouldn't you? Besides, this has the little bastard cold ... although how he got his job will certainly be a bloody interesting line of inquiry once Peter Toh interviews him.'

Alastair shook his head again. 'Fuck *me*, Galahad, you really are a box of tricks today. What else have you got for Uncle Alastair?' he asked, making a 'gimme' signal with his right hand. I rummaged around in my satchel and passed over Thomas's notebook. Alastair took it gently and tapped it on his knee.

'And this is ...?'

'That,' I replied 'is the notebook Thomas sent me before he was killed. It's in a fairly simple substitution cipher.'

'A final confession, hey,' Alastair said quietly as he flicked through the pages. 'And you're giving it to me?'

'Yes. There are a lot of other people who want that book. But I want you to have it.' I paused for effect and pointed at the notebook. '*That* is the way we break this operation; the smoking gun we've both been hunting for.'

He continued to flick back and forth through the pages of the notebook.

'I shall allow you your brief moment of titillation while you hold me in suspense.' He seemed to count to ten then: '*Now*, tell me what this all means.'

I pointed at the envelope and he drew out the final sheets, the translation, leafing through the pages, stopping now and then to raise an eyebrow or whistle softly.

'My my, not as stupid as I thought' he murmured. 'You're actually quite a clever wee thing aren't you, old boy?'

Suddenly, Alastair stopped and looked up, his eyes wide. He stabbed at the page with a finger. 'Do you know what this is?'

I craned my neck to read the words under his nicotine-stained finger.

'Xiào Xiào? Well, I know what it *means* but can't figure it's significance. It appears two or three times in the notebook. Thomas seems to have overheard it but if you see the question marks next to it each time, it looks like he didn't know to what, or whom, it referred. I was going to ask you...'

'Well, I'll bet it's not the fucking *singer*!' Alastair said, referring to the nickname for one of Hong Kong's popular female artists. He leaned forward and I noticed, disturbingly, that his dressing gown had slipped open.

'*Think*, Galahad!' He lit another cigarette. I saw his hand tremble slightly as he did. Alastair Chard was shaken.

He got up and strode over to the desk, rummaging about in a pile of papers until he drew out what he was looking for with a flourish. Sitting back down he waved a colour photograph of a group of men in shirt sleeves, somewhere in Hong Kong, all smiling widely for the camera.

'Second from the right,' he said. 'The little bastard.' He passed the photo to me.

I stared at the photo and felt my stomach lurch.

I looked up from the photograph. 'This can't be right, Alastair,' I said a little shakily. 'It has to mean something, or someone, else... I mean, *diu*! It's unbelievable!'

'It makes *sense*!' Alastair shot back. 'Think of all the rumours that have been swirling around about this smuggling operation for nearly two years then think about the total silence with which that has been met. I told you before: someone is flying some *serious* top cover for this bloody thing. It has to be someone very big and someone very well covered.'

We both sat in silence while we contemplated the enormity of what was before us. If this were true, if this person was involved in the conspiracy, the effects would be tectonic once it became public. All of a sudden we were playing for astronomically high stakes. This was the 'very, very serious shit' Alastair had foreseen and we were about to step neck deep into it.

Alastair suddenly stood and the black cat, surprised, leapt to the floor with a faint hiss.

'Well, my day's fucked now. Thank you,' he growled. 'I've got a lot of work to do so you best fuck off.'

He shook his head, running a hand over the grey stubble on his chin. 'My editor is going to shit himself when I give him my draft. I'll have a fight on my hands to get it published.'

He paused, a wicked grin on his face as he brandished the diary. 'But he won't be able to resist! Once I dangle this in front of his eyes he'll go at it like a randy dog on your leg.'

I gathered up my satchel and headed to the door. 'I've things to do too,' I said. 'Let's stay in touch, Alastair. This is about to get very interesting.'

Alastair held the door open for me and put his hand on my shoulder. He squinted up at me, his face serious.

'Be very careful, Galahad,' he said sombrely. 'I fear you are about to take yet more steps along your own personal road to perdition.' He paused. 'You're an insufferable prick but I would miss you if you wound up floating in the harbour.'

I nodded and gave him a wink. Standing alone on his front step as the door closed softly behind me, I weighed Alastair's last words. He was right. If I survived the next few days, my life would never be the same again. Hefting my satchel I walked off down the driveway, Alastair's huge black cat padding along silently beside me.

37

THE PHONE ANSWERED after three rings and Joey's sleep-roughened voice sounded in my ear.

'Boss? What's up?'

'Sorry to bother Jo,' I said, getting straight to it. 'I've dropped off two packages in the office. They're on your desk. I need you to go in and grab them then take them to Arsenal House. One's for Peter Toh and the other's for someone else I think you know...Can?'

Joey sighed and I heard another woman's voice in the background before Joey muffled the call with her hand. I smiled and rolled my eyes. I hoped it wasn't Irene Sheh in Joey's bed. An image of Joey juggling chainsaws came to mind and I looked out of the taxi window.

The shop fronts on Wan Chai Road were shrouded in a fog that was dropping across that part of the city, their lights diffused by a soft, white shroud and the taxi sped down the road, cutting the fog like an ice-breaker as it carried me to my apartment. Joey came back on the line, now awake and her voice clear.

'Sure,' she said. 'I'll head in and do it now. What are they?

'A photocopy of my decode of Thomas' notebook and prints of the compound photos.'

'Shit, you *did* it? You decoded the notebook? Wow!' She paused briefly. 'Was it what we thought?'

I nodded in the back seat of the taxi. 'That and more. *Much* more,' I said. 'Look, I'll take you through it all as soon as I can but right now I'm racing the clock on a few things. I just need those notes to get to Peter.'

There was silence at the other end of the line for a moment.

'Boss, what's happening? I get the feeling you're not telling me everything... where are you going now?'

I sighed softly and I was sure Joey heard it. I owed it to her. After all she had done, all she'd been through, I owed her the complete truth. But now wasn't the time as the taxi was pulling up in front of my apartment.

'Joey, I've got another meeting with Lee then, if that goes as I expect it to, I'm going hunting,' I said. 'I'll fill you in later. Promise.'

She seemed to consider that for a moment. 'Hunting?' she asked softly. 'What does that mean?'

'It means what it says, Jo,' I snapped, not intending to but not in the mood to justify my already morally questionable choices.

'Look, I'm sorry' I said, my tone softer. 'I'll be in touch. I promise. Just get those docs to Arsenal House. Please.'

Joey acknowledged and hung up. I could tell I had offended her but I really didn't care at that point. I'd make it up to her later. If there was a "later".

Not long after, having dropped my satchel at home but stuffing the automatic into the waistband of my jeans, I was standing on the footpath. The sun had burned off the fog and now the humidity was rising. The roar of passing traffic thundered in my head as buses belched out hot exhaust, trams clanked by, taxis sounded their horns in annoyance and trucks and delivery vans competed for space on the jammed road.

My shirt stuck to me and sweat trickled down my face. I could feel a headache coming on. I pulled at my shirt and checked my G-Shock. Any minute now, I thought.

I had barely registered the time when a black E-Class Mercedes glided smoothly to a stop at the kerb and the bearded gangster who had escorted me to Lee's boat stepped out.

He smiled in recognition, his eyes twinkling, and patted me down. His hands froze on the automatic that he drew out carefully, examined and slid into his jacket. Looking at me in mock disapproval, he smiled once more then opened the back passenger door.

I slid in beside Lee Pak-chun, who stared straight ahead as I sunk back into the upholstery of the seat and let the air-conditioning wash over me. The Mercedes slid quietly out into the traffic of a busy Hong Kong day.

As the car tuned left onto Hennessy Road, Lee pushed a button at his elbow and a glass screen slid smoothly up between us and the front seats. Once he was satisfied, he turned to me.

'You have been busy, Mr Jones,' he said.

'What, no small talk Mr Lee?' I said, gazing back at him, my face composed although my heart was racing.

'Obviously, I know all about the events of a few nights ago,' he said. 'Very well done.' I nodded but immediately felt guilty at tacitly accepting his praise. 'The girl at Mei-ying's house will be very useful I do not doubt,' he said, rubbing his chin.

'Yes, once Peter Toh makes some arrests she will be a key witness. The only witness, in fact, so she's valuable. It's critical we keep her safe.'

Lee nodded. 'I understand Mr Toh has not made any arrests yet,' he said. 'The smugglers' hideout was empty within hours of your discovery and no-one knows where they, or the girls, are.'

'You can't find them?' I asked, a little surprised.

'Mr Jones,' Lee said patiently, as if he was talking to a cranky child. 'We are looking but it was two days ago and Hong Kong is a big place. Let us not forget, no-one knew the compound was there for nearly two years... we certainly did not.'

I conceded the point with a slight nod.

'May I ask why we are taking a drive around town?' I held up my hands. 'Don't get me wrong, I enjoy your company but I presume you want something from this meeting...you usually do.'

Lee sighed. 'You are being boorish, Mr Jones. Please, let's focus on the matters at hand shall we?' I gestured for him to go on. 'Tell me about the Thomas Diary,' he said.

'Is that what we're calling it now? It's got a certain ring to it.'

'Well?'

'I'm sure Angel has told you it's a coded notebook. What she won't have told you – because she doesn't know yet – is that I have deciphered it. It makes for very interesting reading.'

I noticed Lee's fingers dig into the armrest between us and I could see him physically gather himself. 'Such as?' he asked mildly.

'It won't surprise you that the notebook is a record of every transaction and meeting of the conspiracy, at least those Thomas attended, going back over eighteen months. Names, dates, locations, dollars. The lot.' I paused. 'I think he always intended it to be some sort of insurance policy. In the end, he used it as his Last Will and Testament.'

Lee nodded, tapping his fingers on the arm-rest. 'These names: were there any that... stand out?'

'Stand out?'

'Yes. Do any of the names stand out to you? Any that you recognise?'

Lee was eyeing me closely but I didn't blink when I answered.

'No. None stand out. In fact, I don't recognise a single name.'

It wasn't exactly a lie – I didn't recognise any names in the notebook – but neither did I bring up the reference to Xiào Xiào. There was something about Lee's eagerness that was ringing alarms in my head.

Lee pursed his lips and seemed to think about this for a moment. 'No matter,' he said. 'As the notebook is not in my hand, I am assuming you do not intend to give it over to me?'

'Not now. No.'

'That may be a mistake on your part Mr Jones,' he said mildly. 'May I ask where it is?'

'You may, but I won't tell you. Just accept that it's in a safe place with the right person for its purposes.'

Lee turned away and looked out the window of the car. 'What do you intend to do now?' he asked after a long pause.

'You said you wanted the smuggling operation stopped and I am on the way to doing that. Peter Toh has photographs and has a full transcript of the notebook, as does a friend of mine at The Herald. We have a witness. We have the notebook that Peter Toh will, eventually, have as evidence. It's only a matter of time now, Mr Lee.'

Lee played with a ring on his right hand while he looked out the window as Central passed by and we continued to head west. I had no idea where we were going and didn't much care, so long as I was deposited, safe and sound, at home. Finally, he spoke.

'Yes, it does look as if it is coming together,' he agreed. 'I shall just have to trust in your judgment and your methods, Mr Jones.'

'I'm flattered,' I said drily. 'You'll be interested to know,' I continued 'that I photographed David Zhou at the compound. He wasn't there in his capacity as head of CIB.'

Lee waved his hand dismissively. 'That isn't news to me Mr Jones.'

That surprised me. Or maybe it didn't. 'It's not? You *knew* he was crooked?'

'I...*we*... have known Zhou has been corrupt for many years.' He shrugged. 'Since his promotion, it has served our purposes, almost as much as SYO's, for there to be a corrupt policemen at the head of CIB. Because of Zhou, OCTB haven't made a major arrest for many years. Just small fry, whose removal from the game is of no consequence.'

'Why didn't you tell me?' I demanded.

'There was really no need – at least at that point. I was sure you would find out the closer you got to the conspiracy. Besides, I was holding that particular name back for another reason.'

I froze in the seat and my pulse began to race.

'I think you owe me something, Mr Lee, and I think now would be the time to make good on that.'

Again, Lee took the time to think that through. He looked straight ahead, his face impassive but I knew he was weighing his options, looking at his tiles and considering how he would line up his melds in this particular game of real-life Mahjong.

I knew I had the bonus tiles but Lee was a master player and I had the uncomfortable feeling he had held the winning tiles all along. Finally, he turned to face me. I tried hard, but probably unsuccessfully, to keep my expression bland.

'I promised you,' he said 'that I would reveal the identity of the man who killed your father if you brought about the end of the SYO smuggling operation. There is still a way to go, I agree, but, as you say, the end appears near.'

'So...?'

Lee studied me, watching for my reaction, as he spoke. 'The man who killed your father was an SYO 49er. He was a nobody who didn't even have a nickname. His name was Chan Wang-lei. Jimmy Chan... and he died when you were at the Police College. I had him killed.'

I felt sick and my head spun.

By now, I had convinced myself that David Zhou had killed my father. It had all added up, or at least had seemed to. But I had been wrong. My father has been killed by an 'ordinary member' of the triad, just some street punk. That man was long dead and my chance for revenge, the closure I so desperately sought, had died with him.

My disappointment gave over to rising anger as I realised I had been played all along by Lee; he had dangled an identity, knowing its worth to me, to get me to do his bidding and that name had turned out to be worthless.

I clenched my hands as I fought the urge to reach across the seat and strangle Lee, choke the life out of him in the back seat of his own car. Lee could see me wrestling to control my anger, but he didn't look concerned.

'I'm supposed to thank you for having this guy killed?' I asked, my voice strained. Lee just held up a finger and spoke.

'You may if you wish, but it is not necessary. Please, Mr Jones, allow me to go on.'

I nodded mutely and clenched my jaw, but hoped my eyes conveyed to Lee just how close he was to a punch in the mouth at that moment. He spoke again, both hands now resting comfortably on his knees.

'I appreciate this must come as a great disappointment to you,' he said. 'And I imagine, at this moment, you are less than pleased with my sleight-of-hand.'

'You could say that,' I said between clenched teeth.

Lee nodded, as if appreciating a finely delivered debating point.

'Yes. Well, while Chan was the man who pulled the trigger your father was deliberately lured to that place in the old Walled City by a third person. That person worked with your father and was a corrupt policeman who had been a member of SYO since his youth.'

I swallowed and Lee went on, his voice level as he, finally, parted the curtain for me like a master magician.

'That person was David Zhou,' he said.

I exhaled a long, shuddering breath and turned away from Lee to gaze out of the window. We were on Connaught Road, passing the Western Markets, still heading west toward Kennedy Town.

I didn't much care where we were at that point – all I could think of was David Zhou and what I would do when I found him. Zhou had obviously hated my father from the start but had wormed his way into his confidence, all the while plotting to kill him once he had the word from his criminal masters.

That fateful day, he had lured my father into Kowloon Walled City, on the promise of an informant meeting, and my father had walked unknowingly to his death in a rubbish-strewn alley in that densely populated slum. In my mind, I saw my father lying bleeding in the alley. Chan stood over him with a smoking revolver while Zhou planted incriminating evidence then whispered the word 'nuisance' in my father's ear as he dragged in his final, shallow breaths.

I screwed my eyes tight and composed myself before turning back to Lee who was still watching me closely.

'Where is he?' I demanded.

Lee shrugged. 'We don't know. His house is locked and he has not been home for nearly 24 hours, according to his neighbours.' Lee handed me a slip of folded paper. 'His address,' he said as I opened the note and read the handwritten Chinese scrawl.

I nodded, thinking that through. 'They will be waiting to see who it was that had been at the compound that night and what, if anything, it might mean. They obviously know something's up or they would not have relocated the women.'

I thought for a moment. Something still did not add up.

'But why has he gone to ground? They probably didn't even notice a girl had escaped – the others wouldn't have given her up. And, as far as Zhou knows, his cover is intact so why drop out of sight? I told Peter Toh yesterday that Zhou was involved, and even showed him the photos. Yet he hasn't been picked up yet.'

I shook my head, trying to clear it. My mind was spinning and trying to piece the thoughts together in my current state was like a crazed arcade game that was flashing 'Game Over'. I sighed.

'Whatever the reason,' I said 'Zhou has dropped off the screen and I need to find him before Peter Toh does.'

'What do you plan to do when you find him?' Lee asked, mildly interested as if looking at a kid's school science experiment.

'I don't even know how I *will* find him,' I said. 'But if I do, I'll kill him.'

Lee nodded. 'The latter will be entirely up to you, Mr Jones. We do not kill policemen – even corrupt ones. But we *will* assist you to find him. I have already given the order to that effect and my men are combing Hong Kong as we speak. We will find Zhou, I guarantee it.'

'Thank you,' I said, feeling sick at heart at how I had got to this place and where I still intended to travel.

Here I was, sitting in the back seat of a Mercedes with Hong Kong's most powerful criminal overlord, openly talking about killing a man; and a cop at that, despite his corruption.

Alastair Chard was right: I was on the road to perdition and, once there, once I had brought about my final and irrevocable spiritual ruin, there would be no return. That was assuming I survived.

I realised the car had stopped and the bearded gangster was

standing on the footpath, the door open, waiting for me to step out. I looked about, registering where we were and turned to Lee.

'You couldn't drop me at home? Not very polite of you.'

Lee chuckled softly. 'Please accept my deepest apologies, Mr Jones. I have an important meeting to attend in Kowloon and, besides, you look as though you could use the exercise.'

I stepped out onto the kerb and leaned into the car. 'Have Angel relay any information you have on Zhou. You need to find him quick.' Lee nodded and I went on. 'Once this is all done, Mr Lee, I'm out. Nothing to do with you or with your San Ho Hui, *Triple Union Society*, ever again. Clean.'

Lee smiled, almost pityingly. 'No-one is ever out, Mr Jones,' he said. 'And, most certainly, none of us is ever clean.'

With that, he sat back and waved a hand at the gangster standing beside me, who gently closed the car door.

Putting on my Wayfarers against the glare of the mid-afternoon sun that was fracturing the grey clouds rolling in from the south, I turned as I felt a tap on my shoulder. The bearded gangster was smiling at me and holding out the handgun, grip first. I took it and stuffed it into the waistband of my jeans, pulling my shirt down over it.

'Good luck, Mr Jones,' he said, nodding toward my waist. 'I expect you will be needing that very soon.'

I just looked at him as he gave me a final, cheery wave before climbing into the Mercedes that slid out into traffic and away, leaving me standing alone on the footpath.

A group of deliverymen, squatting in the shade of an awning, smoking and drinking cold Cokes, watched me idly. I nodded at them, then walked off in the direction of the MTR, feeling the handgun nestled menacingly in the small of my back.

38

THAT DAY PASSED QUICKLY as I scoured Hong Kong for David Zhou. On my way home I called Fat Johnny Tong and told him to get his network of street kids, hookers, drug dealers and associated other dwellers of Hong Kong's underworld on the case. If anyone could find a missing copper, holed-up in a squat somewhere in the city, it would be Johnny Tong's all-seeing, street-wise army of villains.

That done, I had returned home briefly to check if Angel had picked up Bors.

I was relieved to see the apartment empty and a handwritten note from Angel on the kitchen bench, knowing I was now free to hit the streets for a day or two without worrying about my ever-growing dog and his needs. I had then thrown the handgun, a spare T-shirt, a bottle of water, my camera, Leatherman multi-tool, a few protein bars and a power bank for my phone into my backpack, which I had tossed into the back seat of Prudence's car before driving out into Hong Kong's streets, heading north to Zhou's home address.

Two hours later, wind was whipping the trees, the sky had clouded over and the first fat drops of rain were beginning to fall. I flicked on the wipers to clear the windscreen so I could see Zhou's small apartment block on a busy street in Sham Shui Po.

I was unwrapping a protein bar when a dark sedan pulled up 75 metres from me and outside the block. I froze, protein bar midway to my mouth, as the driver of the car stepped out and looked quickly up and down the street before entering the building.

Peter Toh disappeared from view and I slunk lower in the car seat. The last thing I needed was for Peter to see me at Zhou's house, only to have him put two and two together when Zhou later turned up dead somewhere in the city. Best to let him think I had dropped the whole thing after sending the package of evidence to him.

I felt a tingling at the base of my neck as I contemplated the scene. It was exactly what I would have expected Peter to do – he was, after all, on the hunt for Zhou – but I thought it strange he had turned up alone. Why do that? Why did he not have backup?

I shook my head in annoyance. It was obvious, I told myself: he knew Zhou had gone to ground and was taking the opportunity to search his house for evidence. Still, it was unusual for him to be doing that without a partner so I decided to sit it out and see what happened next. I didn't have to wait long.

Peter exited the building 15 minutes later, carrying an A4 envelope in his hands, unlocked his car and slid in behind the wheel. I watched as he made a short call before he pulled a U-turn then drove off down the street away from me. I munched the last of the protein bar as I switched on the car and pulled out into the street heading after Peter.

It looked like he had found some evidence, I thought, and that was a good thing for him but not for me. I needed to find Zhou before Peter did so I decided to follow him for a while and see where it led. As it turned out, it led nowhere.

I followed Peter Toh for two hours as he drove to various locations in Hong Kong – each time stopping for a short time to enter a building or speak to someone on the side of the road – before driving back to Admiralty and through the gates of Police Headquarters. It looked as if he was up the same blind alley on the hunt for Zhou that I was. I didn't underestimate my old friend: he was an impeccable investigator and tenacious once he got the bit between the teeth. He would soon locate Zhou and have him in custody so I needed a lucky break and I needed it quick.

I had not gone more than two hundred metres and was turning into Jaffe Road when my phone rang. I looked at the contact details on the in-car screen and tapped the steering wheel control to answer.

'Hi Pete,' I said. 'Not entirely an unexpected call. Did you get the package?'

'I did,' Peter's voice sounded tense, tired. 'That's why I'm calling.' He paused then: 'Look, you need to come in and go through this with me.'

'No can do,' I said. 'I'm on a job for a client. Maybe a day or two?' It was a lie but finding Zhou was all that mattered and I couldn't waste time talking to Peter about the evidence he had in black and white – and colour – in front of him.

I heard him draw a breath as he took another pause to think something through. 'I can come pick you up this evening,' he said. 'Let's go for a beer and we can talk about what you've discovered.'

'I can't Pete.,' I said. 'I'm too busy. Paying the bills, you know? Two days, tops. I promise.'

Another pause, only this time much longer and I glanced down at the in-car screen to check if the call had disconnected. I was about to speak when Peter's voice cut into the silence.

'Where's the notebook?' he asked, his tone clipped.

'I'm hanging on to that for a while,' I lied.

Peter sighed. 'I've asked you this before,' he said, his voice cold. 'Who else knows about what you've found?

As I did the last time my friend had asked me that question, I lied.

'No-one, Peter. Just you and me and whoever you've briefed on your team of course.'

There was another long pause and I waited for him to go on as I turned the car onto Hennessy Road and headed east.

'Okay,' Peter's voice firmer now. 'Let's leave it at that. Can't be having any interference on this. Tell nobody Gal. It's essential we keep it between us. Right?

I was frowning as I answered. Peter was definitely sweating on getting to Zhou and making the arrest. I didn't blame him but I couldn't let that happen.

'Sure, Pete,' I said. 'Just us.'

'I'll see you very soon,' he said and hung up.

Sweat prickled under my arms despite the air-conditioning. I could feel a headache coming on and I badly needed a drink and a cigarette. With a swallow, I pushed down on the feeling of unease and, dropping down a gear, swung the car onto Victoria Park Road, to merge with the traffic heading to the east of the Island.

I had been driving for ten minutes, weaving the agile Mini from lane to lane as I negotiated the dense traffic, not really focussing on what I was doing as I picked away at what I would do and what might lie ahead of me when I found Zhou. My mind was wandering and I was brought back to focus when I heard the sound of a siren behind me.

Glancing in the rear vision mirror I saw a police motorcycle swing out from around a truck and fix itself closely behind me. As I watched, the rider swung the bike out into the lane and drew alongside me, signalling with his hand that I should pull over.

I groaned and nodded, looking for a safe place to stop in the hectic flow of traffic on King's Road. I was annoyed at the delay but knew I'd soon be on my way once I received a ticket for whatever was wrong with the car – I had not been speeding so I figured the car had a brake light out or Pru had forgotten to pay her registration.

Spotting a gap in the traffic I turned right into a side street, pulled over and switched off the engine. The street was empty and, apart from a scrawny cat grooming itself on a low wall, nothing moved. The cop pulled up a few metres behind, kicked down the stand of his bike and started walking toward me. I wound down the window and waited.

'ID and driver's licence' he said without preamble, standing slightly back from the door of the car.

I noticed he had raised the visor up but had not flipped up the front section of the modular helmet which was unusual for a routine traffic stop. His eyes were hidden behind dark sunglasses and I could not see his face. I dug around in my wallet and handed over my two cards.

'Good afternoon, Constable,' I said in Cantonese. 'What seems to be the trouble?' The cop ignored me as he eyed my ID, glancing between it and my face. Without another word, he turned and walked back to his bike.

Rain started to patter on the roof and windscreen of the car and I relaxed into the seat to wait for the ticket. Settling back, I glanced again in the rear vision mirror and froze. The cop had pulled out a mobile phone and placed it in the front of his helmet.

He was talking to someone. Why wasn't he using his radio? My heart started to pound as I watched him. Seconds later he slipped the phone into a pocket of his jacket and started walking back toward me.

Sweat ran from my hairline into my eyes. My hand slipped down to the keyless ignition and I rested a finger against the button. The cop had taken two steps when he reached down and unsnapped his holster retention strap, his right hand coming to rest on the grip of his pistol. Another step and he drew the weapon and began to raise it. I stabbed at the ignition button and the car roared to life.

The cop was now three paces behind the car, slightly off to the right and lost in the wing mirror blind spot. I slapped the gear into first and the powerful little car leapt off from the kerb, the rear tyres screeching.

I heard the sound of two shots at the same instant the rear window was pocked by two holes. Spider lines appeared on the glass, and the rounds impacted somewhere in the car with dull thuds. I hunched down into my shoulders and slammed my foot to the floor, furiously working the gears as the car flew down the empty street.

The day had suddenly darkened and rain was falling steadily. I glanced in the mirror in time to see the cop swing onto his bike and speed off after me. My mouth was dry and my heart felt as though it was about to leap out of my chest as the adrenalin coursed through my body.

I did not need to be a genius to work out that had been no random traffic stop; it had been a deliberate attempt at a hit on me and the person on the other end of the phone call had been the one who had green-lit it. Who that was, I had no idea and no time to think about it.

The car sped down the street and I slapped down a gear and swung the wheel hard to the right, to fish tail the car into another small street, its rear wheels scudding in the wet as I fought to control its drift. I flicked my eyes to the mirror and saw the police motorcycle swing into view, the rider expertly leaning the bike and counter-steering as he surged into the turn on the slick road.

Without fully registering it, I geared down yet again and swung left into another side street. I was running on automatic, trying desperately to make space between me and the motorcycle speeding up behind me, but he was too quick and the gap was closing rapidly.

Hugging the right side of the street I sped past a small van but the bike kept pace, closing fast. I scanned ahead, desperately seeking an escape from the long street. I had to keep turning to try and throw off my pursuer – the low, squat car cornered better than he did in the conditions and I knew the longer I stayed on a straight course the quicker he would overhaul me.

Two hundred metres ahead, another van turned out of a street on the right and I geared down again to leap the car forward and around a delivery man on his ancient bicycle, his boxes laden with fruit and vegetables. I was readying myself for a sharp right turn when the bike drew up beside me and I glanced to my left.

The cop had cross-drawn his pistol in his left hand and was drawing a bead on me as he fought to control the bike with his right. I had barely registered that when a shot shattered the passenger window and slammed into my right arm like a hammer blow.

I grunted with the impact but felt no pain and I gripped the steering wheel as if my life depended on it; which it did. A second shot exploded into the car and the driver's window shattered. I swore loudly as the turn sped up into my vision and before I could react it was on me.

I geared down savagely, tapped the brakes and swung the wheel hard to the right, the pain now searing through my right arm. I could feel blood running hot off my elbow and onto my legs.

Risking a glance in the mirror as I entered the turn, I saw the bike overshoot and disappear from view. I accelerated out of the turn, the car fishtailing in the wet, and my eyes widened as I saw a large rubbish truck backing out into the street ahead of me. I flicked my eyes to the mirror and the bike swung back into view. I had a slight lead but he would soon be on me.

As the truck reversed, the space was closing between its rear and a brick wall that ran the length of the narrow street. If it closed I would be trapped.

I slapped at the gear stick, heel-and-toeing the clutch rapidly and the car surged forward, aimed directly at the narrow gap. I wasn't going to make it. I swallowed hard and gripped the steering wheel. A second later I was committed and the car sped into the gap.

The right side of the Mini screeched along the brick wall, the wing mirror snapped off with a loud crack and then I was through. The truck completed its reverse and the gap closed. I checked the mirror and the truck now blocked the entire street as the driver wrestled with his wheel to manoeuvre out of his jam. There was no sign of the motorbike or the cop as I sped away, making a hard left then another to the right in the maze of backstreets.

In moments, I found myself in a busier street with cars queued up, slowly moving toward an entry back onto the main road. I glanced frantically about and spotted an alley 20 metres up and to my left partially obscured by a stack of wooden pallets and piles of bamboo scaffolding. I sped past it then slammed the car into reverse, backing quickly down into the shadows of the alley, hidden by the pallets and bamboo.

Seconds later the motorcycle roared past the alley opening, weaving in and out of the traffic. I sat gripping the steering wheel and holding my breath. If my desperate move had failed to throw off my pursuer I was a dead man.

My heart pounded in my ears and I moved a shaking hand to switch off the ignition. I reached behind me to draw the handgun out of the bag on the back seat. It was quiet in the alley. The hot engine ticked and rain was now falling heavily, drumming on the roof. The automatic sat on my right thigh, my right hand gripping it tightly.

I let out a shuddering breath and prised my left hand from the steering wheel.

Gingerly rolling back the sleeve of my T-shirt, I inspected the wound on my right arm. I could clearly see a small, clean hole on the inside of my right bicep and rolling my arm slightly, grimacing against the pain, I saw the exit wound, from which blood flowed steadily to soak my jeans and pool on the floor of the car. The good news was the round looked to have passed through cleanly but I was losing a lot of blood.

Grunting with the effort, I pulled the T-shirt over my head and reached behind me to drag the backpack onto my lap. I briefly rummaged around in the pack then drew out the bottle of water and the Leatherman. That done, I snapped open the knife blade to cut and tear my T-shirt into strips. Gritting my teeth, I wrapped a long strip of material around my arm, above the wound and cinched it tight using my teeth and left hand. I opened the bottle and sluiced the wound with fresh water then selected two smaller strips and balled them up.

Taking a deep breath, I stuffed a ball into each of the wounds.

I swore loudly as white-hot pain lanced through me and a ball of light exploded behind my screwed-up eyes. I took a few more deep breaths then wrapped the longest strip of material firmly over the wounds and around my arm. Once I had tied that off securely, I leaned back in the seat, breathing slowly to settle myself. I badly needed a drink and regretted not throwing a small hip flask into my backpack.

Shaking, I rolled and lit a cigarette, letting a cloud of blue smoke fug the inside of the small car. Pru hated smoking but the smell of smoke in her car was the least of my worries after what I had done to it.

The rain was blowing in through both shattered windows and I was wet and shaking. I could feel myself slowly slipping into shock.

Checking my watch, I calculated I had been sitting in the alley for nearly 15 minutes. I picked up my phone and tapped Angel's contact. I was beginning to worry the call would ring out, when she answered.

'Well,' she said without greeting, 'my guess is this isn't a social call.'

'You could say that,' I said, drawing deeply on the cigarette. 'I need a doctor who won't ask any questions and a place to hole up, and I need both right now.'

I heard her intake of breath. 'What happened?'

'I was nearly killed by one of Hong Kong's finest – at least I think he was. I'm bleeding and I'm pissed off.'

'Where are you?'

'I'm in what's left of my sister's car somewhere in North Point. South of King's Road.'

Angel thought for a moment then gave me an address. 'Go there. There is private parking and you'll be met at the entrance. The doctor will be waiting.'

I thanked her and hung up then checked my watch again. Nearly 20 minutes had passed since I entered the alley and there had been no sign of any further pursuit, but I could not rule out he wasn't still out there somewhere – in fact, I was sure he was. A guy like that doesn't give up easily.

I entered the address Angel had given me into the maps app on my phone and was relieved to see it was only 400 metres away. If my luck held, I would make it to the safe house in minutes without being detected.

I finished the cigarette and flicked the butt into the rain-soaked alley, then, taking a deep breath, I started the car and rolled slowly, quietly, out of the alley. I turned left, drove out onto the street and was soon pulling into the driveway of the safe house and the steel-panelled driveway gate was closing behind me.

39

I WINCED AGAIN as the needle pierced the skin of my arm, so I bit my lip and looked around the room to take my mind off things.

A bent ceiling fan wobbled drunkenly overhead, beating ineffectually against the humid air in the room and a rusted air conditioner chugged noisily in the corner, dripping water into a bucket on the bare tiled floor. Faded green curtains covered the open louvre window and flapped noisily as the mounting storm outside beat against the glass and sent gusts of rain into the room. The bed on which I lay was an ancient, rickety wrought iron number with a sagging mattress that felt as if it was stuffed with straw. The bed linen was old and musty but at least it looked clean.

'There, that should do it.' The small man in grey pants and plain white shirt said, snipping off the last of the suture thread with a pair of surgical scissors. He sat back and regarded me over the rim of his glasses.

'You've been lucky Mr Whoever You Are. The round passed right through and with minimal tissue damage. I didn't need to debride the exit wound and you were lucky you were wearing a T-shirt. No foreign-body contamination from shreds of material.'

He sat back, smiling then fished around in his bag and held up two small bottles.

'This one,' he said raising his right hand. 'Amoxicillin. Good broad-spectrum antibiotic. Instructions on the bottle.' He tossed me the bottle. 'And this one,' he said tossing the other bottle into my lap 'good old paracetamol...it will take the edge off the pain.'

'Thanks doc,' I said and looked up at the bearded man leaning against the door, his arms crossed and a wry grin creasing his face. 'Any chance of a drink?' I asked hopefully.

The doctor clicked his tongue, shaking his head as he packed his equipment away in his bag. The other man in the room chuckled and left, returning seconds later with a bottle of whisky and a glass. He poured a stiff shot into the glass and passed it to me as the doctor left the room.

'It seems you and I are destined to meet often, Mr Jones,' said the other man, the short but powerfully built bearded gangster who had been floating in and out of my life for weeks.

I took a large sip of the whisky and swirled it around in my mouth, savouring it before I swallowed it and leaned back into the pillows behind me, feeling the whisky wash warm through my body.

'It seems so,' I said. 'Seeing as we're pals, what should I call you?'

The gangster seemed to consider this for a moment then smiled widely, spreading his hands. 'You may call me whatever you wish, Mr Jones,' he said. 'But my name is Ho Li-qiang. Tommy Ho.' He stuck out his hand and I hesitated briefly before taking it, feeling his firm grip as we greeted each other.

'All good gangsters have a nickname, Tommy,' I said, taking another sip of the whisky.

'I am called 'The Panda',' he said proudly, rounding his shoulders and flexing his arms and chest to pull his shirt and jacket tight.

I nodded. 'Yes, I can see why,' I said. 'That is a good nickname.'

He shrugged expressively, still smiling. 'Sometimes people who don't know better think it's gaau gei, *gay*, but they soon realise the error of their thinking. Pandas are fucking strong, man.'

I stood and crossed the room to peer out the window from the corner of the curtains. It was raining heavily and the few trees in the street were being flogged viciously by a strong southerly wind that was flaying the leaves from them. It was dark and the streetlights cast their warm yellow glow that was reflected in puddles of water that pooled on the road and pavement. The street was quiet with little traffic, mostly taxis, and a few hardy pedestrians hurrying their way home, hunched under their umbrellas that they fought to control in the wind.

'So what now?' I asked, still looking out the window.

Tommy Ho grunted behind me. 'No idea,' he said. 'I've just been told to babysit you for a day or two...Longer if Ms Yeung says so.' I turned around. 'I don't mind,' he said happily. 'It's an easy job, there's a typhoon coming and it's safe and warm in here.' He stepped out into the corridor.

'I'll bring you some noodles shortly,' he said, then nodded at the empty whisky glass beside the bed. 'And I will leave the bottle with you. Take rest, Mr Jones.'

As the door closed I moved back across the room and lowered myself onto the bed, groaning as I stretched out and luxuriated in the feel of the pillows and the thick duvet beneath me. I realised I was hungry, and my stomach cramped at the thought of a bowl of noodles but I couldn't fight the weariness that enveloped me. My eyes grew heavy and my body, still shocked at the wild chase, gunshot wound and loss of blood, gave itself over to the fatigue that oozed warm and thick over me. I slipped away into a dreamless sleep.

I panicked briefly when I woke the next morning. My eyes opened to take in the ceiling fan, and the roar of the storm outside beat at my senses. I didn't know where I was and the room spun uncomfortably as I gripped the sides of the lumpy mattress. The feeling passed in moments and I sat slowly, groaning against the sudden pain in my arm as I put my weight on it. I coughed, swung my feet to the floor and shuffled to the window, parting the curtains.

Outside, the day was murky and rain hammered down, whipped into a frenzy by the wind that had strengthened overnight. I walked into the bathroom and splashed water on my face. I winced at my haggard, unshaven reflection in the mirror. I looked like shit and didn't feel much better. The dressing on my arm was tinged pink as the wound wept through the stitches and my arm ached terribly.

I opened and closed my right hand experimentally, feeling my weakened grip and the flare of pain that shot into my bicep. Popping open the lids of the pill bottles, I swallowed down two paracetamol and two Amoxicillin then broke open a new toothbrush that had been left on the counter and cleaned my teeth.

Absently, I ran my fingers through my hair then returned to the room and rummaged around in my backpack that someone had left beside the bed. Pulling out the fresh T-shirt I slipped it on. Feeling a little more human, but with my stomach cramping again with hunger, I grabbed my tobacco pouch, left the bedroom and wandered downstairs to the kitchen.

The room was small but clean and, on the kitchen bench, a small wireless radio played a Hong Kong chat show. Rain beat against the window that rattled in its frame, pummelled by the wind that howled up the street. Outside all was sound and fury but inside, in the homely kitchen of a triad safe house, it was peaceful and I felt oddly comforted.

Tommy Ho sat at a small, laminated table and looked up from his newspaper, his muscular frame straining his white shirt, the sleeves cuffed up to his forearms. Tattoos emerged from under the shirt on both arms. He sipped what looked like green tea from a small china cup and smiled.

'Jou san, *good morning*, Mr Jones. Sleep well?'

I nodded. 'Yes. Thanks, but I'm bloody hungry. What have we got?'

Tommy Ho gestured with his head to the small stove across the kitchen. 'I've made some fish congee,' he said. 'It's fresh and still hot. There's no *Youtiao*,' he apologised, referring to the fried strips of dough that often accompanied the breakfast dish.

I spooned some of the thick rice porridge into a bowl and sat across the table from Tommy Ho who watched me closely, his arms crossed, and that ever-present wry grin on his face. I dipped a spoon into the congee and blew gingerly on it then swallowed the warm, fishy mouthful, savouring its taste. I sighed as my stomach instantly stopped cramping.

'This is good,' I said. 'You must have been up for hours to make this fresh.' The gangster smiled broadly and sipped his tea.

'Any coffee?' I asked and he just shook his head and shrugged apologetically. I was beginning to like Tommy Ho. He didn't say much.

'I'm going to need coffee, Tommy, so can you magic some up?' I asked hopefully.

He sighed and tapped at his phone, waited a moment then told the person at the other end of the line to get to a local franchise and bring me a coffee. He paused and looked at me, crooking an eyebrow in question

'Latte,' I said. 'Double shot.'

The gangster rolled his eyes and repeated the instructions then hung up. I ate the rest of the congee in silence and Tommy Ho returned to his newspaper, every now and then slowly turning a page with a faint rustle.

When I was done I pushed the bowl aside and sat impatiently, tapping my fingers on the table as I waited for the life-giving brew to arrive. Tommy Ho studiously ignored me as he concentrated on his paper.

Twenty minutes later, there was a knock on the front door. Tommy stood and had a brief conversation with the man outside before bringing me the cardboard cup and placing it, with exaggerated formality, on the table in front of me.

'Happy?' he said, bowing slightly.

'Very,' I said as I rolled and lit a cigarette, sipping at the strong coffee and smacking my lips with relish. I blew a cloud of smoke toward the ceiling and watched Tommy Ho closely as I spoke.

'So... Where's David Zhou?'

The gangster sat very still, studying the newspaper then slowly raised his head. He looked at me, his face expressionless. 'Who?'

'Come on, Tommy. Don't jerk me about!'

He sighed and raised his hands. 'Look, Mr Jones, I'm just a soldier. They don't tell me what I don't need to know. I just do what I'm told.'

He sipped his tea and gently lowered the empty cup. 'All I can tell you is we don't know where he is. We've got people out everywhere looking but he's disappeared.' He waved a hand. 'Poof. Gone.' With that, he returned to his paper.

I sipped at the coffee and dragged on the cigarette, enjoying the double hit of both on my wearied body and mind.

I was starting to fidget again as I fretted away at the time passing while David Zhou was somewhere out there, possibly preparing his escape with Peter Toh hot on his heels. I could only hope Peter was drawing the same blanks as I was. I had been through too much to get to this point and I could not bear the thought of losing Zhou when I was so close.

I drummed my fingers on the table and tapped my foot impatiently. Tommy Ho sighed dramatically and turned a page of his newspaper. Finishing the coffee and tossing the cup into a lidless bin in the corner, I stood and parted the flimsy venetians with my hand. The storm was worsening. As I gazed out, my mind turned to the events of the day before.

I realised I had not had time to think through the encounter and I had no idea what it signified; other than that someone wanted me dead. Assuming the cop on the motorcycle really was a policeman that didn't necessarily mean the person he called before coming at me was another copper. It could be anyone, but it had to be someone who wanted me out of the way and the only people I could think would want that were triad.

I picked away at that for a few minutes and got nowhere. If it was a triad, logic pointed to it being SYO but why? They couldn't know of my part in the rescue of the girl from the compound, nor that I had witnessed the landing of the shipping containers. They were unlikely to know I had met with Thomas – unless he had told them, which I doubted. I shook my head and rubbed my eyes. None of this made any sense.

I turned back to the room and sat again across from The Panda.

'Tell me, Tommy,' I said. 'Out of interest. Why did you join 14K?'

The gangster frowned and closed his paper, resigned to the fact he wasn't going to be able to read it in peace while I sat in the room. He looked up at me, a little perplexed.

'Why do you care?' he replied quietly. 'You're a policeman – or you were – so you have seen it all before.'

I shrugged. 'I don't know. We seem to be getting on so well that I thought I should get to know you a little better.'

He smiled at that and shook his head.

'Diu. You are as annoying as my young nephew.' He clasped his hands and rested them on top of the newspaper.

'The usual reasons, I guess,' he said. 'My parents were poor, but hard-working. Good values. I was an overweight kid, bullied at school and I was failing all my classes. I used to play hooky and hang out on the streets all day, often until late at night and always on my own.'

He sighed softly and his eyes clouded as he recalled the days of his youth.

'Anyway, it wasn't long before a recruiter approached me and asked if I wanted to make some pocket money. He was a nice guy. Friendly. He treated me with respect. It was easy at the start. I ran numbers for the betting houses, messages to the 49ers – no mobile phones in those days – and did odd jobs for the society's stores. You know, moving in merchandise and moving out the laundered cash.'

I nodded silently and he went on.

'It really was the first time I felt I belonged anywhere and it wasn't long before I became a Blue Lantern – an uninitiated member. My dad was really mad and my mum just cried a lot.'

He shrugged again.

'Anyway, after a few years of that I was moved up to smuggling jobs then one day I was given my first chastisement job'...

'Chastisement?'

'You know what I mean. Think of your own that Jade Tooth's boys gave you.' He clicked his tongue and looked at the ceiling. 'Sloppy. Amateurs.'

'As I recall, I wasn't in any position to judge the professionalism of their service...'

'Mmm. Anyway, in this case, it was a pawn shop owner who had monkeyed the books and held back a large sum of money...'

'So you were sent to "chastise" him.'

His eyes bored into mine and he sat very still for a moment. 'It turns out I was very good at that.'

I shivered slightly but kept my expression bland. 'I can imagine,' I said.

He nodded and spoke more briskly. 'Before long I was initiated and soon became a Red Pole and the rest, as they say, is history.'

He clapped his hands and smiled.' So there you are, Mr Jones. Now, please, may I return to my newspaper?'

Tommy Ho's story was typical of triad recruitment methods and the young men that attracted their attention. I had certainly met enough of them when I had been in the job, most often across a table in a small interview room, but The Panda was the first I had ever had a 'one-on-one' with.

It didn't change my view of the societies, nor of the men who inhabited them, but I could not help a certain feeling of closeness with this big, affable, and very dangerous gangster. I stood and stretched my back.

'Fair enough, Tommy,' I said. 'I'll leave you to it. You'll shout out if you hear anything on Zhou, right?'

He waved his hand, head down over his newspaper. 'Hai-yah, hai-yah.' *Yeah, yeah.*

I wandered back up to the bedroom and stretched out on the bed after swallowing another two paracetamol and, as the wind and rain battered at the windows, soon drifted off to sleep.

~

The phone ringing on the bedside table jarred in my senses. I opened my eyes, checked my watch and grunted. I had been asleep for four hours. I still felt a little dazed but at least I knew where I was this time. I leaned over and picked up the phone. It was Joey.

'Hi,' I croaked, clearing my throat.

'I've been worried,' my offsider said. 'Not a word from you since we spoke yesterday and you told me you were "hunting".'

I sighed inwardly. I knew what was coming.

'You're cutting me out Gal,' Joey said, now sounding irate. 'You don't tell me what's happening, what you know, where you're going... all I do is drop fucking mail for you at Arsenal House!'

'It's for your own protection, Jo,' I said, immediately regretting my words.

'Diu! Don't you *dare* patronise me, Galahad Jones,' she snapped. 'I'm a big girl and can look after myself!'

'I know, I know.' I said hurriedly. 'But what I'm about to do, if I find the person I'm looking for, will cross the line, once and for all. No going back... and I don't want you involved in it. Full stop.'

Joey was quiet but I could hear her breathing angrily through her nose. 'Okay,' she finally said, I could tell her teeth were clenched. 'I'll have to accept that... but you can't shake me that easily. Call me when you need me.'

With that, she hung up leaving me feeling shamefaced at the way I was treating her, but, I told myself, it was for her own good and that was that.

Time passed and I prowled the house like a caged cat, bored and frustrated, watched all the while by Tommy Ho who seemed to never tire of talkback radio nor ever finish the one newspaper he had.

Outside, the storm had risen again in intensity and Hong Kong was being battered. There was no-one on the street and the city, from my small bedroom window, looked post-apocalyptic.

I rolled and lit another cigarette. I had lost count of how many I had smoked and my chest felt tight, my tongue furry. I popped two paracetamol from their blister pack and, glancing at the whisky bottle on the bedside table I quickly crossed to it and poured a stiff shot, swallowing it back with the pills.

I was leaving the bedroom to stalk around downstairs when my phone rang. I reached into my back pocket and drew it out, surprised to see the contact on the screen. My heart skipped a beat as I answered. Fat Johnny Tong's voice sounded faintly in my ear.

'Mr Jones! Can you hear me?' he shouted, his voice whipped away by the sound of wind and rain in the background.

'Only just, Johnny. What's up?'

'I've got him! I've got David Zhou.'

I sat on the bed. 'Jesus Johnny, that's a bit of news,' I said. 'How and where?'

There was a brief pause at the other end and I could hear running footsteps. Finally, Johnny came back on the line, his voice clearer. 'I just moved into a doorway. Is that better?'

'Yes. Get on with it.'

'I got a call, about 90 minutes ago, from a number I did not recognise. The voice was disguised. Muffled. It was a man and he asked if I was looking for Zhou. When I told him I was he gave me an address and hung up.'

'What then? Come on Johnny, give me details!'

'Patience, Mr Jones. I'm getting to it... I'm cold and I'm wet because of you.'

I sighed. 'Sorry. *Please* go on.'

'The address is in Shau Kei Wan. An apartment block. I called a friend who lives nearby and she got straight over there. I messaged her a photo of Zhou and she called back about 30 minutes ago to tell me she had seen him entering the building from the car park, carrying a shopping bag. I caught a taxi and have been here for five minutes. He's still inside.'

Johnny then read off the address and I couldn't believe my luck. Shau Kei Wan was only two districts east of where I was holed up and, with no traffic on the roads, I could be there in minutes. I stood and grabbed my backpack.

'Stay where you are, Johnny. I'll be there in about ten minutes. Ring me the moment you see any movement.'

Johnny agreed. 'Can you bring me a coffee?' he asked plaintively.

'No, I fucking can't,' I said and hung up, running downstairs to confront The Panda.

'I'm going out,' I said in answer to his surprised look.

'May I ask where?'

'No.'

'Ms Yeung is not going to be pleased. My orders are you are to remain here. Let's face it, if I decide to hold you here you're staying.'

I nodded at that. I certainly would stand no chance against Tommy Ho in a fight. Besides which I had no time for one.

'Look, Tommy... It's Zhou. We've found him and I have to move now or risk losing him. I don't think Ms Yeung would be pleased at that so you're screwed either way.'

Tommy Ho covered his face in his hands and I could hear him muttering Cantonese curses as he roughly massaged his eyes and temples. With a deep sigh, he stopped and looked at me, stepping aside from the door as he did so.

'Have I not told you that Ms Yeung scares me?' he implored. 'I mean, really scares me.'

'She scares me too.' I stepped toward the door. 'Don't worry, Tommy. I'll put a good word in for you.'

'That won't help, you know,' he called behind me as I exited the front door and ran through the rain to the shattered Mini parked in the driveway.

With its rear window pock-marked and both front side windows shattered, the car was soaked by the storm and water pooled on the sodden carpet and the seats. I dropped my backpack on the passenger seat and gunned the engine, turning over my shoulder as the younger gangster, who had earlier fetched my coffee, slid open the barrier gate.

Slapping the gear into reverse, I surged out onto the road, spun the wheel and headed east, through the storm and lowering gloom of early evening, to Shau Kei Wan.

40

MINUTES later I was flagged down by a whip-thin figure in a bedraggled black raincoat. I pulled into the kerb and Fat Johnny Tong clambered into the passenger seat.

His hair was plastered to his scalp making his head look even more skull-like than usual and his thin beard dripped like wet rats tails. He was shivering violently. He looked around the inside of the car in surprise.

'What happened here?' he asked mildly, his teeth chattering as rain poured in the shattered window beside him. 'Not good weather for you to be re-modelling your car.'

I waved a hand dismissively. 'Run-in with a bad guy,' I said. 'What have you got?'

Johnny pointed across the road to a middle-aged apartment block, ten stories high, with a driveway to the left that disappeared down a ramp into a carpark.

The shattered remains of a tree trunk stood near the front gate with the rest of the tree flung across the front fence that had buckled and bent under the force of the impact. Rubbish blew everywhere in the wind that howled down the street and shop signs rattled and banged.

'He's in there,' he said. 'I have no idea what floor he is on – we didn't go in.'

That disappointed me. I had hoped to get inside and confront Zhou in whatever bolt hole he was squatting in. I now had no choice but to wait until he left then either jump him in the carpark or follow him to wherever he was headed. I decided on the latter.

'Have you got any smokes?' Johnny asked.

I indicated my backpack that he had tossed into the rear seat and watched as he hungrily drew out the tobacco pouch, rolled a cigarette and lit it, drawing back deeply on the smoke.

'*Diu*, but that's good,' he sighed.

I thought through my next steps and turned to Johnny.

'Once you've had that you might as well get the hell out,' I said. 'This is down to me now.'

He turned to face me, his eyes squinted.

'What are you planning to do, Mr Jones?'

I shook my head. 'You don't want to know, Johnny. Just get home and keep your head down. Oh, and tell your friend that neither she nor you were here. Right?'

He nodded and dragged again on the cigarette.

'You know, if you plan on taking Zhou in, on him surrendering to you, you're asking a fox for his skin,' he said. 'It won't happen. So I am left wondering what it is you *really* plan.'

I shrugged. 'Let me answer one proverb with another,' I said. '"A cornered dog will leap over a wall". Extreme circumstances call for extreme measures.'

His shoulders slumped and he cupped the stub of the cigarette against the rain. 'I was afraid you would say that,' he muttered.

I looked ahead through the cracked windscreen. The wipers made a comforting slap and squeak noise as they beat uselessly against the downpour.

Johnny flicked the butt of the cigarette through the shattered window and threw open the car door. He stepped out into the driving rain and the wind whipped at his threadbare raincoat. He leaned over and stuck his head into the car.

'Even a dragon finds it difficult to conquer a snake in its lair,' he said. 'Take care, Mr Jones.'

And with that he stalked off into the gloom, hunched over against the force of the storm, leaving me to my troubled thoughts.

41

My legs were cramped and my backside was numb. I was soaked through and shivering, and my right arm throbbed where the wound continued to weep into the dressing.

I also badly need to urinate so I undid my fly, shuffled the jeans over my hips and pissed onto the already-soaked carpet in the footwell. To hell with it, I thought. As my father used to say, in for a penny, in for a pound. Pru's car was already totalled, so piss-stinking carpet would make no difference.

I rolled and lit a cigarette and munched on a protein bar I had pulled from the backpack. Come on you bastard, I thought. Where are you?

At exactly 5:17 p.m. David Zhou walked through the front door of the apartment block. He was carrying a large duffle bag, slung over his left shoulder, and was dressed in jeans and a light blue shirt over which he wore a dark green rain jacket. He had a baseball cap pulled down low over his eyes. He looked briefly left and right then walked down the driveway ramp into the carpark. The duffle looked heavy and he bent slightly as he walked.

I flicked the stub of the cigarette out into the rain and started the car, thankful to be moving at last. In minutes a small, light grey sedan appeared on the driveway and I could see Zhou behind the wheel, his rat-sharp features clear even beneath the ball cap. Without a pause, he turned the car left onto the road and headed east and I pulled in 50 metres behind him – with no cars on the road I felt dangerously exposed but there was nothing for it. The grey sedan sped forward has Zhou accelerated away and through the deserted streets of Shau Kei Wan, heading east.

'Where are you going?' I muttered.

I didn't have long to wait for an answer. The sedan soon turned right and headed up the hill on Tai Tam Road, toward Tai Tam Gap and the southeast side of the Island. I dropped the car back a little more as we entered the winding road scaling the hill. There was no need to spook him and he had nowhere to go on this stretch of road; so long as I cornered briefly after him, I would not lose him.

By now it was dark and the typhoon still lashed out in fury. The trees of the dense jungle on either side of the road whipped this way and that. Leaves and debris rained down across the road and bounced off the car.

By now I was sure Zhou must have seen a car behind him as my headlights cornered each bend just as he disappeared around the next, but he didn't seem concerned. As far as he knew I was just another person trying to get home through the storm.

I rounded a bend in time to see Zhou's car turn left onto Shek O Road. That confirmed it in my mind: Zhou was running, he had to be. I assumed he was headed to a boat pickup somewhere on the coast ahead and turned left in pursuit. The Mini responded to my gear changes and cornered beautifully as I sped along on the dark and winding road, the headlights washing through the tangled, wet mess of the jungle.

I had just glanced at my watch as I entered yet another bend and looked up, my eyes widening in shock as my right foot slammed instinctively down on the brake, the left pumping the clutch as I geared down savagely.

Ahead, Zhou's car was parked, its lights still on, nose into a large tree that had fallen across the road. The car went into a skid and I lost control as the back end slid out to the right. I heard the tyres screeching as the car scudded sideways and I gripped the steering wheel tightly moments before colliding with the rear of Zhou's vehicle.

The centre pillar of the Mini collapsed with the impact in a screech of metal and an airbag went off at my head in a loud explosion, catapulting me to my left, the seatbelt digging deep and preventing me from being thrown across the cabin.

The car came to rest, rocking slightly and I killed the engine. I grabbed my backpack and opened the passenger door. It creaked open a few centimetres then jammed. Sitting back on the driver's seat I kicked furiously at the passenger door, the smell of petrol rising thick in the night air. I was swearing and starting to panic when the door finally gave way and swung open. I tumbled onto the road, staggered to my feet and hurled myself into the jungle on the side of the road.

Panting heavily I looked about. There was no sign of Zhou so I climbed onto the fallen tree and looked up the road. Nothing.

Suddenly I saw a brief flicker of light, off to my left, weaving its way down through the undergrowth of the jungle and, moments later, I made out a track heading off the road into the dark. Drawing the handgun from the backpack, I racked back on the slide chambering a round, slipped the safety, shouldered the bag and headed off after Zhou.

The track was well-worn and clear, even in the dark. It wound its way downhill off Dragon's Back, the mountain ridge that ran the length of that part of the Island, toward the coast. I could see the pinlight of Zhou's torch blinking in and out as he hurried along the path about two hundred metres ahead of me.

It was quiet in the jungle with the canopy holding off much of the rain and deadening the howl of the wind. The sound of crickets filled the air and frogs croaked and burped, while somewhere ahead a Nightjar called.

My pulse was racing and I could hear it pounding in my ears. I tried to control my breathing as I stepped quietly along the path, the gun held loosely in my right hand, my eyes tracking Zhou's torchlight.

I felt, rather than saw, the track level out and, suddenly, I broke from the jungle. Clear ground stretched away from where I stood to the coastline. I paused to gather my bearings and, as I did, the rain stopped and the clouds opened up to shine a bright moon over the scene.

Up ahead Zhou moved on, now hurrying as he neared a small copse of trees that stood silhouetted against the land's edge, beyond which lay the black immensity of the open ocean. Zhou entered the copse and his torchlight disappeared, so I picked up my pace and jogged swiftly across the clearing, breaking into the trees only minutes behind him.

The copse was not thick but more a circle of trees and secondary undergrowth around a clearing on the edge of which stood Zhou, signalling out to sea with his torch. The light flicked on then off and on again. He was oblivious to my movement behind him as he focussed on signalling whoever he was supposed to be meeting.

Straining my eyes I could see, out in the dark and far off to the right, the navigation lights of a small ship. By now Zhou was frantically waving the torch above his head as he sought to attract the crew's attention – the ship was obviously expecting him further down the coast and his signals went unanswered.

I stepped through the trees, the gun raised and steady in a two-handed grip. At the last moment, Zhou sensed me and spun around, a look of shock on his face.

'Drop the torch and step away from the edge,' I said as I moved obliquely across the clearing, the gun trained on Zhou's chest.

Zhou's mouth hung open and his eyes were wide. His right hand crept slowly behind his back.

'Don't!' I snapped. 'Draw it out slowly, thumb and forefinger, and throw it over here.'

Zhou scowled and gingerly drew out his service automatic. He took a small step forward and tossed the gun across the clearing to land in the mud at my feet. I kicked it behind me.

'Now the bag,' I said, indicating the large duffle at his feet. 'Drop it here.' I nodded at the ground in front of me and took four steps back.

Zhou hefted the duffle with some effort and dropped it on the ground in front of me. I waved my handgun at him and he stepped back as I moved forward and crouched at the bag.

Without taking my eyes off Zhou I unzipped the duffle and glanced down. Inside lay tightly packed ziplock bags, each filled with wads of US hundred dollar notes. Bag after bag of them. Stuffed into one end of the duffle was a shopping bag containing some spare clothes.

I zipped the duffle back up and lifted it, judging its weight in my hands. It weighed close to 20 kilograms. It was an enormous sum and obviously intended to be Zhou's getaway cash. I pushed the bag to one side. Zhou finally gathered his wits and spoke.

'You *really* are a nuisance, Jones,' he hissed. 'I can't believe you're still alive after yesterday but you always did have the luck of the devil.'

I frowned. So it had been Zhou on the other end of the bike cop's phone, but it didn't add up. Something was very wrong here.

'Why order a hit on me, Zhou? What prompted it?'

'You know too much,' he snapped. 'Almost everything... the operation, the compound, my involvement...'

I felt faint. Only three people, other than me, knew all of that. How could Zhou possibly know what I had discovered? He had to have been told and I shuddered to think what that meant. Zhou went on.

'So, you're going to take me in now, huh?' An oily grin creased his face. 'Go right ahead, Jones. Take me in; I have insurance in place that will make sure the investigation is killed and I walk free in hours.'

I shook my head. 'I'm not here to take you in,' I said quietly. 'I'm here to finish something that should have been done years ago.'

Zhou's eyes darted. 'What do you mean?'

I raised the gun and sighted it on Zhou's chest, my index finger resting lightly on the trigger. 'You killed my father, Zhou, and now it's time to square that.'

Zhou stepped back and raised his hands.

'No! Don't!' he said, panic edging his voice. He pointed at the duffle bag. 'There's 2.5 million US in that bag... take it. Take it *all*. I'll take my boat and you'll never see or hear from me again.'

I shook my head, my voice hard and cold. 'I don't want your money, Zhou. I want your head.' I took up the first pressure on the trigger as Zhou stepped backwards, tripping over to sit heavily in the mud.

'No, please,' he whimpered.

My stomach churned. The man responsible for my father's death was nothing but a cheap crook and a coward. He made me sick.

'I didn't kill your father. It was the triad... *they* did it!'

'You set him up, you bastard. You had him killed then you planted fake evidence on his body to ruin his name. Then, for years, you've been a viper in the nest. SYO's man on the inside, causing untold damage to the force and our investigations.' I shook my head again. 'Christ knows how many deaths you have on your hands.'

I stepped quickly forward and kicked him, hard, in the ribs.

'Get on your feet, you piece of shit,' I snapped.

Zhou clambered up, his clothes plastered in mud, streaks of it on his face. I grabbed him by the collar of his jacket and jerked him across the small clearing, then thrust him against the trunk of a large tree. I took five steps back and levelled the gun.

He was shaking in fear and mumbling incoherently, then he raised his head and shrieked 'But I have *protection*!'

I shook my head and eyed him mercilessly. 'You have nothing, you bastard. This is where it ends.'

I took the first pressure on the trigger and continued to squeeze. All the years of anger and bitterness, all the loss and failure... it all came down to this moment. My hands started to shake and I clenched my eyes tight. I couldn't do it.

For all I felt about the cringing creature in front of me, I simply could not execute him in cold blood. Christ knows I wanted to, but I couldn't. I lowered the gun. Zhou heaved a huge breath and started to weep quietly.

'That's a wise decision, Gan-Li,' a familiar voice said to my left and I froze as Peter Toh walked into the clearing, his handgun held loosely at his side.

Zhou stepped forward, his arms wide.

'Luo-yang, thank God! This maniac was about to...'

Peter waved his handgun dismissively at Zhou.

'Shut up, David,' he said, his voice calm, almost bored. 'Get back up against that tree and don't move, or speak, unless I tell you.'

I stood rooted to the spot. The pieces of the puzzle were all finally tumbling into place. I had known, or at least suspected, it all along but I still felt sick to my stomach.

Peter turned to me. 'Toss the gun over here, Gal,' he said softly. 'It's over.'

I flipped the gun underarm and it thudded into the mud at his feet. 'How did you find me?'

Peter grinned. 'It was simple really. It did not take much to tip this fool off to your location and the evidence you had on him. I knew he would order a hit and that would certainly have relieved me of the most difficult problem here...had it succeeded'

I swallowed and he went on.

'I'll give it to you, Gal, you're hard to keep track of. I saw you outside Zhou's apartment, then you just disappeared after you followed me around all day. But it was easy to smoke you out by contacting Johnny Tong. All I had to do was sit back and wait then I would have both of you. Quite neat, huh?'

There it was. I had suspected it for a while but had pushed it down deep, refusing to believe what my instincts had told me. After all, it was why I had sent the package of documents, and a long note, to my old friend Station Sergeant Billy Wong as insurance. Peter Toh was bent and I could have cried.

'How long Peter?' I asked, stepping slowly back to the lip of the clearing.

He shrugged. 'Years. At least since you were in Narcotics...'

'A triad plant? I can't believe it ...'

'Not exactly, Gal. You know I've got runs on the board against the triads, including my own, but I've always been on... let's call it a "special assignment".'

I glanced at Zhou who was looking madly between me and Peter like someone at a tennis game. His face was puzzled.

'The smuggling operation...' I said. 'You were always thwarting any investigation. From the start, you were against it.'

'No, that's not strictly correct.' He waved the handgun in Zhou's direction 'That was this idiot's job. I had a much bigger task.'

Zhou finally spoke up. 'You... you're one of *us*?' he stammered to Peter. He rolled his eyes and smiled. 'Luo-yang, this is perfect,' he said, his voice firmer. 'Get rid of Jones and we'll move on just like before.' He started to move toward Peter.

'David,' Peter sighed. 'I found the envelope you left in your apartment, offering me evidence of a high-level conspiracy to buy your own freedom. You even named names.'

He clicked his tongue. 'Sadly for you, I *am* that conspiracy.'

Zhou started to speak but Peter raised his gun and fired a single shot. It took Zhou under the chin, snapping his head back and blowing out the top of his skull, painting the tree behind in blood and brains. Zhou's baseball cap hung in a branch of the tree and his body collapsed into the mud, a river of blood pooling around his destroyed head. Peter turned to me.

'I tried to warn you off, Gal,' he said, his voice level. 'So many times. I wanted you to just walk away because I knew if you kept at it we would arrive at this point.'

'I don't get it,' I said, trying to stall while I edged ever further backwards to the lip of the clearing. 'If blocking the investigation wasn't your job what was?'

I felt my right heel slip into thin air and I glanced over my shoulder. A metre or two below me ran a line of dense vegetation, far below which I could just make out the jagged rocks onto which the surf pounded. My heart sank. There was no way out.

'Come on, Gan-Li,' Peter said, a broad smile on his face. 'You've figured it out by now... you tell me.'

I took a deep breath as the final piece of this mad puzzle slotted into place. 'Xiào Xiào,' I said.

'There, see? I knew you'd do it...'

My mind was working fast. Eddie Lau Ming-yuen was a career politician, known for his moderate stance on a range of issues and for working hard to achieve consensus within the often fractious Legislative Council, Hong Kong's unicameral law-making body.

He was also renowned as a man of the people in a government notorious for its distance from the people over which it ruled. Eddie Lau was loved especially by Hong Kong's poor for his work with charity and his own personal, and sizeable, contributions to a variety of community projects in the tenement housing estates. His personal back-story was a dramatic tale of 'local kid does good'. He had come from an impoverished background - in fact his diminutive size was attributed, as part of the legend, to poor nutrition during his childhood - and spent his childhood running the back streets of Hong Kong, before pulling himself up by working two jobs to support his family while he studied on scholarship. His success in business was legendary and his move into politics, and rapid rise through the ranks, was seen as an inevitability by anyone looking back on it.

His personal life wasn't without its tragedy; he had lost his wife and youngest daughter in a car accident the year before and Hong Kong had mourned with him. More than anything else Eddie Lau was known as a man who could be relied upon not to cave to interest groups and the grip they had on Hong Kong's government and society. He was incorruptible, and Hong Kong's marginalised loved him. He was also Hong Kong's Chief Secretary, second only to the Chief Executive who he was tipped to succeed, and his moniker was 'the Little One'. Xiào Xiào.

'So, the Chief Secretary is a triad operative and your job is to watch his back... make sure no investigation or whiff of scandal gets close to him.'

Peter nodded. 'He's been SYO since before his move into politics. The most successful organised crime plant in our history. Next year he's the frontrunner to succeed the Chief Executive, then nothing will stop us. We'll have our man at the very head of government in the SAR, following which we will seed every department, every organisation and every institution. We'll literally *own* Hong Kong.'

'Only, Eddie Lau went rogue on you and got too close to the slavery operation and Thomas heard him referred to, which means others know...'

Peter nodded again, conceding the point. 'Yes, that was very unfortunate. What can I say? Greed,' he shrugged. 'I'll deal with any leaks inside the society and with Thomas dead, all the evidence you managed to pull together now in my hands and with you gone, the whole wrinkle will be neatly ironed out.'

'And Thomas?' I asked, not wanting to hear the answer.

Peter's face showed mild distaste, like someone stepping around dog-shit on the footpath.

'Well, yes,' he said. 'I admit I had help on that one. Someone I've been keeping for just such an ...occasion. Someone particularly skilled in that sort of thing. I mean, I couldn't very well do all *that* on my own... and the Thomas' fought like hell.'

He stopped and grinned lasciviously. 'At least *she* did. *Diu* what a Tigress!'

I truly hated him then. The thought of rushing him flashed across my mind, but I knew I'd be dead before I took two steps. It was deathly quiet in the clearing with even the wildlife silent. The rain was starting to gently patter down, tapping against the tree canopy.

Peter suddenly pointed at the duffle that lay at my feet. 'What's in the bag?'

I shrugged noncommittally. 'Zhou's clothes.'

He thought for a moment, looking at Zhou's body, then seemed to come to a decision.

'Drop it over the edge. It will look like he was preparing to climb down when I arrived, confronted and killed him when he drew on me. Then you rushed me and…' he shrugged. 'Well, you know the rest.'

I lifted the duffle, trying my hardest to make it look weightless as it tore painfully at the wound on my arm, and casually dropped it over the edge. It thudded into the undergrowth. I turned back to Peter.

'You're making a mistake, Pete,' I said as calmly as I could muster.

He looked amused. 'Oh?'

'Me being taken out of the picture won't change things. Others know everything I do. In fact, identical packets of evidence to the one I sent you are now in the hands of others, including Alastair Chard at The Herald.'

Peter snarled at me, a look of pure hatred twisting his features. 'You lied to me!'

I couldn't help myself: I laughed out loud. 'I *lied* to you? Fuck! How wicked of me, you being a murdering triad scumbag, and all.'

He bit back angrily on a retort, calming himself with an effort, and shrugged. 'Just a complication,' he said. 'Nothing I can't deal with.'

I shook my head. 'No, Peter, it's all coming out in the next day or so. Everything including Xiào Xiào. It will be a scandal even he can't dodge, especially given The Herald has the original Thomas Diary. He's going down and you're going with him. In fact, there are people at Arsenal House, right now, preparing to arrest you and they will be expecting to see me alive and well tomorrow. If they don't they will know what happened and at whose hand.' I hoped to God I was right.

He was furious and, even in the dark, I could see his jaw clenching and his nostrils flared as he fought to control himself.

'Arsenal House? Who?'

I stood silently.

'How did you figure me out?' he asked quietly. 'I mean, nobody else has a clue.'

I shook my head, 'I didn't really. It was just instinct. Your biggest mistake was raising the faked wire transcript with me in the first place.'

Peter nodded. 'Yes, I realised that but I didn't really have a choice.' He waved his hand at Zhou's body. 'This idiot, not knowing I was on the inside, brought it to me to investigate so I knew he was after you. Sooner or later, you'd come to hear of it – from somewhere, if not from Zhou himself. I had hoped to "manage the message", as they say.'

'That got me thinking about the wire,' I responded. 'The apparent lack of anything coming out about the people smuggling operation, but your insistence that the intell was solid, then your reticence to look into it. That troubled me and you knew it would. You knew I'd pick away at it and that worried you. The last time in your office, I could see that, but what I didn't know was why. Then, you figured the next best thing was to control the situation: warn me off Thomas and, when I didn't, to keep anything I found to yourself, insisting I told no-one.'

I paused and shuffled back a little more. A clap of thunder broke the silence around us, and the small clearing was lit phosphorus white by lightning. The wind picked up and it began to rain heavily.

'The clincher came,' I said, 'when the compound emptied out overnight and the only person, apart from me, who knew about the evidence I had was you.'

I shrugged. 'In the end, it was all just a hunch. I could easily have been wrong – I hoped I was – but sending the package of evidence, with a long note from me, to Arsenal House was my insurance policy.'

Peter nodded, digesting all of that.

'You're a clever bastard, Gal, I'll give you that.' He scratched the side of his head. 'You know, I always liked you. But I always knew I had to keep you from coming anywhere near our guy. I was mightily relieved when you left the job, I can tell you.'

He shook his head again and chuckled. 'Then, unbelievably, you stumble onto Thomas and the smuggling operation, and you just wouldn't let it go. I knew you wouldn't as soon as you began to suspect, somehow, that Zhou was involved...'

He stopped suddenly, his mouth snapping shut. He eyed me for a moment then wagged his finger at me.

'Oh, you have been naughty, haven't you? You're working with 14K!'

He laughed, a course cough-like sound. 'You have to be. How else would you know about Zhou and your dad? Where else would you have got your little gems of information along the way to finding yourself watching that landing and the compound?'

He rubbed his chin. 'Mind you, cracking Thomas' role in this was all your own work I think. Kudos.'

He stood silently for a while, looking up at the night sky, letting the rain wash his face as if cleansing himself of what he was about to do.

'The people smuggling I could have controlled, and you would have been none the wiser. A few decent arrests, the girls disappear into Hong Kong, no more shipments for a year or so... job done. But when I saw the translation of Thomas' notebook, with its reference to Xiào Xiào, I knew you were getting close to the one person I had to protect at all costs. You had to go.'

There was so much I wanted to say to him, to ask him, but there was no point. I remained silent, content to let him rant while I furiously tried to work out a way to get out of this alive.

The only thing I could think of was the cliff at my back. It was my only hope but I didn't much like the idea. In the end, Peter Toh took the decision out of my hands. He raised his gun and aimed it at my head. I was staring directly into the muzzle from a range of about five metres. The moon began to cloud over, and the clearing darkened. I drew a deep breath.

'Enough,' he said quietly. 'I *will* get away with this Gal, you can be sure of that.' He sighed. 'What I do now, I do with real regret. Believe me.'

I stepped back and was about to launch myself when he fired. I saw the flash but did not hear the shot. I felt the round take me in the left temple, an explosion of light and pain detonating in my skull, and I dropped over the edge. Falling heavily through the narrow line of undergrowth, backward and face up into the night sky, I plummeted down.

For an instant, I could see the moon and the stars and the banks of cloud that scudded across them, and then I struck a boulder. I heard my left arm snap with a report like a rifle and the pain was instantaneous and unbearable. I bounced, and then my head struck another rock. Down and down into the darkness I fell and that was all I knew.

42

I COULD SEE MY MOTHER. She was stroking my face and calling to me, telling me not to leave. To stay. I wanted to hug her but I couldn't move. My eyes opened and I looked up into Joey's face. She was leaning over me, speaking but I couldn't hear her. Behind her stood Tommy Ho, pulling off his jacket. My mother called again. 'Coming mum,' I said and slipped away.

~

I was spinning. Slowly. Above me the dragon hovered and flapped, roaring its displeasure and its two red eyes blinked at me in the dark. All around me, the air was hot with his breath. I turned my head and screamed. A huge red insect, with impenetrable black eyes in a swollen grey head, was hanging on to me, gripping me with its claws. It looked up to the dragon that opened its giant maw. I was being fed to the great reptile. He roared loudly and I screamed again as I was swallowed, and all was dark.

~

I woke up and slowly opened my eyes, blinking against the bright light in the room. I tried to swallow but my tongue was stuck to the roof of my mouth that felt as if it was full of rocks.

My left arm was suspended in a sling above the bed. My right arm, with a cannula inserted running to a bag of fluids hanging from an IV pole, rested on top of crisp, white sheets. I heard a movement to my left and turned my head. Joey had risen from a chair and stood beside the bed.

'Hey,' she said. 'So you're back with us.'

I nodded slowly and croaked a request for water. Joey poured a glass from a blue plastic jug and held it to my lips. I gulped at the cool liquid, relishing the feeling as it cascaded down my parched throat.

'Where am I?' I mumbled, my mind foggy from the anaesthetic.

'You're in hospital and you've been out to it for two days.'

'Two days? Jesus.' I looked over her shoulder and saw a blue uniform standing in the corridor outside the room. I started in shock and tried to sit up. Joey followed my gaze, then pushed gently down on my shoulder.

'Don't worry. Yes, it's police but Billy Wong's nephew ordered the protection. You're safe.'

I lay back and closed my eyes as Joey recounted what had happened. She had tracked me to the 14K safehouse and, fearing the worst, had persuaded Tommy Ho that I needed help. They had both then tracked me into the hills above Shau Kei Wan and come across three abandoned cars on a bend on Shek O Road, one of which was Prudence's wrecked Mini. After a few moments of indecision, they had headed into the jungle and down the path that led off Dragon's Back...

'How the hell did you find me?' I asked.

'Ah, that's the easy part. Remember on our last call I said you couldn't shake me that easily?'

I nodded, puzzled.

'Do you also remember back when you were sitting outside Kwai Chung after you followed Thomas there? You shared your location with me and, well, you never cancelled it,' Joey grinned and shrugged an apology. 'I didn't see a need to remind you.'

I grunted. 'I'm bloody glad you didn't.'

Joey continued with her tale.

She and The Panda had moved down the track, heading toward to coast, and had barely started their trek when they heard a single gunshot off in the distance. They had looked at each other, standing still in the night, and both had drawn handguns from holsters on their belts. The two of them moved off, faster now, down the path and soon burst into the clearing that led to the small copse of trees. They had moved cautiously bathed as they were in moonlight, stalking low and slow across the few hundred metres of open ground to the copse.

They had not gone much further when it began to rain and, shortly after a clap of thunder and flash of lightning, a second gunshot rang out.

They both froze, staring ahead. In the gloom a figure could be seen running from the copse of trees, making its way diagonally away from the pair and across the clearing toward where the road would appear further down the hill. Joey had studied the figure's movement and determined it wasn't me so she and Tommy Ho sprinted across the last of the clearing to burst into the tree line, Tommy Ho in the lead, his handgun raised and eyes scanning for threat.

They saw Zhou's body and, after prowling the clearing, Joey picked up a series of quickly fading footprints in the mud on the edge of the cliff. She had dropped to her belly and peered over the cliff into the dark.

On a hunch, Joey had signalled to The Panda and leapt over the edge. She slid and tumbled her way through the line of vegetation and onto the rocks below. Finally, clambering over the boulders she had spotted me in the moonlight, lying on a rock shelf with my legs in the surf.

'I thought you were dead,' she said. 'I mean, *damn*, you should have been! Anyway, me and that gangster pal of yours pulled you from the surf edge and called up the rescue chopper from GFS,' she added, referring to the Government Flying Service.

I smiled a little. So the dragon that had 'swallowed' me had been a GFS Cheetah and the 'bug' its crew member on the end of the rescue hoist.

Joey finished her story by recounting how she and Tommy Ho had retraced their steps and raced back across the island to the hospital, arriving only 30 minutes after the chopper had landed and I had been rushed from the LZ into surgery, bleeding heavily from the head wound and the shattered bone that stuck sharp and white through the torn flesh of my left arm.

She drew a breath and sat down.

'I've been here most of the time since.' She nodded through the door. 'Your pal wanted to sit in but the police wouldn't let him in so he's sitting out in the corridor; he has been for about 48 hours.'

Joey ruffled her hair and rubbed her tired eyes.

'I called Billy Wong while you were in surgery,' she said. 'His nephew had a team here in minutes. As soon as I saw you had me delivering a package to Billy at the same time as the one to Peter Toh, I guessed what that meant.'

She blinked twice and swallowed. 'Peter Toh was bent, wasn't he? He shot you.'

I nodded, still unable to believe it myself.

Joey whistled low through her teeth. '*Diu*, who would have thought it?'

'Absolutely no-one,' I said. 'I think that's the point. He was so deep not a soul knew.'

'So he was in on the people smuggling then?'

I shook my head. 'He knew about it but he had a much bigger job... I'll tell you about it soon but right now I need to sleep.' I reached out and took her hand. 'How many times is this now?'

Joey knew what I meant. She shrugged but patted my hand. 'Oh, baak ci, *idiot*,' she said quietly. 'It's what partners do, right?'

She stood, picked up her bike helmet and was about to speak when a voice broke in loudly from the corridor.

'Look, my dear *chap*, I appreciate you have a job to do, I really do.

But I don't give two *fucks* what you've been told. Mr Jones will see me...'

I rolled my eyes, knowing sleep was now out of the question. Joey raised an eyebrow and I nodded.

'Yes, let him in before he huffs the place down...'

Seconds later Alastair Chard ambled into the room, looking for all the world as if he was walking into a cocktail reception, and tossed two copies of The South China Herald onto my chest. I looked down my chin at them then back up at Alastair, who was kissing Joey on each cheek.

'You'll notice, Alastair, that I'm not in a position to pick up either paper and flip through it. Would you mind?'

'Oh, fuck! *Sorry* old cock.' He picked up a newspaper in each hand. Waving his right hand he said: 'This one came out two mornings ago – not long after your best chum, Peter Toh tried to put a bullet in your head...' he stopped and leaned in close to the bed to examine the wound on my left temple.

'Oh *my*,' he breathed – I could smell whisky in the small hospital room and my stomach lurched 'That is a pretty neat job. Just a few stitches and a bloody *awful* haircut.'

He stood up and shook his head.

'You've the devil's own luck! That bullet only grazed the side of your melon. A couple of millimetres more and it would have blown your eye out the back of your head.'

I nodded, thanking all the gods that Peter Toh had always been a terrible shot and I had been moving, in the dark, when he pulled the trigger.

'Anyway,' said Alastair. 'Where the fuck was I? Oh yes...' he waved the paper in his right hand again. 'Exhibit A: the morning after. The big exposé. Names, dates and places. The kicker to it all being the suggestion that Eddie Lau was connected.'

Now he waved the paper in his left hand.

'Exhibit B: this morning's copy. A story of betrayal, of rogue cops and of murder. Good cops on the block, led by Michael Wong, the new *aurea puer* of HKPF, roll up the network, making dozens of arrests. Eddie Lau makes the usual noises: 'speculation', 'baseless and scurrilous allegations' blah, blah. Peter Toh disappears, whereabouts unknown'

I sighed. 'Well done. Alastair,' I said tiredly.

I couldn't bring myself to feel an abundance of joy at the way the whole thing had panned out. Yes, the people smuggling operation had been broken, but at what cost and for how long? Had it all been worth it?

Alastair had the good grace to pick up on my mood and he shuffled a little.

'Well, I just thought you should know.' He patted my shoulder. 'I know it probably doesn't seem like it right now, but you have done a wonderful thing, Galahad...for many, *many* people.'

I just closed my eyes and nodded. I heard Joey whisper something to Alastair and I opened my eyes to watch them both leave the room. Craning my neck I could see past the police guard to where Tommy Ho sat, motionless and implacable, staring at the door of my room.

Sighing deeply I closed my eyes again and, before I knew it, had fallen into a deep and dreamless sleep.

Three weeks later I stood at Star Ferry Pier in Tsim Sha Tsui, looking out across Victoria Harbour. My body ached all over and it was hard to stand, and it hurt to sit. I leaned on the rail trying not to put too much weight on my arms, and Bors sat patiently at my feet occasionally slurping from the bowl of water I had placed in front of him.

It was a clear night and, all around me, people strolled along the promenade. Kids sat together on benches, drinking from cold beers, laughing and talking, and small children darted and weaved between the walkers, screaming in delight at evading their parents. Here and there police, in pairs, patrolled, ever watchful and stern.

Across Victoria Harbour the Island glittered and shone in the night. The neon lighting of the city's buildings blazed brightly, reflecting long fingers of multi-coloured light across the still, dark waters. Hong Kong's famous wooden junk, its red sails raised and illuminated, cut its large hull through the pools of light. Directly opposite me, the zig-zag lights of the Bank of China building stacked and connected their way up into the night sky.

I reached down clumsily with my one half-good arm to the plastic bag at my feet, that held a bag of ice, and drew out a can of beer, cracked the ring pull and sipped at it. Bors looked up briefly at the sound then resumed his watch of the crowds at my back. A brightly lit ferry pulled out from the wharf and chugged off toward Central as my mind continued to pick at the past weeks like an annoying loose thread on a shirt.

My last visitor in the hospital had been Billy Wong – more accurately, Billy and his nephew Michael. Billy had been all smiles but I had seen he was tense and Michael was unsmiling and silent as they both stood by my bed. The visit had been brief and to the point. Billy had kicked it off.

'I'm glad to see you're okay, Mr Jones,' he said.

I moved my left arm, suspended above me in a sling, the surgical pins glinting. 'I've been lucky, Billy,' I said. 'It could have been a whole lot worse.'

Billy Wong shook his head. 'I still can't believe it. Peter Toh! Crooked...'

I glanced at Michael. He watched me impassively. Billy went on.

'When I received your package, especially the note, I did not know what to think. It was all just so mad, I couldn't believe it. But it all hung together so, as you had asked, I took it to Michael. Of course, when we heard you had been shot and that David Zhou was dead there was no longer a sliver of doubt. Michael and a small team moved to arrest Chief Inspector Toh but he had gone.'

Michael Wong spoke, his voice clear and well-modulated. He looked every inch the professional plain-clothes officer. Unlike his garrulous uncle, Michael was clipped and to the point.

Who killed Zhou?'

'Peter did,' I replied. 'I was there, I saw it.'

'Then he shot you?'

'Not immediately. He seemed intent on crowing about what a genius he was. You know, the classic bad guy monologue in a Bond movie.'

'He made admissions?'

I nodded. 'Everything... he knew I wasn't going to walk out of there so he was content to give me the news. Everything you've read about Eddie Lau is true. He's a triad plant – always has been – and it was Peter's job to shepherd him.'

Michael Wong changed tack. 'Did Zhou say anything to you before he was killed.'

I thought of the duffle with the bundles of cash and fixed my eyes on Michael's.

'No, nothing...other than confessing to his role in my father's killing.'

I eyed them both, steadily. 'You know my father was fitted up, right? He was murdered because he was getting too close to SYO, and Zhou planted the evidence the inquiry later accepted.'

Billy Wong shook his head sadly and clicked his tongue. Michael nodded tersely. I got the impression he didn't like me very much.

'Yes, that's clear now,' he said. 'We will be taking formal steps to have your father's name cleared.'

He paused a moment then glanced over his shoulder to where Tommy Ho sat, immobile, on his chair in the corridor, watching the door to my room with an unblinking intensity.

'We will speak again. Soon,' he said and left the room, walking past The Panda without a glance. I saw Tommy Ho's eyes follow the detective, a sardonic grin on his face, before they refocussed on my door. Billy Wong leaned in.

'Forgive Michael, Mr Jones. He's a good boy and a great policeman, but... well, your 'connections' to 14K trouble him.' He scratched his chin. 'To be honest,' he said, 'they trouble me too.'

'Necessary evil Billy,' I said wearily. 'Sometimes you've just gotta swim with the sharks...'

Billy had nodded silently then, squeezed my shoulder reassuringly and left the room, nodding curtly at Tommy Ho as he passed.

A light breeze had picked up across the Harbour and I sipped at the beer, absently scratching Bors behind the ear. I looked down at him, amazed at just how much he had grown in the space of a few short weeks. His paws were still the size of small plates – which didn't bode well for his future growth in my tiny apartment – and a broad head sat on a thick ruff that led to wide, muscular shoulders. He looked like a black and tan lion and passers-by recognised that and gave him a wide berth. I finished the beer and crushed the can, dropping it into the plastic bag, and opened another.

I had been discharged after a week, the hospital insisting I couldn't do so on my own so I had called Joey who had turned up in a taxi and escorted me on the short trip home. With my left arm pinned and in a cast, and my right arm aching badly from the gunshot wound, I could barely care for myself and showering was an issue. Luckily, I thought, I had no-one to impress. Bors was still at Angel's so, as quickly as I could, I set off to do something that had weighed on my mind from the moment I regained consciousness in the hospital.

The walk off Dragon's Back in the heat and humidity had not been easy with my rigidly-cast arm in a sling and jolts of pain lancing through me with every limped step. Eventually, I had entered the copse of trees where I had last seen David Zhou's body and where my friend of many years had tried to kill me.

I was relieved to see no-one around so I moved to the cliff edge and awkwardly shrugged off the backpack I was carrying. I looked about and slowly paced out to the position I thought I had been standing when facing Peter. Then, after clipping the carry handle of the backpack to a belt loop of my jeans with a small carabiner, I dropped to my backside and slithered over the edge.

I had scrabbled about on my knees in the bush for nearly 30 minutes, my slung left arm occasionally, and painfully, knocking the ground when my fingers brushed something. Drawing a breath, I slid forward on my belly and pushed my right hand through a tangle of vine and touched the bag. It was still there! Zhou's duffle was hung up in a dense thicket and my hands were on it. I laughed out loud. The crime scene boys had missed it in the dense undergrowth as they trawled for evidence.

Moving as quickly as I could, I dragged a rope out of the backpack and secured it around the duffle, then, tying a loop at the end, slipped my head and right shoulder through the loop, harnessing me to the bag. That done, I started the long and painful one-armed crawl up the slope and back into the clearing.

I had eventually made it home that night after painfully dragging the duffle behind me for nearly two kilometres to the road before calling a ride-share car. Stumbling into the bathroom, I had swallowed down four paracetamol with a shot of whisky, before moving to my bedroom and squatting back on my haunches to stare at the bundles of $100 dollar notes. 2.5 million US, in zip lock bags, was scattered about the floor of my apartment and no-one, not a soul alive, knew about it.

I should have felt guilt about what I was doing, felt some remorse. My conscience should have pricked me. But none of that happened. I re-packed the duffle, slid it under my bed then dropped off to sleep, utterly unperturbed by what I had decided to do.

~

Over the following days, I got busy with the cash. I took half the hoard and deposited it into my bank account, the teller not even blinking when I passed over the small sports bag. Converted to Hong Kong Dollars the deposit amounted to a little over 8.3 million and I was trembling slightly when I walked out of the bank with the bag still weighed down with a large sum of HKD. The following morning, Jenny Lam's dog shelter received an anonymous donation of 250,000 when she found a black sports bag, wrapped tightly in masking tape, hanging from the front door when she arrived to open up.

That afternoon a new Mini Cooper S was delivered to Prudence's address with a long note from me taped to the steering wheel – I knew I would have a lot of explaining to do but that was a problem for later.

Adele and Joey both received three months back pay, along with a sizeable bonus, into their accounts. Adele had demanded to know where I had got the money but I had deflected her with a kiss on the cheek, and Joey had just eyed me suspiciously but said nothing. I had paid the back rent for the office and organised a complete renovation to start later that month – Adele and Joey had, again, reacted with suspicion then excitement once I laid out the plans for the office facelift; Adele in particular threw herself into the project with enthusiasm.

I had found Fat Johnny Tong in his usual routine of feeding the birds at the Yuen Po Street Bird Garden. I watched him for a while as he tossed out crumbs and whispered quietly to the birds that hopped, cheeped and fluttered at his feet. I waited until he looked up and noticed me before I patted the bench beside me. He shuffled over, sat down and I passed him a fat envelope and watched as his eyes widened when he opened it. I had told him the money was for doctors' bills, rent, food and some new clothes, and that if he shot it into his arm or smoked it I would wring his scrawny neck.

Last, I had drafted a single-page document, that I had signed and given to a speechless Joey, giving her equal partnership in the business and a 50% share of all profits – not that they were something we had seen for a while. She had hugged me then stepped back, her face serious, and told me I wouldn't regret the decision. I already knew that.

~

Over by the ferry gates, a kid with a guitar had started up, the chords and his clear voice echoing across the piers, and small crowd had gathered to listen. Prowling low overhead, a Government Flying Service chopper swung out of its LZ in Wan Chai and roared away to the west. It was a bustling Friday night beside the harbour and I should have felt moderately at peace; after all, everything had turned out well enough. But I didn't.

There was one last piece to this puzzle that had nagged at me for weeks. Rather than easing, the sinking feeling had only increased as the picture became clearer to me during the events of recent days.

I pulled out my tobacco pouch and tried to roll a cigarette, cursing as my clumsy one-handed attempt resulted in the paper tearing and the tobacco falling to the ground. I was about to try again when the guitar music suddenly stopped and Bors growled lowly. A familiar voice sounded at my side.

'Good evening, Mr Jones. It's a lovely night.'

I turned to my left to see Lee Pak-chun leaning with his elbows on the fence rail, looking out across the harbour. Turning slowly around, I saw a semi-circle of young men in smart suits had fanned out around us, one of whom was gently shooing away the kid with the guitar. Tommy Ho was standing to my right. He nodded at the bag of ice at my feet.

'I see you're drinking at 7 Club,' Tommy said smiling and put his hand out. 'May I assist?' I shrugged and passed him my tobacco pouch then turned back to Lee.

'I was just thinking about you,' I said to Lee, accepting the rolled cigarette from Tommy and lighting it.

'Oh? Should I be flattered'

I thought about that for a moment. 'Take it any way you like,' I said. 'I'm sure you flatter yourself enough at the scale of your genius.'

Lee accepted my childish sarcasm with his usual equanimity, his eyes sparkling with mild amusement.

'So,' he said. 'Chief Inspector Toh was crooked.' He shook his head in amazement. 'SYO all this time.'

'You didn't know?'

'Not a clue. Why would he have figured in my planning had we known? Remember; he was to be the one to roll up the slavery racket once you gave him the necessary evidence.' He shrugged. 'Well, that was wrong but it did all end correctly wouldn't you say?'

'That depends on your definition of "correctly".'

'The people smuggling operation has been broken, SYO have suffered a significant blow to their finances that will set them back years which, in turn, will allow my society to once again flourish. So, yes, I would call that the appropriate conclusion.'

I turned to look back out over the harbour and dragged on the cigarette.

A week earlier Eddie Lau, the former Chief Secretary of Hong Kong, had been led away in handcuffs, a grim-faced Michael Wong at his shoulder. Lau's career had ended in shame and with criminal charges that were likely to see him banged up in Shek Pik for a lengthy term. Given that it was now clear Lau had been SYO's highest-placed plant at the seat of government, that had to be to the advantage of both Lee and 14K.

'How long have you known about Lau?' I asked, dropping the cigarette butt into the empty beer can.

Lee considered that for a moment. 'I would not say we *knew*,' he replied. 'At least not definitively. He was extremely well protected both within SYO and by your friend Mr Toh. But there had been one small leak, about two years ago.' He looked at me, studying my reaction.

'So this was never about ending the people smuggling was it? This was always intended to get the dirt on Lau and have him removed.'

Lee shook his head. 'That's not strictly correct. I had no information linking him to the trade, not a shred. But, yes, given the operation was so well covered I assumed his involvement, at least peripherally, and hoped that, perhaps, when you gathered your evidence you might unearth something.'

He smiled and spread his hands. 'As it turns out, when you came into possession of the Thomas Diary my hopes rose.'

He paused. 'You didn't quite tell me the truth when we last met, did you,' he said mildly.

'Xiào Xiào?'

Lee nodded. 'Yes. You omitted to mention that - and I'm not talking about the singer, he said smiling faintly. 'I was very excited at the prospect Lau would have been revealed in the diary and somewhat disappointed when you told me there was nothing of 'particular note' in it.'

He signalled wordlessly to Tommy Ho who dipped into my bag of ice and cracked one of my beers, handing it to his boss. Lee took a long gulp at the beer and smacked his lips.

'Delicious, and so refreshing on a night like this,' he said, enjoying every moment of the encounter. He really was a manipulative old bastard but you didn't get to be Mountain Master of a triad without being like that. 'Where was I?'

'The diary. Lau...'

'Ah yes. Anyway, I was content to let it play because, by that stage, I was hopeful that with the rolling up of the smuggling operation, a link would eventually be drawn to Lau. I had no idea it was in the diary and would happen so quickly. I'm quite delighted actually.'

'I can't tell you how much that pleases me.'

The day after Eddie Lau had been led away to a cell, the Legislative Council had held an emergency session to vote on the election of a new Chief Secretary. The field had been large and the smart money was all on an ageing insider who had the ear of the Chief Executive, but in the end a long-shot had overtaken the field in the home straight and galloped past the post with a resounding majority of votes.

The winner was only in his second term and few had even heard of him. He was a nobody and had come from nowhere to secure the second most powerful position in government. Hong Kong's establishment was in shock but the fix was in; we had a new Chief Secretary. Lee was still watching me closely. I turned around to lean back against the railing.

'The new Chief Secretary,' I said. 'He's yours.'

Lee grinned widely. 'I always knew you were clever, Mr Jones', he said. 'He's not Triad but, yes, we own him.'

He paused briefly and gazed across the harbour. A ferry chugged into its berth, the crew skilfully throwing out the thick hawsers to tie her off, and he turned back to me.

'You are now one of the very few people who know that.' He wagged a finger at me. 'That knowledge comes with certain...risks.'

I shook my head in disbelief.

The whole thing had been about Lee's removal of an opponent and placement of his own man at the heart of government. In fact, there was every chance Lee's boy would become Chief Executive at the next election when the incumbent stood down. In one fell swoop, he had out-manoeuvred SYO and won the glittering prize they had worked so hard, over many years, to achieve. I had to hand it to him. It really was genius. I shook my head at the audacity of it all, and at my stupidity at playing a central role in bringing Lee's plan to fruition.

'What will you do now?' I asked, although I thought I already knew the answer.

Lee finished the beer and dropped the empty can at his feet. 'Perhaps nothing, Mr Jones.' He shrugged and smiled again. 'Perhaps everything. We shall see.'

I had no answer to that and watched mutely as Lee walked away, accompanied by Tommy Ho and one of the semi-circle of young men.

Cracking a fresh can, and patting Bors briefly on the head, I turned back to the harbour. A tap on my shoulder startled me and I turned. Angel stood there, her hair shining and eyes bright, a soft smile creasing her red lips. Behind her stood a young woman, in a smart business suit, who I didn't recognise.

'Well, you did it,' she said softly.

I nodded. 'Yes, I certainly did,' I said darkly. 'You and your boss must be very pleased with yourselves.'

Angel looked hurt at that but her face hardened.

'*Diu*, Gal. Grow up. You, of all people, should know this is Hong Kong and this is the way we roll. Don't come the outraged boy scout with me.'

'You'll forgive me if I'm not altogether delighted by all of this,' I said. 'It's not every day I play a starring role in a triad conspiracy.'

'You went into this with your eyes open! You ended a gigantic sexual slavery operation, brought justice to your father and removed two highly-placed, corrupt policemen. I'd say that was not a bad accounting.'

She was right of course.

I couldn't pretend I was an innocent party in all of this. I had knowingly played along, all to discover who had killed my father and to bring them to justice. I had achieved the first and the second had happened, of a sort. Now I was profiting from a very large sum of neatly laundered triad money. I had no-one to blame but myself so I'd just have to live with it. I was fairly sure my dubious moral compass would soon adjust.

'Who's the girl?' I asked, nodding over Angel's shoulder.

She smiled and raised her hand, gesturing with her fingers. The young woman stepped forward from the shadows and my jaw dropped. It was Chaya, the young woman from the trafficking compound. She moved silently to stand beside Angel.

'Good evening, Mr Jones,' she said in heavily accented English. 'It is a pleasure to see you again.'

I gaped stupidly then looked questioningly at Angel.

'Chaya will remain here,' Angel said. 'She has no-one to return home to and does not wish to go back, so we have arranged a work visa and she will work for us at YunCorp.' She paused and smiled at the young woman next to her. 'She will be my assistant both at YunCorp and in "other business".'

I nodded and smiled at Chaya, who just regarded me solemnly.

'Well I guess that's a big improvement on your previous situation,' I said lamely.

The girl nodded and took three steps back into the dark, leaving Angel and me alone. Angel took me by the arm.

'What happens now, Gal?' she whispered.

That was a question that had exercised my mind for weeks so I had an answer ready. I smiled and took her hand. 'I guess we can start again,' I said. 'You know, slow and soft, see where it leads us.'

Angel smiled. 'I like slow and soft,' she whispered. She stuck out her hand. 'Deal,' she said as we shook on it.

She kissed me on the cheek and winked, then turned away with Chaya trailing after her and the rest of the protection team quickly moving into position around her. In moments she was lost in the crowd and I was left standing alone with a quickly melting bag of ice and a hungry dog.

43

HONG KONG SHONE brightly in the dark of a hot and humid night, moving and dealing and taking life head-on as it always had and always would. From Sheng Shui to Stanley, and Yuen Long to Clearwater Bay, from the cloud-punching office towers and the roar of traffic to the silence of the jungle-clad hills, the city called to me and wrapped its arms around me in an electric embrace.

Distant lightning flickered across the sky, illuminating the low clouds in a flash-bulb moment, and thunder, low and deep, rumbled across the Island. I sighed and gazed westward down the harbour.

Somewhere out there Peter Toh lurked and I guessed it wouldn't be long before we met again. Only, next time, I would be ready for him. A thrill of excitement prickled at me at the thought.

With a groan, I bent and picked up the bag of ice and the last few beers. Looking about, I gave them to a couple of kids sitting on a nearby bench listening to what passes as music these days. They thanked me politely and cracked the ring pulls, smiling widely at their good fortune.

I took a last, long look along the promenade and, with a low whistle and click of my fingers, walked off with Bors trotting beside me toward the Wan Chai ferry and home.

AUTHOR'S NOTE

Hong Kong is my second home. I have loved the city since I first set foot there as a young Lieutenant in the late 1980s. Although I had travelled the world as a child - my father's army postings taking us to places far and wide - I had never seen anything like Hong Kong and I fell instantly in love. Hong Kong became the dragon in my blood from the moment the Boeing 747 swooped and dived between the apartment buildings in the famed Kai Tak Heart Attack. It's true: on those approaches into the old airport, you could quite literally look into apartment windows and see people preparing dinner. Hong Kong has changed greatly in the 34 years since - physically, culturally and, most significantly, politically - but none of that has changed my feelings for the city or its people, feelings only reinforced and strengthened over the last five years of living there, despite the turmoil the city has recently endured.

I have always found Chinese names to be descriptive and poetic - you can be sure each given name is carefully chosen to reflect the parents' views (and future hopes) of their children. Chinese naming conventions used throughout this novel can sometimes be confusing for the uninitiated. They follow the [FAMILY NAME] [First given name-second given name] convention. The family name (or 'surname') as in English is inherited from one's parents and shared with other members of the individual's immediate family. For example Galahad's mysterious girlfriend YEUNG Mei-ying (first name, incidentally, meaning 'beautiful flower' - see my point about 'descriptive and poetic'?). Readers will note most Chinese characters of this novel have anglicised first names, making their names expressed in written form as [English First Name] [Chinese Family Name] [Chinese given names] so, for example Peter Toh Luo-yang.

There are a number or reasons for this but, chiefly, it is due to the long British connection to Hong Kong so the adoption of an 'English' first name for business and social contexts, has become somewhat of a tradition. While it's never really discussed, the anglicised first name, in Hong Kong at least, tends to denote the person has a decent education (that also includes the ability to speak English). There's another, very practical, reason and that is that Chinese forms of address are either very formal or overly familiar, so English first names tend to serve as a 'lubricant' to speed up the process of getting acquainted. Paradoxically, I've always favoured my friend's Chinese names while they prefer me to address them using their English name.

The last point I'd make on this is the delightful habit of Hong Kongers - especially women - choosing colourful, and sometimes unusual, first names. There are a lot of theories around to account for this but I think it's a way to claim their names and truly own them. 'Angel' and 'Swallow' are common and I've been introduced to a 'Treacle'. My barber's first name was 'Cherry' and my personal trainer's was 'Pizza'.

Much has been written about Chinese transnational crime syndicates, commonly known as Triads and they feature in this novel. The term 'triad' - originally a translation of the Chinese term San Ho Hui (or Triple Union Society) has come to be synonymous with the organised criminal gangs - known as 'societies' - that operate in Hong Kong, Macau and other South East Asian countries. Like the Italian mafia, they are highly disciplined organisations with complex organisational structures created to engage in a variety of criminal activities including trafficking (in both drugs and people), prostitution, fraud, political corruption, extortion, illegal gambling and money laundering. As this novel depicts, it is not unusual for triads to run, or be connected to, legitimate business enterprises both as a way to further their commercial success and launder their proceeds of crime. Lee Pak-chun's YunCorp does not exist but it easily could.

There are a number of references in 'Dragon's Back' to triad hierarchy and rank systems, that use numeric codes to distinguish positions within the society – this is the *I Ching* referred to in Chapter Eighteen. The leader of the triad is the 489, or 'Mountain Master' below whom report 438 'Vanguard' or Operations Officers. 426 'Red Pole" are the enforcers of the unit and run teams of rank-and-file members known commonly as 'soldiers' but made up of 'Blue Lanterns' (uninitiated members) and '49ers (ordinary members who have been inducted into the triad by the Incense Master (ceremonies officer). The Panda, Tommy Ho, who you may see again in future books of the 'Dragon' Series, is a Red Pole, and the mysterious and beautiful Angel Yeung, as Galahad found out to his dismay, is the 432 of the triad, the 'Straw Sandal' or Lee's Liaison Officer.

Tommy Ho was recruited in the classic method of the triads who seek out marginalised and troubled youth, taking them under their wing and showing the kids, possibly for the first time, respect and a sense of purpose. It's cynical and manipulative but a very effective recruiting method.

14K and Sun Yee On exist and are two of the most powerful Hong Kong triads, but that's where the similarity with the people and events of this novel end. Everything I have written about specific events and people connected with 14K and SYO is fictional and the product of what my friends formerly of HKPF called my 'fevered imagination'.

I recommend the following excellent books for further reading into triad societies in Hong Kong: Peng Wang's *The Chinese Mafia* (2017) is an excellent study on the origins of the societies in ancient China and their rise in contemporary China. Chu Yiu-kong's *The*

Triads as Business (2002) is my go-to resource on the rise of the Hong Kong triad.

A few words now about Hong Kong Police Force (HKPF). The force has a long and revered history going back to its formation in 1844 and continuing to this day. It is a highly trained, effective police force - arguably the finest in East and South East Asia - and I have nothing but the greatest of respect for the men and women of the force - in particular the General Duties, or 'beat' cops who pound the pavements of Hong Kong for hour after hour, mile after mile.

That said, like every other police force on the planet (some more than others) HKPF is not without its dark episodes of corruption (both low and high) and accusations - some proven, many not - of unreasonable use of force or 'police brutality' as it's more commonly called. It's fair to say that the force's reputation and standing in the community has taken a drubbing in recent years. HKPF has, in particular since the leadership of Commissioner Andy Tsang, been held up to close scrutiny, and wide condemnation, during and following the protests of 2014 and the 2019 riots that arose out of the democracy protest movement. It's a complicated story and not one that I intend to buy into, other than to say I have personal knowledge of the facts behind a number of the 'scandals' swirling around HKPF in 2019 and its aftermath. A few were legitimate complaints of brutality that, as a former policeman, I condemn wholeheartedly, but a great many of the accusations were selective, politically motivated and made out of context of the incident at the time.

The two units responsible for countering organised crime, and the triads, in Hong Kong are the Organised Crime and Triad Bureau (OCTB), and Criminal Intelligence Bureau (CIB) - both part of the Crime Wing of 'B' Department. Both the units do an excellent job of tackling triad and other organised criminal activity in Hong Kong, and are manned by dedicated, hard-working men and women. There's always a 'but' and, like other units of their type worldwide, neither unit is perfect. However, I have not a single shred of evidence to suggest anyone like the villainous David Zhou and Peter Toh ever held command positions in either unit. I certainly hope not!

Finally, while I have tried to be as accurate as possible in all aspects of this novel - much of it drawn from my own experiences - it is a work of fiction and of imagination so mistakes, doubtless, have been made. These are entirely of my making. I also admit to, occasionally and slightly, altering Hong Kong's geography, climate and streetscape. In my defence, I only did so where I felt it enhanced the story and allowed me to neatly tie up a narrative point. I apologise to my Hong Kong friends and beg your forgiveness.

A.C. Edwards
Brisbane, Australia
2023

ACKNOWLEDGMENTS

It's often been said, but writing *is* a solitary, and lonely, activity. Although, I would argue that my characters keep me company and, yes, they *do* talk to me.

I was fortunate in that when I started to write 'Dragon's Back' I was living alone in Hong Kong so walking the ground day and night, then locking myself away with my notes and laptop didn't upset anyone. My beautiful wife of 30 years would often call and message me in Hong Kong demanding updates on the manuscript and would be mildly annoyed when I refused to give her anything but the most general of details of plot and character. I didn't want to spoil the finished product for her.

Now I'm home in Australia, I set up a writing space in the house where I now create my stories - with my old dog, Loki, and monstrous white cat, Murphy at my feet. They are here now as I write. Thank you Liz. For everything!

Thanks, also, to many other people along the way. First, my old friend, fellow paratrooper and writing mentor, Chris Allen - author of the outstanding 'Intrepid' Series - without whose advice and encouragement I would never have even started down this path, let alone stuck to it. Thanks also to my amazing, brutally honest, Test Reader Group - you know who you are - for the 'tough love' critiques you gave me. I owe each of you.

ABOUT THE AUTHOR

A.C (Andrew) Edwards is a former policeman, paratrooper and Special Forces officer. He served in the Australian Army and operated widely across South East Asia and the South West Pacific, including attachments to the Malaysian and Indonesian armies, and other operational deployments. He retired at the rank of Major.

In addition to his military career, Andrew has worked as a security adviser across SE Asia, as a close-protection specialist for several Very High Net Worth individuals and their families, and as a Security Contractor in the Middle East and Afghanistan. He was most recently the Regional Security Director for Asia Pacific for a multi-national company but has now swapped the corporate grind for full-time writing.

Born in Singapore, Andrew has lived and worked for much of his life across Asia Pacific. Today, he lives between Hong Kong and Brisbane with his wife, dog and rescue cat.

www.ingramcontent.com/pod-product-compliance
Lightning Source LLC
LaVergne TN
LVHW091023080826
845145LV00002B/338
9780645867305